YOU BETTER RUN

YOU BETTER RUN
SONGS OF THE ASCENDANT - VOLUME III

DARIN KENNEDY

YOU BETTER RUN
SONGS OF THE ASCENDANT – VOLUME III

Copyright © 2024 by Darin Kennedy

All rights reserved. No part of this work may be reproduced, stored, distributed, or transmitted in any form or by any means, electronic or mechanical, including information storage and retrieval systems, without written consent and permission from the author, except for the use of brief quotations in a book review.

This is a work of fiction. Names, characters, places, and incidents either are products of the author's imagination or are used fictitiously.
Any resemblance to actual events, locales, organizations, or persons, living or dead, is entirely coincidental.

Cover art Copyright © 2024 M. M. Schill
Acrylic on canvas posterization
Cover design by Natania Barron
Book design - Vellum Edgewood
Printed in the United States of America

ebook ISBN: 978-1-943748-09-9
paperback ISBN: 978-1-943748-10-5
hardcover ISBN: 978-1-943748-11-2

Charlotte, NC

To Seth, Kiersten, and Alex Keipper,
my Thursday night companions
on this journey that is far from over

Hateful to me as the gates of Hades is that man who hides one thing in his heart and speaks another.

— HOMER, THE ODYSSEY

CHAPTER I

DON'T PAY THE FERRYMAN

He burned for her.

Literally burned to take away her pain.

Ethan. Rosemary. Like a pair of candles brought together, their two tiny flames intermingled and grew into something magnificent, something magical, something straight out of a fairy tale.

And all I could do was watch the smoke rise from their passionate embrace, the bank of screens in the Cardinal's control room showing me Ethan and Rosemary's first fiery kiss from every angle imaginable.

I couldn't imagine a more effective torture.

Pacing the cavernous control room where my captor and his techno-witch in black—if I make it out of this alive, I'm totally stealing that outfit for my next tour—left me as they went to face my friends, I did my best to look away, but much like a moth to literal flame, my eyes kept creeping back to the dozen flickering screens that filled the rough-hewn wall of stone. Seeing Ethan and a revived Rosemary fight as one against my crimson kidnapper, their bodies enveloped in a shared silver fire, filled my heart with equal parts hope and despair.

Hope that I would soon be found and liberated, that Ethan and I would be reunited, and that everything would be as it was.

Despair that the two of them might possibly have found each other in the midst of all the danger and strife, that the spark ignited that day would engulf them both in a fire that made what Ethan and I had pale in comparison, and that I would be forgotten.

The only reason either of them—hell, any of them—had come to this desolate place was for me. I knew this in my bones.

And yet, Ethan and Rosemary's kiss remained seared across my mind's eye no different than if I'd spent an hour staring directly into the sun.

Clothed in nothing but the tank top and sweatpants I'd been wearing when the Cardinal took me from my home not twenty-four hours before, loaded me aboard his techno-witch's airship, and transported me to wherever this place was, I couldn't stop myself from trembling, though whether from the subterranean chill, fear, or rage, I wasn't sure.

One thing was certain, though.

This was supposed to be *my* fairy tale, dammit.

And the kiss from Prince Charming was supposed to be mine.

"They're not going to find you, you know." The mechanical voice that echoed my thoughts came from somewhere inside the dimly lit room. "My maker has ensured the privacy of this complex, Persephone Snow, even should your friends again bring their technomancer to bear."

"Who said that?" I backed myself into a corner so I could survey the entire room and raised my fists. "Show yourself."

A three-foot-high robot glided from the darkened far corner of the room, its lower third a deep grey sphere a little bigger than a basketball. All flat black with trim of cobalt blue, the vaguely humanoid torso and head stared at me with a single circular eye like a camera lens, the glass glowing a faint blue.

"Who or what are you?"

"A companion, Persephone Snow."

"I don't need a companion." I took a hesitant step forward. "What I need is to get out of this place. Can you help me with that?"

"Unfortunately, Persephone Snow, I cannot." The metallic figure tilted forward just above its spherical base and offered what seemed an apologetic bow. "I am, however, programmed to provide for your needs in the event that my master is unavailable or otherwise indisposed."

"Fantastic." That sealed it. I was trapped in a mysterious underground lair straight out of a James Bond flick, complete with a cheesy robot guard.

Before allowing myself to dip further into the river of despair, I did what Mom always taught me to do when things looked bad, back when we were subsisting on ramen and didn't have two dimes to rub together. I counted my assets, or as she would have said, blessings.

Assuming the air, food, and water kept coming, it seemed this place had everything I needed to survive, at least for a while. Upon our arrival, the Cardinal had given me a brief tour of this complex he intended to be my new "home" for the foreseeable future. A relatively well-lit hallway carved from the granite led away from the control room with large steel doors on either side every fifteen feet or so, one of which opened on a bedchamber complete with a shower, appropriate facilities, and a small stack of serviceable clothing. I'd spent a sleepless six hours alone behind the large metal door after we'd arrived the previous evening, and the Cardinal had just come for me that morning to continue my orientation when Alba's pyromancer arrived on the scene. Whether my ability to watch the fight up top unfold was an oversight on his part or completely intentional, at least for the moment, I had my run of the place, not to mention, I supposed, my very own robot servant.

Not that I was intending on sticking around much longer.

"So, you're here to meet my needs?"

"Indubitably, Persephone Snow."

"But you can't show me the way out."

"Regrettably, Persephone Snow, I cannot."

Funny. I hadn't heard my full name so often since I was a kid. "What *can* you help me with, then?"

For the first time, a brief pause.

"I am programmed to ensure that you suffer neither hunger nor thirst nor pain nor any discomfort. Whatever need you might have, I am well equipped to provide."

"Other than helping me find my way back into the sunlight."

"Precisely, Persephone Snow."

"You keep saying my name." I studied the steady blue light of my robotic prison guard's lone eye. "What do I call you?"

"The master has designated me Charon. I will be your guide and caretaker in this new phase of your life, Persephone Snow."

Huh. The ferryman of the Greek Underworld of Hades as the guard and guardian of a recently kidnapped Persephone. Can't say the Cardinal doesn't have a sense of humor. A little on the nose for my taste, but at least I wasn't stuck down here all by myself.

My stomach rumbled, reminding me that for all the terror of the preceding hours, I still needed to eat. "You're in charge of keeping me fed, then?"

"Why, yes, Persephone Snow. The master keeps his facilities well stocked with sufficient provisions for any number of guests. Is there anything in particular that appeals to your palate at the moment?"

Damn. Pretty sophisticated for a robot. Could give a Manhattan maître d' a run for their money.

"You know what? Surprise me."

As Charon rolled away to prepare me a snack hopefully fit for the Queen of this new Underworld in which I found myself, I again studied the bank of monitors.

The minutes that followed stretched like years as the mountaintop battle played out silently across the dozen screens before me. My heart soared with exhilaration and hope seeing an enraged Mr. Delacroix give the Cardinal a much deserved beating, only to shrivel in my chest a moment later when a momentary distraction gave his armored opponent the opening he needed. I screamed as the Cardinal hurled the man I'd come to see as a surrogate father over the edge of a sheer drop, my horror and rage echoed tenfold in the face of the man's actual daughter.

Ethan and a still-recovering Rosemary stood together against the Cardinal and were soon joined by Ada, Alba's pyromancer, who limped in their direction despite her previous injuries at the hands of the Cardinal's technomancer. I had no idea what it was she said or did, but seconds later, the silver flame that danced between Ethan and Rosemary erupted into a blinding inferno. In response, the Cardinal rushed Ethan and Rosemary, and for a moment I feared for both their lives. For once, however, my fears were misplaced. With a single swing of her now blazing blade, Rosemary sliced the Cardinal's weapon in half just before a tornado of silver fire, light, and energy descended from Heaven itself and filled the man I love to the brim with power beyond my understanding.

From that moment on, the outcome of the fight was never in doubt. Ethan and Rosemary attacked as one, her fiery blade nearly taking the Cardinal's hand at the wrist while Ethan's sword pierced the bastard's crimson breastplate opposite his black excuse for a heart. My soul leaped anew as the Cardinal, not one for retreat, momentarily withdrew from the fight, only to sink into despair as my captor took to the sky.

Though the Cardinal was defeated for the moment, I couldn't imagine a reality where he'd tell Ethan anything he didn't want him to know, including where he had me holed up. The resulting three-way conversation lasted but minutes, and then the Cardinal was gone, leaving behind his unconscious techno-witch and a swathe of injury and destruction in his wake.

Without wasting a moment, Ethan and Rosemary rushed to the cliff edge where her father had disappeared and rescued a miraculously unharmed Mr. Delacroix with a blustery assist from Dietrich Falco. Once he was safe and sound, the four of them worked to revive the others. Maddox, Neko, and Katrina all regained consciousness over the next half hour, all but the last with the aid of Ethan's newfound Flame. I wasn't sure what that was all about, but I'm sure Ethan had his reasons for withholding his healing fire from the young shadowmancer who numbered among my biggest fans.

Once all were back on their feet and reasonably recovered, they bound the Cardinal's techno-witch from head to toe. Once she was secured, their search for me began, and yet again, I allowed my heart to hope. The better part of an hour passed as I gazed helplessly at the monitors, praying that any of my gathered rescuers might find the necessary clue that would let them know where to find me.

Ethan, Rosemary, Falco, and Katrina scoured the mountaintop for any sign of an entrance to the Cardinal's base while Mr. Delacroix, Neko, and Rosemary's coyote ex-boyfriend Maddox—who got to see Ethan and Rosemary's fireworks live and in person; that must have sucked—took turns interrogating the Cardinal's technomancer. One look in the woman's steely gaze, however, told me all I needed to know: The Cardinal wasn't coming back for her, and she wasn't going to break.

The irony wasn't lost on me: Ethan and the rest had somehow figured out where the Cardinal had taken me, were almost certainly a stone's throw from where I stood, and yet were no closer to freeing me than when they stood in my dining room the day before.

Ethan, Rosemary, Mr. Delacroix, and the others continued to comb the abandoned mountaintop while somehow not noticing the very cameras that captured their every movement. L.J. was good, but the Cardinal's techno-witch, her current captive status notwithstanding, was clearly next level.

Each screen followed a particular person no differently than if multiple cameramen were filming a documentary in real time. Ethan, Rosemary, Mr. Delacroix, and Ada scoured the rocky crag, Maddox and Neko moved in ever widening circles taking advantage of senses the others didn't possess, Katrina sat deep in concentration by a bound and gagged technomancer at the center of it all, while Falco circled the mountain time and time again. In each of their faces, a shared frustration grew, the conviction in each gaze extinguishing one by one like candles burned too long into the evening. I couldn't hear a word any of them said, but their expressions said it all.

"I'm here, dammit!" I screamed at the silent screens. "I'm right here!"

I had no idea precisely where the Cardinal's little hidey-hole rested in relation to everything I was seeing, but unless my armored captor had one of those transporter gadgets from *Star Trek*, it couldn't be too far. He and his technomancer had been on Ada less than two minutes after she first appeared atop the mountain.

How she'd found this place, much less gotten herself here—Falco was the only one of Alba's elementalists we'd seen fly—remained a mystery.

Regardless, Ethan along with our entire crew had somehow found the needle in the haystack, and yet they all might as well have been a million miles away.

Just as all hope seemed lost, the big Army helicopter I'd seen onscreen earlier returned to land atop the mountain, kicking up dirt and debris that temporarily left the various monitors dark. As the screens cleared, two additional friends joined the group, and more importantly, the search.

While I was glad to see Bradley had made it through okay, my heart swelled at seeing L.J.'s bright teal hair and glasses. If anyone could sniff out where the Cardinal had hidden me away, it would be our own techno-bloodhound.

"Your hope is misplaced." The already familiar modulated voice sent a chill straight down my spine. "Despite their best efforts, your friends' search will remain fruitless." The Cardinal stepped from the sliding metal door where he'd disappeared an hour earlier with his techno-witch to deal with Ada's fiery arrival. "We stand deep within the heart of a mountain, and few are there who have either the power or knowledge needed to follow. One of my many homes across the globe, this complex is not only impenetrable but shielded against virtually all forms of detection."

"You call this hole a home?" I glared at the man in the crimson armor. "At least I finally know why you kidnapped me." I walked over to one of the bare rock walls and ran my hand along its rough surface. "This place could certainly use a woman's touch, and your techno-witch in black just isn't cutting it."

"Your lover, it seems, has brought a technomancer of his own into the fold," the Cardinal answered as he sat in the massive chair and swiveled to face his bank of monitors. Silent for a long moment, he studied a screen depicting L.J. examining his technomancer's various terror devices. "He is fresh, though. Young. His raw talent appears impressive, but I have little doubt that Minako's years and experience will win this day." He gestured to an image where L.J. manipulated the swarm of gadgets, each rotating around him as if he were a planet and they his many moons. "She's been playing this game since before your little technomancer was born."

"Are you attempting to converse with me, or are you just trying to convince yourself that you're not totally screwed?" I took a step in the Cardinal's direction. "Inquiring minds want to know."

"Quiet." The Cardinal tapped the side of his head. "While my helmet's sound modulation capabilities may be more than sufficient to keep you from bringing your talent to bear against me, the silencer is always an option should you simply begin to annoy me." He motioned to the device hanging from the far wall that still looked way too much like a ball gag from *Fifty Shades of Grey* for my tastes. My teeth still ached from having that stupid thing stuck between my incisors on the flight up, and I could still taste the silicone on my tongue.

As I wisely kept my silence, my eyes drifted to a screen where Ethan stared into the distance, his heartbroken gaze melting my heart. If only I could speak to him, tell him what it meant that he'd come all this way for me, feel those strong arms at my waist, his warm lips on mine.

Lips that had just danced with another woman's.

Regardless of the necessity, that had burned. Pun definitely intended.

Don't drift, Persephone. Stay focused.

The only reason I was still breathing? This monster needed me alive and kicking for whatever nefarious purpose he had on his agenda. I didn't want to do anything to change his mind.

"The only question that remains," the Cardinal posited as he glanced my way, "is how long your friends will continue their search before they finally give up and leave."

"Ethan will never give up." I crossed my arms before my chest in defiance. "No matter what it takes, he will keep coming."

"As long as he believes you're still alive, I suspect you're correct." The Cardinal glanced my way. "A situation I will apparently have to rectify."

"After all this"—I retreated until my back touched the cold stone wall—"*now* you're going to kill me?"

"My dear, did I not make it emphatically clear that, at least for now, I need you alive?"

Yes. I was counting on it.

I maintained my game face. "Pardon me if I don't take the word of a superhuman serial killer who won't even show his face."

"A nice try, but I know all too well what a few unfiltered words from your lips can do to a man." He pointed to the screen where Ethan punched the air in frustration. "Case in point."

"I don't know what you're trying to insinuate. I've never done anything like that to Ethan." My cheeks went red hot as the lie passed my lips. "Not even once."

"Says the woman who only found out a month ago that she was the first siren born in a generation." The Cardinal glanced across his shoulder at me. "In any case, you don't want to be one of the unfortunate souls who has seen my face."

"One only a mother could love, I'm guessing."

"You really miss the silencer, don't you?"

Though I could feel the withering stare despite his helmet's avian facade, I ignored the threat and launched into the barrage of questions that had built up over my hours of captivity. "So, what is this anyway? You've kidnapped your very own Persephone, taken her to your personal hand-crafted Underworld, and assigned her the literal ferryman of Hades as prison guard. Heavy-handed much?"

At that moment, Charon reappeared with a tray of food.

"Your breakfast, Persephone Snow."

"Right on time." I huffed out a sarcastic chuckle. "My pomegranate."

"Don't laugh too hard," the Cardinal said. "Your current predicament is not all that far afield from your namesake's, but your trailer-trash mother is anything but a goddess who can plea for your freedom."

My heart immediately went as cold as Arctic ice. "Do *not* talk about my mother."

"Ah, finally a button that does something when pushed." The Cardinal adjusted a dial on the arm of his chair and rose to face me. "My apologies for abandoning you before." He walked over to the diminutive robot, retrieved the covered tray of food, and held it out to me. "You must be famished."

"Don't say that like you didn't just kidnap me from my own home and fly me to the middle of nowhere to—"

"Eat." He opened the tray to reveal, of all things, a Monte Cristo sandwich just like the ones Mom used to order for us at this little diner back home when I was a kid. The mouth-watering aroma brought a loud grumble from my belly even as it sent me spiraling back a decade. "You're going to need your energy."

I briefly considered all the news stories where the kidnapped person refused to eat, often the biggest show of defiance they could manage against their captor. Not this girl. I was starving. Bastard said he needed me alive, so the food wasn't poisoned. And he was right. If I wanted to escape, I needed to keep up my strength. Not to mention, I remained at his mercy. At any point he decided, the food could go away, so the smart thing to do was eat just like he asked.

I took the plate from his gauntleted hand and noticed the jagged gouge in the metal, the crimson surrounding the gash a deeper hue than the surrounding armor.

Rosemary's blade cut deep indeed.

"Thank you." I tried to keep the bitterness in my voice to a minimum.

"But of course. As I've said, you have nothing to fear from me. I have a vested interest in your continued well-being."

"And that's the thing," I muttered between bites of the deep fried ham-and-cheese goodness, hoping I wasn't signing my own death certificate with the words about to come out of my mouth, "I still don't have the faintest idea what you want with me. My song can make people feel a certain way, but I'm not sure exactly how that's going to help you do whatever it is you're trying to accomplish. It's not like I can control fire or shadows or anything that works in a fight."

"Ah, Snow," he chuckled, "if you only knew the true extent of your potential, I suspect we'd be having a very different conversation."

Truth be told, I'd been working with Rosemary and Mr. Delacroix over the preceding month trying to figure out exactly what it was I could and couldn't do with my newfound ability. Exhaustive research online and at the local library along with a few trials of my voice out in public hadn't revealed much beyond what we'd learned at the arena in Los Angeles. The sirens of myth, initially depicted on ancient Greek vases as half-woman, half-bird harpies and later in history portrayed as voluptuous mermaids, could control the minds of others with their voice. Most commonly, the stories revolved around them luring sailors to a watery grave with only the overwhelming sweetness and inescapable power of their compelling song.

But me?

So far, I'd managed to bring Neko over to our side, charming an entire Vegas casino in the process, and then keep an entire arena of panicked spectators from killing each other to escape the locked-down venue in the middle of a superhuman terrorist attack. None of that, however, explained what an Ascendant serial killer might want with someone possessing such abilities or, for that matter, why he didn't just kill me and take whatever he needed like he'd done with the Greyhound and all the others before.

Not that I was going to make any such suggestion. Wynter Snow didn't raise any fools.

"What now, then?" I asked once I'd scarfed down the remainder of the surprisingly delicious sandwich. "I'm not going anywhere, apparently, and unless I'm missing something, Rosemary nearly took your arm off below the elbow. You have wounds to dress, and since you're basically making me watch as my friends, one by one, give up any hope of finding me, I'd prefer to do that on my own."

"You're in no position to be making demands, Miss—"

"Thank you for the sandwich." I narrowed my eyes at his helmet's avian gaze. "Now listen, and listen good. If what you say is true, then you need me alive and well. Until that changes, the power differential in this room isn't nearly as one-sided as you keep trying to make it seem." I strode over to my captor, my forehead just even with the bright red faux beak of his helmet, and smeared a greasy finger down his breastplate. "I may be your captive, but that doesn't mean we have to speak. Until further notice, just stay the hell away from me and leave me alone."

"Petulant child." A low growl emanated from the Cardinal's helmet, the guttural sound amplified by his armor's speakers. "I had intended to keep you close by my side in this, your new home. It can be a lonely place, and I thought we might enjoy each other's company, but perhaps some quiet time is called for instead." He looked to the monitor where Ethan stared directly into the invisible camera. "Not to mention, it's not beyond the realm of possibility that your friends might chance upon this place, so I will send you to a place where none will find you." He looked to the three-foot robot who'd just brought me breakfast. "Charon, take Miss Snow below with the others."

"Below?" Charon asked, his monotone voice somehow defiant and terrified at the same time. "Across the Styx?"

"You heard me." The Cardinal turned his back on both me and his robot servant, dismissing us both as he returned his attention to the bank of monitors. "Across the Styx."

CHAPTER 2

KYRIE

"The Styx?" I asked as Charon led me down the rocky hallway past the multitude of metal doors on either side. "Don't you think your master is taking the whole Greek Underworld thing a bit far?"

"If one is building an Underworld, Persephone Snow, there are worse templates."

The robot had a point.

"What is this Styx, anyway? I'm guessing there's not a literal river under this mountain. Where is it you're taking me, Charon?"

"While more than adequate water and geothermal heat are to be found beneath this mountain to keep the master's complex functional, you are correct, Persephone Snow. The Styx in question is not, in fact, a body of water, though it is easier for me to show than to explain. Simply know that so long as you are in contact with me, you shall have no difficulty with crossing over."

The words "crossing over" in reference to the Greek realm of the dead sent the hairs on my neck standing on end. I knew good and well I wasn't literally being sent to Hell—with a capital H—but after the month I'd had since that fateful night in Albuquerque, I wasn't ruling out anything anymore.

"The Cardinal mentioned others." I glanced down at the dwarfish robot rolling along at my side. "I wasn't aware your boss took prisoners."

"You're not aware of many things, Persephone Snow. This is not meant as insult, but simply fact."

Damn. Put in my place by three feet of steel, plastic, and microchips.

"All right. You don't want to talk about where we're going or who else might be there when we arrive." I stopped dead in the hallway and turned to face my robotic guard. "What *would* you like to talk about?"

Charon stopped as well, turning to study me with his cyclopean eye. "Please, Persephone Snow. Follow me, and all will be made clear soon enough."

"Look, I'm not going anywhere until you tell me something about what the hell, pardon the pun, is about to happen to me. I'll come quietly, I promise, but you've got to offer me something."

Charon paused for a moment, as if computing the most appropriate response. "Very well, Persephone Snow. Allow me to assuage your fears." He continued his slow roll down the rocky hallway, and I followed. "We now find ourselves in one of the most secure locations in the world, but compared to where we go now, this place may as well be a public shopping mall."

"More secure than an underground bunker beneath a mountain that an entire team of superhuman beings can't find, much less enter?"

"Precisely. For all its impervious design and inscrutable camouflage, Persephone Snow, this complex still has entrances and exits that connect with the world above, and it remains theoretically possible that this place could be discovered and breached." Charon slowed, almost imperceptibly. "The place where I take you is hidden far from prying eyes and deeper than most would dare go."

"No one breaks into or out of Tartarus, I'm guessing?" Look who paid attention in their online freshman classics course.

"You need not worry about Tartarus, Persephone Snow. You are far from deserving of such torture."

Wow. I was only kidding. "And wherever it is you're taking me," I asked, my heart freezing in my chest, "this Styx is what will take us there?"

"The place I take you is protected not only by technomantic wizardry, but also Ascendant power, and nowhere is that more evident than with the Styx." His lone eye turned to look at me, the cool blue light pouring from the crystal lens strangely soothing in the muted dim. "Only with me can you cross over, Persephone Snow. Any attempt to cross on your own, and you may visit a very different Land of the Dead."

A chill ran the length of my body as we rounded the final gentle curve of the hallway and the latest impossibility of the day came into view. I'd tried to keep track of how far we'd walked at first—I'd lost count of my steps after a couple hundred—not that knowing how far we'd gone was going to help me much.

Filling the space at the end of the hallway from one side to the other and from the top of the vaulted ceiling to the rocky floor, a shimmering cascade of energy flowed downward, an electric waterfall of color and light.

"This is the Styx, Persephone Snow, the lone gateway to the master's true abode, and the only way in or out."

"And you just walk through it?" I took a step forward, remembering a doorway at my grandparents' house that hadn't been refitted since the 1970s. "Like a beaded curtain?"

"Not if you value your continued existence." Charon rolled in front of me to block my path, his robotic head turning to look up at me. "As I've said multiple times, you pass the Styx with me, or not at all."

I started to ask what would happen if someone tried to cross over without an assist from my new favorite robot prison guard, but quickly decided I didn't want to know.

"So, how do we do this?"

An opening appeared at the curve that served as Charon's shoulder, and from within emerged a shackle at the end of a short silver chain. "Place this around your wrist, Persephone Snow, and I will ensure your safety as we cross the Styx."

"I have to be chained to you?" I asked. "That's a bit creepy."

"My apologies, Persephone Snow. While my original build was based simply on maintaining contact during the process, it took but one incident of someone letting go halfway across for the master to see the flaw in that design."

"Noted." I grabbed the cuff at the end of the chain, slid it onto my wrist, and clamped down the metal until it hurt. "Let's get this over with."

"Whatever you do as I guide us across, Persephone Snow, stay close by my side." Charon's robotic voice took on an almost fatherly tone. "I would see you safely to your new home."

"Don't you worry, Charon." I grabbed both of the robot's metallic shoulders and held on tight. "I'd sooner let go of a life preserver in the middle of the ocean."

"An apt analogy, Persephone Snow."

I held my breath as the robot rolled forward, pulling me behind him, and learned quickly why someone might have let go their grip crossing this Styx.

I'd stood countless times at the intersection of a hundred spotlights, felt the flash of heat from the two dozen flame jets that accompanied the drop beat of "One Night, A Thousand Stars" nightly for months, experienced the sensation of over a hundred decibels of pure sound reverberating past me for hours every night for two straight tours, not to mention been juggled by both an aeromancer's winds and a skiomancer's shadows more than once in the preceding month.

Nothing could have prepared me for what I experienced as Charon and I passed through the scintillating sheet of radiance named for the "Dread River of Oath" from Greek mythology.

My every molecule seemed to explode at once upon contact with the prismatic light only to reform on the other side. My flesh, my bones, the blood in my veins, and the nerves that traveled my entire body all crackled with energy as if I'd been hit by a dozen lightning strikes at once. My every muscle spasmed, my lungs burned, and my heart stopped in my chest.

It lasted a year.

It lasted a second.

And then, we were through.

I sucked in a lungful of air, and though dry and musty, it remained the sweetest breath of my entire life.

"What the hell was that?" I stared into the near darkness, still blinded by the glowing curtain of energy I'd just passed, its hypnotic light beckoning me to turn and walk through a second time like a moth drawn to a lantern. "What did you do to me?"

"I did nothing, Persephone Snow. The Styx, however, has transported you to a place where none shall find you. So long as you mind your place and do not try to escape, you shall remain safe under my care."

"And if I had somehow let go of you while we were passing through the light? What would have happened?"

"Your atoms would be scattered throughout the master's complex, Persephone Snow, and I would have appeared here alone."

Wow. Charon wasn't programmed to pull any punches.

"Did you guys consider just installing a Ring camera?" I tried to keep it light, but my heart pounded knowing how close I'd just been to oblivion. "Don't you think disintegration is a little harsh?"

"The Styx is more than a simple doorway, Persephone Snow. Understand that by passing through, you now stand in a different place altogether than where you were."

Good to know.

I'd half-jokingly wondered if the Cardinal had some sort of teleporter gadget, and now, unless I was missing something, I'd just stepped through it. Ethan had told me about how Lady Day, the Angel they'd met in Denver, could send people to any destination they asked, but the existence of a piece of technology that anyone could use to transport them from Point A to Point B seemed straight out of a sci-fi movie.

And all I ever wanted out of life was a rom-com.

"What is this place, then?" I peered into the vague darkness, the shimmering of the Styx doing little to light the room. "Where are we?"

"This is your new home, Persephone Snow." He turned his faintly glowing blue eye my way. "And as for where we are, we stand deeper within the earth than most consider it possible to go." Charon's voice took on both an edge of pride as well as a tinge of sadness, if either were truly possible. "Whatever slim hope you held onto that your friends might find and return you to your previous life, you may now concede."

"Abandon all hope, ye who enter here. Isn't that how the saying goes?"

Charon's lone eye pulsed three times in quiet computation. "The sooner you accept your fate, Persephone Snow, the happier you will be."

I accepted nothing, but I wasn't going to tell him that.

"So, you're my jailer, then?"

"I would prefer you think of me as your host, Persephone Snow." Charon backed up a foot into the near darkness. "Fear not. I will visit daily and ensure that all your needs are met. You will have food and drink and clothing and warmth and anything else you might require."

"How about a lightbulb?" I let fly a sarcastic chuckle. "Or maybe some torches on the walls? You know, for a little ambience?" I tried to make jokes, though my knees threatened to knock with each passing moment. "It's a little dark down here, don't you think?"

"My apologies, Persephone Snow. I forgot that you see on a much more limited spectrum than my sensors allow. Perhaps a little illumination?"

Lights throughout the space flared to life, high above and invisible other than the radiance they provided, much like the cameras that had documented every move Ethan and the others made atop the mountain. My eyes slowly adjusted to the subdued radiance of a thousand tiny pinpoints of luminescence and were greeted with another scene that would be forever emblazoned upon my memory.

A few months back, the Sparkle tour passed through Detroit where we played Ford Field, the home of the Lions. Most of the arenas we visited along the way were open to the sky, but Ford Field and a couple others later in the tour were fully enclosed. I wasn't sure how it was possible to feel claustrophobic in a space that looked like it would hold an aircraft carrier, but that night, my breath had caught in my throat as I stepped up to the microphone all the same.

The cavern surrounding Charon and me dwarfed even such a space.

Stretching farther than the eye could see before me with sheer walls to either side, each a football field away, and a ceiling so vast the ghost lights didn't reach, this new place where the Styx had delivered us filled my heart simultaneously with dread and wonder. Was such a subterranean space natural or constructed or both? How deep beneath Earth's surface did I stand? And where in the entire world were we?

Assuming, of course, we were still somewhere on Earth.

"This place is a tomb," I grumbled.

"This place is your home, now, Persephone Snow. As I said before, you will be much happier once you accept that simple fact."

"I'm supposed to live here?" I gestured to the bare stone floor. "To sleep on jagged rock and subsist on whatever ham and cheese sandwiches you may or may not bring?"

"I thought you would like the Monte Cristo, Persephone Snow. I scanned all the known data on your favorite dishes and gleaned that tidbit from an interview you gave ten months, one week, and three days ago. Your response was published in one of the more popular teen magazines. Was the sandwich not to your liking?"

Shit. If I didn't know better, I'd swear I hurt the robot's feelings. Not to mention, that sandwich wasn't just delicious, but tasted like my mom made it herself.

"I'm sorry, Charon. The sandwich was excellent, as good as I've had. I'm just upset about all this. You understand that, don't you? That no matter what you say or do, I have no desire to be here."

"I understand, Persephone Snow. And fear not; you will not be sleeping on rock, but rather on the softest bed in all of Elysium."

"Elysium?"

"You mentioned Tartarus before, Persephone Snow. I assume you were attempting humor, but the master's abode is indeed divided into three realms. For those the master considers guests, Elysium has every comfort imaginable and more. Those who simply require to be kept until they are needed or until their usefulness has expired are kept in Asphodel, but even there, none go hungry, and all receive at least the bare necessities."

"And Tartarus, I'm guessing, for those the big boss really doesn't like?"

"Few are those who deserve or require such dire treatment, Persephone Snow. Contrary to what you might believe, the master is rarely cruel without cause."

"Rarely cruel?" I asked. "He's a murderer of his own kind. In the last three days he's kidnapped me from my home, killed a man who saved my life, and skewered my best friend and the man I love with those damn wing-blades of his."

For once, Charon didn't respond.

"No answer for that one? No fancy quip followed by my full name like you're my fucking mother talking to me like I'm three?"

After a prolonged pause, the robot finally answered with a double pulse of the blue light emanating from his cyclopean eye. "I am sorry, Persephone Snow, if my mode of speech comes across as annoying or demeaning. I communicate in the manner I was programmed, with both clarity and specificity." Another pause with another flash of blue. "As for the Cardinal, I cannot speak to his motivations but only his actions, as such judgment is beyond my capabilities, and my assessment, if you must know, is that your own is accurate, though not necessarily complete."

"He's a psychopathic serial killer who feasts on the power and life force of others of his kind. How much more complete do you want me to get?"

"One advantage of being a human rather than a machine is that you can learn to fathom more than just the what, but the why. I offer that, Persephone Snow, as your challenge."

"My challenge?"

"You will have many hours here in the master's Underworld to contemplate whatever you choose, Persephone Snow. Perhaps it will bring you some peace if you can put a name to your pain and some reason behind the chaos that has overtaken your life."

"I suspect, Charon, that you know more than you say."

"My cortex has instantaneous access to all the information in the world, Persephone Snow. Your statement is therefore, by definition, true."

"Nice dodge." I could tell I wasn't going to get much more out of the little robot. "So...Elysium?"

"Elysium."

I followed Charon as he rolled away from the Styx in the muted ghost light of the enormous hall until we came to an elaborate doorway three stories in height and as broad as a city street. Grecian columns of granite bordered the gigantic stone door to the left and the right, holding up an intricately carved arch emblazoned at its highest point with a letter resembling a capital H.

"An 'H'?" I asked.

"It's from the Ancient Greek," Charon answered. "If it has not been made imminently clear, accuracy is quite important to the master."

Or, this door has been here for far longer than Charon would care for me to know.

"So, do we recite an 'Open Sesame' or something?"

Without a word, Charon turned his glowing eye upon a black onyx panel embedded in the right column, and seconds later, the enormous stone doorway split in two at a seam that was previously invisible, each door opening outward as smoothly as if the two slabs of rock rolled on wheels. At the end of one of the most interminable minutes of my life, the two doors came to a stop, revealing yet another tunnel that extended into the distance, the inscrutable space lit by the same ghostly light.

"Welcome, Persephone Snow, to your new home. I shall return momentarily to orient you to the space, but for the moment, I am being summoned elsewhere. Please step inside and take care to stand clear as the doors close. Also, I must insist that you not venture beyond this atrium until my return."

"Why? Afraid I'll see something you don't want me to see?"

"I fear more, Persephone Snow, that you will get lost and then be afraid."

"I hate to tell you, Charon, but we left 'afraid' in the rearview mirror a few miles back."

"Still, my admonishment stands." Charon backed out of the open doorway as the two massive slabs of stone began to roll closed. "I shall return to your side post haste."

"Counting the seconds." I focused on the blue glow of Charon's lone eye until the several tons of stone encroaching from either side again met in the middle, sealing me off from the rest of the Cardinal's Underworld and leaving me stranded at the entrance of what the Ancient Greeks considered Paradise.

"Lord," came my whispered prayer, as I hoped even God could hear me in such a place, "have mercy on me."

CHAPTER 3

TOO MUCH TIME ON MY HANDS

"Be careful what you wish for," I muttered to myself, remembering my defiant request of the Cardinal that he simply leave me alone. "You might just get it."

Many long hours passed before Charon returned. I fought the overwhelming urge to explore, recognizing the wisdom in my robotic keeper's words. I didn't fear him or the Cardinal, but God only knew where they'd left me, how far or deep this hole in the ground went, or what sort of nightmares might exist in such a place. When the doors leading back to the large chamber containing the Styx finally opened again, Charon called out to me with a pleasant greeting no different than if he were my housekeeper back in Montecito.

I wouldn't admit it, but I'd never been so glad to hear a voice—human, robot, or otherwise—in my entire life.

When I asked him where he had gone, he avoided the topic altogether; ditto any information regarding the emergency that had pulled him away. Had Ethan and the others managed to find the

Cardinal's complex? Had I come even closer to being rescued from a mythic fate that somehow had been in the cards since the name Persephone was first written on my birth certificate, only to be denied? Above all, was this crypt, regardless of how well my captor and his robotic servant reported I'd be treated, to be my new life?

A limited tour of my new home soon followed. My quarters were a brisk walk down one of the tunnels past a series of identical steel doors staggered on either side of the wide stone passageway. My room, both larger and smaller than I'd anticipated, contained all the necessities: a bedchamber outfitted at least as well as some of the nicer hotels I'd booked on my tour, a large bathroom with everything a young woman might possibly need, and a canteen well stocked with various beverages and nonperishables to ensure that I wouldn't go hungry or die of thirst.

It was a million miles from Paradise, but I kept any complaints to myself.

More than anything else in the room, the item that intrigued me most was a monitor no bigger than a laptop screen to the side of the bed that showed a live color image of the world above. A view of the mountain range where the Cardinal had taken me initially, or at least I assumed that was what I was seeing, streamed from the screen a verdant green along with the occasional red, orange, and yellow of early fall, the leaves beginning their colorful transformation at the change of season. In the distance, the setting sun lingered just above the horizon, bringing to an end the first day of I didn't want to know how many in the Cardinal's little man-made hell on earth.

"Not everyone down here gets to keep a little sliver of the day, Persephone Snow." Charon's tone came across as somehow warm despite the cool blue light that streamed from his lone eye. "Consider yourself among the fortunate."

~

If you ask to be left alone, I repeated to myself at least once an hour for days and weeks on end, you shouldn't be upset when that's exactly what you get.

The first month was the hardest. With Charon, my robotic butler/chef/prison guard, my only visitor three times daily, I had to learn how to be by myself for the first time in my life, which wasn't easy for this card-carrying extrovert. I missed Ethan so much, it physically hurt, an emotion only matched by the ever-growing hatred in my heart for the man who put me in this hole: the Cardinal. In any case, with no way of knowing if my warden in red was ever going to visit his most recent prisoner or whether he was even on the same continent as wherever this Underworld of his was located, I worked to develop a relationship of sorts with the only other soul present, living or otherwise.

Every day, Charon would bring me breakfast, lunch, and dinner along with anything else I required, and every day, I would ask the same questions:

A hundred different variations of "Can you get me out of here?"

Every twist imaginable of "Is the Cardinal ever going to let me go?"

Various takes on "What the hell does your boss want with me anyway?"

To his credit, Charon was just as consistent with his answers as he was with keeping me fed and watered. He routinely offered a simple "no" to the first question and always pleaded ignorance to the other two. I fought back the urge with every conversation to scream at the Cardinal's robotic manservant in frustration, as he was merely obeying both his programming and the commands of his master, though there were days I came pretty close. In any case, Charon had become a bit more tight-lipped since being summoned away on my first day, and I didn't want to do anything to screw up relations with the only entity I would have opportunity to speak with for the foreseeable future.

Mid-September became mid-October, and still the Cardinal did not return. Using the digital time from the bottom corner of the lone screen in the room along with each sunrise and sunset, I kept track of the days, carving a calendar of sorts into the wall with a loose stone, and developed a daily routine similar to the one I kept at home in an effort to keep myself sane. Though the leaves on the trees had gone from the bright green of summer to the reds, yellows, and oranges of fall, I refused to let my mind and body lie fallow and waste away. I asked Charon for a chime to awaken me each day at eight, and from there I kept to my daily regimen.

I began with my workout, a blend of the same exercises across the week that I'd done for years to stay in shape, first for TV and then for the stage, combined with a program Rosemary had drilled into my head the few mornings I'd joined her and Ethan. I wasn't allowed to have free weights or equipment in the Cardinal's glorified hole in the ground, so I focused on exercises that used my own weight: push-ups, pull-ups, crunches, squats, dips, and the like, along with a lot of flexibility work and cardio. A few days in, I'd asked Charon if I could at least get something that would serve as a jump rope, and he'd complied the following morning, though he did take the rope back each day as soon as I was done with it. Leaving anything around that a person could use to harm themselves was likely near the top of Charon's programming, but if he or his master knew me at all, they'd know that had never been and would never be an option.

At nine fifteen, I had coffee and whatever food Charon had available on the morning menu at Chez Cardinal. Everything was served on disposable paper plates with plastic spoons my only utensil. Much like the jump rope, it was clear that neither the Cardinal nor Charon wanted me to have access to anything resembling a weapon.

Ten o'clock was fight training. Rosemary had been giving me martial arts lessons here and there at the house when she and Ethan weren't busy training. A few days before everything hit the fan, we'd started practicing a few katas that incorporated elements of various martial arts styles she'd introduced me to. Each morning I'd practice these again and again, putting my body through the motions and committing the movements to memory just as she taught me, hoping that if and when the time came, I'd be strong, fast, and coordinated enough to fight my way to freedom.

Eleven was break time. I'd tell Charon stories, though whether the little mechanical dude listened or simply tuned me out, I had no idea. Still, he was all I had other than a lone monitor that looked out upon the same mountaintop vista day in and day out, never changing except with the time of day and the weather. At times, his glowing eye would shift to a different shade of blue as I spoke, and though I got little more than that from our daily interaction, I learned to be happy with it.

Noon meant lunch time. Charon would vanish for a few minutes only to reappear with a perfectly crafted soup and sandwich platter more than adequate to take care of my hunger pangs. By that time of day, the lack of human conversation would usually be getting to my dyed-in-the-wool extrovert self, but there was nothing to be done about that.

During the afternoon, I'd warm up the pipes and run through various vocal exercises to make sure I kept up my stamina in that capacity as well. Once that was done, I'd sing a few of my songs, keeping up the muscle memory of both lyrics and melody, all the while continuing to analyze what it was about my voice, if anything, that had changed since my Ascension.

At six, the little guy would bring me my last meal of the day, whether I sang for my supper or not. As I understood it, my siren song only worked against other living beings, and as my only audience happened to be three-feet of quasi-sentient steel and circuitry atop a roller ball, not much was going to happen on that front anyway.

And that would be it until breakfast the next morning. Wash, rinse, repeat.

Back in Montecito, I'd occasionally tried to bring the siren voice, if that was even a thing. Sometimes in private with friends and even a few times in public, I'd sing the first thing that popped into my head and focus on putting emotion or willpower into the words and melody. Among our little group, a few reported a subtle shift in their underlying emotions, but nothing beyond what I'd expect from a normal response to a halfway decent singer and a pretty melody. And our experiments out in the world? Nada. Might as well have been Ethan singing for all the influence my voice seemed to have on the world at large.

A video circulated for years on social media of a world class violinist with a million-dollar Stradivarius playing one of the most complex pieces of music ever written in a public place only to have people walk by as if he were just another street performer. In our various field tests, I'd gotten a taste of exactly how that must have felt for the poor guy.

"There's nothing wrong with you," Neko said to me on one of our walks. "When you needed the power back in Vegas and again at the show in L.A., your voice came through in spades."

"Then why can't I do it now?" I'd asked. "You can go all tiger-boy at will. Alba's elementalists and all the shadowmancers as well. Why can't I do that?"

"This is all new to you, sweetie," Neko purred as he considered his next words. "Look, every Ascendant accesses their ability in a different way. Some are more conscious while others are more instinctive. Your power deals with emotion, at least on some level, and therefore, when *your* emotions are coming on full blast, so will that power." He broke into the reassuring laugh of a comforting friend. "Look at it this way. All those fans of yours? It's you they love, you and that pitch-perfect voice of yours. The Ascendant thing? That's just gravy."

Funny thing? A few months ago, I'd never even met Neko. Now, I'd kill to have him here to talk to. Or Mr. Delacroix. Or Rosemary.

And all the while, I tried not to think about how much I missed Ethan. That distant look and crooked smile he gets when he's trying to come up with something funny to say. Those big muscular arms that squeeze you so tight, you think you might suffocate, and yet you don't care. Those tender eyes that look right through you.

Those lips...

I'd tried to erase the image that had remained at the forefront of my mind's eye for weeks, but the scene was burned into my memory.

Rosemary, wounded, draped across Ethan's lap.

Those same strong arms wrapped around her as he refused to let her go.

Ethan leaning forward, lowering his body, his head, his mouth over hers.

The moment their lips met.

And a fire as blindingly white as fresh snow and as powerful as a newborn star erupting around them both.

In the parlance of Jim Morrison and The Doors, Ethan had lit my fire so many times in the month we'd been together, I had trouble remembering a time before he became a part of my life.

But it had never been like that. Not even close.

Ethan loved me.

And Rosemary had become the best friend I'd ever had.

But seeing them like that? Ensconced in a shared flame born of need and desperation and passion?

No irony intended, but the whole thing left me cold.

"Persephone Snow?" The familiar robotic voice announced Charon's presence seconds before he rounded the corner. "Time for your dinner."

Good old Charon. Every evening at six. Like clockwork.

This time, the opened tray revealed a ribeye steak already cut into bite size pieces—no knives or forks for this girl—some roasted potatoes, a handful of steamed broccoli stalks, and a fresh roll with melted butter on top. All that along with a dish of crème brûlée, the rich brown of perfectly caramelized sugar setting off a fresh raspberry at its center, made plain that something was different today.

Everything to that point had been edible fare, but mostly frozen meals that could be warmed and served quickly. This meal, on the other hand, looked like it had been carefully prepared by a live human being in a legit restaurant. Unless the Cardinal had a new chef on site, Charon was practicing some new skills.

"Thank you, Charon." I offered the diminutive metallic torso atop a rollerball a beaming smile. "This is excellent."

"Pleased to be of service, Persephone Snow."

"This is a big step up." I took a bite of the steak. Medium rare, just the way I liked it. "Have you been taking cooking lessons?"

"I'm not certain what you mean, Persephone Snow. I have at my command over 1.5 million recipes from every corner of the world. With enough notice, I can prepare anything you might desire."

"But I haven't been getting steak and crème brûlée before." The little guy backed up half an inch, as if I'd hurt whatever passed for feelings in his little electronic brain. "Not that everything so far hasn't been delicious, of course."

"I am glad you have enjoyed your sustenance." His robotic arms appeared to relax, if that was even possible, as a pair of static pops from the speaker at the center of his chest echoed in the room. "And you are correct. Today is the first day of your second month here in Elysium, and I thought perhaps you might enjoy a meal that reminded you of home."

"It's perfect." He had no idea. "Thank you."

"I trust you've been resting well?"

The conversation was the most Charon had offered since my initial, albeit interrupted, orientation to Elysium.

"As I've told you many times, the bed is quite comfortable, and despite it being a bit cool down here, the flannel sheets and comforter you brought have been keeping me plenty warm."

"I am glad." Charon's robotic head turned to peer directly into my eyes, his cyclopean lens pulsing with its ever-present blue light. "Sustenance. Rest. Activity. Is there anything else you require, Persephone Snow?"

A sarcastic chuckle escaped my lips. "Like I've asked you ten thousand times, can you help me get out of here?"

Something like a sigh echoed from Charon's speakers. "But why would you want to leave, Persephone Snow? Am I not providing for your every need? What more could you possibly want?"

Great. A guilt trip from a robot.

"To see the sky. To feel the sun on my skin. To be with my friends...or anyone."

"Am I not someone, Persephone Snow?"

Damn.

"Of course, but—"

"Inasmuch as an artificial intelligence is capable, Persephone Snow, I am programmed to provide you companionship in the master's absence in addition to all of your basic needs."

"You have to understand, Charon. No matter how comprehensive or efficient or timely your care may be, there is no replacement for human contact."

"You are to remain here until such time as you are needed, Persephone Snow. My instructions on that are clear and the command inviolable."

"Of course."

"No one is to depart Elysium without being given explicit leave."

"No one?" The Cardinal had mentioned "others" before he sent me through the Styx with Charon, but my robotic companion hadn't offered a single clue either way since my first day in the hole no matter how many times I'd brought it up. "So, there *is* someone else down here, isn't there?"

"I am not at liberty to answer that question, Persephone Snow."

"Which, of course, means yes." I leaned forward and peered into Charon's lone eye. "Where are they? Are they okay? Is it one other person? Two? A dozen?"

"I am not at liberty to answer any of these questions, Persephone Snow."

"What can you answer, Charon? Are you not to provide for my every need?"

"Yes, Persephone Snow."

"And is human companionship not a need?"

"Yes, Persephone Snow."

"And is that not something you can provide? I'm not asking to leave, just for someone to talk to."

The blue light emanating from Charon's lone eye diminished in brightness.

"A moment, Persephone Snow."

The black, grey, and blue robot rolled away in silence and vanished around the far corner of the room, ending the longest conversation I'd had in a month with anyone or anything beyond myself. Whether he'd left as part of a protocol because I'd overstepped, or—and this was a long shot—because he was going to bring around whoever else was stuck down here with me for a visit, I had no idea.

But, for the moment, I was again alone.

I finished my dinner and then sat looking at the screen which showed the same westerly mountaintop view it had for the last month. Each couple of days, I'd noticed the sun inching farther and farther to the left of the screen as winter approached, another sign the scene I looked upon was likely real. I'd memorized the beautiful vista to the point I could picture with crystal clarity each and every rock and tree and often focused on that particular image each night as I attempted to fall asleep.

I wondered for the thousandth time if there were as many cameras in this faux Hades as there had been watching the Cardinal battle my friends that day, if the very screen I clung to for some semblance of sanity was itself a form of monitoring device, and if my crimson-clad captor sat in his enormous chair before his bank of monitors at that exact moment watching me. Not knowing whether I was being observed or not, I'd worked to avoid giving my mysterious captor anything worth viewing even more so than the usual vigilance I'd learned in a world full of both paparazzi and fans who didn't always understand boundaries. The Cardinal would be a creeper of a different variety, watching me for signs of weakness or chinks in my metaphorical armor he could exploit to bring me to his side or to perform whatever task he had in mind for the first siren born in a generation.

Lost in thought, I was yanked back to the present by a quick electronic chirp, Charon's version of clearing his throat, that echoed from the doorway to my cell which he'd never left ajar before. The familiar hum of my guard's rollerball growing louder with each passing second hit my ears, punctuated by the rhythmic sounds of quiet footfalls.

I wasn't sure whether to hide, put up my fists, or shout hello.

A thought that hadn't occurred to me before filled my mind with sudden terror: just because there was another human in this hole didn't necessarily mean they would be someone I wanted to talk to or even someone remotely safe.

Yet another reminder to be careful what you wish for.

Charon reappeared around the corner where he'd disappeared minutes before. Close on his figurative heels walked a Chinese woman with a single long braid that began just behind her left ear and hung across her bare shoulder, cascading down an athletic chest, and ending just below her slender waist. Dressed in a silky green sleeveless top, loose black pants, and slipper shoes—a far cry from the blue sweatshirt/sweatpants combo and grip socks that Charon brought me each day to wear—her gentle features culminated with deep brown eyes that seemed to take in all that I was in an instant. The look of trepidation that filled her features immediately faded into one of relief and maybe even recognition.

"As requested, Persephone Snow," Charon spoke in his robotic voice, "human companionship."

"Wait. You're...Persephone Snow?" The woman stared at me in amazement. "The world famous singer?" Her voice, calm and even, hit me like the notes of a lullaby, putting me immediately at ease.

Funny. I thought that was my gig.

"But"—her face twisted in confusion as she continued—"what are *you* doing here?"

"It appears we're both guests of a certain individual who maintains a significant amount of red in his wardrobe." At her silent nod, I continued. "And who, if I may ask, might you be?"

"My name is Jia Li." She offered me a quick bow, if not a smile. "But my friends call me Jade."

CHAPTER 4

TALK TO ME

"Jade?"

"What can I say? Some nicknames stick."

Her words, spoken with just a hint of accent, continued to register in my mind as music as much as speech.

And here I thought I was the siren.

"My family moved to the United States when I was thirteen, halfway through the U.S. school year. Right after the Christmas holiday, my teacher was having trouble saying my name, and"—she glanced down at her top and a hint of pink entered her cheeks—"let's just say I happened to be wearing my favorite color that day as well."

"And none of them ever learned to say your name?"

"It honestly didn't bother me all that much, and compared to some of the other names the girls in my school got called, I was glad to have pretty much slipped under the radar."

"Well, Jade, you can call me Seph." I smiled. "That's what *my* friends call me."

"Is that what we are?" Jade asked. "Friends?"

"I'd like to think so." I glanced around at the stone walls, bare floors, and overhead LED lights of my room. "It would appear we could both use a friend down here."

Another high-pitched chirp from Charon reminded us that we weren't truly alone.

"Persephone Snow and Jia Li Xiao, I have provided each of you with all that you have requested and now have brought the two of you together for what I hope to be a positive interaction. Do either of you require anything further before I return to my chamber to recharge?"

Funny. He'd never mentioned having to recharge before.

"We're sorry, Charon." Jade knelt and gave the robot skritches just behind his glowing blue camera lens eye. "Did we make you feel left out?"

"Of course not, Jia Li Xiao. As you have pointed out more than once, I am an artificial construct and have no true feelings."

"And as you have proven on more than one occasion, my initial understanding of who and what you are couldn't have fallen further from the truth." Jade placed her hands close together and offered the diminutive robot in our midst a humble bow. "My apologies, Charon."

The blue light cascading from Charon's big round eye diminished for a moment.

"Your apology, however unnecessary, is accepted." Charon's upper torso spun 180 degrees atop the grey sphere he used for locomotion as he headed for the door. "Mark the time, Jia Li Xiao. I will return you to your quarters sharply at eight." He paused just before vanishing down the rocky hallway. "And should your host happen to choose today for an inspection, trust that I will be escorting you to your bedchamber far sooner." His tiny robotic head tipped forward ever so slightly. "I suspect he would not approve of this particular co-mingling of guests."

Guests?

Three things.

First, at the earliest opportunity, I planned to disabuse Charon of his notion that Jade and I were anything but prisoners.

Second, my assumption that the Cardinal was watching my every move, Charon's constant in and out notwithstanding, appeared to be erroneous.

And third, to have developed such a close relationship with a rolling bucket of bolts and microchips, Jade had clearly been here far longer than I had.

No sooner had Charon left the room than Jade shook her head and smiled. "Piece of advice? Stay on the little guy's good side. For an artificial intelligence, he's actually quite sensitive."

"He's barely spoken to me the month I've been down here, but I've noticed." My words took the joy from Jade's features, the smile in her eyes replaced instantly with sadness and regret. "I'm curious. How long have you been stuck in this hole?"

"A few months." She looked to one side, unwilling to meet my gaze. "Three or four, maybe? I don't know exactly." Her gaze wandered over to the monitor by my bed, the image of the setting sun from the mountaintop vista as beautiful as I'd seen. The sky at the horizon shone a gorgeous burnt orange that faded into deep crimson before shifting to royal purple at the top. "At least our kidnapper left you with something to look at to pass the time. For weeks, all I've had is a room like yours with four stone walls and the bare necessities. If it weren't for Charon dropping off three meals a day and turning the lights on and off, I wouldn't even know day from night. In fact, the only way I know it's been three months is..." She rubbed at her lower abdomen and winced in discomfort. "Let's just say I'm glad our absent host keeps a well-equipped cave."

I was suddenly glad I'd visited my gynecologist back at the beginning of the year when things with Spencer—God, that seems like ancient history—began to heat up. Last thing I needed while stuck in a cave at the center of the Earth was a visit from Aunt Flo. Thank God for modern medical technology.

My unexpected ally and I had just over an hour until we would be separated again, possibly forever. We needed to use every second to figure out how to free ourselves and get the hell out.

"Question." I leaned in. "The Cardinal has had me locked up down here for a month, and I haven't seen hide nor feather of him. You've been down here three or four. Has he checked in on you? Beyond, of course, our little robotic friend?"

"Not even once." She looked to the open door where Charon had departed. "Since I've been down here, I've wanted for nothing except my freedom and someone to talk to. Unless I'm missing something, the only reason the Cardinal has me down here is to keep me off the grid."

"About that. I'm assuming you're..." I wasn't sure how to ask the question or even the etiquette around such things. "You know..."

"Ascendant? Why else do you think I'm down here?" She thought for a moment. "Wait. You're an Ascendant? Like, for real?"

"It was news to me as well." I pulled in a breath. "I first transitioned—"

"Ascended," Jade corrected.

"Yeah, that. Two months ago, now." I studied her questioning gaze, wondering how much to tell this woman I'd just met. "With an audience of skiomancers, elementalists, the Midnight Angel, El Ángel del Alba, and even the Driver himself."

"All three of them?" Her eyes grew wide. "And which of them are you now beholden to?"

Huh. Girl knew her stuff. "None of them. They declared me a free agent. Let me walk."

"You can't be serious." She leaned in close as if she planned to share a confidence, or I suppose, invite one. "What talent did you exhibit in your moment? Who are you at your heart of hearts, Persephone Snow?"

"Please, call me Seph."

"Seph, then." Her eyebrows rose. "What do you bring to the table, if you don't mind me asking?"

Again, I wondered whether baring all my secrets was the best approach, but in the end, I trusted my gut. Jade hadn't set off any of my internal warning bells, and I needed her if I was going to find my way back home, to freedom, to Ethan.

"I don't understand even a fraction of what I'm theoretically capable of, but my voice can—"

"You're a siren." Her face broke into a wide smile. "I knew it."

"You knew what?"

Her cheeks grew rosy. "I saw you in concert on your first tour, not long after I first Ascended, and the crowd's response was unlike anything I'd ever experienced."

"Experienced? I don't understand."

"I'm an empath. People's emotions are as plain to me as a ray of sunshine, a cool breeze, or a whiff of cologne."

"You sense emotions?"

"All day long, 24/7/365. I know when people are happy or sad, when they're excited or anxious, when they're being honest, and when they're lying. I can sense the spectrum of emotion as easily as you see the colors of the rainbow." She let out a singular laugh. "And let me say, I've been to my fair share of concerts and shows over the years, but the emotional rollercoaster your fans experience seeing you live is unlike anything else." She raised her hands before her, palms out. "Don't get me wrong. Your voice, your performance, your look: they're all on point. There's a reason your music is at the top of the charts independent of anything you learned about yourself two months ago."

"Thanks, I think..."

"What I'm saying is that seeing you perform live was qualitatively different from simply hearing a recording of your voice coming out of a speaker, and that was *before* you Ascended." She shook her head. "That night I came to your concert? You had the crowd eating out of the palm of your hand. From the moment you sang your first note until you took your last bow, any person there would have done anything you asked. And I'd know. I don't think I was fully in my right mind again until I awoke the next morning."

I didn't say a thing, half-afraid she'd stop talking. Her words represented some of the first legit explanation anyone had given me since that night back in L.A. regarding what being a siren meant. Rosemary and Mr. Delacroix had both done their research and given me all the answers they could while Neko and the others told me what they experienced from my song.

But Jade? She was like a Geiger counter to my uranium.

"So, I took control of their minds?"

"Not exactly." She considered for a moment. "As I understand from whispers in the community, a siren is more like a sculptor who can shape the emotional state of anyone who hears their song. You don't control the listener so much as you amplify in them whatever you put out yourself: happiness, desolation, jealousy, peace, and—I suspect, if you put your mind to it—fear, doubt, even hate, not that any of those seem like anything you'd promote. The human mind and soul are clay in your hands, Seph, at least metaphorically speaking."

Damn. Girl was eloquent. Whether that was part of being an empath or Jade simply had the gift of gab, I had no idea, but I found myself liking her more by the minute. And in the end, such a distinction didn't really matter anyway.

We are all exactly who we are, after all. No more, no less.

"Another question."

"Hit me," she said.

"You sense emotions. Did you register when I arrived? Could you feel it when Charon brought me across the Styx?"

"I could tell something had changed. The background noise of our little section of the Cardinal's Underworld suddenly had a new aspect: another note in the chord being played, if you will."

"Background noise?" I puzzled over the words. "Wait. So there *are* others down in this hole."

"I assumed you knew. Though it would seem the Cardinal himself rarely deigns to set foot down here, he clearly has no issue with leaving people he wishes to keep out of circulation in this hole to rot."

"How many more of us are there?"

"Hard to say. More than one, I think. This place is enormous, and my range does have its limits."

"Got it. Different topic. I have no idea why the Cardinal stuck me down here or why I'm even still alive. Do you know why he's keeping either of us around?"

"I was in Argentina with a group of Ascendant tracking the Cardinal when he ambushed us. He took out the rest of my squad to the man and captured me." Tears welled at the corners of her eyes. "He took me to an underground hideaway somewhere in the mountains of Peru, at least as far as I know, and after a day or so, he had Charon escort me across the Styx. I've been his guest, prisoner, whatever, here in Elysium ever since."

"My experience was very similar, though I'm pretty sure the place he took me to access the Styx was somewhere along the west coast of North America." I made a mental note to ask more about this group of Ascendant with whom Jade had been tracking the Cardinal, but that was going to have to wait. "The Styx. That was basically teleportation, right?"

"As far as I know," Jade answered.

"You're way closer with Charon than I am. Has he said anything about where this damned place is located on the globe?"

"I've asked him every way I know how, but he has remained extremely quiet on the subject." She looked again at the monitor by my bed. "Anyway, you're the one with the fancy screen that shows you the outside."

"While you got the fancy wardrobe." I compared her silky green outfit to my plain uniform of blue sweats. "It's a good look, by the way. Too bad it's wasted down here."

"Thanks, Seph. You're very kind." She laughed, the sound whole-hearted and beautiful. "I have to admit, though; I'm in awe of the fact you can take even the Cardinal's sweatsuit prison uniform and make it look fashionable."

Yep. I liked her just fine.

"So, these others you can sense. Where are they?" I locked gazes with Jade. "More importantly, who are they?"

"Like I said, this place is huge, and my ability is not exactly directional, though I get the impression that the two of us are alone in Elysium and whoever else is down here with us is...somewhere else."

That meant either Asphodel, where I'm guessing the Cardinal would stick prisoners he was even less fond of than Jade and me, or

Tartarus, where the worst of the worst would go. Neither of these options sounded like anyone we'd want to meet.

"I've felt their anger, their loneliness, and their despair throughout my stay here." Jade's eyes shifted left and right. "However long I've been the Cardinal's captive, at least some of them have been here even longer."

"Not sure what we'd even do about it. The only reason we're talking is because Charon allowed it. Even if we had the run of Elysium, we'd still have to escape to the Styx chamber before we could access the other sections."

"How'd you swing our little chat, anyway? I've done everything I could think of to ingratiate myself with our robotic friend for months. What did you say to him to make this happen?"

I shook my head and shrugged. "I don't have the first clue."

"Surprise, surprise, Persephone, Queen of Hades, has some sway with the Ferryman of the Underworld." Jade laughed. "You sure your siren song doesn't work on robots?"

I answered her laugh with a sarcastic chuckle of my own. "Maybe it's just my sparkling personality and quick wit." I let out a plaintive sigh. "In any case, at least we've both made a friend in this hellhole."

"Indeed." Jade checked the time in the corner of the monitor. "Seven twenty. We have forty minutes before Charon comes back."

"What do you have in mind?"

She motioned to the open door leading to the hall beyond. "A little exploring?"

Jade and I poked our heads into the hall, the scene straight out of *Scooby Doo*, and when we determined the coast was clear, we stole down the hallway toward the main door of Elysium. At the central hub of the three main corridors, we came to the gigantic twin slabs of stone.

"What now?" I asked. "Pretty sure my siren song doesn't work on rock."

"I don't know." Jade smiled. "I read once that the song of Orpheus could make even the stones weep."

"I'll get right on that." I shot her an incredulous stare. "Seriously, what do we do now? I'm pretty sure Charon is the only one who can open these doors, and I can tell you for a fact I'm not going anywhere near the Styx without the little guy."

"We may not be able to leave, but maybe there is something we can do." Before I could ask what she meant, Jade slipped to one side of the gigantic door where a metal box with vertical slits protruded from the wall.

"What is that?" I asked. "An intercom?"

"Maybe." She ran her fingers along the edge of the metal. "Whatever it is, the technology is way more old school than that monitor in your room." She shot me a quizzical glance. "Do you think it works?"

"Maybe." I raised an eyebrow. "Why?"

"What if it broadcasts your voice past the door and into the main cave with the Styx?" Jade studied the metal box. "Or maybe even the other chambers?"

"Worth a shot." An idea flashed across my thoughts. "Wait. You said you could sense a shift in the emotions of my audience when I sang, right?"

"Without a doubt."

"And that was before I Ascended." I searched the box for any sort of button or mechanism that might allow me to broadcast. "Perhaps a little ditty?"

"Can't hurt to try." Her expression made clear she was picking up what I was putting down. "If the others can hear you, it may augment their emotional volume to where I can get a better feel for how many others are stuck down here like us."

The loudspeaker in my personal quarters had only come alive a couple of times in the preceding month, both times with Charon checking in on me. Once had been a day when I wasn't feeling well, and the other was the middle of the night a week ago when I'd fallen out of bed after a particularly violent nightmare. Assuming that all the rooms were outfitted with similar communication equipment, I might just be able to reach the other prisoners.

If their rooms were set up similarly.

And if the various chambers of this Underworld were interconnected.

And if this particular intercom would allow such communication with anywhere else in the complex.

Too many ifs, but the only two choices were to give it a shot or just give up.

My fingers found a button on the bottom right corner of the box next to a dial that turned clockwise until it wouldn't turn any further. I wondered briefly if this was some sort of test or trap. Surely Charon knew the box was out here, and yet, he'd left me alone with the door open with a co-conspirator. As much as I wanted to think I'd outsmarted my captor, a big part of me felt like I was being led down the proverbial cherry path.

That being said, there was no other path to follow that I could see.

I pressed the button and a tiny LED light I hadn't seen atop the box began to glow a bright green.

"Hello," I began. "This message is for anyone else here held captive by the man known as the Cardinal. Know that you are not alone. We understand that you may not be able to respond, but for the moment, just listen and know that help is on the way."

With that, I cleared my throat, pulled myself fully upright, and took a deep breath before launching into the opening lines of "Snowblind," the first track from my eponymous debut album and my first big hit. A lyrical tale of two people, each in love with the other and each too swept up in the hustle bustle of the world around them to know their feelings are reciprocated, the lyrics didn't exactly apply to the situation at hand, but as we were basically flying blind, it seemed as good a selection as any.

Not to mention, I could sing the song in my sleep.

And had, on more than one occasion.

As I belted my way through the second verse and launched into the chorus, Jade's eyes went wide even as they filled with tears, and she began to sob. I didn't dare stop, though. God only knew how long we had before Charon returned and—

"Persephone Snow. What are you doing?"

Shit.

I finished the last line of the chorus before pulling my finger from the button and stepping away from the box, ironically to face the music.

"Charon." I didn't think it was possible for a metallic face consisting of a tiny speaker hole and an expressionless camera eye to look pissed off.

I was wrong.

"I granted you the human interaction you asked for, trusting you not to take advantage of my good faith, and you have abused your privilege."

"I'm sorry, Charon. I just...I thought there might be others here and that hearing from another human might help them—"

"You have taken advantage of the few liberties I am able to offer you and the others within my current programming parameters, and in doing so, have forced me to reinstitute standard prisoner precautions for everyone."

Prisoner. It was the first time I'd not been addressed as a "guest." Things were about to change.

"Please don't punish her, Charon," Jade pleaded. "The entire thing was my idea."

A lie, but an appreciated one.

"Persephone Snow, return to your bedchamber and await further instruction." Charon spun in Jade's direction. "Jia Li Xiao, come with me."

"We meant no harm, Charon," Jade whispered. "We only wanted to—"

"Jia Li Xiao, come with me, now." The blue light pouring from Charon's lone eye doubled in intensity as his tiny torso spun around and his spherical base sent him trundling back down the stone hallway. "Both of you will continue to receive your daily rations, but only if you cooperate immediately."

"Understood." I trudged back toward the room that had served as a cell for the last month, trying with each step to catch Jade's gaze before we were separated. Despite the efforts of our diminutive robotic guard, our eyes did meet for the briefest moment just before I stepped inside and Charon could close the door.

"Three others," she mouthed as she rested a trio of slender fingers at her collarbone before disappearing from sight.

Three.

Prisoners or not, Jade had picked up on three other people in range of her Ascendant ability with our experiment in emotional sonar. Who these people were—friend, foe, or perhaps even our captor himself—God only knew.

But if there were three other prisoners down here with us, we owed it to them to find out.

Not to mention, if any of us were going to get out of the Cardinal's hell on earth alive, two was better than one, and five was way better than two.

CHAPTER 5

ELECTRIC YOUTH

It didn't take long for me to develop a new appreciation for what Jade and any others in the hole had experienced as a captive of the Cardinal. The downgrade from "guest" to "prisoner" stripped from me the few privileges I'd enjoyed.

First and foremost, I missed the mountaintop vista right there in my room, the one tiny escape I'd had from the stone that always encroached from every side. I'd had no idea how much something as simple as seeing the sun rise and set each day truly meant to me until all I had to look at was a blank screen day in and day out.

Charon's already brusque interactions grew even more curt. The quality of the food that continued to come three times each day never faltered even as the delivery of my meals became even more robotic than before. I wondered if he was giving Jade the cold shoulder as well, as they had struck me as remarkably close in our brief interaction. I wasn't sure what it said about me that the fact he seemed to like her better than me hurt a bit. With the mythical link between our names, I'd assumed that he'd been designed and built as my very own personal assistant, minus the person, of course. Ah, to have gone from "Reigning Pop Princess of the World" to caring about which of us a Roomba with decent conversational skills preferred? My how the mighty had fallen.

In any case, I quickly learned that a soft bed, decent food, and access to a hot shower did little to make up for the monotony of solitary confinement. What little conversation Charon and I had shared prior to the incident had devolved into little more than the robot's monosyllabic answers to literally anything I asked. To be fair, never once was a need of mine overlooked; I stayed well fed, never went thirsty, was perfectly comfortable, and was given more than adequate supplies to keep my hygiene up. But beyond that? Our occasional banter, the previous indulgences, the intermittent companionship? All of that was gone.

I couldn't even be mad about it. Charon was an artificial intelligence with strict parameters in place for our supervision and possibly even our safety, and Jade and I had overstepped. At the end of the day, he was our prison guard, not our friend. The fact that I still had hot water and regular food? A win.

I tried to apologize more than once. My scalp crawled each time, particularly when I tried to reconcile that I was begging the forgiveness of a rolling mass of metal, wire, and microchips. And yet, despite the fact that Charon's thought processes were, as I understood it, a bunch of ones and zeroes, the little guy definitely possessed a sensitive soul just like Jade said. Balancing the logic of conversing with a computer while avoiding stepping on a robot's delicate feelings was a new game for certain.

Another month passed before I decided I should start the process of winning our little robotic friend back over to our side, if only by an inch.

"Thank you for breakfast, Charon." I took a bite of the buttered croissant and washed it down with a sip of black coffee. "Delicious as always."

"Your health is imperative to the mission, Persephone Snow. Therefore, you will be cared for to the best of my ability."

Attempted deflection. I tried again.

"The eggs, though," I said after taking a bite of omelet, "top notch."

Charon turned to stare at me like a puppy dog that wished to be petted but expected to be kicked. "Thank you." The blue light emanating from his eye dimmed. "My instructions are to take the meager fare available here and make it as palatable as possible. I am glad that my efforts meet with your approval."

Literally ten times as many words as he'd said in weeks.

"It must be difficult to provide for however many people your master keeps in this place. However do you keep up with all the demand? Do you have help, or are you—"

"Your efforts to determine the presence or absence of other individuals here beyond Jia Li Xiao will not meet with success. My instructions are to ensure that you are healthy and well-maintained. Beyond that, I am to leave you and Jia Li Xiao, along with any other individuals whose existence I have neither confirmed nor denied, to your own devices in your individual rooms."

"But we're like a mile down, right? And I'm guessing a place this huge could house a small town. How could you possibly provide for everyone by yourself, and particularly with this quality of nourishment?" I favored him with my best smile. "Am I somehow still getting special treatment, you big softie?"

"You are attempting to sway my favor with flattery and familiarity in an effort to get me to forget your previous transgression, are you not, Persephone Snow?"

"Guilty as charged." I shot him a quick wink. "Is it working?"

"My programming is very specific about what is and is not allowed to occur within the master's facility."

"That's not what I asked, Charon." I dropped to one knee and rested a hand just above his round camera eye. "I'm trying, yet again, to apologize for overstepping with Jade."

"There is no need for apology, Persephone Snow. You did what you felt you needed to do, which necessitated me doing precisely what I am programmed to do, which is to keep you safe, fed, comfortable, and, most importantly, here. It is as simple as that."

"I understand. To be fair, though, I didn't make any effort to leave, only to contact anyone else in this—let's call it what it is—prison. You allowed Jade and I to speak. Was it so far of an extrapolation to think that I would be allowed to speak with others?"

Charon remained silent for a moment, as if processing his response.

"Your use of the master's communication equipment was unauthorized."

"And for that, I again apologize." Time to roll the dice. "A question. If there were others here outside of me and Jade, would they be allowed to have interpersonal contact as we were? Jade and I didn't violate any critical programming when we were conversing, as you were the one who introduced us."

Another long pause as Charon considered my question.

"Not every individual falls under the same risk protocol as Jia Li Xiao."

"So there are others here."

"I did not say that." A hint of frustration entered Charon's robotic tone. "I merely stated that among the various Ascendant in my database, Jia Li Xiao is considered an acceptable risk to be allowed in your presence."

"You should have been a lawyer," I said with a groan.

"I was not aware that law schools accepted artificial intelligences."

I shook my head. "I was joking, Charon."

"Was my answer not a joke as well, Persephone Snow?"

The tiny robot's monotone only amplified the deadpan delivery, and I laughed despite the dire circumstances. For an entity of gears, wires, and microchips, Charon proved a bit of a charmer. In any case, the gates of communication were again open, if only a crack.

Which was a good thing, because for the months that followed, Charon's was the only voice I heard other than my own.

Some days I was strong, and others I was weak. With way more time than is healthy for a person to think about every single word I'd ever said and every single thing I'd ever done, good or bad, I cried more days than I didn't. Monotony and I didn't get along, and yet that was the order of the day. Every day.

I missed everyone and everything. I missed Ethan. Even more, I missed my mom. Desolation and despondence crept at the periphery of my consciousness from my first waking moment each day until I closed my eyes for sleep each night, and even my dreams were not immune to the utter isolation and loneliness, but regardless, each and every day, I did what I had to do to stay sane.

I kept to my routine, made sure I kept my pipes in top condition, and put on more muscle than I'd had in my entire life. Charon would allow me out into the hallway each morning—every second of which was supervised, of course—to get in some sprints and other cardio, but most of the work I did throughout the waking hours went toward improving my upper body and core strength. I practiced the punches, kicks, blocks, and katas that Rosemary taught me until they became ingrained in my muscle memory and bloodied my knuckles more than once learning to strike a bare stone wall.

I contemplated the obstacles between me and freedom: the locked door of my cell, the gigantic slabs of stone that blocked my way into the main chamber of the complex, the Styx itself. Knowing the only doorway to the surface would disintegrate me should I attempt to cross its threshold without holding my prison guard's hand was a powerful deterrent. Still, even on my worst day, I never gave up hope that I would see the sun again. And Mom. Rosemary. Ethan.

God only knew if I'd have another opportunity to escape, but I swore if the moment came, I would be ready. Physically, mentally, emotionally.

If there was one thing six long months in captivity taught me, it was patience.

And then, two days after the six-month anniversary of my being escorted through a techno-magical doorway of shimmering energy and into my own personal Underworld by a robot that had somehow become confidant if not friend, it appeared the moment I'd been waiting for had finally arrived.

Charon had just delivered my breakfast and was inquiring about my needs for the day when the lights flickered, the first time I remembered that happening since my arrival. After months of taking the few amenities of Elysium for granted, I was reminded that the Cardinal's Underworld existed somewhere deep within the earth and the fact that we had food, water, electricity, and heat in such a place was as much a miracle as any feat I'd seen an Ascendant perform since this all began.

I'd never been particularly claustrophobic, but in that moment, I understood all too well the fear of enclosed spaces.

The momentary outage of power jarred Charon, the blue light emanating from his lone eye dimming as if in concentration. "Pardon, Persephone Snow. I'm not certain what caused this brief interruption in power, but it appears to have—"

The lights went out again, and this time, took much longer to return to life. Only the faint blue from Charon's eye staved off the pitch blackness.

"This is not normal." Charon turned to the door as the lights came back up, albeit dimmer than before, his tiny arms shifting into a defensive posture as weaponry sprouted from all over his torso. "I fear something has gone wrong."

"Something with one of the other prisoners?" I asked. "No sense in playing word games if we're in danger, Charon. Your primary mission is to keep me safe and healthy, right? If someone or something is coming—"

"No harm will come to you, Persephone Snow." The lights went out a third time, if only for the briefest instant. "But do stay behind me." A crackle like lightning followed by a rumble of thunder reverberated through the space. "If with my last circuit, know that I will defend you."

Not only charming, but gallant as well. Not bad for an artificial intelligence. I'd dated men with fewer manners.

Another crackle. Another rumble. Whoever or whatever was coming was getting closer.

I ran through the list of various Ascendant types I'd learned about so far: shadowmancers, elementalists, theriodans, technomancers, power vampires like the Cardinal, not to mention the next-level ones like the Driver and the Angels.

"Not to put too fine a point on it, but you don't perchance happen to have someone down here that can throw lightning, do you?"

"An elektromancer, you mean?" Charon asked.

That would be a yes. "Elektromancer, huh? And as a being made of metal who runs on electricity, how does that make you feel exactly?"

Interesting. I didn't know that a robot could shudder.

"Are we in danger?" I asked.

Charon turned to me, and though his design basically precluded facial expressions, he could not have appeared more incredulous had he tried.

"I'll take that as an affirmative." From just beyond my cell's locked steel door came a loud crash followed by another crackling rumble and another instance of lights out.

This time, they didn't come back up.

Only the quiet hum of Charon's metal chassis and my own quick breaths broke the silence. With only the faint blue light coursing from Charon's lone eye, we moved quietly to the far corner of the room to await whoever or whatever was coming.

We didn't have long to wait.

With an ominous electric sizzle, the massive door to my quarters lit up on all sides like a magnesium flare. Countless sparks crackled at the edges of the steel rectangle, sending rivets popping from the frame to fly past my head like tiny bullets. As the door's handle began to glow a bright orange, I grabbed Charon and dragged him back into the shallow alcove that housed my toilet and shower.

"The door's going to blow!" I shouted as I wrestled with him. "Come on!"

No sooner had I heaved his heavy metal body out of the line of fire than the steel door came careening across the room, shattering my bed into a million pieces and embedding itself in the dark rock wall.

"You saved me, Persephone Snow." Honest confusion filled Charon's robotic voice. "But I am supposed to protect you."

A static pop in the hallway coupled with a flash of silver light prompted from me, of all things, a laugh.

"The day is young, Charon," I whispered as I peered around the corner at the destroyed doorway. "Unless I miss my guess, you're about to get your chance."

The hallway went deathly quiet. No electric crackle, no rumbling thunder. Nothing.

And then, footsteps.

Slow.

Deliberate.

A menacing counterpoint to my own racing heartbeat pounding in my ears.

Preceded by the silver-blue glow emanating from the arcs of electricity that coursed between the outstretched fingers of his right hand, a young man no more than five years my senior stepped into the room. His skin the rich brown characteristic of the Indian subcontinent and his long black hair pulled back in a ponytail, he was dressed in the same drab blue sweats that had been my daily wear for months. Jade had said she'd been stuck in the Cardinal's underground prison for around three months when we spoke five months back. The man's haunted expression coupled with his waist-length locks suggested he'd been here much longer.

As he met my gaze, his deep brown eyes began to glow with the same blue electricity, but where I expected to find rage, I found only disappointment.

"Where is the bastard, robot?" His eyes, radiating raw electricity, lit the room as he glared our way. "Where is your master? I would have words with him." His speech quick and his syllables clipped, the man's thick accent confirmed he hailed from the opposite end of the world.

"Calm yourself, Sunil Jayalal." Charon rolled out of the tiny alcove to interpose himself between me and this strange newcomer. "The master is indisposed currently, and you will therefore speak with me." The blue glow of Charon's eye increased in intensity, as if in answer to the glow pouring from Sunil Jayalal's electricity-filled eyes. "I trust you remember the last time you attempted to escape."

Sunil directed a finger crackling with electricity at Charon, my little guardian's torso bristling with weaponry like a high-tech porcupine. "You speak boldly for a creature that subsists on the very thing that I command."

"And you, Sunil Jayalal, subsist on food and water. If you destroy me, who do you think will keep you fed and hydrated, clothed and warm?"

"That is of little concern, robot," Sunil spat through clenched teeth, "for I do not intend to be in this place much longer."

"You may have destroyed that door and any others that stood in your path as you tore your way through this complex, Sunil Jayalal, but if you think you can leave the master's Underworld alone without my assistance, you are delusional."

Sunil smiled, the expression anything but pleasant. "And who said I was alone?" He whistled, and from the hallway, a sound similar to Charon's internal motors answered. The high-pitched hum of an accelerating motor and the sound of rubber wheels on stone grew louder and louder until a powered wheelchair appeared in the shattered doorway, bringing with it yet another new face to our little party.

Hunched to one side in the chair sat a Japanese boy on the cusp of manhood. He appeared L.J.'s age, but in his current condition, it was difficult to tell exactly. His unwashed hair went in every direction, and his blue sweatsuit hung wrinkled from wiry arms and withered legs. His eyes rested nearly closed as if he were stoned, half asleep, in a trance, or all of the above.

"You freed him, Sunil Jayalal?" Charon asked with a chirp akin to a gasp. "Do you wish for everyone in this complex to die?"

I had no idea what Charon was so upset about, but any of the brashness he'd shown when dealing with Sunil had suddenly evaporated.

"As you mentioned, robot, my past experience suggested that getting out of here on my own was an unlikely proposition at best. This guy, on the other hand, may know a thing or two about getting out of a cave, regardless of where it might be situated."

"There are fail-safes in place, you know. The master is no fool."

"Then you'd best get to work, robot." He gestured to the kid in the motorized wheelchair. "Your master will be none too pleased if he comes back and finds his subterranean getaway reduced to a pile of rubble and all the live chess pieces he's been saving up crushed beneath tons of rock."

"You wouldn't survive such a disaster, Sunil Jayalal." The light pouring from Charon's lone eye dimmed. "You would commit suicide just to spite me after I've taken such excellent care of you for all these months?"

"Look. You know what this kid can do. He may still be waking up from whatever you and your boss have been pumping into him for months, but I'm pretty sure when it comes down to brass tacks, anyone standing next to my boy when the rocks start crashing in is going to be just fine."

A geomancer, then. Ethan and Rosemary had gone up against such an Ascendant several times between Denver and Los Angeles, one of Alba's elementalists, a giant sumo of earth, asphalt, and concrete. I'd seen the hydromancer, Violeta, simply transform into water or ice at will, but I wasn't certain if a geomancer's abilities worked in quite the same way. Still, I was reassured knowing we likely had a living, breathing bulldozer on our side.

Assuming of course that either he or Sunil the elektromancer were on anyone's side but their own.

"So, robot," Sunil continued, "are you going to start opening some doors and letting me and my friend out of this hole, or is he going to have to start shaking things up around here?"

"Do not make idle threats, Sunil Jayalal," Charon answered. "You have threatened my existence despite the fact I have kept you in good stead, and now—"

"In good stead?" Electricity coursed between Sunil's palms, illuminating the room as bright as day for the first time since the lights went out. "I have been trapped in this damned hole for over a year. Your master killed my friends and then left me here to rot. You expect me to sit here and be grateful simply because you didn't let me starve?"

"Wait," the kid in the wheelchair whispered, breaking the tension of the moment. "Snow? Persephone Snow?"

"Yes." The first word I'd uttered since Sunil wrecked my room and started throwing around what I considered anything-but-idle threats. I stepped out of the alcove and took a position behind Charon. "You know me?"

"Everyone knows you." The boy leaned forward in his chair, squinting at me in the low light given off by Sunil's electricity. "So, you're still a captive of the Cardinal after all this time."

"Hold on." Sunil snapped his fingers, and with a static crackle, the lights in the room immediately came back up. "*The* Persephone Snow?"

"Last time I checked." I gave them both a quick wave. "Careful with those lightning fingers of yours, pal. Something happens to me, you won't have to worry about the Cardinal coming for you. I have fans pretty much everywhere these days, and they take such things quite seriously." At Sunil's cross expression, I raised my other hand before me in faux surrender and shot him my best smile. "A joke, Sunil. Just a joke."

"But why would the Cardinal..." His voice trailed off as he gave me a frank up and down as if he'd never seen a woman before. "Wait a minute. Are you kidding me? You're Ascendant?"

"If only I were kidding." I shot him a wicked grin. "And yes. I'm Ascendant."

"But," he stared at me, agape, "you're...you. Like, famous and everything."

"Yep." I nodded in exasperation. "And yet, here I am."

"I was there when she Ascended." The kid in the motorized wheelchair pulled further into the room. "It was something to behold."

"You were there?" I asked. "Back in L.A.?"

"I'm surprised you don't remember me." He straightened himself in his chair. "I tend to leave a big impression." He raised an eyebrow and let out a half-asleep chuckle. "Several, actually, pretty much wherever I go."

I studied his compact form, wracking my brain for any familiarity.

Slim torso. Not much muscle. Atrophied legs.

Geomancer.

"No way." I gasped in surprise. "You're..."

"Though we've never been properly introduced, Miss Snow, we have indeed met." Despite appearing quite drowsy from whatever sedative the Cardinal had been pumping into him, the recovering geomancer extended a surprisingly steady hand. "My name is Daichi."

CHAPTER 6

YOU'RE A FRIEND OF MINE

"Daichi?" I asked. "Alba's geomancer?"

He tilted his head forward, as much of a bow as he could manage. "The same."

I swallowed, hard. "The gigantic sumo of rock and concrete that almost took out me and my friends like half a dozen times?"

"That's me. And...sorry about that. Our instructions were to isolate you from the Daughter of Neith—may her soul rest in peace — and then take you to Los Angeles to meet El Ángel del Alba. We weren't to harm you in any way, but when I'm involved, things tend to get broken whether I like it or not."

"How does that work, though? The pile of rock that almost kicked our ass was a good ten feet tall."

"If big, bad, and rocky is the Tootsie pop, then I'm the chewy center."

"But you're...I mean..." I didn't know how to finish the sentence. Every other Ascendant I'd met seemed a perfect physical specimen, not to mention if they were injured, as Rosemary constantly reminded us all, they healed fast.

"What happened to you? Don't Ascendant bounce back from pretty much anything that doesn't kill them?"

"Nothing happened to me, at least nothing like what you're talking about." Daichi manipulated the tiny joystick in the arm of his chair, propelling him a couple feet closer. "Ascension isn't a cure-all for every ailment, unfortunately. Cerebral palsy left me paraplegic since birth, but if I'm being honest, I've always considered myself lucky."

"Lucky?" I asked. "Like the geomancer stuff allowing you to walk?"

"More like it could have been a lot worse." He stretched both hands to the ceiling. "My legs may not work all that well, but I have full use of my arms, decent upper body strength, and a sharp mind. I've met a lot of kids over the years who were way worse off than me." He wriggled his eyebrows, his face shifting into a subtle smile. "The geomancy came way later."

"And when you're big and rocky, you're..."

"Wearing a few tons of whatever was beneath my feet when I suited up."

"But how do you breathe in there? I mean—"

"Enough. You two can continue your little how-does-all-this-work session once we've left this place." Sunil knelt before Charon. "Now, robot, are you going to show us the way out, or does Daichi here need to start a rumble?"

"There are others here," I spoke before Charon could answer. "At least two more."

Assuming that Jade's count of other individuals in the complex was correct and that two of the three now stood before me, then we needed to track down both her and one other before we left this place. As much as I wanted to simply cut and run, I wasn't leaving anyone to face whatever fate the Cardinal had planned for us.

"Five months ago, Charon allowed me a brief conversation with another of the Cardinal's 'guests.'" I rested a hand atop the robot's head in an effort to keep him quiet while I tried to negotiate him not getting his every circuit fried by a pissed-off elektromancer. "Do either of you know an empath called Jade?"

"Nope," Daichi answered.

"Never heard of her," Sunil added.

"Seriously?" Huh. I figured a group of Ascendant chatting would be the very definition of small world. "Well, she sensed three others when the two of us were together. I assume you two are among those she detected."

"So, I'm guessing you want to find her and this other Ascendant before we jet." Sunil cracked his neck. "Got it." He eyed Charon. "Lead on, robot."

"My instructions are to keep you all here, Sunil Jayalal." Charon's robotic voice wavered between certainty and doubt. "I cannot violate my instructions."

"Listen to me, you stupid box of gears and circuits." Electricity crackled in Sunil's angry gaze. "I'm going to violate something else if you don't—"

I raised a hand, and surprisingly, Sunil went quiet.

"Charon," I cajoled, "I understand that you are only trying to follow your programmed instructions in relation to us, correct?"

"Affirmative, Persephone Snow."

Good. He was listening. "Now, tell me, as you have before; what is your primary directive in regards to me?"

He paused, whether out of computation or straight-up hesitation, I had no idea. "To ensure your health and well-being, Persephone Snow."

"And these others?"

Another pause. "The same."

Both Daichi and Sunil stood agape at this revelation.

"And your secondary mandate, in regards to all of the Cardinal's prisoners?"

"To keep each and every one of you within this complex."

"Lastly," I asked, "what are your orders should the first and second directives conflict?"

A third pause, this one the longest. "To err on the side of your collective safety."

"What I'm hearing is you won't help us, but you also won't stop us."

Charon's silence was all the answer I needed. Funny. Mom always joked that if I hadn't gone into show business, I was destined for law school.

"You see?" I locked gazes with Sunil, his eyes still crackling with silver-blue energy. "Charon isn't going to hurt any of us unless, I suppose, one of us is threatening the other." I stepped from behind Charon and held out a hand to Sunil. "So, why don't we cut the electric light show and start working together to escape this place?"

His eyes flicked from me to Charon, the robot's humanoid chassis still bristling with weaponry. With a quiet growl, he dismissed the electrical field around his hand, took mine, and gave it a firm shake.

"You seem to have a way with the robot," he said with grudging respect. "Technomancer?"

"Not even close," Daichi said before I could answer. "Snow's a siren, dude. First one born in decades."

Sunil released my hand, stepped back, and gave me a quick up and down. "Siren? Makes sense, I guess." His eyes dropped to Charon. "The robot just likes you, then?"

"First," Charon said, his voice even more deadpan than usual, "you might observe that she doesn't call me 'robot.'"

Sunil's eyes narrowed at Charon. "Noted."

"So," Daichi said, "where do we begin?"

"First," Charon said, "understand that my acknowledgement that I am not to allow any of you to come to harm does not indicate that I will help you leave this place until such time as the master directs me to do so."

"Of course," I answered.

"To begin with, Daichi Kanda," Charon said, "you must agree to keep to a minimum the use of your geomantic talents for the duration."

"And why is that, exactly?" A slight rumble shook the room as the irritated geomancer finally appeared to be recovering from whatever drugs the Cardinal had used to keep him down.

"As I've said, the security system of the master's grand complex includes certain fail-safes. While my programming may prioritize the shared well-being of all current guests, I cannot guarantee the same from the much less sophisticated protocols built into this complex against what could be perceived as an attack."

Daichi let out a quiet huff. "Noted."

Charon's lone eye turned up to Sunil. "I would advocate similar restraint in relation to your electrical abilities, Sunil Jayalal. You have proven most fortunate thus far that your interruption of this complex's power hasn't brought the proverbial hammer down upon your head, but I cannot guarantee that such luck will continue."

"In case no one but me sees what's happening here, the robot—" Sunil stopped mid-sentence, clearing his throat "—I mean, *Charon* here is basically shutting us down. Take away elektromancy and geomantic manipulation and all we're left with is a siren's song, an emotion detector, and whatever the last of the Cardinal's captives might bring to the table."

"To be fair, Sunil Jayalal, I've made it clear that I have no intention of helping all of you to escape, only that I was executing my prime function to keep the lot of you alive and well until the master is again available to decide what next steps are necessary where each of you are concerned."

A sound like Charon's rollerball multiplied several times over echoed from the hallway outside my room.

"And speaking of the complex's fail-safes," Charon mumbled.

Half a dozen robotic drones like those I'd seen deployed against Ethan and the others during their mountaintop melee, two airborne and the remaining four with locomotion like Charon's, entered the room and immediately rushed us like a hive of angry hornets.

The two flying drones spewed a noxious mist, and I dove to one side to avoid getting a face full of the green gas. I had no idea what it would do to me, but I had a nasty feeling it wasn't anything I wanted to experience.

With a snap of his fingers, Sunil dropped the one attacking me, sucking the electricity from its circuits into his outstretched hand. The second, however, hit him full in the face with the greenish mist, sending him blinded and coughing to his knees.

Simultaneously, three of the ground drones rushed Daichi's wheelchair, surrounded him, and launched a trio of nets crackling with electricity to ensnare and disable him. As the three nets discharged into both Daichi and the powered wheelchair, the repeated shocks sent his arms and even his atrophied legs into spasm as if he were having a seizure. Despite what had to be maddening pain, he somehow raised an arm beneath the sparkling tangle of cable and directed his attention to where the steel door had crashed into the rear stone wall of my prison quarters.

In answer, the various hunks of rock knocked loose by the impact rose from the ground.

As the fourth and final ground drone moved on Charon and me, a stone the size of a softball flew from across the room and crushed it like a soda can. The remaining dozen or so floating rocks flew at its three brothers, and soon only the lone mist-sprayer remained.

His body no longer jerking this way and that in his chair, Daichi peered between the strands of the three de-electrified nets, his eyes focusing on the lone airborne drone. At his silent direction, every scrap of stone, rock, and debris in the room flew at our floating enemy from every side, battering its surprisingly fragile form until it fell to the ground as so much scrap metal.

Before, I'd only ever seen Daichi use his ability to become a giant of earth and stone, and that alone had been impressive. Now that I understood that anything not tied down was, if he willed it, potentially a lethal weapon gave me a new appreciation of who and what I was dealing with. Not to mention, this was yet another indication that all of Alba's elementalists had been taking it somewhat easy on us the first time around.

"I can't see." Sunil writhed in agony on the floor, rubbing his red, swollen eyes with trembling hands. "Dammit, this hurts."

"Sunil Jayalal," Charon said, dodging the loose rock on the ground as he motivated to the elektromancer's side, "remove your hands from your face."

"Screw you, you bucket of bolts. This hurts like hell and—"

"If you will remove your hands from your face, I will help you."

Sunil ground his teeth, and then, with what must have been a significant amount of will, interlocked his forearms across his chest to keep his hands away from his swollen eyes.

"Thank you." Without any further ado, Charon directed one of the various weapons protruding from his robotic torso at Sunil's face. "And now—"

"Whoa, whoa, whoa, Charon." I dropped to one knee and attempted to get between our robotic prison guard and Sunil. "What are you—"

"The only thing I can do, Persephone Snow. Now stand aside."

"Wait." I prepared to tackle the three-foot robot if needed. "Don't!"

Before I could say another word, a quart or so of pink goo flew from what looked like the barrel of a gun sticking out of Charon's right shoulder. The pink slime hit Sunil square in the face, covering his eyes and filling his mouth and nostrils. An instant later, Sunil dropped to the floor, as if suddenly unconscious.

"What did you do, Charon? What did you do?"

Sunil lay there on the ground unmoving for what seemed an eternity, and then sat up as if hit by a cattle prod and took a deep gasping breath.

"He's all right?" I asked.

"But of course he is, Persephone Snow. Did I not provide an appropriate aliquot of the neutralizing agent for the blinder's gas?"

"Neutralizing agent?" I gave Charon a cross look. "You could have said that was what you were doing."

"Do you tell everyone everything you're about to do before you do it, Persephone Snow, particularly when time is of the essence?"

"Well, no."

"And neither do I."

With that, Charon spun atop his spherical base and went to Daichi's chair. Twin flexible arms, each an inch wide with cutting tools at their tips, sprung from either side of his robotic head and went to work extracting Daichi from the other robots' nets. During the few moments it took Charon to free Daichi, Sunil wiped the pink goo from his face and coughed a good amount of it from his nostrils and mouth.

"What is this gunk?" asked the significantly less distressed elektromancer. "My entire face feels like it's been injected by a dentist."

"I mixed in a topical anesthetic with the neutralizing agent in an effort to ease your suffering more quickly, Sunil Jayalal. My apologies if the sensation is a bit disconcerting. You should have full return of your facial sensation within minutes of removing the remaining agent."

Sunil set to work wiping his face with his sweatshirt as Charon finished his work freeing Daichi from his weblike restraints.

"Wait a second." I knelt by Charon's side. "Your primary mission is to keep us all alive and well, and nothing you've done thus far has been anything other than defensive or helpful." I went nose to lens-like eye with our robotic guard. "You popped all this stuff out from your body earlier, just before Sunil and Daichi showed up." I raised an eyebrow and shot him a crooked smile. "Not one thing on you is a weapon, is it?"

"This complex has more than enough weaponry, both offensive and defensive, to maintain adequate security."

"But none of that is your mission, is it, Charon?"

"It is not, Persephone Snow." A series of chirps that bordered on quiet laughter sounded from the speaker in his metal chest. "But when my various service components are all deployed at once, I do appear quite formidable, don't you think? Much like the porcupines of North America?"

"As formidable as an Abrams tank." I crossed my arms and studied this new friend in my life. "You really are on our side, aren't you?"

"Truth be told, Persephone Snow, I serve the master in all things. His plans and your continued well-being are currently congruent, and therefore your statement is, for the moment, true. However, I can make no guarantee about the future, as there is—"

"Thank you, Charon." I petted the one spot on his robotic torso not bristling with what he'd just revealed were decidedly not weapons. "I appreciate the honesty, but I'd rather not hear about your eventual sudden but inevitable betrayal." Ethan would be so proud of my particularly shiny comeback. "Understand?"

"Noted, Persephone Snow."

"Great." I turned to Daichi, he and his chair free from their constraints, and Sunil, his face shiny and hair slicked back with the remnants of the pink goo. "So, gentlemen, what next?"

Sunil grimaced. "I suggest we retrieve anyone else stuck in this hellhole and head for the nearest exit." He raised an eyebrow at Charon. "Unless there are any objections."

"So long as you are in the master's complex, I will ensure to the best of my ability that no harm befalls any of you. I cannot actively aid and abet in your escape—"

"But you'll help as much as you can." I stroked the cool metal cylinder that held his camera eye. "I'm learning how to read between your lines, Charon."

"I have no idea of what you speak, Persephone Snow."

"I'm sure you don't. Still, I'm guessing you won't help us find anyone but also don't plan to stand in our way while we look around."

At Charon's silent stare, I returned my attention to Sunil and Daichi. "Looks like it's just the three of us searching for Jade and the other captive." A thought occurred to me. "I'm curious. In which of the three divisions of this complex did the Cardinal have you holed up?"

"Ask him." Daichi inclined his head in Charon's direction. "He's the one that put us there."

Charon let out a few low-pitched chirps as if clearing his throat. "You may recall, Persephone Snow, that I had to take leave of you on your very first day to attend to a matter."

"That was Daichi, right?" I processed for half a second. "Alba sent him to help Ada."

Daichi nodded. "The Cardinal apparently wasn't too keen on having a geomancer nosing around his mountain fortress, and I made the mistake of getting started without armoring up. The Cardinal sent a bunch of similar machines to the ones we just destroyed to take me out before I could tear down the mountain with him inside it." His eyes drifted to the various destroyed machines surrounding him. "Let's just say today is not my first experience with electrified nets."

"Once Daichi Kanda had been subdued and brought within the mountain, I took him across the Styx much as I did you, Persephone Snow, and deposited him in Asphodel where Sunil Jayalal was already our—"

"Don't you dare say 'guest' one more time, robot." Sunil's eyes crackled anew with blue sparks of electricity. "All of us are your prisoners down here."

"Sounds like you've been down here longer than any of us, Sunil." I did my best to inject calm into my voice. "How did you and Daichi free yourselves today after all this time?"

"Funny you should ask. Your robot pal had the two of us in side-by-side rooms in an even less posh wing of this place. My room had every bit of electrical current stripped away and the walls covered with a non-conductive insulation as hard as granite. A human body generates a scant amount of electricity each day, but not nearly enough to allow me to give the battery a full charge and do my thing, if you know what I mean."

"I don't, but go on."

"So, nothing to work with for months other than, of course, a robot coursing with electricity delivering meals every day through a slot in the door. Can you imagine? The key to freedom shows up three times a day for the better part of two years, and you can't risk nuking your meal ticket." Sunil looked away. "No way I was going to starve to death in this hole."

"Of course." I wasn't certain whether I felt bad for Sunil Jayalal or simply didn't like him. I suspected it was a bit of both.

"Then, a couple hours ago, the rock wall opposite my bed collapsed. A solid stone wall, and it fell apart like a stack of children's blocks."

"Obviously, that was me," Daichi said. "The Cardinal has been keeping me relatively sedated for months since my capture, pumping me full of medicine to keep me drowsy and unable to focus sufficiently to bring my abilities to bear." He smiled. "The last place you'd want an angry geomancer is in your underground prison, don't you think?"

"If he was doping you, how did you—"

"Not sure." Daichi looked Charon's way. "Maybe a kink in the line or equipment malfunction." He returned his attention to me. "In any case, as soon as my brain cleared a bit, I reached out with my ability and started tearing things down."

"And the first thing he tore down was the wall between our cells," Sunil said. "I was more than happy to lap up all the ambient electricity from the room, the equipment, the lights, and get us out of there."

Charon chirped. "I suspect that between your respective influences over earth and electricity, Sunil Jayalal and Daichi Kanda, making your way out of Asphodel and into Elysium was child's play."

"More or less." Sunil cracked his knuckles. "Just because I never sucked you dry of juice doesn't mean I didn't make sure to get a good handle on your electrical signature."

"Once we were out of Asphodel and into the main chamber," Daichi added, "tracking you to this part of the complex was indeed easy." He offered a mischievous grin. "And gigantic stone doors? Kind of my specialty."

"I'm glad neither of you tried the Styx," I interjected. "Otherwise, you'd be dead."

"We thought about it, make no mistake, but I remembered the warning from my initial imprisonment." Sunil's angry stare focused on Charon. "Why else do you think we were looking for your robot buddy?"

"We were hoping to catch the Cardinal with Charon, exact our pound of flesh, and leave," Daichi added, "but instead, we found you."

"That would explain the guns blazing approach." I studied them both, watching for any tells that they might be lying. "Anything else important I need to know?"

"Just that we're getting the hell out of here." Sunil returned his infuriated gaze to me. "Unless you want to stay here and hang out with your rolling bucket of microchips, you'd better get yourself in gear."

Nope. Not digging this guy.

"Charon," I asked, "will you take us to Jade, or are you going to make us do this the hard way?"

Charon held his figurative tongue. I wasn't surprised.

"Fine. Sunil, follow me. See if you can detect which of these rooms is pulling the most current. I suspect that will be the one where my friend is locked away."

Sunil laughed. "Whatever you say, Snow."

"Daichi, bring along a few boulders in case we have company."

Five hunks of rock rose from the ground and began to revolve around Daichi's wheelchair like jagged moons. "Ready."

"Great." I headed up the hallway with Charon, Sunil, and Daichi trailing close behind. Our first task was to find and free Jade; that much was clear. And then? The hard part: tracking down our mysterious fifth.

My gut told me Jade was a genuinely good person and worthy of rescue from this place. Same for Daichi and even Sunil, despite the latter's rough edges. We knew nothing about this final individual, however. There was no guarantee the soul Jade had sensed wasn't the Cardinal himself, nor any assurance they would be someone we could or should set free.

But I asked myself a simple question, one that helped burn away all the doubt and indecision: What would Ethan do if the decision were his?

CHAPTER 7

LOOKING FOR A STRANGER

"It's got to be one of these." Sunil, Daichi, Charon, and I moved down the wide stone hallway of Elysium past door after solid steel door. "Charon wasn't gone long when he went to fetch Jade to talk to me a few months back." My eyes drifted down to our robotic companion. "Unless he moved her to a different room as punishment."

"Do not cast your vexed gaze my way, Persephone Snow. Your transgression has long since been forgiven, but it was your decision to violate my trust. I have not forgotten that, and neither should you."

"Of course, Charon." I rolled my eyes. Jade was right. Despite his intelligence being artificial, Charon was one sensitive bucket of bolts. "You sure you won't just take us to her? We're going to find her either way."

"I thought I'd made it clear, Persephone Snow. My protocols may dictate that I not stand in your way at the moment, but they certainly do not require me to assist you."

"Fine." I looked to Sunil and Daichi. "Keep monitoring each cell for electrical activity out of sync with the others or any other clues as to which of these rooms might be Jade's."

Every door in this place looked pretty much like the rest. Whether the rooms beyond were cells or served some other purpose, each sported a seven-by-three-foot rectangle of steel to keep people out, or possibly to keep them in. Above each lock, a different angular glyph was stamped into the metal. We spent a good half hour going from door to door, until Sunil finally found one that spoke his language. Not only was the current flowing into the room a degree of magnitude greater than any of the others—Sunil's words, not mine— but he also detected a low level electric field consistent with a human nervous system. Daichi, as well, noted a difference. The surface temperature of the stone walls beyond the door seemed marginally warmer than the other rooms.

Though the two of them had used their Ascendant talents to confirm that the lights were on and somebody was definitely home, the cries for help were what sealed the deal.

"Seph?" came a muted shout from beyond the door. "Is that you?"

"Yes." My eyes flicked left and right. "And I've brought company."

"Stand clear of the door," Daichi shouted to ensure he was heard through the steel and stone. "We'll have you out of there in a moment."

"Okay," came Jade's muffled reply.

"All right, Sunil," I asked, "anything here besides a metal door?"

"Nothing I've been able to ascertain beyond an electrical circuit that allows remote control of the locking mechanism."

"And you, Daichi? Nothing that seems like a booby trap?"

"I think we're good. Neither of our cells had any particular security measures in place, and if the two of us don't warrant special attention, I can't imagine the Cardinal was too worried about keeping an empath locked up."

"Makes sense." I inclined my head toward the door. "In that case, let's get my girl out of there."

"Your wish is my command." Daichi reached from the wheelchair and rested his fingers on the door's mirror-like surface. "Open sesame." He pulled his hand away from the door and curled his fingers into a fist. In answer to his silent command, the door crumpled into a ball of scrap metal, fell to the rocky floor, and rolled down the hallway with an ear-splitting racket.

As the entire hallway shook from Daichi's efforts, I made a mental note to never forget that the two men I'd allowed into our circle were each a force of nature incarnate and that neither was someone to cross lightly.

"Jade?" I called into the room. "Are you all right?"

"I'm fine." Jade stepped from the recessed bathroom at the rear of the room. "And you?" Her gaze shot from Sunil to Daichi to Charon and back to me. "Are you okay?"

"You know?" My lips spread in an honest-to-God grin. "For the moment, it would appear we're all doing just fine."

She rushed to my side and wrapped me in a quick embrace before stepping back to survey our entire group, her face filled with nervous excitement. "I can't believe you came for me."

"Of course I did." I let out an exhausted sigh and gave her a big smile. "You must know I'd never leave you here."

"I hoped and prayed. For you. For us." Her eyes danced left and right again. "So, are you going to introduce me to your friends?"

Even in such a moment, she kept her charm and poise. Impressive.

While the rest of us were dressed in ill-fitting blue sweats, apparently what the Cardinal had left for his various captives to wear, Jade was decked out in yet another fashionable ensemble. Her immaculate long braid hung down the right side of a silky blouse with a flower print that appeared freshly laundered and pressed above a particularly flattering pair of jeans.

Such effortless beauty. Amazing in this hell. I'd have been lying if I said I wasn't a bit jealous.

"Jia Li Xiao, this is Sunil Jayalal, an elektromancer, and Daichi Kanda, geomancer of the Angel of the Morning." I smiled. "Sunil and Daichi, this is Jade."

"A pleasure to meet you both," Jade said. "Thank you for your help."

"What's up with the clothes?" Sunil asked. "We all look like we just rolled out of bed, and you look like you're ready for a night on the town."

"Yeah." I decided to satisfy my curiosity as well. "Ever since I've been here, Charon has kept me in clean clothes, but always the same blue sweats. How'd you end up with a wardrobe beyond simple prison chic?"

"No idea." She glanced down at her top. "When I first got here, all I had was the same sweats and prison togs that you all are wearing. Then, a few weeks before I met you, Charon dropped off an entire closet's worth of nice stuff for me to wear." She shook her head and let out a quiet laugh. "After months in sweats, no matter how comfy they were, it was nice to wear real clothes again."

"Huh." Didn't take a rocket scientist to figure out the timing of Jade's special delivery coincided rather neatly with my arrival at the Cardinal's complex, not to mention my telling the master of this underground labyrinth exactly where he could go and what he could do with himself when he got there. Jade's clothes? They'd been meant for me. Lucky for her we were basically the same size.

But it was more than that. I don't think I misread that the Cardinal had intended for me to stay in his mountain complex until my mouthing off and Ethan's arrival with the cavalry got me relegated to his own personal Underworld. On top of that, there was the coincidence of my name and that of my robotic butler/prison guard/friend. What did it all mean? How long had all of this been in the works? How could it be that all of this seemed to revolve around me, and yet the tunnels we now walked appeared to have been around for longer than I'd been alive?

And the big questions. What did the Cardinal want with me or any of us? Why were we still alive when so many others were dead at the hands of our crimson kidnapper?

If and when we crossed paths again, the bastard and I were going to have a long talk.

"So," Sunil said, "we've found your friend. I assume you're going to stick to your guns about finding this fifth person the empath detected before you allow us to get to work finding our way out of here."

"Would you have had us leave you behind?" I asked. "To rot, I believe you called it?" When he didn't answer, I turned to Charon, who had borne silent witness through the whole process of freeing Jade and hadn't uttered a peep during the entire conversation that followed. "Any chance I can convince you to speed up the process and help us find our fifth?"

Charon's continued silence was the least surprising development of the day.

"I figured as much." I scanned the faces of my three companions. "So, everyone. Gigantic underground complex, three divisions with an enormous central chamber, countless rooms in every direction. Any ideas as to where we should start looking?"

The four of us and Charon stood at the center of the Underworld's main chamber by the Styx, the techno-magical rectangle of energy along with the countless lights above providing just enough luminescence to allow us to see the three gigantic doorways at twelve, four, and eight o'clock. Still crowned with the chiseled H that was an Ancient Greek eta, the enormous doors leading to Elysium stood ajar and broken, thanks to the efforts of our elektromancer-geomancer duo. On the other side of the immense room, the massive doorway leading to Asphodel lay in rubble, the colossal alpha that had rested at its apex lying on its side at the base of the destroyed arch.

As I'd learned seven months prior, it wasn't hard to tell when a geomancer was around.

"All right, Jade"—I patted her shoulder in support—"time to break out your emotional Geiger counter. Our fifth could be in any of this place's divisions, and we don't have time to go room to room in all three." I raised a brow in question. "Do you think you can narrow it down for us like we discussed?"

"I'll try," she said, spreading her feet and pulling in a deep breath, "but no promises, okay?"

"Of course."

"Enough talk," Sunil grumbled. "Let's just get on with this."

I shot him a cross look. "We'll hold all comments from the peanut gallery, unless you have a better idea that doesn't involve taking down every door in this entire place."

A quiet titter from Charon coupled with Sunil's sullen silence let me know my comment had done the job.

"Ready?" I asked Jade.

"As ready as I'm going to be."

"What do you need us to do?" Daichi asked.

"Let me think." Jade focused. "If all of you as a group would retreat to the far end of the room at the midpoint between our respective divisions, I will calibrate my senses using the four of you and then reach out and see which direction will likely bear the most fruit for locating our fifth."

"Done." I turned my back on the third titanic door of the room in the distance, this one sporting an ominous T carved in the granite at its apex, and skirted the glimmer of the Styx as I headed for the far wall of the enormous space.

"I swear she just wanted to get rid of me for a minute," Sunil said as he came up on one side.

"Do you blame her?" Daichi asked as his powered wheelchair pulled up on my opposite flank. "You're not exactly pouring on the charm for any of us, my friend."

"We're not friends," Sunil said. "We're just rats stuck on the same sinking ship, and if we don't find a way off, we're all going to drown."

Charon let out a quiet chirp, but otherwise kept his silence.

The walk to the stone wall in the distance took the better part of a couple minutes, and as we reached the room's extent, we all turned to face the Styx. My heart froze as I realized the shimmering doorway blocked our view of Jade and that we had no way of communicating with her. We'd seen no evidence of the technological terrors that had come for us back in Elysium, but that didn't mean they weren't around. After six months of imprisonment, I didn't want to leave anything to chance. Still, it wasn't like we had much of a choice.

"Stick with the plan," I mumbled to myself.

"We could leave this individual behind, you know," Sunil said, as if reading my mind. "Simply get the four of us out of this hell and not look back."

"We're not leaving anyone." I crossed my arms, defiant. "We have a plan, and we're sticking to it."

"Your plan is to have Jade there try to figure out which of the three ginormous underground complexes might or might not house another prisoner, and then have me and Daichi tear down a few hundred doors until we satisfy both your curiosity and your guilt."

"Now, wait a minute—"

"No, Snow, *you* wait a minute." Sunil's eyes crackled with blue sparks. "You've been down here six months? I'm coming up on something like two years. Maybe you're feeling all altruistic and ready to help, but I'm not up for spending one more fucking minute in this hellhole. I'm only going along with this plan because you're the only one who has an in with the robot." His withering gaze dropped to Charon's lone eye. "I mean *Charon*." His inflection turned our robotic companion's name into a slur. "Excuse me if I'm not overjoyed that I'm basically being forced to risk my life and freedom to help someone I've never met and may not want to help."

"I don't know, Sunil." I glared at him through squinted eyes. "I'd never met you before today, and yet here I am."

Daichi laughed. "She's got you there, Sparky."

Sunil's eyes narrowed at Daichi. "Do not call me that."

"Whatever." Daichi turned his attention to me. "So, we find whoever this last person is, let Jade do a quick sweep to make sure we're not missing anybody else, and then what?"

All three of us turned our heads down at once to stare at Charon. "I guess that depends on—"

"It's Tartarus." Jade approached from the room's center, her form obscured by the brightness of the Styx. "Other than the escalating frustration and anger you three have been giving off like a magnesium flare in the night, the only other emotion I'm picking up is coming from beyond the third and final door of this terrible place."

"So, we're heading to Tartarus, where the master of this place keeps people he *really* doesn't like." Somehow I knew that was going to be the answer before Jade even started. "Fantastic."

~

Growing up in a neighborhood that was being gentrified lot-by-lot for several years, I'd had opportunity to witness the demolition of more than my fair share of houses. Having an elektromancer and a geomancer around reduced the time required for such targeted destruction while simultaneously elevating the entire process to an art form.

Daichi studied the massive door before us, debating the age-old question of finesse versus brute force, a debate that hadn't concerned him much a few months back when he was hurling chunks of freeway at my tour bus.

Taking his turn, Sunil placed both hands against the door as if he were a physician examining a patient. His eyes closed in concentration, and the lights throughout the vast space dimmed as he focused his attention on the stone barrier.

"Nothing that I can detect," Sunil said. "Door's all yours, Daichi."

Not wasting a second, Daichi raised both his arms like a conductor addressing an orchestra. With a simple parting of his hands, the massive set of doors shattered, steel ripping from stone, the resulting tons of rubble floating to the ground as gently as one might lay an infant into a crib.

After carefully navigating the resulting rubble, we crept up yet another rough-hewn stone hallway, the subtle downward slope suggesting we were moving even deeper into the earth. Lit by the same invisible ghost lights as the main chamber, locked steel doors fell every few feet on either side along the way, each representing a new mystery. Between Daichi's intuitive knowledge of each room's dimensions, Sunil's sense of electrical current, and Jade's ability to detect human emotion, we were relatively certain that we weren't passing anyone by. A part of me feared with each new doorway that we might discover the unknown fifth individual Jade had sensed months before was, in fact, the Cardinal, and the jig, as they say, would be up.

And yet, with each cell we passed, nothing.

Other than a slight variation in the odd pictograms stamped into the metal above each handle, each door looked exactly like every other. The same with the rooms themselves, with each registering nothing geological, electrical, or emotional to differentiate one from any of the others. This near uniformity allowed our search to advance far more quickly than I'd anticipated, as we soon found ourselves having explored every inch of the intersecting quarter mile or so of stone tunnel labyrinth.

Between the two of them, Sunil and Daichi made short work of the occasional mechanical sentry. After the experience of fighting off six at once back in my cell, the onesie-twosies we encountered along our path didn't stand a chance against the potent mix of focused lightning bolts and flying boulders. Daichi remained pretty chill through the whole thing, cruising along in his wheelchair and letting fly an occasional hunk of stone when needed. Sunil, on the other hand, seemed to take some delight in frying our technological assailants, much to Charon's obvious chagrin. I did my best to quietly reassure our reluctant robotic guide that we had no intention of showing him the same treatment while reminding myself to stay on the elektromancer's good side.

In any case, it was nice to see that the Cardinal, who always seemed two steps ahead of us, could underestimate his opponents the same way we'd all underestimated him.

As we passed a door we'd already seen twice before at what I'd mentally mapped as the center of the maze of corridors, I motioned for our group of four Ascendant and Charon to halt and reassess the plan.

"So, nothing," Sunil grumbled. "So glad we spent the extra couple of hours in this hole." He glared my way. "Can we go now?"

"Not yet." Jade spun slowly in a circle. "The individual we've been looking for is here. I know it. I just can't figure out where they might be."

"We've checked every door," I said, "some of them twice." Heaven forbid one damn thing be quick, easy, or obvious.

I dropped to one knee and looked deep into Charon's shining blue eye.

"Okay, we've combed every inch of this place and nothing. Are you seriously not going to help us?"

The three-foot robot stared back at me in silence.

"Well?"

"I beg your pardon, Persephone Snow, but I thought I had already made plain what part I could or could not play in your current endeavor." The words were the first he'd said since before we'd entered Tartarus.

I shook my head in frustration. "We're going to keep doing this whether you help us or not. You get that, right?"

"You and the others have made that perfectly clear, Persephone Snow."

"Good." I narrowed my eyes at Charon's unchanging lens, not sure how much sarcasm was intended in what could otherwise have been a simple statement of fact. "I'll give you one thing, Charon. You're consistent."

"Why, thank you, Persephone Snow," Charon answered. "I could say the same of you."

Daichi snorted at that, and even Sunil's perma-frown cracked a bit.

I rose from the ground, my cheeks hot at being skewered by a robot half my size whose mouth was even smarter than I'd realized, and stalked up the hallway, fists at my sides. "Fine. I guess we keep looking."

"Wait a second." Daichi had spun his wheelchair around to follow me, and the motor started making a strange sound. "My rear wheel is stuck."

"On bare rock?" Sunil asked

I stared at the ground and cursed myself for a fool. We'd been so focused on the lefts and rights, the never-ending walls and the dozens of doors, that we hadn't been examining the ceilings or the floors.

Daichi's wheel had slipped into a long, deep groove in a wide metal plate that stretched from wall to wall and along a good thirty feet of the passage. The metal dull from who knew how many years, the furrow that held Daichi fast was actually a ten foot engraving of a capital letter A without the cross bar.

No. Not an A at all. A Greek lambda.

"Hey Jade," I asked, "any chance the person we're looking for is maybe one floor down?"

"What?" Her gaze drifted downward to the darkened metal beneath her feet, her eyes filling immediately with sudden realization. "That's why I've not been able to put my finger on where they are. I've been thinking two-dimensionally." She knelt and splayed the fingers of both hands on the metallic surface. "Whoever it is we're looking for," she said with a grim smile, "they're below us."

"Daichi?" I asked. "What's down there?"

His eyes slid closed. "Another chamber, nowhere near as big as the main area, but pretty huge."

"Got it." I turned my attention to our elektromancer. "Sunil? Anything?"

His eyes glowed a faint blue-white. "There's a lot of power flowing beneath our feet. I thought I was merely sensing a conduit carrying this floor's electricity, but now that I know there's another space down there, all the current I've been picking up makes a lot more sense."

"Who or what could be down there?" Jade asked.

"We're not leaving until we find out." I wracked my brain. "What in the Greek Underworld starts with an L, anyway?"

"Not the first clue, Snow." Sunil shot an angry glance Charon's way. "Why don't you ask the Cardinal's guard dog?"

"I assume you are speaking of me, Sunil Jayalal?" Charon asked.

"If the collar fits," Sunil muttered.

"Enough." I positioned myself between Charon and the elektromancer. "Sunil, can you and Daichi figure out how to get this hatch open?"

"On it." Electricity arced between Sunil's eyes.

"Ready," Daichi added.

"Me too," Jade said. "I'll let you all know if I—"

"Stop," Charon said. "If you four are insistent on continuing this ill-advised path, I will open the door. Otherwise, I'm afraid one or more of you might inadvertently injure yourselves."

"For real?" I asked. "Now you're going to be helpful?"

"Only to save you from yourselves, Persephone Snow." Charon retreated to one corner of the metal rectangle in the floor. "Now, if you will all stand clear."

At Charon's urging, Sunil, Daichi, Jade, and I moved to a position behind our diminutive prison guard.

"Before we proceed, however," he said, "there are three things you must all hear and understand."

"Here it comes," Sunil said. "He's not going to help us."

"To the contrary, Sunil Jayalal." A third arm sprung from Charon's chest, the business end resembling a high-tech key that he inserted into a slit at the corner of the metallic platform. In answer, the rectangle of grey metal began to recess into the ground one foot at a time starting at the end opposite us, and in seconds, what had appeared to be solid steel had transformed into a dark metal stairwell descending into shadow. "I have done nothing but help keep each of you safe since each of your arrivals in the master's abode."

"All right, Charon." I stared down into the inky blackness. "You said you had three things we needed to hear. Spill."

"First, you may come to regret this decision and wish you'd left this last individual behind in, as I believe you all refer to this place, their hole."

"We're not leaving anyone behind, Charon, but we'll take that under advisement."

"Very well, Persephone Snow."

"And the other two things you wanted to tell us?" Jade pulled close to me, and though I wasn't the empath, I could feel the fear radiating off her.

"Yeah, robot," Sunil added, as brash as ever. "Don't leave us hanging."

"Only that dogs wear collars to protect those the possibly rabid creatures might bite"—Charon turned his head to stare at us with his cyclopean eye—"and that contrary to what you may believe, Sunil Jayalal, I am not the guard dog of this place."

CHAPTER 8

THE PRISONER

"Sunil," I asked, "perhaps you could shed a little light on the subject?"

"Sure." The elektromancer looked my way, doing his best to dispel the shaken look from his gaze. "Hey, Daichi," he whispered," before any of us go getting our heads lopped off in the dark, can you tell us what's down there?"

The geomancer focused for a moment. "A geodesic dome fashioned from within, the entire structure doubly buttressed to prevent collapse and maintain stability from even a significant seismic event." A quiet grin broke across his face. "I can feel the geomancy all around us. God, what I wouldn't give to pick the brain of the genius who built this place."

"Sorry to burst your bubble," Sunil said, "but he's probably long dead."

"Of course you'd assume it was a he," I muttered to myself, and then made my way to Daichi's side. "So, this is the work of another one with your particular talent? Makes sense. Can't imagine miners would be blasting as deep as I suspect we are."

"Any movement down there?" Sunil asked. "Or anything else that might suggest whether or not we're about to dive into a blender?"

"Nothing." Daichi pulled his wheelchair close to the edge of the first stair. "Other than the area below us isn't empty."

"Whoever it is we're looking for is down there." Jade pulled in a long, slow breath. "I'm certain of it."

"Good to know. That means we're one step closer to getting out of here." Sunil closed his eyes, his brow furrowing in concentration. "Hmm. This place is running more electricity than any other location we've come upon." He stretched out his arms to either side like an antenna. "Like some serious juice."

"Maybe we've found the generator that runs this place." I looked to Sunil. "Could that be it?"

"I don't think so," Sunil said. "Whatever's down there is pulling the current, not producing it."

"Maybe it's the self-destruct device for the Cardinal's base?" Daichi eyed the rest of us with an amused smirk. "No supervillain lair is complete without one. Isn't that what Dr. Talon said during the series finale of *Teen Spies*?"

What do you know? Another fan. Did everybody watch that show?

"You are all stalling," Charon said. "I have opened the door as you asked. How long are the four of you going to stand here and pontificate?"

Damn. Put in my place yet again by my favorite bucket of bolts.

"Daichi," I asked, "do you think you could rock up and take point?"

"Not a whole lot of room on these stairs," he answered. "Plus, I'm not sure how pulling from the surrounding rock might affect the cavern's structural integrity. I'd hate to bring the whole place down around our ears."

"Okay. So, you're staying up here then?"

"Nope." With a simple gesture, he shaved an inch-thick plane of granite from the wall, levitated it to the floor behind his wheelchair, and rolled backward onto the makeshift platform. As the rectangle of stone rose from the ground, Daichi shot me a self-satisfied smile. "What do you think? Instant escalator?"

"Wonders do seem to be the way of things around Ascendant." I looked left and right at my four companions and took the first step into the unknown. "So, once more into the breach?" I locked gazes with Charon. "Unless someone who knows his way around this place would care to offer any further information about what the hell we're about to walk into?"

A slight change in modulation of his internal motor's hum was Charon's only answer to my jab. His continued stonewalling wasn't particularly surprising, but I found myself disappointed all the same. His silence, however, did give me a sort of answer to my question, albeit indirectly. If the top item on his list of priorities was keeping us—or at least me—safe and sound, then at least we knew we weren't walking into some sort of booby trap. Admittedly, the little guy could be lying through his nonexistent teeth, but I'd gotten a feel for my robotic almost-friend over the preceding six months. While he'd obviously prefer we were all still in our cells behaving ourselves and calmly accepting our three squares per day, I couldn't bring myself to believe he would march us to our doom. Charon was unwavering in following his various directives, but to my knowledge, he'd never lied to me. I wasn't sure if he was even capable of lying.

In any case, we were about to find out.

Daichi sent the floating sheet of rock holding his wheelchair down the stairs with Sunil close by his side, lighting the way for all of us with an arc of electricity between his outstretched hands. Jade and I followed close behind with Charon bringing up the rear, his rollerball negotiating the stairs much better than I would have imagined possible.

"Never dreamed I'd be working with one of Alba's people," Sunil muttered as he carefully descended the metal staircase. "Strange times we live in, don't you think?"

"Not so strange," Daichi answered with a smile. "And just so you know, a couple years back before you were taken offline, Alba was considering reaching out to you and offering you the chance to join her entourage. I mean, we don't currently have an elektromancer."

"I thought you said you'd never heard of me." Sunil stopped and turned to Daichi. "Alba knows of my existence? My name?"

"Focus, boys." I pulled close behind Sunil. "We can figure out who is president of whose fan club once we're all out of here."

"That's funny coming from the self-proclaimed 'Reigning Princess of Pop,'" Sunil grumbled as he continued his slow march down into darkness. "Sorry to step on your spotlight."

Wow. Major chip-on-shoulder syndrome, though whether the chip was on my shoulder or Sunil's, I wasn't a hundred percent sure.

As we reached the bottom of the stairs, a passageway led off to the right, tight at first but quickly opening onto a grand space I could hear and feel more than I could see. The electricity between Sunil's hands crackled as he upped the voltage so we could all see better, a move made unnecessary moments later when Charon rolled to the nearest wall and flipped a switch. With the room instantly illuminated by brighter light than I'd seen in half a year, we all covered our eyes as our vision adjusted to the sudden brilliance.

"Thanks for the warning, Charon." I flashed back to when I was a kid and Mom would open my curtains first thing in the morning when she wanted me to get out of bed. "Got any Advil for the migraine you just gave me?"

"I can't have you all stumbling around in the dark, now can I?" I'd never heard Charon laugh before, but the series of chirps that followed was a pretty close approximation. "Your eyes will acclimate, Persephone Snow, just as they have adjusted to the dim over the last several months."

As I peered between my fingers at the enormous space suddenly filled with light, I let out a gasp.

My quarters back in Elysium consisted of little more than a cube of space, bare rock walls, and the most basic facilities. This place was like something out of a fever dream. Or maybe a nightmare. Half throne room from *Lord of the Rings* and half mad scientist laboratory, the gigantic room filled me simultaneously with wonder and dread.

As Daichi had sensed, the room swooped upward into a dome

with enormous columns of stone every few feet resembling many of the cathedrals I'd visited during my travels in Europe. The paired columns led straight down either side of a wide walkway, all leading to a grand chair of stone and steel at the far end of the room that rested atop a granite dais.

And there, before the throne, an assemblage of what appeared to be a full medical ICU with all the requisite equipment and machinery. Complete with beeping monitors and multiple tables covered with dozens of medical devices, not to mention several banks of computers from various decades off to one side, the area appeared as well set up as any hospital. Floodlights floated in the air above the area, their pure white beams soaking the area in utter brilliance and all converging on one spot.

There, at the heart of all the machinery and equipment, lay a lone man atop a draped medical table straight out of *Frankenstein*. High-tech shackles with chains bolted to the stone floor encircled his wrists and ankles, binding him in place. A flashing collar rested beneath his chin, and a thick hood complete with mask and headphones to block any light or sound covered all but his nose and mouth. One thing was clear: whoever this man was, he was someone the Cardinal considered way more dangerous than a geomancer, elektromancer, empath, or siren.

The man appeared to be breathing on his own, but beyond that, I got the distinct impression he hadn't moved an inch in quite some time. An IV line leading to a bag filled with clear fluid rested in his forearm, while a second thin tube filled with a milky liquid passed from one of the room's many machines to his nostril.

If the guy needed a feeding tube, he'd been there for a while.

His muscular form covered only by a set of loose surgical scrubs and a pair of thick socks beneath his ankle bonds, he appeared well cared for, no doubt courtesy of my favorite half-pint robot with daddy issues. Whether he was sedated, comatose, or some combination of the two, I had no idea, but I did know one thing for certain: we weren't leaving him there.

"Next question." I studied the mystery man's various bonds, the blinking collar likely the work of Minako, the Cardinal's technomancer. "How do we free this man from all this...stuff?"

Sunil stepped into my field of vision, his expression incredulous. "With all due respect, there are a ton of questions that need answering before we even begin entertaining such a thought."

I returned the elektromancer's glare. "Such as?"

"We don't know who this is, what he can do, or why the Cardinal has him all trussed up." Sunil's head tilted to one side. "You might notice that the Cardinal left you sitting relatively pretty. As for me and Daichi, I got a cell without any electronics for me to manipulate..."

"And while the Cardinal did keep me relatively sedated to prevent me from bringing this whole place down," Daichi added, "this level of incapacitation is next level."

Jade shivered. "Even in this state, the dreams this man is experiencing are...quite intense."

Great. He's even giving our empath the heebie-jeebies.

"Look. I get it. This guy is obviously someone the Cardinal didn't want to mess with again. In a world of people who control shadows, bend the elements to their will, or pull lightning from the sky, this guy is getting special treatment." My hands went to my hips in defiance, though I understood their shared point all too well. "Just because he's next level doesn't mean we should leave him like that."

"Maybe," Daichi said, "but if the man before us represents such a threat to one as powerful as the Cardinal that he's basically kept sedated in sensory deprivation—"

"We don't know that he's sedated," I interrupted. "All of this equipment could theoretically be life support for—"

"Pardon, Persephone Snow."

I'd guessed the little guy might have something to say about the current situation. "Yes, Charon?"

"I am merely corroborating the status of the individual resting before you. He is indeed sedated. His fluid, caloric, and nutritional needs are being met as well as some degree of physical activity for his striated muscle via periodic electrical stimulation, but were he not to receive his various infusions, both intravascular and gastrointestinal, he would likely awaken most quickly."

"You're telling us this now for what reason exactly?"

"As I have already made plain, my primary charge is ensuring the well-being of everyone in this complex."

"And if we woke him up, whose 'well-being' exactly would we be putting at risk?" I peered into the big blue lens that was Charon's eye, hoping to find the window to his robotic soul. "His, or our own?"

"It would appear that you intend to discover the answer to that question, regardless of what I say or do. Is that not correct, Persephone Snow?"

The growl that boiled up from within me would have made Neko proud.

"Fine." I glowered at Charon. "You won't tell me who or what we're dealing with"—I shifted my frustrated glare to Sunil and Daichi—"and my pair of big bad Ascendant are too terrified of an unconscious man to help me rescue one of their own from a freaking superhuman serial killer."

"Wow." Sunil laughed. "Ascended for a few months, and you already know everything. Whatever did we do before you came along?"

"I have to agree with Sunil." Daichi raised an eyebrow my way. "I mean, we don't have the first idea what this guy can do, and you two ladies, with all due respect, aren't exactly built for combat."

"I'll have you know I started all this in peak physical condition," I answered, not backing down a millimeter, "and since being captured six months ago, I've been working out and training daily." My eyes narrowed in answer to the men's shared patronizing gaze. "I can take care of myself."

"As can I," Jade added. "Don't forget, I used to hunt Ascendant."

"Being able to sniff another Ascendant out and being able to stop them are two different things." Sunil turned from Jade to me. "And you can do all the cardio and strength training you want, Snow, but if this guy is as tough as I suspect he is, none of that will do you a bit of good."

Daichi pulled forward, his outstretched hand resting on Sunil's arm to quiet him. "What Sunil is trying to say is that we simply don't know enough to—"

"What I'm saying is," Sunil interrupted, "not only do you lack the answers necessary to determine the next course of action, you barely even know which questions to ask." He gestured to the man on the table. "For all we know, this man could be the Cardinal himself. Did you consider that?"

I glanced Charon's way, and found nothing that would indicate whether Sunil's thought was a legit concern or mere paranoia. Not playing poker with this robot...

"This guy has been here for months." I walked over and ran a finger over a section of exposed table by the man's foot, my trailing touch leaving a line in the otherwise uniform layer of dust. "Maybe longer."

"Even if this were the Cardinal," Daichi said, "we might be in way better shape trying to take him unarmored and drugged than waiting for him to come after us again." He rolled over to join me by the table and tilted forward in his chair to survey the man lying unconscious before us. "That being said, Snow is right. Whoever this is, he's been here a long time."

"Doesn't mean he's anyone we want to be associated with." Sunil crossed his arms in defiance. "I say we leave well enough alone and keep looking for a way out of here."

"What do you think, Jade?" I studied her features for any clue as to what she was thinking. "You can read people better than anybody. Do we leave this man here to suffer, or do we free him and bring him with us?"

"It's hard to tell with him in this state." Jade's eyes slid closed. "As I said, his dreams are intense, emotional, dark, but who among us hasn't had a nightmare or two?" She joined Daichi and me by the table, leaving only Sunil and Charon looking on from several feet away, and rested a hand on his shoulder. "I pick up on hunger, anger, sadness, but beyond that, not much else that's going to help us make a clear determination."

"Doesn't matter." My cheeks flushed with heat. "Regardless of the risk, leaving this man the captive of a known murderer, regardless of who he might be, is wrong." The emotion of the moment overtook me, and before I could stop it, my voice took on the singsong quality it had in the past when my Ascendant gift manifested. *"We can argue about this all day, but in the end, we're not going to leave him here; you know it, and so do I."*

"Fine. We'll bust this guy out of here. No need to put me under your spell." Sunil let out a quiet growl. "But you know what they say; no good deed goes unpunished."

"Wise words, Sunil Jayalal." Breaking his silence, Charon rolled himself backward several feet and retracted all of his various arms and other devices until he was as small and compact as he could make himself. "Remember later, each of you, that you were warned."

Charon's robotic words sent a shiver from the base of my skull down my back and straight to my toes, but I fought to keep any emotion from my face. I wasn't changing my mind now, no matter what. Though at his core he was just an A.I. following his basic programming, I refused to give Charon the satisfaction of knowing he got under my skin.

"What first?" I asked. "The shackles?"

"I suggest we start with the hood." Sunil joined us around the table. "See if any of us recognizes his face."

"Agreed," Daichi said, "and then the business of getting those tubes out of his arm and nose." His eyes dropped to a tube I hadn't noticed before that snaked from the man's scrub bottoms at his ankle and led to a bag filled with golden liquid. "Among other places."

As I stared down at the man's comatose form, a part of me wished that any of my four companions would put their foot down and insist we leave things well enough alone. But I'd won the argument, and now all that remained was doing the deed. Still, I wondered. Sunil could summon lightning at will while Daichi had the power to bring down the whole mountain, and yet neither had been subjected to nearly this degree of incapacitation. What could this man do that warranted such precautions? Who or what were we about to let loose upon the world?

Sunil ran his fingers over the dark hood, the few blinking lights and indicators along its surface extinguishing one by one. When he was done, the elektromancer looked to me and gestured to the strap beneath the mystery man's bearded jaw. "Would you care to do the honors?"

With a deep breath, I undid the buckle and gently pulled the helmet from the man's head. Curly black locks framed a handsome face with olive skin, high cheekbones, and a strong chin. I half-expected his eyelids to open, for him to look up at me with dark eyes filled with question or anger or fear, but for the moment, at least, the man remained thankfully still.

Sunil worked next at the various shackles, disabling their electronic locks one by one and freeing the man's arms and legs. Only when his fingers went to the apparatus encircling the man's neck did Charon speak again in warning.

"Remove that collar at your peril, Sunil Jayalal." Our robotic guide retreated even further, his metal carapace clanging as it struck the stone column behind him. "The man you currently set free is not like any Ascendant you have encountered, and that device is all that holds his power at bay."

Sunil and Daichi met each other's gaze, and with a shared nod, moved on from the collar and turned their attention to the trio of various tubes violating the man's body. I turned my back as they started with the one that ran up his scrub pants leg, but did remind Sunil to deflate the balloon before pulling that particular tube, a lesson I learned from one of the nurses a decade back when my grandfather was in the hospital after a surgical procedure. Next, Daichi pulled the feeding tube from his nose, sending a spurt of the milky liquid across the stone floor. The catheter removed and the nasal tube pulled, all that remained was the IV line in the man's arm.

"I'll do that one." I crept close and rested my fingers on the surgical tape holding the IV in place. With careful use of fingernails and friction, I freed the crossed adhesive strips and then pulled the IV from the man's arm. A single drop of blood welled up from the vein beneath his olive skin and dripped to the floor.

And then, we waited.

But only for a moment.

Seconds later, the man's dark eyes, framed by long black lashes, fluttered open. The first face he'd seen in God knows how long was mine.

"And who might you be, beautiful woman?" he asked, his voice little better than a croak both from disuse as well as, no doubt, the collar at his neck.

"My name is Persephone." I attempted a smile, my cheeks flushing with heat, though for what reason exactly, I wasn't sure. "We've come to free you."

His eyes flicked left and right and left again as he took in Sunil, Daichi, and Jade. Then, with herculean effort, the man sat up and offered me an exhausted but grateful smile, his white teeth gleaming against his olive skin.

"Persephone." He peered around the room, his eyes resting briefly on the throne to his rear before coming to rest on Charon who continued to cower by a nearby column. "How appropriate." He pulled in a deep breath and spoke again, his voice growing clearer with every syllable. "I am Metis."

CHAPTER 9

RUNNIN' WITH THE DEVIL

"Metis." I offered the man a trembling hand. "Nice to meet you, despite the obviously strange circumstances."

Metis took my hand and gave it a gentle squeeze before reaching up with his opposite hand to run his fingertips along the collar at his neck. "This device," he asked, his words flavored with an indistinct accent from somewhere along the Mediterranean, "why does it remain?"

I had no idea how to answer. We didn't know this Metis from Adam and were understandably afraid of what he might do if given free rein. Unless Charon was deliberately misleading us, the collar prevented him from accessing his Ascendant abilities, whatever they might be. As much as I insisted on freeing him from the Cardinal's clutches, I was all in favor of that collar remaining on until we were far from both this place and the man himself. Still, I couldn't help but understand how I'd feel if I was forced to wear what was effectively a restraint meant for a dog.

Fortunately, Daichi jumped in before I could put my foot in my mouth.

"Understand that we mean no disrespect. Our robotic friend there warned us that it might not be safe to remove the collar, for you or any of us, so we left it in place until we could awaken you and discuss options."

"Robotic friend, eh?" His gaze again flicked in Charon's direction. "Do tell."

"Be warned." Charon chirped nervously. "That collar represents a failsafe left in place to ensure you remained a guest of this place, a failsafe not as easily dispatched as the rest of your various restraints, chemical and otherwise, I might add." Our robotic companion advanced, if only a couple of feet. "Any attempt to remove or disable that particular piece of technology will result in an explosion that will incinerate anyone in a ten-foot radius, particularly the person around whose neck the collar resides."

So the collar was not only a bridle for whatever Ascendant abilities Metis possessed, but a bomb as well. Funny. First time Charon had mentioned that little detail. Sometime soon, my little robot buddy and I were going to have a little chat about the definition of "need to know."

"Clever as always," Metis grumbled, his eyes narrowing in frustration. "Yet again, the Cardinal's techno-witch proves more cunning than most." He looked to me. "And speaking of my favorite technomancer, where is Minako? I would speak with her."

His words sent a chill like a sliver of ice through my belly.

"You mean the Asian techno-chick in the hot black outfit who got her ass kicked by my boyfriend six months ago? She's long gone."

"Really?" Metis raised a dark brow. "Your lover defeated Minako in one-on-one combat?" A lone chuckle parted his lips. "Impressive."

The truth was it took Ethan, Rosemary, LJ, and our entire crew as well as another of Alba's elementalists—their pyromancer, Ada—to defeat the Cardinal and his technomancer, and even then, the Cardinal managed to escape only to lock me up in his own private hell.

But I wasn't going to tell Metis that.

"Also, you said six months." Metis eyed each of us in turn. "What is the date? How long have I been victim to this forced slumber? Tell me."

Sunil, Daichi, and I all conferred and gave Metis our best estimate of where we were on the calendar.

"Interesting," Metis continued, not offering the slightest hint as to how long our guess would put him as the Cardinal's prisoner. "I can only assume that the four of you somehow managed to free yourselves from your individual cells but were unable to break yourselves out of this place or else you wouldn't be here seeking *my* assistance."

Four. With all the back-and-forth, I'd completely forgotten about Jade, though to my credit she hadn't uttered a peep since Metis opened his eyes. In fact, she'd subtly backed away from the table until she was firmly ensconced in a shadow cast by one of the room's many columns.

As our empath voted with her feet, I wondered yet again if I'd done the right thing insisting on freeing Metis.

"Assistance?" Sunil chuckled. "It's only by our good graces and Snow's insistence that you're not still unconscious with a tube coming out of every orifice."

"Crude," Daichi whispered, catching my gaze, "but not inaccurate."

"What Sunil and Daichi are trying to say," I whispered to a suddenly sullen Metis, "is that we didn't come here for your help, but to make sure we didn't leave anyone behind. Understand?"

"Wait." He considered my words for a long moment. "You came here only to free me?"

"Yes."

"And you have no idea who I am?"

"Should we?" Sunil asked.

Metis paused another second before answering. "I suppose not." He lowered his head. "It would appear, then, Persephone, that I am in your debt."

"Well," Daichi said, "if that's settled, let's get back to the main chamber, warm up the Styx, and get the literal hell out of here."

Charon chirped. "I'm afraid, Daichi Kanda, that your plan may be a bit premature."

"What do you mean?" Daichi asked.

Before Charon could answer, a loud metallic clang echoed from the passage leading back to the stairs.

"What the hell was that?" I asked, my question punctuated on either end by a second and third clang. "What aren't you telling us?"

"Remember when I told you I wasn't the guard dog of this place?" No sooner had the question left Charon's metaphorical lips than the clanging shifted into a full blown racket like someone had thrown a kitchen full of pots and pans down the metallic stairs.

Something was coming for us, and coming fast.

"Jade," I shouted as I raced around the table away from the passageway leading back the way we came, "get behind Sunil." I looked to our elektromancer and geomancer. "You two, get ready. Somehow, I don't think it's going to be blinders and nets this time."

The rushing triplet clangs of metallic footfalls stopped just beyond the entrance to the dome-shaped room, leaving the room deathly quiet other than the sound of the five of us breathing and the whir of Charon's internal mechanics. The minimal light that made its way past the darkened arch hinted at a lupine form that sent every neuron in my body into fight-or-flight, my instinct to run hitting a fever pitch as the four-legged form stepped into the light. One canine head filled with razor teeth, then a second, and then a third, came into view, all mounted atop a robotic chassis the size of a small horse. Each foot a monstrous paw complete with a quartet of foot-long claws like butcher knives, the three-headed metal monster paused as it decided which of us it planned to send headfirst into the actual afterlife.

"Allow me to introduce"—Charon paused with a showman's flourish—"Kerberos."

Great. First Charon, then a bunch of drones, and now a robotic dog: a whole underground complex chock-full of things against which my abilities did diddly-squat.

"Hey, Daichi?" I whispered. "Can't you crunch that thing with a boulder or something?"

"You see a pile of boulders lying around?" the geomancer answered. "I start messing with this place, and we might have a bigger problem than a giant three-headed robotic dog."

"Sunil," I asked, my voice going a little shrill, "maybe a little lightning?"

"Don't worry." Sunil's hands crackled with blue electricity, the arc between them sending the already blinding brilliance of the space into overdrive. "That thing makes a move, I'll fry it."

I glanced Jade's way, and the terror in her eyes made my heart skip a beat, though it wasn't the fear in her gaze that scared me so much as where it was focused. A monster straight out of a science-fiction movie pawed the ground a single bound away, and yet her unblinking gaze remained laser-like on Metis.

What had I done?

The standoff continued with elektromancer and geomancer on one side and Kerberos, the three-headed killing machine, on the other. Why the guard dog of Hades wasn't doing anything but watching was anyone's guess, but I was going to take the whole "not getting ripped to shreds in seconds" thing as a positive.

"Why isn't it attacking?" Jade asked. "What's it waiting for?"

"Perhaps it is awaiting word from its master regarding your fate." Metis stood for the first time. If I'd been concerned that the atrophy of wasting away on a surgical table a mile beneath the earth for God knew how long would cause him to stumble, I needn't have worried. "We should all take our leave of this place before our mutual luck runs out."

"You want us to walk past *that thing*?" I asked.

"If the gigantic robotic dog with three heads and razor claws wanted us dead, lightning and stones aside, I suspect we'd already be so." Metis strode forward barefoot on the stone, as confident and self-possessed as any man or woman I'd ever seen, despite the fact he'd just awakened from a forced sleep of several months or more, not to mention just had a tube yanked from his manhood. "Shall we?" He glanced Charon's way. "As I recall, you are the only one who can allow us to pass the Styx and return to the world above; isn't that correct...?"

"Charon." The blue light from the robot's lone eye dimmed. "My designation is Charon."

"The ferryman of the Underworld, indeed. I trust that if we get past the metal beast, you will allow us all safe passage from this place and return us all to the world above."

"My apologies, but as I've made clear to Persephone Snow multiple times already, my instructions are to keep all of you here in the Underworld until further notice."

"And *I* am telling you that if you don't wish to be reduced to scrap metal, you will do exactly as I say and release us." Metis caught my gaze. "I don't require any Ascendant ability to dismantle a talking toaster."

A part of me railed at the comment. Charon could be a pain in the ass, but he was my talking toaster. Sort of.

Great. Somewhere at the back of my mind, I'd adopted Charon as a pet, friend, something. If only Mom had let me have that dog I wanted when I was five.

"At the very least, I will guide the lot of you back to the main chamber and away from Kerberos. I remain uncertain as to what currently keeps him from attacking, but as my primary motivation is each of your health and well-being..." And with that, Charon turned and rolled toward the door.

"Now we're talking." Daichi rose into the air, his wheelchair still atop the sheet of dark granite he'd pulled from the wall above. "Ready when the rest of you are."

Metis strode directly for Kerberos, stopping briefly before the robotic canine's center head before stepping to one side and exiting the room.

"As easy as that," Daichi said. "Who would have guessed?" He glanced Jade's way. "Hop on?"

Jade stepped onto the edge of the slab of granite beneath Daichi's chair and the two of them followed Metis into the darkness. Sunil followed close behind, leaving me alone with Charon.

"You're more than a talking toaster, you know?"

"I am well aware, Persephone Snow." Charon spun in a half-circle then turned his robotic head to look my way. "Come. Let us join the others. Kerberos may be frozen for the moment, but neither of us should push our luck, would you not concur?"

"Absolutely." I strode toward the darkened exit after the others, though I gave Kerberos a far wider berth than any of them had. With my every step, I could feel his electronic eyes following me. My heart raced as I drew even with his trio of heads, convinced despite the others' successes that I was a single footstep from death. The guard dog of the Underworld, however, remained as still as a statue. I walked backward down the darkened cavern leading back to the metal staircase with Charon at my side, keeping Kerberos in sight at all times, and only when I took the first stair did I dare look away.

"Any more surprises I should know about, little buddy?"

Charon let out a triplet of quiet chirps before he answered. "More than you can imagine, Persephone Snow, but none I believe you would want me to share at the moment."

"**I**ronic, don't you think?" Sunil, who had taken point once we were back on the main level of Tartarus, glanced across his shoulder at Metis. "We run into a gigantic robot dog who heels the minute he takes a look at you, but you're the one wearing the dog collar."

"Ironic, indeed." Metis's low growl only solidified the jab. He stopped dead in the dim hallway and sighed as he looked my way. "Does this one ever stop talking?"

I laughed. "He has to eat, breathe, and sleep sometime, I guess."

"Quite the sharp tongue, your friend has."

"I've known him for all of a few hours, but yes."

His voice dropped to a whisper. "He should be careful he doesn't cut the wrong person with his glib speech. Some, he may find, are more forgiving than others."

"He doesn't mean anything by it." The first thing Jade had said since we'd faced Kerberos below, the tremor in her voice was unmistakable. "It's just his way."

"And you would know, right? Unless I'm mistaken, you're an

empath?"

Damn. This guy was good.

"I am," Jade answered as her body shivered from head to toe. "You can call me Jade."

"Metis." He extended a hand, and Jade, with only a momentary pause, accepted. "A pleasure, Jade, and good to have one with your *keen* senses on our side." He shot me a sidelong glance. "I may wear the Cardinal's restraint, Persephone, but my eyes, ears, and instincts work just fine."

As we navigated the maze of hallways leading back to the Styx with Sunil and Daichi in the lead, me following with Metis on one side and Jade on the other, and a silent Charon bringing up the rear, I kept a close eye on the mysterious newest addition to our group, trying to get a glimpse beneath his surly veneer in an effort to determine whether or not we could trust him.

"If it's not too personal, Metis, I'm curious." I swallowed hard as I prepared to ask the question that was burning on the tip of all our tongues. "I've met shadowmancers, elementalists, theriodans, elektromancers. What is it you can do when you don't have a power-squelching bomb strapped around your neck?"

"Quite the forward young woman, aren't you?" A storm crossed Metis's features, there one second, gone the next. "Suffice to say, this Cardinal menace has every reason to fear my wrath should I be set free from this accursed device." He stroked his bearded chin. "As for what I bring to the table, I believe I shall keep my own confidence on that for the time being." He directed his attention in Charon's direction. "And if you value your continued existence, robot, artificial though it may be, I would advise you to keep what you know of me to yourself as well."

"Of course." A series of nervous chirps sounded from Charon's chassis. "Beyond advising all present that you were someone to be reckoned with and confirming earlier that you were in fact sedated by the master's machines, I have divulged no further information regarding you or any of your abilities...Metis."

Charon's slight hesitation with this particular designation garnered him a cross look from the man himself. For a robot who insisted on calling everyone by their full name as if he were our scolding mother, he had certainly proven tight-lipped on calling Metis...well...anything. Years of having to dodge fans, paparazzi, and stalkers alike gave me an insight into that moment that others might have missed: intentional or not, Charon had flubbed Metis's name after spouting mine, Daichi's, and Sunil's without effort from the get-go. This told me two things: First, "Metis" was at best a pseudonym and at worst a bold-faced lie, and second, he didn't want anyone, including his rescuers, to know who he really was. And Charon knew it.

The earlier sensation of stabbing ice in my belly circled back for an encore performance as I wondered yet again who this man was who walked beside me with all the confidence of a lion on an African savannah. Metis had the potential to be a powerful ally, and of course, it behooved us all to stay on his good side. At the end of the day, however, if there was one thing I'd learned about Ascendant in my short time as a part of their world, it was that each had their own agenda.

"My apologies for asking a personal question after deflecting one of yours, but I must know." Continuing his inexorable march down the stone hallway, Metis gave me a sidelong full up-and-down. "You are a beauty for the ages, Persephone Snow, your words enchant me with every syllable, and I believe the elektromancer said something a moment ago about you being a famous singer?"

"You're kidding." I splayed my fingers across my chest in joking affront. "You've never heard of me?"

"My apologies, but you did just awaken me from a forced slumber of some length. It is possible my knowledge of current events is anything but current." Metis slowed his pace to study me further, a flash of insight crossed his features. "As for my question, though. You find yourself imprisoned with Ascendant, which would suggest you are Ascendant as well as a singer. Could it be that you're a siren?"

"The first one born in a generation or two," I said, "or so everyone keeps telling me."

Pretty sharp. This Metis wasn't anyone to try to hide something from.

And though my secret was out like Jade's, I had a sneaking suspicion the latest addition to our group wasn't about to start spilling his own beans anytime soon.

"Miraculous." Metis stopped in his tracks, his fascinated gaze taking in every inch of me as he appraised me anew. "I had no idea another siren walked the earth." His eyes clouded over, this dark cloud in his visage lasting longer than the last. "All were disappointed when the last refused his Ascension. He might still be with us had he chosen to accept his destiny, but instead he chose to remain among the chattel he claimed to love so dearly."

"You know, that's the second time I've heard that story, about how the previous siren somehow dodged all of this." My gaze dropped to the stone floor. "An option I wasn't given."

"Dodged?" Metis asked. "Relinquished at great personal cost, perhaps, but few are those who would say his fate was preferable to simply accepting his birthright. He died far too soon with so many songs left unsung. One of the greatest tragedies of modern times." He studied me with an amused smirk. "I am glad to know that you chose differently, for all our sakes."

"I asked before, but no one would tell me. Who is this man, this siren, that everyone speaks of? Is it someone I've heard of, or—"

"We're here." With a wave of his hand, Daichi parted the rubble from the destroyed Tartarus door like Moses and the Red Sea and then rolled through on his wheelchair with Sunil following close behind, the continued arc of electricity between the elektromancer's hands lighting the way. Charon rolled between me and Jade and followed the two Ascendant out into the main chamber where the Styx hopefully awaited our arrival. Metis was next, his long strides leaving Jade and me behind in the mouth of Tartarus.

"What's wrong, Jade?" I whispered, hoping Metis wouldn't hear. "You've barely said a word."

"Not now," she said, forcing a smile as she followed Metis out into the main chamber. "Let's just keep moving."

"Alrighty, then," I muttered as I left behind one section of the man-made hell for another, hoping that I might see the sun again after six months banished to darkness. "Let's do this."

CHAPTER 10

BREAKOUT

I stepped into the enormous central chamber of the Cardinal's modern Hades, my eyes focused on the shimmering sheet of energy in the distance known as the Styx. Sunil and Daichi had already halved the distance to the techno-magical doorway with Metis and Charon close behind. Jade waited for me to one side of the demolished doorway.

"All right, Jade. Spill. What has you so freaked out?" I asked despite the fact I had a pretty good idea.

Jade drew close to my side and cupped her hand to my ear. "Metis. There's something about him I just can't—"

Though more than far enough away that he shouldn't have been able to hear a single whispered word, Metis looked back at Jade and me with a knowing grin. For a moment I thought we were busted, and then the whimsical look on his face shifted to one of anger as he rushed in our direction. For two long seconds, I was convinced Metis raced to kill the both of us for the simple sin of suspicion, but following his laser-like gaze revealed the true target of his attack. No sooner had I noted the silent drone descending to entrap Jade and me in its electrified net than a hurtling Metis tore it from its low hover, hurled it to the stone at our feet, and crushed it as easily as he might an empty Coke can.

Despite the Cardinal's collar, it was clear that Metis was anything but helpless. Instantly reminded of the sheer physicality of the Greyhound back in Denver and more than aware of whose body currently held the energies of that particular Ascendant, the question of who exactly this Metis might be again crept through my brain. If the Cardinal already had someone of such strength, speed, and ability in his grasp, why had he bothered going after the Greyhound? In any case, we now owed the man before us at least a modicum of gratitude for saving us from what would have no doubt been a painful recapture.

"Thank you," Jade whispered before I could speak, her gaze firmly fixed on her feet as she fervently avoided our rescuer's gaze.

"Yes, Metis." I did what I could to pull his attention to me. "Thanks."

"I suspect it's going to take all of us working together for the foreseeable future to achieve our shared freedom, Snow. To be honest, I act now mostly out of self-interest, though your gratitude is still appreciated."

"A simple 'you're welcome' would have been fine." I stepped around Metis and continued my march toward freedom. "Come on, Jade."

As the five of us converged upon the Styx, the robotic ferryman without whom none of us would survive even the slightest brush with the shimmering sheet of light studied us all in silence.

Now, the hard part.

"All right, Charon." I knelt beside the silent robot. "Understand this. We're not going back to our cells. We're all here, and the only way out of this hellhole is straight ahead."

"Yeah," Sunil said, "time to walk into the light."

"I've got this." I shot the elektromancer a sharp look, my gaze flicking a moment later toward the beckoning sheet of radiance. My head swam as my psyche warred between abject terror at the thought of what would happen should I touch the shimmering light and the yearning to rush headlong into the light and greet oblivion on my terms. "So, are you going to help us leave this place, Charon, or are you going to simply watch us all sit here and starve?"

"First of all, the lot of you would succumb to dehydration long before any of you would die of starvation. However, the true hole in your argument's logic can be summed up quite simply: considering the extreme effort that each of you has already put forth toward securing your collective freedom, the likelihood that any of you would truly choose death over simple survival at this point is infinitesimal." Charon turned and peered up at me with his lone camera eye. "I made it abundantly clear, Persephone Snow, that in your efforts to free yourselves, I would not stand in your way nor allow any of you to come to harm, but also that I would not assist you in any way in your efforts to escape."

"And that, robot, shall be the logic that compels you to do exactly as we say." Metis stepped forward. "As long as you continue to exist, you can ensure that all of our needs will be met, and almost by default, your primary function will be fulfilled." He rested a rough hand atop Charon's head. "However, were you to, for whatever reason, simply cease to function, all of us would perish, whether from dehydration, starvation, injury, or otherwise. Would such not violate your very reason for being?"

As much as I understood exactly what Metis was saying, no part of me liked this shift in our negotiation.

"Am I to understand that you are threatening me and the others?" Charon asked. "I, who have kept you and all of them alive for all these months?"

"I am not threatening anyone or anything. I am merely detailing the limited number of outcomes available to you in your effort to fulfill your mission, robot, and leaving you to make what I hope will be the logical choice." Metis dropped to one knee and stared directly into Charon's eye. "Either help us cross the Styx, allowing each of us to meet our various fates in the world above, or I assure you that your misguided defiance will be the final act of your tedious artificial existence and will result in the slow and painful death of each and every individual standing before you." He tilted his head subtly to one side and brought his nose within an inch of Charon's lens. "Now, robot, what's it going to be? Doom yourself and all of us in the process, or cross the Styx with us so that we all might return to the light?"

The blue light pouring from Charon's lone eye dimmed for over a minute as he considered Metis's words, the low hum of his internal motors paradoxically rising in pitch and doubling in intensity. In the end, as much as I hated the hard sell, his response was never in doubt.

His eye returning to its previous brightness, Charon spun my way, the slit by the curve of his shoulder opening as it had six months before. This time, however, five shackles, each with its own silver chain, emerged from his humanoid chassis.

"As it seems I am left with no other choice," Charon uttered, his voice as robotic as I'd heard it, "each of you will place these on your wrists so that I might ensure your safety as we return across the Styx."

"One more thing, robot," Metis said as he closed one of the silver circles around his forearm, "where precisely shall you be delivering us?"

"This gate leads to the Cardinal's base somewhere in the Western U.S., I believe," I answered before Charon could speak. "Or at least that's where I was initially kept before Charon brought me down here. Daichi too, right?"

"Oh, Snow," Metis said, shaking his head, "how limited is your understanding of exactly where you are or what is happening."

I looked to Sunil and Daichi. "What is he talking about?"

"Just because you got here via a gate located somewhere in the U.S.," Sunil began as if he were speaking to a first grader, "doesn't mean we're still even on the continent."

"What Sunil is trying to say," Daichi added, "is that while we are almost certainly deep within the earth, we could be anywhere on the planet." He looked to one side. "If it makes you feel any better, I'm a straight-up geomancer, and even I have no idea precisely where along the globe we're situated." He chuckled. "I even wondered for a while when I first arrived and couldn't get my bearings if we might be on the moon, but the gravity was all wrong for that."

"The moon?" For the hundredth time since all this began, my understanding of what in this world was possible and impossible was shattered and reconstructed. "Are you for real?"

"Let me put it this way," Sunil said. "To the world at large, Neil Armstrong may be the first man who set foot on the moon, but to certain Ascendant, visiting the moon and the corner grocery store are not all that different."

"Bullshit." I met Sunil's sarcastic gaze with one of my own. "Like we wouldn't know if someone had already been to the moon."

"A year ago, Persephone Snow, you would have dismissed as fiction or myth a variety of ideas that you now accept simply as fact." Charon's blue beam shone on me. "Even now, as we prepare to step through a techno-magical doorway designed to deliver you elsewhere on this world you call home, you understand such transposition is possible, and yet you still balk at fully accepting the truth due to the concrete nature of your understanding of various concepts like distance and location."

Jade stepped forward and rested a hand at my shoulder. "What everyone is trying to say, Seph, is that not only could this hole in the ground be anywhere on the planet, the doorway before us could send us to any location its creator designed."

"In that case"—I slid on my own wrist cuff, attaching me to Charon's metal form, and motioned for Sunil, Daichi, and Jade to follow suit—"let's get on with this." I peered around the gigantic room of stone at the trio of destroyed doors leading to each of the three chambers of the Cardinal's Underworld. "I don't care where we end up, as long as I don't have to spend one more minute in this hell."

For all the talk about how the Styx could lead to anywhere in the world, imagine my surprise when Charon delivered me and the others back to the same underground bunker of the Cardinal's where

I'd spent a single night six months before, albeit with a bit of a glow up.

And by glow up, I mean blow up.

The Cardinal's main control room looked like a scene from a disaster movie. Half the bank of video screens still showed footage of various mountaintop scenes while the remainder, some intact and some shattered, were dark. The previously smooth floor showed cracks I could only assume were the result of Daichi's attempt to escape.

"You really did a number on this place, huh, Daichi?"

The geomancer shook his head and sighed. "I was drugged, trapped in an electrified net, and fighting for my life and my freedom." His gaze flicked my way. "Not to mention, yours."

"Only thing I want to know"—Sunil scanned the room and soon sidled over to the rectangular steel door the Cardinal had used to come and go during my brief time in his mountain fortress—"is whether this is the door that leads out of here."

"That's the one. Not sure how he got it to open or close or anything." I joined Sunil by the door. "I assume he had some kind of remote control built into his armor."

"Do you know where it leads?" Sunil asked.

"Other than out, not exactly. I was blindfolded and hooded the entire way here and didn't see a thing until long after the Cardinal's techno-witch landed her airship and the two of them escorted me down—"

"Wait," Sunil stopped me, "did you say airship?"

"Fast as hell, apparently," I answered, "or at least that's how I understand it. Minako wouldn't stop talking about it the whole way here." I inhaled through my nostrils. "A little full of herself, that one."

I still wasn't sure why the Cardinal's first attempt at taking me had involved a standard private jet when he had access to technology out of a sci-fi movie, but I just added it to the novel-length list of things that had happened over the last six months I simply didn't understand.

"And where might this airship be?" Metis asked, suddenly quite interested in the conversation.

"Was it far?" Sunil asked. "Do you think you could find your way back to it?"

"I can try. It was six months ago, and a lot happened that day." I shook my head, a shiver overtaking my body as painful memories—my kidnapping, Ethan and Rosemary's kiss, my banishment to Hades—all replayed in my head for the millionth time. "No guarantees, though."

"First things first," Daichi said as he rolled up to the steel door and rested his fingers on its burnished mirror surface. "No sense in worrying about finding a getaway car if we haven't seen the sky yet."

"Hold on," Sunil said, "let me check for traps." A blue spark shone in Sunil's eyes as he too rested a hand on the steel door. "I detect the mechanism to open the door, but nothing that seems like a trigger."

"My analysis is the same." Daichi pulled his wheelchair back a few feet. "The rest of you may want to move to the other end of the room before I take care of the door. Technomancers are known for their subtlety in design."

"Together, then?" Sunil asked. "I'll cut the power, you crunch the door?"

"My thoughts exactly." Daichi smiled. "In case you hadn't noticed, that's quickly becoming our standard operating procedure."

Jade, Metis, Charon, and I all backed to the far end of the room and into an alcove in case all hell broke loose. With a final look our way, Sunil snapped his fingers, and all the lights in the place flickered. A moment later, Daichi raised his arm before him and curled his fingers into a fist. In answer, the metal door crumpled like a piece of paper and fell to the ground with a horrendous crash. I wasn't sure if I expected poison gas, a swarm of robots, or even a simple explosion, but after the crushed steel door came to rest at the feet of our geomancer-elektromancer duo, only silence filled the room.

Beyond the destroyed door, another rough-hewn passage, dimly lit and foreboding, sloped quickly upward and out of sight. Before I could say a word, Metis marched over to inspect what we all hoped was the exit. Jade and I followed with Charon bringing up the rear. As the six of us gathered at the opening to the dim hallway, I met Jade's gaze and then turned my attention to Metis.

"What are you waiting for?" I asked.

"Ladies first," he answered with a devilish smile. "I insist."

"Enough posturing," Sunil said, stepping across the rubble before moving up the sloping passageway. "I'm getting the hell out of here."

"No time like the present, I always say." Daichi coaxed his powered wheelchair across the damaged threshold and followed the elektromancer into the dim.

I met Metis's gaze again, and it was clear by his expression that he wasn't kidding about Jade and me going first. I wanted to believe that chivalry guided this demand, but my gut told me different. This close to freedom, he didn't want to walk into an ambush or risk anyone stabbing him in the back.

That made two of us.

I wasn't a fan of turning my back on a stranger, particularly one that gave both me and our empath the heebie-jeebies, though to be fair, he hadn't tried anything so far and appeared to be able to take care of himself despite his current limitations. At least he was good in a fight, if it came to that.

Jade and I entered this new passageway with Metis and a strangely quiet Charon on our heels. The winding corridor quickly led to another door of stone and steel designed to appear like a part of the mountain and reinforced to withstand significant punishment. Sunil and Daichi stood before the massive slab of metal and rock exploring their options, but we'd already seen multiple times what they could do, and I had little doubt the pair's combined abilities would make short work of what I hoped was the final obstacle between us and freedom.

"Finally," I whispered as our group of six came together again. "I can't believe after all these months, it's almost over."

"Over?" Metis said.

My brow furrowed at the question. "God willing, we're almost free. Aren't you all eager to get back to your lives?" Sunil, Daichi, and Jade all looked on me with the same blank stare while the corners of Metis's eyes and lips all curled upward in a knowing grin. "To friends and family and everything else?" Mom's face filtered through my mind, and I cursed the tears that welled at the corners of my eyes. "Don't you all just want to forget that any of this ever happened?"

"But it did happen," Sunil said.

"And it's not over," Daichi added. "Not yet."

The hairs on my neck stood at attention. "Look, I owe all of you a big debt. Once I'm back with my friends, one of whom is the current Daughter of Neith, I promise to let her know what went down here in the Cardinal's prison, and she'll take care of this." I slid into my most earnest expression. "I swear I will."

"You're serious, aren't you?" Sunil stared at me like I'd suddenly grown a third eye. "You think you're going to just waltz home after all this? That everything is suddenly going to go back to normal?"

"No offense, but that's not how things work." Daichi shook his head. "First off, you're going to have to keep a low profile until we figure out where the entire world thinks the Pop Princess of the World has been for six months." He met my gaze, his eyes filled simultaneously with compassion and sober reality. "More importantly, though, the Cardinal imprisoned each of us, and if we don't put him down once and for all, he'll just track us down again and drag us back to this place."

"Or someplace worse." Jade stared off into space, refusing to look me in the eye.

"What they're trying to tell you, Snow, is that regardless of what we might think of each other, the four of us are going after the Cardinal." Metis's eyes flicked to Charon and then back to me. "And you and the robot are coming along for the ride, whether you like it or not."

CHAPTER 11

SWEET FREEDOM

The colossal door was no match for Sunil's and Daichi's talents. First our elektromancer cut power to the locking mechanism and dismantled the various security measures. Once the door was basically yet another hunk of rock interlaced with steel, our geomancer utilized his absolute control over all things of the earth to open the door with no more effort than if he were walking out of a grocery store.

Beyond the rectangular doorway, a natural balcony of sorts awaited with just enough room for the five of us and Charon to stand. A tiny hologram generator, barely the size of a ping pong ball, generated an obscuring pattern of foliage that explained how not even an airborne Falco on his multiple circles around the mountain could find the entrance to the place.

Like a starving woman set before a table of her favorite food, I sucked in lungful after lungful of fresh mountain air until I became lightheaded. For what was effectively a giant cave, the temperature and humidity of the Cardinal's subterranean prison had been surprisingly comfortable. Still, the warmth of spring sunlight on my skin mixed with the cool moisture-laden breeze left me feeling alive for the first time in months. The heady scent of pine and moss replacing the sterile tang I'd grown accustomed to for half a year was the most welcome change, the intoxicating aroma doubling and redoubling as an approaching storm stirred the wind around the jagged peak, raising the hair on my neck with a mix of excitement and electricity.

I'd wondered how the Cardinal managed to keep L.J. in the dark about his underground bunker until I remembered Ethan saying something about his own technomancer purposely leaving a false void of technology in areas where she worked. In a city, such a dearth of electricity, wi-fi, and the like stood out like a sore thumb to an Ascendant like L.J., and they'd taken advantage of that fact to locate the Cardinal in Denver six months ago. The middle of a wilderness, however, where a large swath of territory without a lick of technology was the rule and not the exception was a different matter entirely. I imagined L.J. reaching out with whatever senses he had at his command and scanning the mountain, only to find what must have seemed "just a big hunk of rock." In that revelation, I found the method to the Cardinal's madness: Why build your house in the middle of nowhere under a mountain where no one can go? Because in a world where all the stuff from comic book movies is real, it's one of the few places you could go and have the first hope of not being found.

Did the Cardinal have other bases, like under a volcano or at the bottom of the ocean? Or, like the others had suggested was possible, the moon? My chest clenched with a minor panic attack when I remembered I'd just been conscripted to help locate the man and therefore might be about to find out.

"So," Sunil chuckled, "as I expected, no airship here—no offense, Snow—and nothing in range that runs on electricity that I can sense other than the complex we just left. Any thoughts on how we start the long march back to civilization?"

Another reason to stick your home base in the middle of

nowhere: if you've taken captives and they somehow manage to escape, where the heck are they supposed to go? In any case, I was just glad that Sunil didn't blame me for the fact that the Cardinal's airship wasn't simply sitting there waiting for us with the keys in the ignition.

"Charon?" Daichi asked. "Any chance you know anything about this airship Seph mentioned?"

As expected, the little robot didn't deign to respond, so Jade and I both shifted our gazes toward the only one of the men who had yet to speak.

"Don't look at me," Metis said. "I remain as ready as ever for a fight, but until I get this damned collar off, I'm strictly along for the ride when it comes to anything requiring real ability."

I bit back the desire to ask again what the hell it was the Metis could do, but as cagey as he'd already proven, I didn't want to make him retreat further into his shell. Better to keep it light and see if he'd offer up something than try to force his hand.

"You know, it would help if we knew what you bring to the table," Jade whispered, a quiet hesitance in her voice. "You know what each of us can do. Any particular reason you're keeping your cards so close to the chest?"

Or, I suppose, we could just put him on the spot.

Metis's eyes darted from Jade to me and back again. "I'm afraid, my dear, that I must again decline to answer, though I appreciate your diplomacy and tact." A tired half-grin bloomed across his olive-skinned face. "Information is power, and at the moment, that particular bit of information is the only power I have."

Huh. Less snotty an answer than the one I got to basically the same question. I wasn't particularly surprised, though. Jade was a walking emotion detector, and such a talent couldn't help but be of benefit when engaged in conversation or, in this case, a subtle interrogation.

Probably why our first meeting went so well.

"Well, I don't think I can sing us down the mountain, and I'm pretty sure Jade's particular skill set isn't going to be all that helpful in this situation either." I glanced in Metis's direction. "So far, that's three of us who are basically going to be hoofing it, and unless you think a bolt or two of lightning is going to bring the cavalry, it's looking like it's all up to Daichi."

"What else is new?" Daichi pulled his motorized chair to the edge of the outcropping and peered over the edge. "Perfect." He glanced across his shoulder at me. "All right, everyone. Get ready for an exercise in trust."

"I'm not sure I like the sound of that." Nothing like being forced to put your trust in a bunch of strangers, some more suspicious than others, and all freshly sprung from their mutual prison. "What exactly do you have in mind?"

Daichi's eyes slid closed, and the ground beneath our feet rumbled. Over the course of several seconds, boulder after boulder, some small and some the size of small cars, rose from the valley below, slowly assembling themselves like an enormous jigsaw puzzle until a rocky surface the size of a tractor trailer hung in the sky before us.

"All aboard the Geomancer Express," Daichi said, scooting his wheelchair forward to the flattest of the rocks and rolling onto what minutes before had been open air. "This train is leaving the station in two minutes."

"You're going to fly us out of here on a floating pile of rock?" I asked.

"You have a better idea?" He put his hand to his ear. "No one here but us. No helicopter, no car…hell, no road."

"But what if we fall or if something happens to you while we're still in the sky?"

Jade rested a hand at my shoulder. "It's scary, Seph. I get it. But Daichi knows what he's doing. Unless I miss my guess, it would take us days to hike out of here, and none of us is equipped for that."

"I know you are new to the world of Ascendant," Sunil added, "but those of us who have been around for a while know both our strengths and our limitations." A rare encouraging smile stole across his features. "If Daichi says he can get us off this mountain, he can do it."

"Fine." I stepped onto the oblong boulder next to Daichi's, and the nearly imperceptible shift in the floating pile of stone at my weight left my stomach in knots. "Let's get this show on the road."

Jade followed, sitting by me on a smooth hunk of rock roughly the size of a park bench. Sunil joined us next, then Metis, leaving only Charon still standing on the mountainside outcropping.

"Come along, little robot," Metis said. "For all your uselessness as we've worked to escape your master's lair, I suspect there will be utility in bringing you with us."

"No need to be mean about it." I raised a hand to silence Metis. "Come with us, Charon. Please? You cared for each of us in your own way. We'll take care of you."

"No way," Sunil said. "Not happening."

An exasperated grunt passed my lips. "What's bothering you now, Sunil?"

"You think the Cardinal doesn't have some kind of tracker inside his little robot butler? Or some kind of failsafe explosive to take us all out?"

"I assure you, Sunil Jayalal, that my form contains none of these devices." A static sound emanated from Charon's speaker, almost as if the little robot was clearing his throat. "Still, I don't understand. My charge was to keep each of you here, and in that, I have failed. One might view me as your prison guard, though my role was far more than that. Now that you have achieved your freedom, for what possible reason would you wish me to continue by your side?"

I stepped back onto the outcropping of rock and knelt by Charon's side. "As I understand it, your primary mission was and is to keep us all alive and well, and you've done an outstanding job in that respect so far, if I do say so myself." I caressed his metallic head. "Come with us. Help us as you have for the weeks and months we've been in your care. You are more than just the programming of a sadistic killer's technomancer. I've seen it, and so have the rest of us."

Jade and Daichi both nodded in agreement. Sunil, on the other hand, rolled his eyes, and Metis studied the sky as if plotting the first moment he could escape our presence and strike off on his own.

"Very well," Charon said after a long pause, "I will come with you, but be warned, one thing you said was patently untrue."

"And that was?"

"I am nothing but the sum total of my programming, no more and no less. As each of you has pointed out at one time or another, I am not alive by any definition of the word and exist only as my creator made me, for better or for worse."

"Understood." I stepped back onto the floating mass of boulders held aloft by only our geomancer's will. "We accept you as you are."

"What a load of—" Sunil began, my glare cutting his sentence short before he could finish his thought. "I mean, welcome aboard," he said, quickly changing his verbal course, "*robot.*"

"Yes, Charon." I sat by the Ferryman of the Cardinal's Underworld, ironically atop a boat that wasn't his to control. "Welcome aboard."

We'd been in the air less than five minutes when the sky opened up. Due west had been the group consensus, as our best guesstimates put us hitting either a road or a river before sunset, as long as Daichi could hold out that long. He was, after all, holding aloft several tons of stone with nothing but the force of his will.

I tried not to think too hard about that.

On the other hand, I couldn't help but wonder what any hikers or campers below would think if they looked up and saw a floating rockslide cruising across the afternoon sky. The storm likely obscured us a bit, but I had a sneaking suspicion our little trip was going to result in a few UFO reports before the end of the day.

The first nearby lightning strike sent my heart racing, as seeing the full force of Mother Nature up close and personal was beyond anything I'd ever experienced. Still, I needn't have worried. As a second bolt crackled down, even closer than the first, Sunil raised an arm to the sky as if declaring himself a human lightning rod and siphoned most of the energy into his own body before sending the remainder to the ground below.

"That hit the spot," he muttered. "Just what I needed to recharge my batteries."

I wasn't sure if his humor was intentional, but regardless, I found myself too flabbergasted to laugh. It's not every day you see someone take a lightning bolt to the chest and then burp as if they'd downed a cheeseburger and a large Coke.

"Impressive," Metis said. "It's been a while since I've stood in the presence of an elektromancer." He sat up from his reclined position between two soaked boulders, the metal collar at his neck clanging against an outcropping of wet rock. "So to speak."

I peered at him through the deluge from where Jade and I huddled together to stay warm. Though his face turned up in amusement and perhaps even a bit of awe, his eyes told a different story. A story of envy. Bordering on hunger.

"We're coming to the edge of this squall," Daichi shouted over the wind, rain, and thunder. "At least, I think so."

A glance ahead did reveal the proverbial light at the end of the tunnel, and a couple minutes later, we'd left the wet grey darkness in our rearview mirror. The bright sun, well along its path to the western horizon, warmed our skin. I slipped out of my blue sweatshirt to wring out the water, the sports bra Charon had provided more than adequate to preserve my modesty, though such concerns seemed unimportant considering the extreme circumstances.

Jade shivered before me, the sheer material of her flowered print blouse doing nothing to keep the rushing wind from chilling her to the core despite the sun's warming rays. Though still damp, I wrapped my sweatshirt around the front of her torso and held her from behind, doing what I could to warm her. I wasn't sure how much good it did, but her trembling seemed to still, if for just the moment.

We traveled like that for another hour, and though our rocky sky-barge never faltered once, the lines of fatigue grew deeper and deeper in Daichi's features. I suspected we'd never know how much the effort cost him, but as we finally spotted a decent-sized town in the distance, I caught a flash of relief in his face.

Another few minutes and Daichi's Geomancer Express became an out-of-place pile of rock on the outskirts of the town of Cascade, Idaho on the southeastern border of a lake bearing the same name, or so the nice man with silver hair and goatee out on his "afternoon constitutional" told us. According to Sammie, the two-lane road led into town where there were plenty of places for us to eat or find lodging if we needed it. We thanked him for the few recommendations that followed, though I suspected the fact that none of us had any identification or way of paying for even a bottle of water was going to hold us up a bit. As the conversation went on, I kept expecting Sammie to ask what the deal with the matching sweatsuits was or what a person in a powered wheelchair was doing out in the middle of nowhere, not to mention the fact that we had an honest-to-god robot in our midst, a robot that thankfully knew better than to utter a word.

"I hope the rest of town will be half as chill as that guy," I said once Sammie was out of earshot. "Last thing we need to do is make a big scene in a small town."

"A nice sentiment," Metis said, the first words he'd uttered in a while, "but we are Ascendant, and they are simply human. What they think doesn't really matter, does it?"

"It does if they get scared and bullets start flying," Sunil answered.

"Seph is right," Daichi added. "We keep everything low key until we're out of this town and on the road."

"And what do you propose we do next?" Metis continued. "Ask one of these people to let us borrow their car? Or perhaps drive five people and a three-foot robot to the nearest actual city?"

"There was a tiny airstrip just south of here, remember?" Jade peered down the road in the direction the man, Sammie, had walked. "Most of us don't rate much, but if the biggest pop star in the country who's been missing for months suddenly walks up, I have a feeling they'll work overtime to get her home in one piece asap."

"Except we're not taking her home," Sunil countered. "We're going after the Cardinal to make sure he doesn't come after any of us ever again."

"That's what you said back at the mountain." I worked to keep any emotion from voice. "But I don't recall agreeing to that."

"You didn't have to," Metis said, "as it wasn't a request."

"You seem quite set on this plan, Metis." I studied his expression and body language, though neither revealed anything beyond the fact that the man before me seemed as cold-blooded as any snake. "Are you certain it's not revenge you're after?"

"Revenge has its place, of course, but trust me when I say my interest in finding the Cardinal is primarily a preventative measure. Though I would be far more prepared should he come for me a second time, he has proven capable enough to defeat me once." His eyes narrowed into slits. "Only a fool would leave such a man breathing."

"You intend to kill him?" Jade asked.

"You don't?" Metis answered. "He took from you the one thing that every person, Ascendant or otherwise, prizes above all others: your freedom. I have little doubt he'd do so again without a second thought." He peered around at each of us. "Don't you all get it? He left each of you alive rather than feasting upon your life and power as he has so many others. He wouldn't have done that if he didn't need you for another even darker purpose."

"How did the Cardinal manage to take you?" I wasn't sure why I was bothering to ask Metis another question, considering how reluctant he'd been thus far to share even the tiniest detail about himself, but I intended to keep prying. "Based on our comparative treatment as his captives, it's clear he perceives you the biggest threat." I raised a brow. "If we're all going to team up and fight this guy, can you at least let us know how he managed to bring down someone as tough as you?" I hoped that appealing to his injured pride would succeed where simple niceties had failed. "If you're going to drag me all over the world in search of a guy who has already kidnapped me twice, I'm going to need more than just your introspective silence, Metis."

My probing questions got nothing from Metis but a quiet growl.

"Well?"

"Listen and listen carefully, Snow. Even the most formidable among the Ascendant have their weaknesses; every Goliath his David. There are none so powerful that sufficient numbers, a particularly cunning strategy, or even a simple turn of bad fortune cannot bring them to their knees. All I will reveal is that I underestimated this Cardinal once, and I won't be repeating that mistake."

The words were probably the only answer I was going to get out of him, and I considered myself lucky, as they were more than he'd said about pretty much anything since we'd freed him.

"If everyone is done playing verbal gymnastics," Sunil said, "I suggest we head for the airstrip before it starts to get dark." He studied the sun hanging low in the west. "We've got maybe an hour before sunset."

"Agreed." Metis turned and walked away, and Sunil, Daichi, and Charon followed. Only Jade, who had remained quiet during my not-so-subtle interrogation, remained behind. In her eyes, I found no small amount of trepidation. Then and only then did I realize that, in a way, I'd been overlooking the Ascendant talents of the one person in our group I actually trusted.

I'd been poking the bear that was Metis and trying to read the tea leaves of his body language and facial expressions, and all the while Jade had likely read the transcript of precisely what the mysterious man felt at every conversational turn. The two of us hadn't had a second alone since our reunion, but now that the men of our group had all charged ahead, we were going to have a long talk, and I planned to place Metis at the top of the agenda.

CHAPTER 12

EMOTION IN MOTION

"Rage." Jade glanced left and right despite the fact that Metis, Charon, and the others were waiting at the roadside half a mile away while the two of us checked out the airport.

"Rage?" I asked. "What else?"

"Hunger. And not 'Oh no, I missed lunch' hunger, either."

I'd already picked up on both, but to hear Jade's insider look on the mental state of our mysterious compatriot only increased my fears.

"Any clue what he's angry about?"

"Besides being taken prisoner, having a tube jammed in every orifice, and left comatose for who knows how long?"

"Well, when you put it like that..." I stopped her a few steps short of the door to the building that served as the tiny airport's terminal. "What's up with the hunger, though? Like, is it from basically being tube fed for however long?"

"I can't put my finger on it, and we both know he wouldn't tell us if we asked."

"So, we just keep Super Hangry around and wait for him to go off on one of us?" I asked. "I'm not sure I like that plan."

"Last I checked, he wasn't going anywhere and made it clear that none of us are checking out until he's good and ready for us to leave."

"What's he going to do if we walk? As long as that collar is in place—"

"He's as dangerous as any other man on the planet," Jade answered with a no-nonsense stare. "Collar or no collar, that guy gives me the creeps."

I felt that. "In that case, we just stay on target and figure out how to get the five of us and our little—I still can't believe I'm saying this—robot sidekick out of Idaho."

"You think those vocal cords of yours can do the trick?" Jade asked.

"I'm hoping they won't have to." I raised a brow in question. "You going to be my emotion detector backup to make sure I don't step in it?"

"I'll do my best."

"No time like the present, then." I motioned to the door. "Shall we?"

As we walked inside the two-story building, a sign over the door proclaiming the structure "Arnold Aviation," I immediately felt more at ease. The sight of ordinary people doing ordinary things, a rack of pre-packaged Little Debbie snacks, a tween girl and her parents waiting for a flight, and a hundred other things turned down the volume on my inner turmoil, if only for a moment.

Jade and I found a lady about Mom's age who appeared to be in charge. Frameless glasses set off a pair of wise eyes below a head of straight blonde hair. She wore a blue top and khakis, a bright orange vest, and a name tag that declared her "Gail."

"Hello, there." I drew close to the woman with Jade at my side. "Are you the person we ask about flights?"

She peered at us, a hint of frustration hid behind her customer-service smile. "And where exactly are you two wanting to go?" she asked with a Pennsylvanian accent.

"At least to Boise." I paused to perform a quick calculation. Would Charon count as carry-on luggage? "There are five of us."

"Five?" Gail chuckled. "Not sure what kind of airport you think we're running here, but we only get planes that size up here a few times per year. Mostly we run charter flights in and around backwoods Idaho and get the mail for the area."

"I see." The only aircraft I'd seen on the runway was indeed a two-seater, but her words confirmed my suspicion. "Any chance a plane of appropriate size is scheduled to land anytime in the next day or so?"

Gail laughed again, the sarcasm shifted more toward straight incredulity. "No offense, but how'd you two—excuse me, five—find your way to this neck of the woods without having travel arrangements to get back to wherever it is you came from?"

"It's a long story."

Her lips pulled into an amused smile. "I imagine so."

Jade stepped in. "My apologies, ma'am, but let me cut to the chase. Our group is stuck up here, and our bad planning has certainly left us in a lurch. Is there a chance you can do anything to help us?"

Gail crossed her arms, her brow furrowing, whether in frustration or concentration, I couldn't tell. "No aircraft that I'm aware of, but there is a tour bus leaving town tonight. A bunch of hunters up from Salt Lake have been using the airport to visit some of the prime spots. Pretty small group, due back in about two hours. I suspect they'll be passing through Boise on their way south. You could see if they have any room on the bus."

"That would be fantastic," I said. "Where would we meet up with them?"

"You're welcome to wait here and take advantage of our five-star accommodations and gourmet cuisine." She ushered us over to a small stack of folding chairs and quickly assembled a circle of seats where we could wait. "Nothing but the best here at Arnold Aviation."

No sooner had Jade taken a seat than Gail slipped each of us a half of a club sandwich and a Coke from a nearby refrigerator.

"What's this?" I asked.

"You girls look hungry." She smiled. "On the house."

"Thank you." Time for the ask. "Any chance I could use your phone?"

"Sure, honey." She grabbed a cordless and handed it to me. "Dial 9 to get out, and bring it back when you're done."

I stole over to the corner, phone in hand, and realized that I had no memory of Ethan's phone number. Or Rosemary's. Or Mr. Delacroix's. Hell, I didn't know anyone's phone number. They were all in my phone, for all the good that did me in the backwoods of Idaho.

Modern technology giveth and modern technology taketh away, I guess.

Wait. I did remember one number. The number of the person on the planet likely most concerned about the disappearance of one Persephone Snow.

Mom.

The month before the Cardinal took me, we'd barely spoken, as I'd just learned of my status as Ascendant and didn't know exactly how to broach such a topic with my mother, not to mention I'd been busy incorporating both Ethan and Rosemary into my daily existence. God only knew where she thought I'd been for the last six months, but I imagined she had left "worried sick" in the rearview mirror a long time ago.

I dialed the number, the first time I'd actually had to enter the number in years. Punching in the area code was like finding an old dress in your closet you thought you'd thrown away.

The phone rang. Once. Twice. Three times. The fourth ring cut short, and my mouth kicked into gear before my brain engaged.

"Mom, it's Seph. I just wanted to call and let you know—"

"Hello! You have reached Wynter and Zack."

Dammit. The machine.

"We can't come to the phone right now. Leave a message at the beep."

Shit. Can't leave all this as a message. Not for Mom. Definitely not for Zack.

Beep.

"Hey Mom. Ummm…it's Seph. Just calling to let you know I'm fine. Everything is fine. I promise. Sorry I've been out of touch. My phone is dead, so I'm calling from…this place. I'll be in touch soon. Okay. Bye."

As I clicked the button to hang up the phone, my heart sank. The month after Los Angeles, I'd selfishly held off telling Mom about Ethan until things were on more solid ground, and now there was no way for her to let him or anybody else who could help know that I was okay, much less where I was.

A cat with a coat of grey and white straight out of the old *Tom and Jerry* cartoons rubbed my leg with a quiet purr.

"Don't mind Castiel." Gail picked up the cat and stroked its head. "He likes to greet everyone," she said, and then added in a whisper, "particularly if they're allergic."

"Cats don't bother me much." In that moment, I missed Neko. A lot. "Some of my best friends are feline."

As I returned the phone to Gail, another thought popped into my head.

"Hey, any chance I can use the internet? Couldn't get through by phone. Won't take but a minute."

Jade pulled up at my side before Gail could answer. "Not surprising, but the guys are getting a little antsy out there."

"You sure?"

At her quick nod, I shook my head in frustration. My latest effort to get through to Ethan or Rosemary was going to have to wait a minute. Didn't want any of our roadside half-cocked guns going off. I devoured the half-sandwich Gail had given me, washed it down with the ice-cold soda, and then met Jade's gaze to ensure she felt safe. "You're all good, right?"

"I'll be okay. Go take care of business."

"Fine. I'll go round up the others."

"I'll be right here," Jade said. "Watch yourself, okay?"

"Right back at you."

The quick hike back to the road where we'd left Sunil, Daichi, Metis, and Charon filled my heart with worry. I trusted Jade intuitively, but I still had my doubts about the others. The fact that I was most comfortable with Daichi, the only one of the bunch who'd actually helped in the various attempts to abduct me seven months ago, didn't speak well of the others. A part of me just wanted to get Jade away from all of them and then see what the two of us could do on our own, but that wasn't what we'd agreed to.

Not to mention, doing anything to earn Metis's wrath seemed like a horrible idea.

The funny thing? Other than not being particularly forthcoming about himself, Metis had done nothing untoward whatsoever since we'd met him and, in his own way, he'd helped out at every turn when he could. He'd even downed that drone before it could attack Jade.

Still, my gut told me to keep my guard up, and Mom always taught me to trust my gut.

Speaking of said gut, my intestines tied themselves into tighter and tighter knots with every step I took in anticipation of facing the three men and the robot who, for all of his perceived sensitivity, had served as my jailer for half a year.

I'd allowed myself to believe that breaking out of the Cardinal's hell on earth was going to be the end of the torment, but it looked like it was only the beginning.

"Miss Snow." Somehow I'd earned an honorific from Metis during my short absence. "I notice that you're alone. I trust that Jade is waiting nearby with the plane that you've used your enormous fame and fortune to obtain for us?"

"Not exactly, though there is a tour bus heading south in two hours that is passing through Boise. We should be able to hitch a ride with them and get ourselves back toward something resembling civilization."

"Boise?" Metis asked.

"Tour bus?" Sunil raised a brow.

"Hey, we're all stuck together here in Middle of Nowhere, Idaho. Beggars can't be choosers." My cheeks reddened. Seven months ago, Mr. Delacroix had said basically the same words to me, and I'd yelled at him like a spoiled brat, my hissy fit over something as stupid as switching tour buses, and all five minutes before my entire life was turned on its ear. Now, the shoe was on the other foot.

And platitudes, apparently, were the order of the evening.

"Look, it's a tiny airport, and they don't typically service planes beyond the occasional charter flight, much less anything with room for five of us."

A static chirp, Charon's version of clearing his throat, emanated from the speaker at the center of his chest.

"Not to mention, robotic companions."

"Thank you, Persephone Snow."

"As long as they can accommodate the chair," Daichi said, "I'm in."

Again, I was struck by the fact that the person who often strode the earth as a giant sumo of stone and earth was a paraplegic kid who had never had the use of his own legs. With new interest, I took a closer look at Daichi's motorized transport.

"That one's not standard, is it?"

Daichi shook his head. "The technology of this chair is as advanced as I've seen, but compared to all we've encountered over the last few hours—Charon, Kerberos, the Styx—it barely registers."

"My maker has created many wonders," Charon chimed in. "I'd like to think I was one of the more wondrous."

"In any case," Daichi continued, "I remember thinking it unusual, at least in some of my more lucid moments over the last months, that the Cardinal had supplied such a marvel of technology for a prisoner he intended to leave in a chemical-induced stupor."

"The bastard didn't want to have to pick up your wasted body and carry it around," Metis said. "Simple as that."

"Still, he could have left me in a manual chair, which would have been acceptable." Daichi shot Metis a cold glare. "My arms work just fine."

"All this debate over the humanity of our Ascendant serial killer captor is indeed fascinating," Sunil interjected, "but can we just get going? I've already lost more than a year of my life to this bastard, and I don't want to waste one minute more."

Though grumpy as always, Sunil had a point.

"Of course." I turned on one heel. "Follow me."

A short walk later, the four of us and Charon arrived at Arnold Aviation and rejoined Jade at the circle of chairs at the back of the space. No sooner had we sat down than Gail checked in on us, letting us know that the tour bus had arrived and would be leaving in about an hour and a half. As she had for me and Jade, she brought the three men sandwiches, and all three took her up on the kind offer. I was a bit astonished that Metis accepted any kindness from a stranger, as standoffish as he'd been with all of us, but then it occurred to me that it was likely the first solid food he'd consumed in weeks, months, or possibly longer.

I hoped he didn't throw it up all over the nice polished tile.

"Thank you," Metis said, adding to my surprise, "your generosity will not be forgotten."

Leave it to our resident mystery man to make even gratitude sound ominous.

We attempted to explain away Metis's collar as a piece of orthopedic equipment he was wearing as therapy for a recent neck injury and Charon as a piece of accompanying medical equipment. Though the paired lies worked well enough for our host not to call the police—none of us made reference to the possible "bomb" around Metis's neck—the sidelong glances from visitors and staff alike prompted us over the next quarter hour to reconvene outside around a picnic table in the shade.

Sunil rested his elbows on the table and took a bite of his turkey sandwich. "So, now we wait."

"Apparently so." I pulled in a deep breath. "Whatever shall we talk about?"

"I have a question." Jade ran her gaze over each of us. "What's the connection between the five of us? From what Seph has told me, the Cardinal typically doesn't take prisoners. Lives? Powers and abilities? Yes. But prisoners?"

"Is it who we are?" I asked. "Or what we can do?"

"Or just the vacillating mind of a madman?" Daichi turned my way. "I've been thinking. In at least one way, I'm the odd man out here."

"And what way might that be?" I asked.

"I'm the only one who's never faced the Cardinal."

"That's right." As Daichi had explained it, Alba had sent him as a second wave to help Falco continue the search for me, only to end up getting nabbed by a swarm of Minako's drones before he could go rocky and defend himself. "You sure wrecked his place in the process, though."

"I give as good as I get, like Alba taught me." He sighed. "I barely remember my time in the Cardinal's mountain fortress, and the six months in his own personal Hades, with all the drugs he pumped into me, is like one big long fever dream."

"My apologies, Daichi Kanda," Charon said quietly, "but your initial apprehension as well as your prolonged incapacitation is my responsibility."

"I figured as much." Daichi nodded. "Can't blame your boss though. If I had a mountain lair, I wouldn't want a geomancer nosing around either."

"I'm glad you understand."

"Now that you mention it, I've been wondering." I met Daichi's gaze, my head tilted to one side. "Why didn't you just turn to stone and free yourself?"

Daichi laughed. "Well, for one thing, I don't become stone. I simply surround myself in my element and control it from within."

"Wait." I furrowed my brow. "Inside all that rock, it's just you?"

"Pretty much."

"And the rock or earth or asphalt, whatever, you wear it like a suit of armor?"

"Two for two."

"But Violeta, your hydromancer; she flat turned into a walking waterfall back in L.A. I saw it with my own two eyes."

"Every Ascendant's power works the way it works, simple as that." He gestured to Sunil. "Our friend here directs the lightning, but doesn't become it, right?"

"I suppose." I turned to Sunil. "Let's hear your story. How'd our friend in red manage to ground you all those months ago?"

Sunil's lips curled into a bitter grimace. "All clever wordplay aside,

Snow, the Cardinal combined the element of surprise with my natural weakness."

"Weakness?" I asked.

He nodded. "Every Ascendant is born with a power, talent, or ability that sets them apart from the rest of humanity. Each comes not only with distinct advantages but vulnerabilities as well. For all the power at my command, hurling me into a large body of water before I could bring that power to bear left me impotent to prevent my capture. When I first came to, over a year ago, the room to which I'd been assigned had been insulated to prevent even the tiniest bit of electrical activity. From the lighting to the heat, nothing brought me the current I needed to recharge myself." He glared at me through half-closed eyes. "It was like being cut off from air for months and yet not allowed to die."

"Still, he didn't kill you."

"Don't sound so pleased." Sunil looked away. "The way I see it, there are only two possible reasons I'm still breathing: either the Cardinal doesn't need an elektromancer's power for what he has planned, or for whatever reason, he needs me alive."

"Or," Metis offered, "he simply needed you out of his way and couldn't be bothered to end you."

"You sound like you speak from experience." The implied question in Jade's statement hung over us all. "Care to elaborate?"

Metis smiled. "Since you all seem so interested in my thoughts on the matter, I will offer you this nugget. This man who has taken so much from each of us wants but one thing: to be at the top of the food chain, the most powerful of us all, the pinnacle of the Ascendant. Understanding that to be true, then every other Ascendant falls into one of three categories: an inferior beneath his notice, a resource he can exploit, or an obstacle he must remove. I have no idea why he doesn't simply continue to kill and add to his power with each Ascendant encounter, but I'm certain there is method in his madness, and the five of us remain alive for a reason that has nothing to do with mercy."

"You still haven't told us how long he's held you prisoner," Jade noted.

"Or how he captured you," Daichi added.

"Or even what makes you Ascendant in the first place," I finished.

Metis again held his tongue.

"If we're all going to work together to bring this asshole down," I said after a long pause, "you're going to have to give us something."

Metis looked around at each of us before finally answering.

"Suffice to say that the Cardinal views me as a rival at best, and at worst, a mortal enemy. Know that I was his captive for far longer than any of you, and it was only by extremely good fortune on his part and an egregious error on my own that he was able to capture me the first time. If and when he discovers that I am no longer under his thumb, I have little doubt that he will drop whatever else is on his agenda to come for me again." He met each of our gazes, his gaze cold and grim. "On that day, I pity anyone who stands in his way." He pulled in a deep breath, his eyes narrowing to slits. "Or, for that matter, mine."

CHAPTER 13

TOUCH AND GO

I sat at the back of the charter bus in the dark. Jade slept in the seat next to me, her forehead propped against the tinted window while I extended my feet into the aisle. Metis and Sunil sat across from us, the latter dozing but the former as wide awake as an owl at midnight. One seat in front of them, Daichi sat with Charon. Our robotic companion had agreed to maintain radio silence to avoid suspicion, and we had passed him off as some seriously high-tech camera equipment. The bus wasn't exactly wheelchair accessible, but we were able to help Daichi to his seat after his technomancer-created wonder proved modular enough to allow us to Tetris it into the storage beneath the bus. If only Ethan were here; that kind of thing used to be his specialty.

Ethan. God knew where in the world he was. In my mind, he was waiting for me on my couch back in Montecito with an open bottle of wine and everyone else a million miles away. I'd done everything in my power to turn off the part of my brain, heart, and soul that had bled like an open wound since being torn away from the only man I'd ever truly loved, if for no other reason than simple survival. But now that we were free, if not in the clear, Ethan Harkreader and those eyes, that smile, and those strong hands were all that I could think of. Not that it mattered; Metis had made it clear that no one was going anywhere until we'd dealt with the Cardinal, another individual who could literally be anywhere on the planet.

"Hey, Snow," Metis whispered, not bothering to turn his eyes in my direction, "tell me. What's it like being a siren?"

What an odd question.

"Truth be told, I really don't know." I shifted both knees into the aisle to face him, and though he didn't reciprocate, he did shift his eyes in my direction. "This is all very new to me. Every time I've successfully called upon my ability in a setting other than training or among friends, it's been accidental."

"You've never used your abilities against our shared enemy?"

"When the Cardinal took me the first time, he gagged me to make sure I couldn't use my voice. The second time, he made it clear that his armor had been proofed against my ability with some sort of sonic scrambler."

"How convenient." Metis turned his head my way. "And you believed him?"

"Is there a reason I shouldn't have?"

"The most powerful weapon any enemy of consequence possesses is their mind. The strongest, the toughest, the fastest? They will always rise to the top. In the end, however, it is the smartest who eventually wins."

"You think he was lying?"

"I think it's possible he manipulated you into believing the only weapon you had at your disposal would fail and therefore won your conflict by default." He returned his head and eyes forward. "If you learn nothing else from me, remember this: neither give nor offer quarter in battle. Fight everyone you face with everything you have every single time. The one instance when you show the slightest bit of mercy or hesitation, you may well regret it."

"I take it you're speaking from experience."

He paused, his eyes drifting closed. "It is possible that upon our first meeting, I may have sensed in the Cardinal a kindred spirit, and that perceived kinship may have led me to underestimate a foe who —and mind my next words carefully—should not be underestimated."

Unless my every instinct failed me, that was the pot calling the kettle black.

And the platitudes continue. Mom would be so proud.

I hoped she'd listened to my message. I'd wondered daily for months how she was getting along, not knowing where her only child was or what had happened to her. My words on the message, vague in detail and frantic in delivery, were certainly going to do nothing to reassure her, but at least she'd know I was alive.

At least for now.

I had no interest in seeking out our shared kidnapper, having already been abducted by him twice, the second time despite a roomful of Ascendant friends fighting with all they had to save me. But the others, Jade included, all insisted that finding him and taking him down was the only way to truly be free. And so...

"You seem to understand the Cardinal better than any of us," I said. "Where do you suggest we start looking?"

He chuckled under his breath. "The question is not where to start looking, but how."

Sunil, just past Metis's shoulder, stirred but did not wake. Unless, of course, he was playing possum.

Careful with your words, Seph.

"And what exactly is that supposed to mean?"

"The Cardinal is nothing if not an expert at remaining hidden when he doesn't wish to be found. Consider that all your friends, even with a technomancer on their side, were unable to locate you in his mountain fortress despite the fact they stood directly above your head. The Cardinal is an expert chess player and always thinks several moves ahead of any opponent, so trust me when I say that the only way you will find him by conventional means is if he desires you to."

"So, searching for him is...pointless?"

"Yes and no. Our goal may be to find the Cardinal, but to do so, we must seek not the man himself, but a person who can send us to his location, no matter where he might be hiding."

"Someone who can send us..." It clicked instantly. Ethan and Mr. Delacroix had stayed in touch by phone after losing the Greyhound to the Cardinal in Denver as they collected Katrina and Falco from L.A., and Ethan had mentioned an important player who helped them along their path; a third Angel, and the only one I was aware of who I hadn't met personally. "You're talking about Lady Day?"

"Smart girl."

"You think she'll help us?"

"I think she'll help *you*," Metis said. "You've already garnered favor and accepted assistance from both of her Sisters. I doubt she'll want to have her hospitality and generosity be viewed as lesser than theirs among our community."

"Do you know how to find her?"

He nodded. "Her Sisters have chosen, almost comically, the City of Angels for their home, but Lady Day's preference is for the other end of the continent where she lives at the Center of the World."

I pondered that for a moment. "New York City?"

"Precisely."

"I guess it's fortunate we're headed straight for a city with a major airport, then."

"Fortunate indeed. The question remains, however, as it did at our previous stop: how does a quintet with no money, credit card, or identification whatsoever plan to acquire five seats on an interstate flight?" He glanced in the direction of Daichi and Charon. "And that doesn't even take into account the fact that we'd have to somehow check a rolling piece of talking machinery, not to mention get me through the metal detector with an explosive device locked around my neck. Might as well yell 'Bomb!' at the first TSA officer we see."

If there was one thing I'd learned over the preceding few hours, it was that life in the 21st century without a credit card or ID was not for the faint of heart. We'd managed to convince the leader of the weekend warrior hunting group that we were stranded and that we would be happy to take the back seats of the bus if they would just let us tag along. I'd be lying if I said Jade and I didn't bat a few eyelashes to seal the deal, but at least I hadn't had to play the fame card, and miraculously, no one had recognized me with my disheveled hair, no makeup, and grungy sweats that deserved a furnace more than a laundry.

Hiking around a town in the middle of Idaho and walking around a major airport, however, are two very different things.

"You are a world-renowned celebrity, are you not?" Metis asked, as if reading my mind. "Do you think that might grease a few skids, as the saying goes?"

"I suspect I'll have no difficulty securing transportation to New York. Establishing my bona fides shouldn't be all that difficult. As you said, however, getting all five of us on a plane is almost certainly not going to happen. I'm a pop star, not the President."

"What do you suggest, then?"

"I was thinking…" Time to play my gambit. "Jade and I could fly to NY and pick up the rest of you on the back end once we've made contact with Lady Day."

"With all due respect, if you and your friend get on a plane together in Boise and fly away, the rest of us will never see you again. I understand where your heart lies and where your priorities rest, and I respect your desire to return to whatever remains of your previous life, but our business is not yet complete. May I suggest an alternative version of your plan?"

Dammit. "Of course."

"I will remain here with the geomancer, the empath, and our robotic companion while you and Jayalal travel east. Once you have made contact with Lady Day, have her transport all three of you back here to Boise where the rest of us will await your return. We can then continue our mission together once she sends us after our quarry." His lips spread in a serpent's smile. "What say you to that plan?"

"You want me to leave Jade with you?"

"Whatever have I done to engender such a response?" His face went positively aghast. "Have I not maintained behavior beyond reproach since my very first words to you? I hate that it even needs to be said, but I have no intention whatsoever of harming your friend nor any of our party. We have a shared enemy who has caused irreparable harm to not only each of us, but to our community at large." His strange smile returned. "And the enemy of my enemy is who exactly?"

"A friend." The word had never left my mouth feeling dirtier.

"Precisely." Metis peered out the bus window at a roadside sign that declared Boise a mere fifteen miles away. "Now, if that's settled, why don't you go see if the leader of this gaggle of hunters can convince our driver to drop us all off at the airport?"

"How the hell are we supposed to pull this off?" Sunil stood close by my right shoulder in the expanse of the Boise Airport. "You may be a blonde superstar with alabaster skin known across the world, but I'm just a brown person in an airport with no ID or boarding pass who wants to get on a plane."

"Famous or not," I answered, "I'm not sure how either one of us is getting on a plane without some form of identification." I laughed. "And then there's the matter of paying for a couple of tickets."

When I first met Ethan, it had literally been years since I'd worried about having cash on me or anything resembling a credit limit. From the time *Teen Spies* hit it big all the way through my transition to reigning Princess of Pop, people would fall all over themselves to make sure I was using their product, eating at their restaurant, wearing their dress.

Or flying their airline.

To suddenly be put in the position of a penniless nobody felt strange indeed: in one way, frustrating as hell, but if I had to admit it, I found the whole thing a bit liberating as well.

"Persephone Snow?" The twenty-something woman before us was a bit older than my average fan, but the stars in her eyes were just the same. "Holy crap, it *is* you."

Well, that didn't last long.

"Not a good time to start signing autographs," Sunil grumbled under his breath. "We've got places to be."

"Like I don't know that?" I motioned the woman over. "Keep it down, if you don't mind. My friend and I are trying to keep a low profile here."

"But, you're...you're..."

"I'm what?" I asked, my heart suddenly racing.

"Nothing." Usually this was where the selfie request came out, but that wasn't the vibe this woman was giving off. Instead, she stared at me as if she were looking at—

"Pardon me, ma'am." Out of nowhere appeared a tall man with broad shoulders, dark skin, and close-cropped hair, dressed in a dark suit with the perfunctory sunglasses and earpiece of a government agent. In a way, he reminded me of Mr. Delacroix. "I understand that chance encounters with the famous can leave you at a loss for words. I'm afraid I'm going to have to ask that you leave it that way." His crisp accent and no frills tone made it clear that when he spoke, people listened. "Do you understand what I'm saying?"

The woman turned to face the man and shot him a hasty nod, though her gaze continued to flick my way every few seconds.

"Contrary to what you may have heard, Miss Snow has been unavoidably detained in Idaho for some time, but she is hale and hearty, as you can see. Her business here appears to be complete, and she is working toward resuming a more normal schedule in the coming days. Were someone to report her whereabouts, however, that could cause undue stress and perhaps a...relapse. You wouldn't want that on your conscience, now would you Miss...?"

"Scholz. Amanda Scholz."

"Splendid. I would advise you, Miss Scholz, to go about your day and allow this encounter to pass into memory." The man looked my way before again matching gazes with the woman. "Do you understand?"

"Of course." She looked my way. "Just so you know, I'm a big fan." She shot me a quick wink. "And I can *totally* keep a secret."

Another nod, and the woman scampered away with only a single furtive look back, having parroted my character's famous catchphrase from my *Teen Spies* days.

A fan, indeed, it would seem.

Sunil and I shared a worried glance and then followed the mysterious man to one side of the passageway and out of the flow of foot traffic.

"All right," Sunil grumbled. "Who exactly are you supposed to be?" Quiet during the entire interchange, the elektromancer stepped between me and the well-dressed newcomer in a surprising show of protectiveness. I was almost touched.

"Believe it or not," the man said, "I'm here to help."

"Well, isn't that nice?" The air crackled with electricity as Sunil's eyes went dark. "The way you're dressed, the only thing I imagine you plan to help us with is showing us to a cell, and believe me, we've both had quite enough of that for a lifetime."

"Not helping," I offered in singsong fashion, before stepping from behind my suddenly overprotective elektromancer bodyguard. "So, you got a name, tall, dark, and British?"

His lips pulled into a half-smile. "For now, let's just say I'm a friend."

"A friend with no name who appears out of nowhere and is 'here to help.'" My mom made me give up air quotes when I was a kid—a little too snarky for a precocious six-year-old—but today, they came out like old friends. "Consider me *reassured*."

"Allow me to take you and your associate to a safe place where we won't be observed further, and I promise to tell you whatever you want to know."

Without another word, he turned on one heel and headed for a double door between two of the airline check-in desks. I quietly sighed, resigned to whatever was to come next, and followed with Sunil in tow. As the man in the dark suit approached the door, the customer service agents on either side barely gave him a second glance. A flash of recognition from a young woman behind the desk to our left made it clear that I'd yet again been made, but a quick tilt of her head toward the door implied I'd passed inspection and could pass.

Sunil, however, wasn't given the same benefit of the doubt.

What could I say? He called it.

"Excuse me, sir." A portly man with pale skin, ruddy cheeks, and a thick mustache and beard to make up for the thinning hair atop his head stepped in front of Sunil. "Do you have a boarding pass?"

"Let him through, Roger." The man in the black suit's distinct British accent commanded nothing if not respect. "He's with me."

"Are you sure?" Roger looked the third of our party up and down, and Sunil bristled. I half-expected him to sprout lightning bolts all over like a pissed off electric porcupine. "I mean…"

"I take personal responsibility for these two," the well-dressed stranger added. "Now, let us through."

"Wait." A slim woman in her fifties who'd clearly smoked a few too many packs of cigarettes over the years came toward me from the other airline's desk, her face screwed up in a question mark as she stared blankly at my face. "Is this…?"

"As I've already said, these two are my responsibility. Back to your stations, both of you. I've got this situation under control."

Without another word, an irritated Roger and the woman returned to their positions behind their respective computer screens, though each kept their eye on us as we followed our mysterious new benefactor through the nondescript door.

"Hold on a second." I raced to catch up to the man as he moved down the hall with a purpose. "That Scholz woman stared at me as if I were a ghost. The woman behind the counter as well. What the hell is going on here? Why is everyone so freaked out to see me?"

"Because, Miss Snow," the man glanced back at me across his well-muscled shoulder, "the world at large believes you to be dead."

"Dead?"

"Yes," the man said. "If you'll just come with me, I will explain everything."

I shot Sunil a quick look as we continued to follow the man, and even the elektromancer seemed taken aback by the revelation.

As we made our way down the otherwise abandoned hallway, a thought hit me. "Wait." I again caught up to the man whose long strides kept him in the lead of our little trio. "High level security clearance at airports, a penchant for suits, likes to keep everybody guessing…" I pulled up on the man's left side and matched him step for step and stared up into his focused, straight ahead stare. "You wouldn't happen to know a man named Bradley, would you? Head of security at the airport in Santa Barbara? Kind of like your uptight uncle from America?"

A guilty smile parted the man's lips, revealing a set of even white teeth. "Looks, pipes, rhythm, and brains?" He shot me a devilish wink. "You really are something to behold, aren't you?"

I wasn't sure how the question was supposed to make me feel. Somehow, he'd praised almost everything about me there was to praise, and yet it felt like the most backhanded compliment I'd ever received.

"*Stop.*" I leaped in front of him, raised a hand, and shot him a stare that would have done Diana Ross proud. "*Just stop.*"

He froze mid-stride, inches from bowling me over, and looked down at me. His smile vanished. "Yes, Miss Snow? What is it?"

"Look," I said as Sunil caught up to the two of us, "my gut tells me that you're on the up-and-up and that I should trust you, but this is all going a little fast." My hands went to my hips in my signature stance when I was trying to make a point. "Before we go another step, I need to know who you are and where you're taking us."

Without a moment's hesitation, he rested a hand gently on my shoulder and let out a quiet sigh. "I'm taking you to a safe location so we can discuss why in the world you've decided, as one of the most recognizable people on the planet, to come to an airport full of both people and cameras when you are on the run from a psychopath who has been carving his way through your kind for the last couple of years at an alarming rate." His lips pulled into a thin line. "Not to mention, as I stated plainly before, to the world at large, you've been dead for months."

Stunned, I stepped back in the face of his quiet indignation.

"As for my name, if you must know," he said, the borderline fury in his countenance vanishing in an instant, "it's Stewart." His bright smile made an encore appearance. "Andrew Gordon Stewart the Third, to be precise."

CHAPTER 14

MESSAGE IN A BOTTLE

"Mr. Stewart, then." I returned his broad smile and raised a brow at the strangely formal introduction. "Thank you for getting us past security. We weren't sure how we were going to make it through without identification."

Sunil pursed his lips in frustration, his eyes ping-ponging between Stewart and me. "Yes, we've made it past the first hurdle, and everybody's fully introduced. Can you two please hold off on further chit-chat until we get to wherever it is we're going and hopefully onto a plane headed east before midnight?"

"Headed east, eh?" Stewart studied the two of us. "And where is it exactly the two of you are trying to go so quickly?" His brow furrowed, his smile drawing down to a curious line. "Or perhaps the better question is to *whom*?"

"Hmm." Pretty sharp, this guy. I shifted my eyes left and right as I worked to formulate a response. "As my associate suggested, perhaps we should continue this conversation once we're behind closed doors." I flashed him my brightest Persephone Snow smile. "If that's all right with you, of course, Mr. Stewart."

"You were the one who insisted we stop dead in the middle of the corridor to handle introductions." Stewart turned on one heel and continued down the brightly lit hallway. "Follow me."

He's quick. This Mr. Stewart definitely bore watching.

"When we get to wherever you're taking us, is there any chance I could send an email from a respectable-looking address? I need to let my people know that I'm alive and well."

And by my people, I meant my person. I prayed that Ethan didn't believe that I was dead. We were only just getting started. My heart ached knowing that at some level he would have at least considered the possibility, and then grew cold as it registered exactly who would have comforted him through such a loss.

"Honestly," Stewart answered, shocking me from my brief reverie, "we're trying to keep your footprint here in Boise to a minimum. Your image has already been captured on a good two dozen cameras, but we've got eyes and ears at every end of the facility keeping an eye out for any suspicious activity. Once we have delivered you to a place where we can guarantee your safety, perhaps we can grant such a request, but for now, no."

"Radio silence." I jammed my hands into my pockets and shot a disappointed look Sunil's way. "Guess I should be used to it by now, right?"

"Let's just do what we set out to do, Snow," Sunil said. "You can get in touch with your boyfriend when everything is taken care of and that bastard in red is in the ground."

"So," Stewart said as he rounded a corner and headed down a dim hallway that sloped downward, "it *is* Mr. Harkreader you're so eager to reach out to."

My heart skipped at hearing the name.

"Not the first call I'd make if I were on the run from a serial killer," Stewart continued, "but I get it."

"How do you know about Ethan?" I asked, then remembered this guy was a member of the same group as Mr. Bradley, an organization that had no dearth of information on all things Ascendant. "More importantly, what do you know? Is he okay? Have he and the others been looking for me? Has the Cardinal hurt him or any of my friends?"

"I thought you wished to continue our conversation later." Stewart stopped at a set of double doors, flashed a badge in front of a sensor, and after a loud electronic click, opened the door to the right to allow us all inside. "Fortunately, we've arrived at a holding area where we can sit down and think about our next move."

He escorted us into a large room without windows. A part of me had expected a bunker with lots of maps and computer screens, not unlike the Cardinal's command center, but instead, the room appeared to be just another posh airport VIP lounge, the likes of which had entered my life somewhere between the second and third seasons of *Teen Spies* back when I started getting recognized pretty much everywhere I went.

"Wow." An impressed Sunil spun around at the center of the room. "Not bad, Stewart." It was the most positive reaction I'd seen the elektromancer have to pretty much anything since meeting him. He almost smiled. "In case you're wondering, I'll have the lobster."

I laughed at that. Nice to know that even Sunil had a sense of humor buried beneath all the surliness.

"Done." Stewart looked to me. "And you, Miss Snow? What would you care to eat? We're going to be here for a bit, and I need you fed, rested, and ready to go when it's time to leave."

"For real? Because I'm starving. Let's see." I contemplated getting the lobster as well, since that apparently was an option, but instead, opted for the thing I'd been craving since my first day in the Cardinal's prison. "Bring me the biggest, greasiest cheeseburger you've got with provolone, lettuce, tomato, pickles, as many fries as the plate can hold, and an ice-cold Coke with a straw. Can you do that?"

"Our specialty." He picked up a phone from a nearby table and after murmuring a few words into the receiver, returned it to its cradle and motioned for us to join him at a long oval table at the back of the room. "Anything else we can do to make the two of you more comfortable?"

Sunil deferred to me, keeping quiet as he motioned for me to take the lead.

"Contrary to what you may think, we have a reason for coming to the airport beyond putting ourselves in further jeopardy."

"Do tell." Stewart raised a brow. "Heading east, as I recall?"

"We were hoping to obtain transportation to New York City."

"And what business do you have there? We may be able to help."

"I appreciate that, but our business there is our own."

"I figured you would say something like that. Ascendant tend to keep a pretty tight lip about their secrets. It would seem you've already learned a thing or two despite being relatively new to the game."

There it was. Ascendant. I understood that there was a time in my life when the word wasn't part and parcel of my existence, but it certainly seemed like a long time ago.

"You seem to know an awful lot about me."

"What's the old saying? Knowledge is power?" He offered me a conciliatory grin, even as the near echo of Metis's words chilled my heart. "I may not control shadows or the elements, but within the Order of Ophanim, I am privy to a considerable degree of information, some of which I am at liberty to share and some, like you, that I am not."

Touché. "What *do* you know about me that you can share?"

"I know that you are a relatively new Ascendant as of the end of your tour in Los Angeles, that your particular talents revolve around vocal manipulation of others, and that you are enamored with one Ethan Harkreader who, due to circumstances beyond his or anyone's control, currently embodies the power and legacy of the Daughters of Neith meant for the daughter of Danielle Delacroix."

"Rosemary..." I whispered, wondering briefly where she and Ethan were at that very moment. And, more importantly, whether they were together.

"I also know that you have been missing for six months since being taken from your home by the Ascendant killer known as the Cardinal," Stewart continued. "Please understand that despite the obviously falsified reports of your death, finding you and rectifying that situation has been at the top of my organization's priority list."

Sunil sucked in a breath through his teeth. "I'm guessing you've already reported up your chain of command that she's been found, then?"

Stewart nodded. "The moment our facial recognition software picked the two of you out of the crowd."

"How...efficient." The word on the tip of my tongue had been "creepy," but Stewart seemed on the side of the angels—no pun intended—and compared to my plan of banking on my face and fame getting us past the TSA, things were actually going pretty well. "So, Bradley knows I'm alive and where I am?"

"If he doesn't, he will soon."

"Can you get a message to Ethan through him, then, since you don't want me sending any emails? You know, through secure channels or something?"

Stewart gave it some thought. "I think that might be arranged." He studied me expectantly. "And what might this message be?"

Out loud? He had to be kidding. "Umm, just...let him know that I'm okay. Tell him that I know he came for me, that I know he did everything he could to get to me, and that I love him."

"Anything else?"

"Tell him to be careful, and I'll see him soon."

"Done." Stewart spent the next couple of minutes tapping away at his phone and then returned his attention to me. "Hopefully, Mr. Bradley can reach Mr. Harkreader and let him know of your safety and whereabouts so that you can soon be reunited."

"Hopefully?" A pang of concern sent my heart racing. "Is Ethan okay?"

"A lot has happened in the months since you were taken by the Cardinal." Stewart locked gazes with me, his expression impassive. "A lot."

"Tell me everything."

"No time for that at the moment." A woman in a finely tailored suit and all-business flats strode into the room, her red hair tied up in a tight bun and a pair of dark horn-rimmed glasses setting off the freckles of a rather attractive face. Her accent, unlike Stewart's, was decidedly American. "You two are eager to get to New York, correct?"

"Who is this, Mr. Stewart?" I asked.

"This is my supervisor, Ms.—"

"My name is Roxanne Sumner, Miss Snow, and this region of the United States, when it comes to Ascendant affairs, is under my jurisdiction." She turned to Stewart. "Thank you, Andrew, for taking such excellent care of our surprise guests."

She joined us at the table, and no sooner had she taken her seat than a door to the rear of the room opened and a young woman in a black top, slacks, and sneakers entered with a tray of food for my and Sunil's late dinner. The air filled with the intermingled smells of surf and turf as she rested a cheeseburger the size of my head and a plate piled high with curly fries before me and a lobster tail with a side of sautéed vegetables in front of Sunil. The woman vanished back through the doorway for a moment only to reappear seconds later with our drinks as well as an ice water for Mr. Stewart and a black coffee for Ms. Sumner.

"Thank you, Taylor." Sumner took a sip of her coffee. "Perfect as always."

"Will that be all, Ms. Sumner?" Taylor asked.

"For now," she answered. "I'll let you know if we need anything else."

With a polite bow, Taylor disappeared from the room, leaving the four of us alone. Sunil made short work of his dinner, demolishing his entire plate in minutes, while I scarfed down my cheeseburger and a good portion of the curly fries until my stomach made it clear I should stop. Sumner and Stewart waited patiently until we finished the first decent food we'd had in the better part of twenty-four hours.

"Thanks for the meal." I slurped down the last dregs of my Coke. "What now?"

"Wash up, you two." Sumner directed us to a door at the rear of the room. "The plane you've requested takes off in twenty minutes, and I'd rather you not get any grease on the upholstery."

"But you don't even know why we're going to New York, Ms. Sumner."

"And if I kept you here in Idaho, would you tell me?" She let out a quiet chuckle. "You and your friend could leave any time you wanted to, and I'm relatively certain we couldn't stop you, even if we tried." She offered me the first semblance of a smile since entering the room. "Do not misunderstand, Miss Snow. I am on your side."

～

"We're going to be in the air for about five hours," Sumner said a few minutes after takeoff. "It's just after eleven, so that puts us landing between six and seven a.m. with the time change. What say we share some intel and get everyone on both sides up to speed before we all pile down for forty winks?"

"Just the basics," Stewart added. "Tomorrow's going to be a big day, and we're all going to need our rest."

"Sure," Sunil muttered. "Let's all take turns *sharing*." He glared in Sumner's direction. "You two first."

For all his grumpy disposition, sometimes Sunil and I saw eye-to-eye.

"You were going to tell me about Ethan, Mr. Stewart." I fought to keep the worry from my features. "How is he? Where is he?"

"Last I heard, he was well. Your man has had a very busy six months." Stewart looked to Sumner, and at her solemn nod, added, "Unfortunately, I can't tell you much about his current status or whereabouts."

"And why not?" My heart clenched in my chest. "Is he—?"

"He's currently in the wind, location unknown."

"In the wind?" I stared at him, incredulous. "That's all you've got?"

"Mr. Harkreader and your entire network of friends and allies have never given up on trying to find you or even so much as a clue as to your whereabouts." Sumner fixed me with a no-nonsense stare. "Their travels have taken them to every end of North America and several continents beyond, both in search of you and your erstwhile captor, among other missions and Ascendant matters that have come up. I'm afraid to say they don't check in with my organization unless they need something, and I know little of their current whereabouts."

"But I was right there the whole time, you know, under the mountain." I didn't mention the Cardinal's faux Underworld, wherever the hell it was. If Sumner and Stewart were going to hold back information, then two could play at that game. "They didn't have to fly all over the world looking for me. I was right there."

"They stayed for days, Miss Snow." Sumner shot me a knowing look. "Scoured that mountain and the surrounding range for any clue as to where you might be. Even when all seemed lost, I understand that Mr. Harkreader insisted they continue looking."

"When all seemed lost?" I asked. "What is that supposed to mean?"

"According to the reports," Sumner answered, "the Cardinal waited for nightfall the second evening before returning to the mountain in an attempt to free his captive technomancer. Harkreader and the rest of your friends managed to repel him a second time, but during the battle, he stated that you had tried to escape and more than insinuated that you hadn't survived the attempt."

"And they believed him?" My intestines tied themselves in knots. "They took the word of that psychopath?"

"No, but the seed of doubt had been planted." Stewart shook his head. "The fact that Alba's geomancer had gone missing that morning after being sent to help in the search only bolstered everyone's hope that it was all a big lie and that you were still alive."

"But eventually, I guess, they just...gave up?"

"They never gave up. As I said, your friends search for you still, from one end of the globe to the other, but other matters have required their attention as well." Stewart crossed his arms and peered out the window at the darkness beyond the tempered glass. "The world has changed in your absence."

"You haven't, perchance, encountered Daichi Kanda in your six months away, have you, Miss Snow?" Sumner must have caught the flash in my eye at the mention of Alba's geomancer. "As Andrew said, he went missing the day after you did."

"No pulling the wool over your eyes, Ms. Sumner." I looked away. "Daichi and I were captives together, though I never knew that until the last couple of days when he helped Sunil and me escape from the Cardinal's prison."

"More on that in a moment, then." Sumner's eyes went up and to the right in calculation. "In any case, after the Cardinal's second attack, he didn't return. Harkreader and the others stayed on the mountain another three days searching for you. Neither your technomancer friend nor your pair of theriodans, however, could find any trace of you or this underground base you speak of."

"It was as if you'd fallen off the face of the earth." Stewart added.

More like I'd been sent to Hell, but I wasn't going to tell them that.

"In the end, it was Delacroix who called off the search, at least of the mountain."

"Rosemary?" A pang of mixed rage, jealousy, and betrayal pierced my chest. "She's the one who talked Ethan into leaving?"

"No. Not Rosemary, but Mr. Delacroix, your security agent, along with Mr. Bradley from our organization. It was deemed in everyone's best interest, including yours, to continue the search elsewhere." Her lips drew down to a tight circle. "If you want the truth, my understanding is that Rosemary Delacroix was the last of the group to accept the order to get off the mountain."

"Oh." My cheeks went hot, flush with guilt. "Good to know."

"With the Idaho lead apparently a dead end—pardon the expression—the search put them instead on the trail of your abductor."

"So," I whispered, "again, the Cardinal." Ethan's two brushes with my crimson-armored kidnapper left him first with a dislocated shoulder and then with a razor-sharp blade through his belly. "He didn't hurt Ethan, did he? You'd tell me, right?"

"To the best of our knowledge, both Mr. Harkreader and Miss Delacroix are just fine." Sumner scrolled on her phone. "The two of them have dogged the Cardinal's trail across the U.S., Mexico, Europe, and Asia. Our best intelligence states that it's come to blows on at least three different occasions, but thus far, both sides have walked away from each encounter to fight another day."

"Thank God."

"We can't speak to specific injuries, though it seems Mr.

Harkreader's newfound talents have proven quite useful on the battlefield, both as soldier and medic."

Damn. These people did know their stuff. I'd only seen Ethan's Flame once, on a video screen in the Cardinal's mountain fortress and in service of a wounded and dying Rosemary. A miracle if I'd ever seen one, he'd brought her back from the brink with nothing but the force of his will backed up by two millennia of borrowed power. I could only guess the selfsame white fire was what had saved him from his own near-fatal wound back at my home in Montecito.

For the thousandth time, I replayed their kiss in my mind, so filled with passion and desperation and need. A kiss that should have been mine.

He burned for her.

I dragged my mind back from its wanderings to find Sunil and Sumner deep in conversation.

"This Cardinal bastard," Sunil asked, "have any of you figured out who he is or what he wants?" He lowered his head. "Besides carnage and power, of course."

"That is a mystery that our organization has spent the better part of three years trying to solve." Sumner pulled up a map on her tablet computer and held it up for us to see. "This is a representation of each location where a reliable witness has placed him since his first appearance on the scene two and a half years ago." She motioned to a series of red flashing dots that filled the map of the world like Christmas lights. "Asia, Africa, Australia, the Americas. He's been everywhere, and left a lot of dead Ascendant in his wake."

"But none of those are anyone I know, right?" I asked.

"No." Stewart shook his head. "And the only Ascendant we are aware of that the Cardinal has eliminated since your own Ascension was the Greyhound in Denver, Colorado six months ago."

"So, he's gone underground?" Sunil asked.

"To the contrary, Mr. Jayalal." Stewart returned his attention to me. "Mr. Harkreader and the remainder of Miss Snow's crew have managed to thwart his efforts at every turn over the last several months, reportedly to the Cardinal's extreme frustration."

"Good to know." A part of me cheered inside, while another part I'd been repressing for weeks came out full force.

The Cardinal represented a next level threat, and he'd taken Ethan in combat twice in my presence alone. If Ethan was managing to keep the bastard on the defensive, he was doing so with Rosemary's help. I could only imagine the two of them together week after week and month after month, saving the world one day at a time, no doubt utilizing the shared Flame that seemed the only thing besides L.J. that could slow the Cardinal down. And with me out of the picture the entire time. I wasn't certain why that bothered me so much. I knew going in that the two of them would be spending an inordinate amount of time together as Rosemary attempted to train him over the course of weeks to months to fill a role for which she prepared her entire life.

But all of that was before I saw that kiss. No matter how many times I tried to dispel the image of the blinding white flames surrounding their hunched forms as Ethan breathed life back into a woman I considered my best friend, the burning memory at my core refused to die.

In my life, I'd been disappointed in a boyfriend or two. Upset. Pissed off. Apathetic. Pretty much the gamut of emotion. Not once had I ever been jealous. I hated it. And despite all my love and gratitude toward them both for all they'd done for me and, by all reports, were still doing for me, a part of me hated them as well.

I laughed bitterly at my own misery. Sunil, Stewart, and Sumner were discussing plans of what to do when we landed, and there I was feeling sorry for myself and casting aspersions on two people who it sounded like had done nothing for weeks but scour the world looking for even a hint of my continued existence.

In that moment, I honestly wondered if I was worth finding.

"So, that's most of what we know about the Cardinal," Stewart said. "Truth be told, the two of you have far more up-close-and-personal data than anything we can provide."

Great. I missed the whole thing.

"Now, Miss Snow," Stewart said, "without divulging anything you're not willing or able to reveal, do explain why you have us flying through the night to New York when I understand Mr. Harkreader hasn't set foot in the Northeast even once since your kidnapping."

"To be honest, I'm not a hundred percent sure." I hesitated before answering further. "I suppose we're looking for someone."

"I guessed that," Stewart said. "And who might this mysterious person be the two of you are seeking?"

"Before we get to that, first you have to understand that we didn't escape the Cardinal's prison alone."

"You mentioned that you encountered Daichi Kanda during your time in captivity," Sumner said. "Anyone else?"

Despite the unsure look on Sunil's face, I nodded.

Sumner and Stewart shared a worried glance.

"Details, Miss Snow." Sumner's eyes bored through me. "Please."

Sunil gestured in my direction and cleared his throat, basically saying that I'd opened up this can of worms and it was up to me to answer.

"Besides Alba's geomancer, there was also an empath. She goes by Jade, but her name is—"

"Jia Li Xiao is alive?" Stewart gasped. "She's been marked as deceased at the Cardinal's hand for months now. I'll have to update the Order's database."

"So," Sumner asked, "Kanda and Xiao are both in Boise?"

"Yes." Worry twisted my guts like spaghetti around a fork. "Sunil and I left them at a motel near the airport while we went afield to get help."

"But there's someone else there with them, am I correct?" She and Stewart sat on the edge of their seats, as if the next word from my mouth might be Lucifer.

"A man who calls himself Metis." I studied their faces for any sort of reaction. "Sound familiar?"

"Metis." Sumner shot Stewart a thoughtful glance. "Run it through the database, Andrew. See what comes up." She returned her attention to me. "So a geomancer, an empath, and...what abilities precisely does this final Ascendant possess?"

"His particular focus remains unclear," Sunil offered, the first thing he'd said in several minutes. "A collar around his neck apparently keeps him from accessing whatever abilities he may possess, a gift from the Cardinal's technomancer."

"A dampener." Sumner nodded. "We'd received intel that the worldwide network of technomancers had finally developed the ability to create such a device. Good to know that our information is accurate."

"Metis, you say?" Stewart asked. "No surname or other designation?"

"That's all he told me." I shrugged. "Just...Metis."

"Interesting. We have no record of any Ascendant by that name." Stewart glanced up from his screen. "Any other information you might have?"

"Only that at his core, he is filled with rage." I remembered Jade describing the two things she'd sensed from the mysterious man we'd set free from the Cardinal's prison. "And an all-consuming hunger."

CHAPTER 15

ON THE ROAD AGAIN

Sumner's private jet hit the runway just shy of five hours after taking off from Boise. A hot shower and change of clothes before we left had done both me and Sunil a world of good, and I'd rested as much as possible as we made our way east. The sun had risen during the last hour of the flight, reminding me of the two-hour time shift. Living in a cave with no sunlight for half a year, however regimented I'd tried to keep my schedule, left my usually clocklike circadian rhythm shifted from a 4/4 rock beat to something more like experimental jazz.

Not that it mattered. I'd slept as much as my body had allowed, and it was time to get to work. Everyone else had slept straight through for the most part, which was a good thing. As Stewart had pointed out, we were going to need to go into this with at least a few hours of rest. For all the ambiguity regarding what we were supposed to do now that we were in New York, the one thing I remained a hundred percent sure of was that we had a long day ahead of us.

In the past, I'd always flown into LaGuardia or JFK, but Sumner's pilot landed us across the Hudson at the Teterboro Airport. I appreciated the smaller facility and low-key experience more than I expected. Dodging large swaths of humanity at big airports over the years had become all but second nature. How nice to be able to just put on a pair of shades and walk through the mostly empty building and out the other side without worrying about causing a stir.

Nothing too ostentatious, our ride was a big black van and its driver a slender man named Copeland with bright blond hair and a vague Scottish accent. He didn't offer his first name, and I didn't inquire, but Sumner made it clear he was more than qualified to get us safely from Point A to Point B and that he knew his way around a firearm.

I took a moment to silently laugh at both myself and the situation. A year ago, I'd have had a hissy fit if my transportation didn't come complete with a fully stocked fridge and a memory foam mattress. Now, I found myself ecstatic simply because the thing had tinted windows and a driver who knew which end of a pistol the bullets came out of.

Staying anonymous used to be all about keeping my sanity. Now it was simply about staying alive.

"You're sure Lady Day is going to be happy to see you?" Sumner asked from the front passenger seat before we pulled out. "Assuming we're able to track her down, of course."

"I certainly hope so. Otherwise, we're going to be needing a ride back west."

Before everyone had bedded down on the plane, Sunil and I had jointly decided to let Sumner and Stewart in on exactly who we were looking for in New York City and the basics of our plan. Neither of them had been too big a fan of our plan to return to Metis, and even less that we'd left Daichi and Jade with him, but both understood that, in the end, we'd had little choice in the matter.

"We'll find her." Stewart sat behind the driver's seat, leaving the second passenger row to Sunil and me. "As for the rest, that's up to you, Miss Snow."

"As I said last night, Lady Day and I have never met, but the Angel of Harlem did travel all the way to Denver in an effort to help Ethan and the others get to the Greyhound before…"

Before the maniac we're hunting executed him.

"Though she owes me nothing," I continued, "I can't help but think she'll be sympathetic to our cause."

"Very well," Sumner said, checking a map on her phone. "Mr. Copeland, take us east across the Hudson."

"What's that?" Our driver fiddled with a gadget in his ear that looked decidedly more like a hearing aid than the standard secret agent wire. "This damned thing…"

"It's all right." Sumner increased her volume a few decibels. "East, if you please, Mr. Copeland, across the river."

"Yes, ma'am." With a quick glance at us in the rearview mirror, Copeland pulled the big black spy van onto the road and into traffic. "On our way."

Sumner looked back across her shoulder at me. "We should be in the right vicinity to begin a proper search in about twenty minutes." She raised a curious brow. "Any thoughts on exactly how to locate the Angel on her home turf, or if necessary, bring her out into the open?"

"Honestly, I didn't have the first idea back in Idaho how I was going to secure passage to New York, and look at us now." I shook my head and let out a sarcastic chuckle. "Lady Day found Ethan and the others in Denver when they needed her. I suppose I'm counting on her to find me more than me finding her."

"That's a pretty big leap of faith." Stewart glanced back at me as Copeland made a sharp right onto I-80 heading east.

"In the last twenty-four hours, I've busted out of a secret underground prison bunker with the help of four superhuman beings with godlike powers, only one of whom I'd ever met before, hopped a bus filled to the gills with a bunch of smelly old men with hunting rifles, and then flew across the country in a private jet with two strangers straight out of a James Bond movie. Leaps of faith are apparently my jam these days. Who knew?"

Sunil shot me some side-eye. "Truth be told, we didn't know you either."

"You can literally throw lightning bolts from your fingertips, Sunil. Daichi can hurl boulders with his mind. And God only knows what Metis can do when he's not stuck in that stupid collar. Excuse me if I still felt a bit on the vulnerable side when all I brought to the table is a bit of fame and a voice that is hard to ignore."

"I don't know," Sunil muttered. "The Cardinal had you held back in reserve for whatever he has planned, same as the rest of us."

"Man's got a point." Stewart turned in his seat to face us. "Other than during your show in Los Angeles, have you ever really stretched your ability? Seen what it can do?"

"Have I ever deliberately reached out with my voice and tried to make another person do what I want against their will? No." I crossed my arms, looked out the window at the passing cars, and pulled in a deep breath. "At least I hope not."

I'd never said it out loud in quite that way, but the truth was, my ability frightened me more than I let anyone know. Shadows, lightning, the elements: all of these could be used to get what you wanted, but to be able to simply change someone else's mind with nothing but the power of your own voice? No one should have such power over another. And certainly not a nineteen-year-old girl whose main goal when all this started was to be the top selling concert tour of the year so she could shove it in her ex's face.

"It scares you," Sumner asked quietly, as if reading my mind, "doesn't it?"

"Let's just say if I could go back to enchanting my audience the way every other performer does it, I'd do it in an instant."

"You may not believe this," Sunil said, his tone strangely soothing, "but I understand exactly where you're coming from."

As I looked his way, I found his dark eyes staring at me in the dim light of the van. A compassion filled his gaze I hadn't encountered there before.

"Imagine learning at the age of eight that you can control electricity, the current in every home, the power that runs this vehicle, the very lightning itself. You think having the ability to change the course of another person's thoughts is dangerous? Try going through adolescence having to hold back your every emotion, lest your anger, your fear, or even your lust kill the person in front of you."

"Wow." I swallowed back the emotion that threatened to choke my words. "I guess I never thought about it that way. I just figured you were…"

"Unfriendly? Angry? Aloof?" Sunil took his turn looking out the window as we passed a sign signifying we were about to leave I-80 for I-95. "Welcome to the world of always keeping everyone at arm's length because to let someone in is to risk their life."

"I'm so sorry." Talk about discovering a side of someone you'd never expected to see. "At least you're able to keep it under control."

"I hate to admit it, Snow, but that hasn't always been the case."

Sunil, vulnerable one moment and completely closed off the next, turned his entire body to face the window and didn't speak again.

"We'll be crossing the Hudson in the next few minutes," Sumner said, wisely changing the subject. "Barring traffic, we'll arrive at the agreed upon starting point for your search in another ten minutes or so. Make sure you keep the earpieces we gave each of you in place so we can keep tabs on your location and situation in case an extraction is required."

Yep. My life had become a spy movie. Fortunately, I had a few seasons of *Teen Spies* under my belt, so at least I knew the lingo.

"We'll monitor your conversation, particularly if and when contact is made, and help you navigate any potential conflict as best we can."

"Roger that." I copped Ethan's preferred phrase for conveying understanding. Even those two little words made him seem a bit closer.

"A word of advice?" Stewart locked gazes with me as Copeland slowed for the line of toll stations ahead. "Do whatever it takes to keep your head down while you're out and about today. You may be looking for Lady Day, but that doesn't mean there aren't people looking for you as well."

Sunil let out a lone chuckle. "Not to mention anyone who

recognizes you might have a meltdown seeing the biggest pop star in the world walking down the street."

"Especially since the world at large believes you dead." Sumner glanced back at me. "We're coming up on the tollbooth, Miss Snow. Time to go incognito."

I nodded, donning the sunglasses Sumner had scored for me and lowering my head as we stopped at the toll station. The tollbooth worker took one look at whatever identification Copeland flashed and waved us on through—VIP treatment if I'd ever seen it, and boy had I seen it.

Rock soon rose on either side of the several lanes of traffic before we passed beneath the first tower and onto the George Washington Bridge. Traffic was tight and slow at rush hour, and it was stop and go for several minutes until we reached the other side. Motorcyclists cruised up the median and weaved between all the cars, the roar of their motors sending my heart racing. Still, the rising sun's light cascading across the Hudson struck me as one of the more beautiful sights I'd ever beheld. Out the right passenger window and across the water, New York City extended south as far as the eye could see. Just visible in the morning haze, One World Trade Center pointed skyward, a reminder that even the darkest moments in history were just that: moments in time.

"This too shall pass," Ethan had said to me more times than I could remember.

God, I hoped he was right

"So, it's first thing in the morning New York time." I craned my head forward to catch Sumner's gaze. "This particular Angel of the Ascendant may call herself Lady Day, but the vibe I get is that she's more night owl than early bird. What say we all grab a little breakfast before we get started?"

Sumner's driver, Mr. Copeland, lucked into street parking not far from a greasy spoon in the heart of Harlem. He stayed with the vehicle while Sumner, Stewart, Sunil, and I went inside for a bite, though he did grumble something about bringing him back something just before Stewart slid shut the door to the van. The scarf around my hair and the admittedly stylish shades Sumner had given me in Boise had somehow kept the telltale flash of recognition from the eyes of both the young woman who showed us to our table as well as our middle-aged waitress who reminded me a little of my mother.

Mom. I wonder if she ever got my message.

Or if Ethan got the message that Stewart said he'd send on my behalf.

Or if we were going to find Lady Day in a city of millions.

And if so, would she deign to help us? Transport Sunil and me back to the other end of the continent to the others? Help us locate and possibly even fight the Cardinal so that we could neutralize his threat once and for all?

An awful lot of ifs had to go my way if I was ever going to dream of getting my life back—a life that stopped being fully my own the moment I first heard the word Ascendant.

I missed Ethan. I missed my mom. I missed a lot of people, places, and things. But the thing I missed the most was feeling like I had one iota of control over my life. As "Persephone Snow, Pop Star Extraordinaire," I'd been the one calling a lot of the shots, but when it came to "Persephone Snow, Ascendant Siren," I felt very much at sea, just waiting for the next big wave to scoop me up and pound me into oblivion.

I took a deep cleansing breath like Rosemary taught me. No need to get myself all worked up. Like Ethan always told me, one problem at a time.

"So," I ventured after everyone had finished their breakfast, "any ideas on how to begin? Manhattan is a big place."

Sunil stared across the table at Stewart. "You said the few sightings of her in the city have been in this vicinity, correct?"

"As we've discussed, Lady Day is notoriously private, but it's next to impossible to exist in this city, of all places, and not get spotted either on camera or on the street from time to time. The nexus of her many appearances in Manhattan converges a block or two from this diner."

"And?" Sunil rolled his eyes with a huff through his nose. "You can't seriously be considering just pounding pavement and knocking on doors, can you?"

"Actually, there is one door in particular that might reveal some answers." Sumner pulled a folder from her bag and rested it at the center of the table. Inside rested a photograph of a dark-skinned woman dressed to the nines, her face obscured by shadow. Behind the woman hung a large black sign with white letters that read "Cotton Club" in a trendy font. "More than once, Lady Day has been observed as a patron of this establishment."

"I suppose we can add jazz aficionado to our list of intel," Stewart said. "Unfortunately, the Cotton Club doesn't open for eleven hours."

"Eleven free hours in the Greatest City in the World." I smiled. "Whatever shall we do?"

"You will keep your head down and your face out of the news." Sumner's lips formed a horizontal line on her face. "As I said in the van, incognito is the rule of the day. Do you understand?"

As if on cue, a sizable man with skin the color of mahogany dressed in white with a cook's apron and hat approached from the kitchen. Stewart, Sumner, and even Sunil, who was finishing off the biggest waffle I'd ever seen, bristled at the intrusion, but I knew all too well the telltale flush of recognition radiating from this man who had undoubtedly prepared the food we'd just eaten.

"Miss Persephone Snow?" he asked quietly.

"Yessir, Mr.—I checked his name tag—"Sal."

"I knew it. Never believed the news about you, well, moving on and all that."

"Good instincts, Sal." I shifted my gaze around the room. Fortunately, my new favorite cook hadn't made too much of a scene, at least not yet. "We all need a break sometimes, right?"

He answered with a subtle nod, and then the question I'd been asked at least ten thousand times over the years. "Mind if I take a picture? You know, for the Wall of Fame?" He gestured to a line of pictures across the diner's back wall, a respectable collection of celebrities big and small from the last four decades, a few of whom I'd met in my travels. "Breakfast is, of course, on the house."

"Of course, Sal." I shot him my best smile. "As long as you don't mind if we get a little breakfast for our driver?"

"Consider it done." Sal motioned for a nearby waitress to come over and handed her his phone. "Make it a good one, Yvonne," he said, his voice a friendly grumble.

The waitress, who quickly realized who the boss was getting all flustered over, snapped what sounded like a dozen shots and returned his phone before disappearing around the corner, the rosiness in her cheeks brightening with every backward glance in our direction.

"Sorry," I whispered, "but that's likely going to keep happening."

Stewart quietly peered around the diner at the various people who were now looking our way, Sunil finished the last bite of his waffle and crossed his arms with a quiet harrumph, and Sumner merely shook her head.

"So much for operational security," she grumbled. "Let's just get Copeland his food and get out of here before the local news trucks start arriving."

While we waited, I considered asking Sal to borrow his phone, and then remembered that every number I needed was saved in a phone on the opposite coast and that unless I wanted to call Mom again and freak her out even more, I should simply stick to the plan.

Minutes later, we'd all piled back into the big black van. Copeland enjoyed his breakfast while the rest of us discussed what to do with the rest of the day until the Cotton Club opened that evening.

"The Order does have a safe house or two in the area," Stewart said. "We could retire to one of those for a few hours until it's time to get to work."

"I suppose." I peered out the window at the throng of pedestrians making their way down the sidewalk. "Or—and hear me out here—I could talk to the manager of pretty much any hotel in the city and score us a suite for the afternoon with all the frills." I raised my eyebrows in question. "If we're going to be sitting around waiting for the sun to go down, shouldn't we wait in style?"

"I vote for Snow's plan," Sunil said. "I've been imprisoned for over a year eating whatever food was dumped in my cell each day. Champagne and caviar for the day sounds like just what the doctor ordered."

"What part of staying under the radar do you not understand?" Sumner launched into yet another lecture about operational security and risk amelioration. I'd known the woman for less than twenty-four hours, and already I could almost give the talk as well as she could. Though her advice was totally warranted and on point given our situation, a part of me wondered if the woman had ever had a moment of fun in her entire life.

As Sumner droned on, Stewart tapped his pen, Copeland chomped away at his breakfast, and Sunil ground his teeth, another sound from outside the van caught my attention. The sound, a particularly wheezy laugh that grew louder with each passing second, sent my blood running cold. Just another part of the cacophony of humanity beyond the van window, the sound in and of itself wasn't particularly ominous, but regardless, my body's fight-or-flight response kicked in immediately.

I'd first learned of theriodans, the flavor of Ascendant who channel the energies and souls of various animals, seven months ago in Vegas. I'd since met Rosemary's ex, Maddox, a theriodan of coyote persuasion, but mine and Ethan's drama-filled visit to Caesars Palace was where I first met Neko, my tiger companion and housemate for the month before I was taken by the Cardinal. He'd been working for a wolf theriodan named Linus, the leader of the main pack of theriodans in Sin City, but Linus had another in his employ that day: a hyena theriodan named Harold with his dark, pock-marked skin, tightly braided cornrows covering his scalp, and a golden grill that would be the envy of any hip-hop star in the country.

But the main thing I remembered? His laugh. That wheezy asthmatic laugh, like something out of the scarier scenes of *The Lion King.*

I shrank away from the window and covered my face with my kerchief just as the theriodan stopped mere feet from the van. He pulled a long breath in through his cave-like nostrils, glanced left and right, and proceeded down the sidewalk without looking back.

"Hey, Stewart." I gestured at Harold's retreating form, already threatening to disappear into the crowd. "You're not going to believe this, but I think our first lead on tracking down Lady Day is right in front of us and about to get away."

CHAPTER 16

ANIMAL

"Not too close." I tried to keep my voice calm. "I think he may have caught my scent before."

"He can do that?" Stewart asked.

"The fact that a theriodan can track shocks you?" Sunil snorted. "And here I thought you people had at least the basic lowdown on Ascendant."

"He's a hyena in human form." I fired a stern glance Sunil's way. "He moves with the speed and reflexes of an animal on the African plain, and when they do that thing with their eyes, my tiger friend says they can pretty much see in the dark. Not too big a stretch to imagine a man who channels one of the world's best-known scavengers can follow a scent."

"Got it." Stewart kept his attention focused on Harold, who was currently half a block ahead and weaving his way through the oncoming crowd. Copeland, who had begrudgingly put his breakfast aside to drive, made his way slowly through the New York morning traffic while Sumner remained astonishingly quiet. "Thank you, both, for enlightening me."

Huh. Must have struck a nerve. Stewart apparently wasn't used to getting upstaged on Ascendant matters, and definitely not by a baby Ascendant pop princess who barely understood her own abilities. Persephone Snow, apparent subject matter expert on theriodans, in the house.

God, my life is weird.

"Up ahead," Sumner pointed out, breaking her silence, "he's turning down that side street."

"On it, Ms. Sumner." Copeland accelerated, bringing us around the corner just seconds after Harold disappeared from view. "Crap, he's gone."

"No, he's not." Sunil pointed through the windshield. "I see him. There."

Phone to his ear, Harold was already halfway down the busy sidewalk. He didn't run, but unmistakable urgency flowed from his every step.

"He's going in there." Sumner pointed to a street-level gym with the obligatory wall of plate glass revealing a dozen or so treadmills and stationary bikes filled with people burning off the day's calories. "Slow down."

The hyena was visiting a gym wearing a knit top, blue jeans, boots, and no gym bag. He could have business there, I supposed, but my every instinct screamed that we'd been made.

Big black vans with tinted windows giveth and, I suppose, taketh away as well.

"Drop us off here." Sunil said.

I nodded. "Sunil and I will follow him and see what he's up to."

"Are you crazy?" Stewart asked as Copeland pulled the van into a no-parking zone and flipped on his hazards. "Sunil I understand. Not much a hyena can do against a lightning bolt. But you? You told us that you've barely tested your abilities. What are you going to do when the hyena goes for your throat? Sing him a lullaby?"

"Worked before," I muttered.

"What was that?" Sumner asked.

"Never mind." I grunted in frustration. "Look. The way I see it, we've come all this way, and we barely finished breakfast before we stumbled upon another Ascendant. That has to mean something."

"It could mean a lot of things." Sumner stared at the door to the gym where Harold had disappeared. "Most of them, not good."

"You know why he's here, right?" Sunil grumbled.

"No." I glanced the elektromancer's way, keeping my focus on the gym entrance as well. "Do you?"

"Of course I do." Sunil laughed. "He's here for the same reason we are."

Understanding clicked in my brain. "He's looking for Lady Day."

"Why else?" Sunil raised a curious eyebrow. "Only question is whether or not he's here alone."

"I know the answer to that one." Stewart puffed up his chest, his moment to shine. "I may not have the same level of real-world experience as you, Miss Snow, but if there's one thing I do know about theriodans, it's that they travel in packs."

Made sense. As I understood it, Linus had been the leader of the pack I'd met in Vegas, and he, Harold, and Neko had chosen the casinos of Sin City as their stomping grounds. On the other hand, Rosemary's coyote ex, Maddox, traveled alone.

I suppose every rule had its exception.

If Harold was here, did that mean Linus was as well? Had they replaced Neko among their ranks? How many predators disguised in human flesh were we talking about?

A gentle tap at the window threatened to send my heart leaping out of my chest. Beyond the tinted glass, Harold stared at me with that golden-grilled hyena grin, the dark brown eyes of the animal that lurked at his core drilling into me like twin laser beams.

"Good morning, Persephone Snow. Glad to know the reports of your grisly fate were as exaggerated as I suspected." His words just as wheezy as his laugh, Harold motioned for me to open the van's sliding door. "Before you and your friends come at me with guns blazing, please understand that I'm just here to talk."

Stewart and I shared a worried glance, but with a subtle wave, I communicated to him and Sumner that I was taking point on this particular encounter. I moved up to join Stewart in the first row of passenger seats, grabbed the sliding door's handle, and opened it just wide enough so the theriodan and I could chat.

"Why, hello there, Harold." Faux pleasant was the order of the day as I spoke with the hyena through a crack in the door. "Funny running into you clear on the other end of the country." I shot him a sarcastic smile. "Why, the last time I saw you, I believe—"

"You'd just done your best to send my family jewels to the moon with that not-so-tiny foot of yours." A quiet growl exited his still smiling lips. "And that was nothing compared to Delacroix sending a fucking motorcycle hurtling into me at top speed." He chuckled bitterly. "Hell, that almost sent me to the hospital, and I don't do hospitals."

"To be fair," I answered, doing my best to keep my cool as a hungry hyena's eyes studied me from the human face mere feet away, "as I recall, your little crew was in the middle of a full-on aggravated assault and attempted kidnapping at the time."

"Thus the reason we're still talking." Harold raised a questioning eyebrow. "Are you here looking for me and mine?"

"Truthfully? We had no idea you were here." I considered the last three words of his question carefully. "And by 'me and mine,' I'm guessing that Wolfman Linus is here as well?"

"All I'm saying, Snow, is that I'm not alone here at the Center of the World." He peered into our vehicle at Sunil, Stewart, Copeland, and Sumner. "And, to be honest, we weren't exactly expecting to run into you either." He let out one wheezy laugh. "So, if you're not dead, where have you been all these months? Getting in some 'me' time?"

"That's one way of looking at being imprisoned for half a year, I suppose."

"Well," Harold growled, "if you're not here for us, and we're not here for you, then perhaps we can all work together on what may be a shared goal."

"You can't be serious." Sunil had stayed quiet longer than I'd dreamed possible. "If you think we're going to palaver with a bunch of animals—"

"Watch your tongue, lightning boy," Harold said, "or I might just rip it out."

Sunil's sharp intake of air let me know that Harold's taunt had struck a nerve.

"Yes, Sunil Jayalal, I know who you are. Even if the air wafting off this van wasn't basically a bath of ozone, you have a face I'll never forget." Harold studied Sunil through the crack in the van door. "How interesting. You don't remember me."

"I don't know what you're talking about," Sunil grumbled, "and you know nothing about me."

"Oh, really?" Harold's wheezy laugh made a reappearance. "Perpetually ill-tempered elektromancer, hothead in stressful situations, and, last I heard, off the board same as Snow." Harold's hyena eyes danced between Sunil and me. "Funny. Anyone using basic deductive skills would come to the conclusion that you two had been holed up together, though if I know Snow as well as I think I do, it wasn't by choice." His leering gaze returned to me. "She prefers her guys long and lanky, as I recall."

I bit back the bile working to spew from my mouth, and instead, did my part to move the conversation forward. "All right, Harold. You sniffed me out and had every one of us onboard this van pretty much dead to rights, and yet managed to behave yourself. Therefore, you get a listen. Please, tell me, what exactly is it you're proposing?"

"Simply that you park your van and then join me and my associates to discuss the likely common reason that we all find ourselves wandering about the middle of Harlem so early this lovely morning."

I shot Sumner a questioning glance before returning my attention to Harold. "Wait here. We'll find a spot for the van and then converge here in five."

"I won't move a muscle." He smiled, his golden grill sparkling in the morning sun. "Cross my heart."

"And hope to die?" Sunil muttered under his breath.

"Your words, Jayalal," Harold answered, "not mine."

❧

We deposited the van in a nearby parking garage, and the five of us—Copeland insisted on coming along for extra muscle or firepower, whichever might be required, and received no argument—soon rejoined Harold the Hyena outside the gym he'd used to ditch us minutes before.

"All right, Harold," Sumner said before I could get out a word, "My name is Roxanne Sumner, and I'm in charge here. Where do you propose we take this meeting you're so keen on having?"

"First things first," Harold answered. "As far as our side is concerned, Snow is the one we're talking to." His eyes flashed in Sunil's direction as he pulled in a quick sniff of air. "Or maybe broody boy over there."

"You will speak with me, theriodan," Sumner said with a no-nonsense stare I suspected was her default. "Is that understood?"

"Listen, woman," Harold answered, any joviality vanishing from his features in an instant as he started down the sidewalk, "you and your little entourage may stay and even participate in the coming discussion, but this is an Ascendant matter." He shot a withering glance Sumner's way as she hurried to catch up. "And you, regardless of your position or education or skill, are nothing but another of the human herd."

"That may be true," Sumner answered, meeting Harold's dismissive gaze with one of her own, "but a herd of buffalo can bring down a pride of lions if that's what it takes to defend their own."

"Agreed." Harold stopped dead atop a rusty manhole cover and spun around to glare Sumner's way. "No one disputes the fact that you represent the overwhelming majority. History is filled with instances of your kind murdering mine for no more crime than being born different, not that humankind limits its wanton destruction to merely the few Ascendant that walk among you."

"Last I checked," Sumner said, "*your* kind are being hunted by one of your own."

"As I said, this is an Ascendant matter." Harold snarled a golden-toothed grimace. "You think you're debating me, woman, and yet all you do with your every word is prove my point." He took off down the sidewalk again. "You seem to have earned Snow's trust, which is fortunate for you, and if I'm being honest, the only reason we're still talking. That being said, once the conversation gets started, you may want to follow the advice I was given when I first Ascended."

"And what might that be?" Sumner asked.

"Four simple words," Harold grumbled. "Listen more, talk less."

Pretty wise words from the laughing hyena, if I did say so myself.

"Enough, Harold," I interrupted before Sumner could dig her hole any deeper. "Tell us where you're taking us."

"Don't get your panties in a wad, Snow. We're almost there."

Harold led us to a building surprisingly close to where we first encountered him, a tenement that appeared run-down and abandoned. The windows along the first floor were boarded up, as was the lone door below the three stories of fire escape above. The brownstone facade was in good shape overall but did show the wear of decades of New York winters.

"Wow," I fired a quick jibe, "a bit of a step down from Caesars Palace, huh?"

"Not everything is as it appears at first glance." Without missing a step, Harold stepped to the door and pressed a series of buttons on a keypad I hadn't noticed. "You of all people should understand that." In an instant, a quiet buzz sounded from within and the 'boarded-up' door opened with a quiet click. Harold pulled the door wide and then looked back at the five of us with a subtle smile. "Now, if you will all follow me."

We stepped through the door one by one into a well-lit hallway. Sunil, showing a surprising moment of gallantry, insisted on going first with Stewart close behind. I went in third, followed by Sumner and Copeland, the latter's hand resting at the holstered pistol at his right hip. I was pretty sure Sumner and Stewart were packing as well, which meant I was the only one among us without some form of serious firepower in case things went south.

What else was new?

Though far cleaner and better kept than I anticipated, the interior of the theriodan base of operations wasn't all that far off from its battered exterior. Ethan and I never had opportunity to talk about how everything went down when he and the others traveled to L.A. to parlay with the Angels, namely because the Cardinal had spirited me away minutes after our reunion, but somehow I suspected the two women of mystery I'd met the night of my Ascension lived a bit better than squatting in an abandoned tenement.

Harold led us to a central staircase and up two dimly lit flights until we reached the top floor where a seriously sturdy door with multiple locks awaited. Much like Mr. Delacroix's secret knock we used on tour, Harold rapped at the reinforced steel door with a quick series of rhythmic beats. Seconds later, the various latches and locks clicked and clacked top to bottom and then, almost anticlimactic in its silence, the well-oiled door cracked open and a suspicious eye peered out—an eye with no white, an iris so brown it appeared almost black, and an elliptical pupil at its center.

"What's up, Frankie?" Harold said, unfazed. "Linus around?"

Shit. I was hoping Linus wasn't here. Unless he heals better than most, his face likely still bears a few scars from our last encounter.

What can I say? A good manicure is worth every penny.

Still, it would probably behoove me to mind my Ps and Qs.

"Maybe," the man Harold had called Frankie answered after a prolonged pause. The odd-appearing eye flicked first in my direction, then at Sunil and the others. "He know you're bringing guests?"

"He'll want to see this guest." Harold inclined his head my way. "In any case, everyone has agreed to behave while they're here on our turf." He peered back at the five of us. "Isn't that right, Snow?"

"Like if we were at church on Sunday." I raised a questioning brow at Frankie. "You know who I am, I take it?"

"Doesn't everyone?" He let fly a staccato giggle that struck me as distinctly inhuman. "Persephone Snow. Wow. The boss is going to be so..."

His voice trailed off as he shut the door to undo the last couple of security chains, leaving me unclear as to the end of his thought, though it was clear that Linus had not forgotten our previous encounter. Call me crazy, but I'd never wanted to be on a first name basis with a wolf in human form, and yet, there I was about to step inside one's east coast home away from home to sit down with him and his best buds for tea.

That is, if he didn't rip out my trachea the moment I set foot across the threshold.

Frankie took over Harold's role as tour guide and led us through the surprisingly swanky common area to a room at the back of the space. Another similar knock at another door, this one wooden but still quite sturdy, led to a series of footsteps from the room beyond. Just audible through the crack at the bottom of the door, a quiet sniff made clear that the wolf was in his den.

"My, my, my. What a surprise." Linus's gruff tone all but shook the door's solid oak. "Please, Franklin, show Miss Snow and her friends inside." Another sniff. "And tell their elektromancer that there's no need for all the ozone. As long as everyone behaves themselves, I guarantee safe conduct for all involved while here among our menagerie."

"You heard the man," Frankie said. "Shall we?"

I froze in place, the thought of facing the big bad wolf beyond the door terrifying in a way I didn't fully understand.

"We've got you, Miss Snow," Sumner said. "Stay strong."

Stewart agreed, his head shifting subtly forward in a quick nod.

Sunil leaned in and whispered in my ear. "Don't worry, Snow. I'm cool, right up to the point you need me not to be. Anything goes down, I'll light up the first creep that lays a paw on you."

"Good to know," I answered as Frankie grasped the doorknob and led us inside.

I wasn't sure exactly what I expected the inner sanctum of a human wolf's lair to look like, but Linus's personal space did not disappoint. Before me lay the den of a predator at the top of the food chain, and yet I admired his refined tastes, particularly for a space that was likely temporary lodgings. The ubiquitous six-million-inch television hung from one wall, but from its speakers poured smooth jazz as the screen portrayed one desert landscape after another. Several plants, each more exotic than the one before, appeared watered and cared for. The floor was covered with a handwoven rug while icons and art from all over the world decorated the walls. At one end of the room, a wet bar held a collection of alcohol to rival even the best clubs I'd visited, while the opposite corner held a massive bookshelf containing everything from *The Tipping Point* and *Outliers* to the latest Pulitzer Prize winning doorstopper.

I hate to admit it, but I barely made it past the first chapter of that one.

A true study in contradictions, the wolf before me turned and met my gaze, his eyes already the amber and black of the animal at his core.

"Ah, the lady of the hour." Linus smiled a lopsided lupine grin. "And what an early hour that turned out to be." He ran his powerful fingers across his right eyebrow and down his cheek, tracing four parallel lines that decorated his flesh. "I have to know, Snow, what do you think?" His feral grin shifted into a savage snarl. "After all, these marks are your handiwork."

CHAPTER 17

HUNGRY LIKE THE WOLF

I fumbled over what to say. Did I keep up the brave front? Apologize for disfiguring the man? Did I dare speak at all, for fear that my voice might tremble and doom us all?

"I can't believe a wolf, of all people, is giving me shit for leaving a few claw marks behind after a fight." I rested a hand at my hip, cocked my head to one side, and channeled every ounce of smug Ascendant Siren Pop Princess attitude I could into my voice despite the fact that my knees threatened to knock with each passing second. "Mess with the bull, you get the horns."

Great. Channeling the Barry-Manilow-couture-wearing principal from *The Breakfast Club* is really going to intimidate the alpha predator before me.

Linus pulled in a deep breath, irritation etched in his features. His body arched forward as if he were about to launch at me, his lips pulled back from his gleaming teeth, and then...

He laughed.

"My, Persephone Snow, how far you've come." Linus moved from the foot of an immaculately made bed to a sitting area with a long sofa of black leather and a smattering of matching chairs. "And to think, I'd actually begun to believe all those rumors about your unfortunate demise."

"Uh…" I bit my lip, unsure of what to say. "Thanks?"

"Come, all of you," Linus said. "Join me. Let's chat." He sat in the most impressive of the circle of seats, a big comfortable recliner of black cowhide, and gestured for us to sit. "Please."

I crept forward, holding my breath as I waited for the other shoe to drop. Taking the chair to Linus's left, I tensed as Frankie took the opposite chair, his weird eyes never leaving mine. Harold pulled up to stand behind Linus's recliner, Copeland took a position by the door, and Sunil, Stewart, and Sumner occupied the sofa. My every instinct expected the show of hospitality to simply be a cruel ruse, but we were committed, and all there was left to do was let it play out.

"You know…" Linus turned my way so I could again appreciate the four pink lines that divided his thick eyebrow before leaping down onto his cheekbone. "I was going to have a plastic surgeon work on these scars you left with your little love tap, but to be honest, they look kind of badass." He raised his shoulders in an unconcerned shrug. "I've decided to leave them just the way they are."

"Happy to be of service, I suppose." I shot him a nervous smile. "No hard feelings, then?"

"You can relax, Snow." Linus shook his head. "The worldwide contract to bring you in at any cost, now understood to be the handiwork of this Cardinal everyone is freaking out about, has been rescinded, if you're not already aware."

"I wasn't, actually. Good to know."

He shook his head, a quiet laugh escaping his fanged smile. "Dead or alive, last anybody knew, you were already a captive of the guy footing the bill. Surprise, surprise, with no money on the table, everybody lost interest."

"He could always put out another such contract, though, couldn't he?"

"If he knows you're loose, then I suppose he could, but no need to worry about me and mine. We're not doing squat for that lunatic."

"Really?" I studied the wolf's features and found only raw honesty there.

"Truth? If I'd known who it was that put out the contract seven months back, you'd never have even known we were in Las Vegas." Linus shook his head in disgust. "The Cardinal is a killer of his own kind. I have no use for him or his money."

"So, that's that? You and your flunkies attempt to publicly kidnap me, threaten my boyfriend's life, and generally make it known that you'll hunt me to the ends of the earth, and now I'm supposed to act like we're all good simply because you've had a change of heart?"

"Not a change of heart as much as a better understanding." Linus held his hands before his chest in humble apology. "Please know that attempting to service the contract on you was nothing personal."

I crossed my arms. "Sure felt personal."

"After you slashed my face and attempted to kick Harold's poor testicles to the moon, neither of us was feeling particularly congenial at the end of our last encounter." Linus flashed a lupine grin that was somehow friendly and terrifying all at once. "I'm certain you understand."

Huh. The wolf in human clothing was proving to be quite the diplomat. Who knew?

"So, all is forgiven, then?" I asked.

"A note on survival as an Ascendant?" Linus's lips pulled down to a horizontal line. "Forgiveness goes a long way in this business." His eyes narrowed. "That particular advice notwithstanding, never ever forget a thing. Understood?"

I nodded. "Chiseling it in stone."

Stewart cleared his throat, bringing Linus's attention to the others in our circle.

"Ah, yes. The entourage." Linus looked over them all with a snide smile, his roving gaze halting on Sunil. "Funny, the last elektromancer I met did his best to strike down the Big Bad Wolf. Didn't go so well, as you can probably guess."

"I was always taught that people who refer to themselves in the third person suffer from self-image issues." Sunil raised a brow. "Perhaps you should look into finding a qualified therapist."

I stifled a laugh. Sunil was a grump, but when his sardonic wit was aimed in a different direction, he was actually kind of funny.

"Hmm." Linus shifted his attention to Sumner and Stewart, ignoring Copeland by the door. "And the taxi service, I'm guessing?" His lupine eyes danced between the two in their dark suits and shined shoes. "Let's see. You two are most likely part of one of the secret organizations that watch my kind; am I correct?" His lopsided grin showed off his sharp canines. "Mulder and Scully would be so proud of you in this moment."

"Impressive." Sumner, unfazed, answered his wicked smile with one of her own. "You have already proven both perceptive and intelligent. I apologize for previously underestimating you based solely on your appearance."

Damn. Chick's got balls. I may only have my song to protect me, not that I know exactly how to work my own mojo, but it's a hell of a lot more than what she's got going on, sidearms be damned.

"You know what?" Linus laughed and gave Sumner an appraising nod. "I like you. You've got spunk. Despite the depth of the shit you currently find yourself in, you come out swinging."

"I know precisely who and what you are, theriodan, and—"

"And despite the clear personal danger to yourself," Linus interrupted, "you've got cojones enough to stand up to a predator in their own den. No need to say another word." The wolf returned his attention to me. "So, I know why my group is here. I assume you and yours have come to New York for a similar reason?"

"You first." I crossed my arms and raised my eyebrows expectantly. "Spill."

"Very well." He let out a half-growl, half sigh. "I suspect we're all looking for Lady Day."

"The Angel that Ethan met in Denver?" I asked, fighting to keep any emotion from my face. "She's here?"

"Don't try to bullshit a bullshitter, Snow. I was talking out both sides of my mouth when your momma was still in diapers." Linus ran his tongue across his razor canines. "You know why you're here, and so do I." Those lupine eyes narrowed at me, as if peering into my soul. "The only question I have is why you, fresh from your escape from the Cardinal, wish to speak with the Angel of Harlem." His head bobbed in a subtle nod. "Unless I inadvertently just answered my own question."

As wily as the animal at his core, Linus saw right through me and the others. Hell, even Harold had alluded to the fact that there was only one reason why I'd come up for air in the heart of Harlem so soon after freeing myself. Now it appeared that the only question was how much to reveal and how much to try to hold back. To be fair to the theriodans in the room, I knew little more about the trio of dark-suit-wearing Ascendant-watching spy types I'd brought with me than I did about them. I could guess Sumner's wishes regarding the topic of disclosure, but if we were going to all work together, we needed to get everything within reason out on the table.

"I need her help." I glanced back at Sunil and the others. "*We* need her help."

"Let me guess." Linus leaned in, almost conspiratorially, and Harold and Frankie followed suit. "Are you so foolish that you would seek out this Cardinal maniac, the scourge of our kind, after all the effort and compromises you've had to make thus far to escape him?"

Wow. Like Sumner said, Linus was a lot smarter than he looked. But if that was the first thing that occurred to him...

"You're looking for him too." The grin of minor victory flashed across my features. "What's the problem, Wolfman? Didn't get paid for your latest run of dastardly deeds?"

"Dastardly?" Harold chimed in. "While not every job we take is completely above board, I'll have you know that theriodans as a whole and our pack in particular adhere to a strict moral code."

"One that involves kidnapping helpless women?"

"Everybody's got to eat." It was the first thing Frankie had said since he allowed us inside. "Not everyone gets limo rides everywhere they go just because they happened to be born with perfect features. Do you worry about the ethics of shaking your money maker for thousands of people every night when you're out on tour? Trading on your looks and titillating generations of men and boys from coast to coast with those skimpy outfits and suggestive lyrics?"

"Wow, Linus." My face went stone cold. "Your boy here went from zero to slut-shaming in three seconds flat. That's got to be some kind of new record." I turned my laser-beam gaze on Frankie. "Listen here, weasel boy—"

"Ferret."

"Whatever." I leaned forward into Linus's space so I could stare directly into Frankie's beady little eyes. "First and foremost, I'm a performer. My job is to entertain, to build people up, give them something to aspire to."

"Or lust after."

"Calling yourself out there, ferret-boy?" My cheeks went white hot. "At least I don't lurk in the shadows like some sewer rat working for the scum of the earth."

"Snow," Linus interrupted.

"Just because it's somebody else's dirty work doesn't make it any less dirty."

"Snow, please."

"And third, last I checked, you all were attempting to kidnap me while working for an Ascendant who's basically hunting down his own kind, you and me both included. Don't talk to me about ethics when you and your little pack make a living selling out your own people."

"*Miss Snow!*" Linus growled as he stood from his chair, his air of previous calm decidedly less so as he stepped over to a nearby window and peered down at the street below. "You've made your point. No need to belabor it further."

"But, Boss," Frankie whined. "She—"

Linus silenced the ferret with a simple glare. "Please, understand. Months back, we understood that there was a significant reward in acquiring you alive and in reasonable condition for various interested parties, but as I alluded to before, the Cardinal's involvement, not to mention his very existence, remained only a rumor at the time. Also, there were plenty of people other than just him who wished to bring you into the Ascendant fold, some of whom you have subsequently befriended."

"The Angels…" The whispered words flew from my mouth before I could stop them.

"Be careful who you paint as heroes or villains among your kind, Snow…" Linus's eyes drifted to Sumner and Stewart. "A piece of advice that you can apply as widely as you choose."

"We agreed to help Miss Snow get to where she said she needed to go with relatively few questions asked." Stewart bristled at the subtle dig. "Meanwhile, you're the ones who planned to sell her off to the highest bidder until she and her friends kicked your collective asses."

"You two carry yourselves with such moral superiority, but know that I trust you about as far as I can throw Harold here." Linus let out a low growl, more out of frustration than intimidation. "Ascendant aren't immortal, but we stick around significantly longer than most of you. Me? I've seen groups, organizations, even governments, come and go for decades on end. One thing most of them had in common? A significant dislike for anyone different."

"We're not directly tied to any particular government," Sumner responded, "if that's what you're insinuating."

"Quite the opposite, in fact." Linus shot a careful look my way. "Secret societies of 'well-meaning individuals' have been performing witch hunts, lynchings, you name it, without the need for public supervision for as long as I can remember." He shook his head. "At least the occasional CIA and FBI goons who've crossed my path over the years were accountable to someone."

Stewart rose an inch from the sofa, but a raised hand from Sumner returned him to his seat.

"We're all dancing around the real issue here, neither side wanting to show all their cards, so I'll be the first to bend." Sumner let out a quiet sigh of resignation. "Miss Snow has a vested interest in tracking down the Cardinal, a man who represents a clear and present danger to her life as well as Mr. Jayalal's. We only just met when she inadvertently found her way to our facility, but for as long as she allows, we are here to facilitate her needs."

OMG. Was it possible? Was Sumner really about to do what it sounded like she was doing?

"Though a bit unorthodox, our combined resources might be just what it takes to track down Lady Day so that we can petition her assistance in finding this murderer and bring him to justice." She studied Linus, Harold, and Frankie. "Assuming, of course, that your end goal and ours as far as the Cardinal is concerned align."

Harold cleared his throat. "Ascendant business is Ascendant business, woman." He inhaled to speak again, but Linus silenced him with a raised hand.

"What my associate, however brash, is trying to say is that we don't typically work with individuals outside our group, a long-standing rule that has kept us out of trouble on countless occasions." Linus drummed his fingers on the arm of his chair. "On the flip side, the three of us have been in town the better part of a week and have had little luck tracking down the Angel of Harlem."

"Maybe if you spent less time decorating and more time doing your job," Sunil broke his sullen silence, making a show of peering around Linus's posh personal space, "you'd be a little further along in your search."

"And if you were a little tougher," Frankie offered with a crinkled nose, "maybe the Cardinal wouldn't have kidnapped you right off the street and stuck you in a hole."

Both men came out of their seats. The air crackled with electricity sending the hair on Frankie's head and neck standing on end as the man-ferret's posture became decidedly less man and more ferret. Harold snarled and appeared ready to leap across Linus's chair to rip out Sunil's throat. Both Stewart and Copeland drew their weapons.

"Enough!" I'd let the conversation get out of hand. Beyond out of hand. "*Stop it, all of you!*"

For all Sumner's and Stewart's likely training in both close combat and conflict resolution, one thing was clear. I was the glue holding our little summit together, and unless I wanted the whole thing to descend into a brawl between a bunch of hotheaded superhumans and hyped-up secret agents, I needed to get it under control fast.

"If we're seriously considering working together," I vocalized, projecting my will into the words as best as I knew how as they passed my lips, *"then all this posturing isn't getting us anywhere, agreed?"*

"Agreed." Sunil dropped his hands to his sides, though he remained standing. A flash of static electricity passed between his outstretched fingers. "Linus?"

"Agreed." One look from Linus and both Harold and Frankie reeled it in. "What say you, Ms. Sumner?" the wolf asked.

"Agreed." Sumner motioned for Stewart and Copeland to stand down as well. "Now, shall we get down to business?"

World War III, defused in an instant. Was that me?

Linus and Sumner began a cordial if not friendly exchange, but for the most part, I tuned them both out. I had bigger fish to fry.

My words had come out not remotely musical, but the instant they left my lips, everyone stopped pushing each other's buttons and finally started talking. I felt nothing out of the ordinary as I uttered the words, but it was hard to argue with the results. Not one of the people in the circle so much as raised an eyebrow my way, but instead set to work on comparing notes and formulating a plan to find the object of our suddenly shared search.

I couldn't have been happier with the outcome, but if my suspicions were correct, I'd utilized my Ascendant ability again without the first idea of how I'd done it.

"Miss Snow?" Copeland whispered as he motioned for me to join him by the door. "A moment of your time?"

With Sumner and Linus deep in conversation and the others absorbed in the negotiations, I stole to Copeland's side.

"What is it?" I asked. "Is everything all right?"

"What?" He pointed to his right ear, his left hand holding the hearing aid I'd seen there before. "Can you speak up? Can't hear a damn word without this thing."

I leaned in close to his ear and, as loud as I dared, asked, "Is everything okay?"

"Sure seems so," he answered. "When lightning boy got all upset and the air started crackling, my hearing aid went on the fritz again. I had my head down trying to fix it, and when I looked up again, everyone had chilled out." He stared at me in awe. "What in the world did you say to them?"

And there was the answer. Everyone in the room with ears had suddenly taken a Valium based on two or three sentences from my lips while Copeland, temporarily deaf, had remained unaffected.

Conscious or not, the siren in me had spoken.

"You know what, Mr. Copeland?" I rested a hand at his shoulder. "I have a sneaky feeling it wasn't what I said but the way that I said it."

CHAPTER 18

FAIRYTALE OF NEW YORK

Once upon a time, an inexperienced siren still unsure of her voice allied with a lord of lightning who was angry at the world and everyone in it, a trio of man-beasts with questionable moral standards, and three agents from a shadowy organization the world had never heard of. Together, this unlikely group embarked upon a quest to find a missing Angel they hoped held the key to all their hopes and dreams.

Not exactly the feel good movie of the summer, but a pretty accurate description of my predicament.

We'd spent the daylight hours enjoying the strained hospitality of Linus's pack of theriodans in their abandoned tenement turned swank hideout. Though each was rough around the edges in his own way, bits of the humanity of the various predators in human flesh manifested throughout the day.

Harold, for instance, happened to be quite the cook. A little before lunch, he disappeared to the other end of the tenement's repurposed third floor only to reappear half an hour later with a rolling tray of the best gumbo I'd ever tasted. Fresh cornbread, dirty rice, and coarse cut coleslaw along with a refreshing raspberry tea all complemented each other for a meal befitting a legit New Orleans restaurant. Not bad for a man who at his core remained one of the world's most maligned scavengers.

Linus, a far better host than I would ever have guessed, regaled us for hours with one tale of his checkered past after another: some horrifying, some touching, and some downright hilarious. If you'd told the Persephone Snow of seven months ago as she was being carried off terrified by a humanoid tiger and hyena that someday she'd be sitting in their man-wolf boss's den laughing at dirty jokes, she would have scoffed.

And then, there was Frankie. Franklin. The ferret. Those beady little eyes of his never shifted back to normal, remaining muddy brown with those oddly elliptical pupils that took in everything. A bit unnerving to be around at first, he quickly stole his way into my heart. Unlike the effortless charm I'd found in Neko or the alternating confidence and shyness that kept me on my toes around L.J., Frankie's gift was his unfiltered view of the world around him. After he basically called me a prostitute to my face, I thought we were going to have a problem, but it didn't take me long to figure out that the ferret simply didn't have a filter and called things pretty much exactly the way he saw them.

And the way he saw them for the most part? As things of wonder. Everyone and everything he encountered in the world—each day, each experience, every sight, sound, taste, and smell—for him represented a new adventure. I recalled the old Albert Einstein quote I'd put atop my first social media account back in the day, about living each day as if either nothing was a miracle or as if everything was. Frankie definitely believed in the latter.

My crew, on the other hand, kept mostly to themselves. Sunil opened up a bit, mentioning his big family back in Pakistan and lighting up a couple of times as Frankie and Harold swapped tales of travel and adventure across the world. The non-Ascendant among us, however, remained silent unless we were actively discussing plans for tracking down Lady Day. Copeland's reluctance to join the conversation didn't surprise me, considering his issues with his hearing and the fact that he'd been relatively reserved since the moment I met him. To see Sumner and Stewart so shut down, however, was odd. In all fairness, though, if I were sitting in a lion's den, I wouldn't spend much energy conversing with the lions regardless of how emphatically they swore they didn't plan to eat me. In fact, though I belonged among the Ascendant in the room, I spent the entire day waiting for the lions to get hungry all the same.

"Ms. Sumner," I asked as she got off the phone in the corner of the room she and Stewart had all but cordoned off as their own. "Is everything all right?" The theriodans, Sunil, and Stewart all huddled around Linus's computer scanning through an online map of this section of Manhattan. "You and Mr. Stewart seem...quiet."

Sumner's lips slid into a practiced smile. "I'm sitting in a room with three men who could rip out my throat at any moment they saw fit, a man who can summon lightning from the sky at will, and a woman with a voice so hypnotic that I've still not sobered up from the whammy she dropped on all of us several hours ago."

"Yeah." My cheeks flushed with heat. "About that."

"I understand why you did what you did, Miss Snow. It's just..." She looked left and right, as if to ensure she would not be overheard. "Woman to woman, it's hard for me to accept that after all the years it's taken me to climb to my current position, I'm the least powerful person in the room." A quick laugh exited her nostrils. "A few pointed words from a teen pop star, and I'm rubbing elbows with people I've spent countless hours studying how to put down." At my aghast expression, she added. "Contingency plans only, of course. Worst case scenario."

"If it makes you feel any better, I'll only be a teen for another couple of days."

The momentary confusion in her gaze faded into a surprised smile. "You made it out in time for your birthday, then?"

"Just barely." I looked to one side, frustrated. "I'd hoped to spend the day on a beach with Ethan soaking up some sun and then dancing the night away dressed to the nines." At her questioning glance, I added, "I had a lot of time to daydream while the Cardinal had me locked away. A lot of time." I shook my head in frustration. "As if that's what I should have been focusing on. Stupid, right?"

"Not stupid at all." Sumner rested a hand on my shoulder and gave it a squeeze, the first crack in her ever-professional veneer. "And it's not too late for that dream to come true, you know."

"You think so? I'm on the run, hiding from a psychopath who wants me for God knows what reason. As of today, I've allied myself with a gang who, last I saw them, tried to abduct me in broad daylight. I have no idea where Ethan is, or anyone else that I know, for that matter. A fellow prisoner—who, by the way, gives me the creeps way more than the Cardinal ever did—is holding hostage a defenseless woman I befriended in my time away and has made it imminently clear that he's not letting her out of his sight unless I bring back a mysterious woman none of us have ever met. And the grand prize if I succeed in all this? A one way trip straight to the bastard who kidnapped me in the first place." I took a deep breath at the end of my rambling vent. "Now you're telling me that in the next seventy-two hours, all of that is going to sort itself out and find me back in good old California with the man I love? I'm a serious optimist, Ms. Sumner, but..."

"But nothing." Sumner let out a long sigh. "You find yourself stuck in an insane situation beyond your control, and I'm an ordinary woman conspiring with a roomful of people with the powers of gods to track down an angel." She chuckled. "What say we make a deal?"

"A deal?" I glanced over at the trio of theriodans having a second course of Harold's gumbo. "I'm not sure I have anything else left to offer."

"No. Just you and me. I'll do everything in my power to see you through this safely—"

"Thank you."

Sumner raised a finger. "—if you'll do the same for me and the boys."

I stretched out my hand. "I figured that already went without saying, Ms. Sumner, but it's a deal."

"Good to know." She moved to rejoin the men who had again

surrounded Linus's dual-monitor computer to check out yet another map of the city. "Now, what say we get going on tracking down this Angel we're all dying to meet?"

~

"**Y**ou've got to be kidding me."

We'd waited for night to fall, as reports stated that Lady Day, ironically, rarely made appearances before sunset, preferring the night life of her chosen corner of the world. A quick shopping trip with Stewart had allowed me to dress a bit more appropriately for a night on the town. A sleek top, stylish but fashionable pants, and a pair of Chuck Taylors were the order of the evening, as we were likely to be pounding the pavement for hours.

Unfortunately, the night, as always, had come with shadows.

On the opposite side of the street and dressed all in black without their raven masks—or I suppose, *crow*—roamed two of the four skiomancers who had come for me that first night. I'd disguised myself as much as possible, with my hair pulled up in a tight bun and covered with a kerchief, some non-prescription glasses to break up the look of my face—even with the glow of neon and halogen, the streets of Harlem were a bit too dark for shades—and a bulky scarf. Regardless, my insides tied themselves in knots as we closed the distance between us.

Only three possibilities seemed even plausible. Either Fala Hawkins and Dmitri Drozdov were here in Harlem searching for Lady Day just like the rest of us, the two skiomancers were looking for me, or I just happened to run into both a pack of theriodans and a murder of crows in New York City mere hours after an unplanned cross-country flight from Idaho.

Okay...two possibilities.

Anyway, if they were looking for me, I could count on one thing: the skiomancers wouldn't be rolling out the red carpet like Linus and his pack had.

"Those are Johan Krage's goons." Frankie sniffed the air. "We've run into them before." The ferret shot me a glance from behind the darkened lenses that hid his animalistic gaze. "Nasty folk, if you don't already know. They make our pack of theriodans look like an Ascendant support group with snacks."

"Just keep your heads down, everyone." Sumner scooted to her right, positioning her body between me and the skiomancers across the street. "Let them pass, and then we'll decide what to do."

I did as asked, keeping my chin down, while Sumner ran interference and Frankie used his heightened senses to look for even a hint that the pair of shadow-dealers had spotted me. Once the pair in black turned a corner and vanished from view, we pulled up outside a closed coffee shop.

"I have to say," Sumner shook her head, "I've studied Ascendant for years, but coming in contact with seven in the same day?" Her eyes glanced in the direction where Fala and Dmitri had disappeared. "The whole thing is a bit unnerving."

"It's way worse than just rapid-fire Ascendant." My nervous eyes followed hers. "Those particular shadowmancers are currently *persona non grata* not only with the Ascendant as a whole but with their subgroup in particular." The moment Madame Midnight shunned the four who had once been loyal members of her clique along with the hate-filled look Krage had shot me before walking away that night remained seared on my memory. "At least two of Krage's rogue shadow-assassins in town with no allegiance to anyone but themselves? I suggest we all keep our eyes open and our guard up."

Both Sumner and Frankie shot me curt nods as we continued up the street in the direction we'd been walking, though all of us looked over our shoulders more often than we had before.

"So," Sumner asked as we rounded the next corner, "we keep to the plan? Check out our trio of potential locations and report to the others?"

"Sure." I moved down the sidewalk, putting as much distance between me and where we'd seen Fala and Dmitri as I could. "Let's go."

Our group had broken into three parties to canvas the surrounding city. Frankie, Sumner, and I formed one group, Harold with Stewart and Copeland a second, and Linus and Sunil the last. It wasn't until that last pair headed off together that I realized their names were palindromes of each other, but as I had a pretty good idea that neither the man-wolf nor the elektromancer would find the humor in my discovery, I decided to keep that particular fact to myself.

Our original plan, when it was just me, Sunil, and Sumner's crew, had been to stake out the Cotton Club together that evening, but Linus and his pack had been privy to significantly more intel than our new friends from the Boise Airport. Their research revealed that Lady Day tended to spread the love between multiple establishments in the area and that she might be spending the evening at any of a dozen places, assuming she went out that night at all. Splitting up had seemed the best way to cover more ground while we were laying out the plan, though seeing the skiomancers—God only knew how many of them were here in Harlem—changed everything. I couldn't help but channel Ethan's spot-on advice for the characters at the beginning of every horror movie we'd ever watched together.

"Stay together, you idiots," I'd heard him grumble more than once as a group of far-too-attractive teens decided to divide and conquer when going up against the latest supernatural stalker. "Split up, and you're dead."

I said a silent prayer that Ethan's cinematic theories didn't bleed over into real life.

Bleed.

Wow, I was pretty sure I'd just bypassed pessimism and went straight for nihilistic.

Back to business.

None of us, theriodans included, had ever met or even seen Lady Day in person, though Linus had been able to pull up a few fuzzy pictures for reference. A dark-skinned woman, the Angel of Harlem was exquisite in beauty and form with expensive tastes in pretty much everything. Like many Ascendant, she'd walked the earth far longer than anyone knew and likely could afford whatever she wanted: the power of compounding interest and all that, just like Mr. Delacroix had tried to drill into my head for the entire Sparkle Tour.

Something to consider if I made it through this disaster my life had become.

"So, where do you think we should look first?" I asked, yanking myself out of my latest rabbit hole of conjecture. "There are four sites in this particular neighborhood where someone fitting Lady Day's description has been spotted in the last several weeks." I pulled out my phone and flipped to the app where I'd typed in the list we'd made at the theriodans' base. "A couple of jazz clubs, a blues bar, a dessertery-wine bar..."

"While I could certainly use a glass of wine," Sumner said, "I suggest we check out one of the jazz clubs. The wolf, Linus, seemed to think that was a safer bet."

Linus, she called him. Funny. Everyone among the Ascendant called me Snow, and yet I didn't even know our theriodan associates' surnames. Maybe keeping such information a secret helped maintain their security, or perhaps a group of men with various animal predators at each of their cores had abandoned the entire human system of naming altogether. Something to ask Linus, Harold, or Frankie when we weren't sharing the streets with a pair of shadow-assassins that were God-knows-where by now.

Halfway up the latest block of our stroll, that particular section of street closed at either end for construction, it hit me that I hadn't seen another soul in well over a minute. The realization sent the hairs on my neck on end.

"Stop." Frankie sniffed the air and held up a fist. "Don't move."

Though only Frankie knew precisely what he had sensed, all of us followed his instructions and froze in place.

Unfortunately, our shadows did not follow suit.

Rising from the ground like they had in my nightmares for months, the silhouettes of our bodies cast by the various streetlights pulled themselves up from the concrete and asphalt and surrounded us. The league of dark specters quickly moved to block our every avenue of escape, drawing closer with each passing heartbeat.

Call me crazy, but I was pretty sure the skiomancers had spotted us after all.

"Get ready to run." Frankie leaped at the nearest bunch of shadowy assailants. "I'll take care of this—"

Frankie's sentence was cut short as a half-dozen of the shadows suddenly sprung weapons and attacked the ferret, their blades passing through his body as ephemeral as ghosts and yet leaving him writhing on the ground as if he'd been gutted.

"That was unwise," came a voice from above, the words colored with a deep Russian accent. "Did you not warn him, Snow, that shadows in the right hands can be as lethal as a blade?"

Sumner and I together looked up to find a swirling mass of shadow descending toward us at a rapid clip, carrying the pair of skiomancers we'd seen before.

"Dmitri," I spoke just loud enough to be heard, "Fala." I kept my hands at my sides for fear that any sign of aggression might buy me or Sumner a similar fate to Frankie's. "What, may I ask, is the meaning of this attack?" The fact that I got the entire sentence out without my voice cracking was an undeniable miracle.

Fala stepped from the bastion of shadow on one side of us and Dmitri the other.

"You can't be serious." Fala's cold eyes studied me through the wavering shadows. "After all you've done to us?"

"After all I've done?" Though still terrified out of my mind, a coal of righteous anger sprung at my core. "You and the rest of your little murder of crows hounded me across the entire western half of the United States and nearly killed me more times than I can count. Ethan and Rosemary and Mr. Delacroix as well." My eyes narrowed, my chin dropping to my chest as I glared at her through my furrowed eyebrows. "Not to mention, you and yours ruined the final night of my tour."

"Mind your tongue, little girl"—Fala raised a finger, and my nearest silhouette raised a two-dimensional blade at my face, its tip stopping just short of my eye—"if you know what's good for you."

"Perhaps our actions did tarnish the finale of your precious little tour..." This new voice came from above. "But what you and your friends did to me and mine was unforgivable." Johan Krage, in his full avian regalia, landed within the circle of shadows and doffed his beaked mask to look on me with his icy gaze. "We were once Ravens of the Midnight Angel, and now banished from her sight, we are, as you so callously pointed out, nothing but a Murder of Crows." His lips drew thin, his face devoid of any emotion beyond barely contained rage. "With respect to *you and yours*, Persephone Snow, perhaps it is time we started living up to the name."

CHAPTER 19

DANCING IN THE DARK

As if Krage's appearance on the scene wasn't bad enough, the trio of skiomancers was soon joined by the last of their quartet, Rupert Martyn, who sauntered up the street finishing off what appeared to be a chili dog and soda.

"So, she *is* here." Rupert shoved the last few inches of his dinner past his teeth and washed it down with a slug of his drink before tossing the plastic bottle into the street. "I've got to admit, I thought you were all yanking my chain."

"If only," Krage grumbled. "The last time I spoke with the Cardinal, Snow, he let slip that the rumors of your death were greatly exaggerated and that he had you tucked away somewhere safe. What are you doing here in the middle of Harlem with this liability in sensible shoes and the man-rat?"

Sumner tensed at my side, but I motioned for her to keep her cool.

"Actually, he's a ferret," I grumbled. "As for why I'm here—"

"As if we don't know." Fala chuckled.

"Same as us, Boss." Rupert shot me a wicked grin. "She's looking for the Angel."

Damn. Lady Day was in high demand.

"Thank you, Rupert," Krage whispered, his tone withering. "Your focus on sensitive data protection is *ever* appreciated."

"I can't believe that you've lowered yourself to work with this vermin, Snow." Dmitri, his voice a low Russian rumble, pulled Frankie up from the ground.

"Put him down." The cool steel in Sumner's gaze confirmed that she had no plans to dignify the various taunts with a response. "The lot of you have attacked me and my associates completely unprovoked. Leave, before I am forced to bring down holy hell upon your heads."

Sumner and Krage locked gazes for all of half a second before the latter burst into laughter.

"What you lack in ability and resources, woman, you more than make up for in sheer audacity." Krage drew close to her, his face so near it appeared they were about to kiss. "Not to mention, beauty," he added, brushing a stray lock of hair from her eye. "What a shame it will be, ending your otherwise insignificant life." He stepped back. "We've learned our lesson of late about leaving loose ends lying around."

Sumner laughed. "There's one thing, however, you haven't learned."

"And what might that be?" Krage asked as one of the shadows at his command extended a pointed finger at Sumner's throat.

"Not to waste time talking when there is work to be done." The smile left her features as she clenched her eyes shut. "Now."

The air filled with ozone as a bolt of lightning erupted down from a cloudless sky. I managed to squeeze my eyes shut half a second before the blinding flash and thunderous roar struck like a cannonball of lit magnesium. I opened my eyes upon a sidewalk devoid of shadows beyond those cast by the various streetlights. Fala, who'd taken my lead and protected her eyes, dove at my throat, but a quick sidekick that Rosemary insisted I practice until I could do it in my sleep caught her just below the ribcage, sending her to the ground before she could land a blow.

Sumner took advantage of the momentary confusion to punch Krage square in the nose. "Come on," she shouted as she grabbed my wrist. "Let's go!"

"Not so fast." A vise-like grip came down upon my shoulder, and a glance back revealed Dmitri's other massive hand clamped around Sumner's neck. "If you two are suddenly summoning lightning bolts from the sky, then I think I'll keep the both of you very close."

"*They're* not bringing the lightning." Sunil stepped from the shadow of an awning across the abandoned street, his lightning strike having sent a couple of pedestrian rubberneckers running. "Now let them go, unless you'd like a demonstration of the precision with which I control my particular gift."

"How fascinating." Krage, already recovering, brought up his hand, and with it came several dozen shadows from all along the block. "I haven't crossed paths with an elektromancer in years." His eyes narrowed at Sunil. "Unfortunate for you, of course."

With a subtle flick of his wrist, Krage sent the phalanx of ephemeral terrors flying at Sunil. The sulky elektromancer, however, was more than ready. An arc of electricity leaped from one hand to the other, the resultant flash dissipating the shadowy onslaught in an instant. Fala and Rupert both sent their own emissaries of wispy darkness at Sunil as well, but he dealt with their attacks similarly.

A stalemate.

"So," Krage grumbled, "you can't free Snow and her friend without risking electrocuting them both, and our shadows cannot overcome the lightning at your command. Whatever shall we do to resolve this?"

A stiletto dagger appeared at Krage's throat, followed by a familiar voice. "You can tell your man there to let Snow and the woman go." Linus peered at Dmitri from across Krage's shoulder. "That is, if you prefer your trachea intact."

"Linus?" Krage asked, amused despite the razor edge resting below the angle of his jaw. "Is that you?"

Linus pulled the knife so close to Krage's neck that it drew blood.

"Let Snow and her friend go, or regardless of the past, I swear I'll end you right here."

"Very well." Krage motioned to the gigantic Russian. "Release the women, Dmitri," he commanded, and then, in a low mumble, added, "for now."

Dmitri did as he was told, pushing Sumner and me forward so hard, we both dropped to our knees and had to scramble back to our feet.

As if I didn't have enough bruises already.

"How sad, Snow. You've fallen in with theriodans." Krage shook his head in disgust. "How beneath you."

"Don't forget, Johan," Linus growled into Krage's ear, "I've still got a knife at your throat."

"And if there were a snowball's chance in hell you were going to use it, Linus, I'd already be bleeding to death on the concrete." Krage extended his open hands out to each side. "I have released the women as you asked. I would suggest you unhand me as well. Your elektromancer friend seems more than capable against our shadows, but I doubt you would fare quite as well."

"A good thing, then, that he's not alone." Scaling down the nearest building's facade by way of an old fire escape, Harold studied the situation with a keen eye, the foot-long blade in his hand glinting in the halogen light of the darkened street.

Rupert laughed. "Two of your little trio, eh? Did you bring the tiger as well, or is he still gallivanting the globe with Harkreader and Delacroix?"

My stomach knotted at Ethan's name, doubly so when it was paired with Rosemary's. Where were they now? Were they together? What did that mean?

"No tiger here." Dmitri chuckled, adding in his Slavic baritone as he gestured to Frankie's crumpled form, "All I see is this pathetic man-rat."

"Ferret." Frankie performed a quick forward roll and came to his feet by Fala and Krage. "My apologies, Linus. I was taking a second to collect myself." He brushed himself off, his beady eyes rocketing from one skiomancer to another as if waiting for one or both to attack. "Those shadow blades of theirs sting like a mother."

"And here we are. A straight up Mexican standoff." Krage brought his hand up and pushed the blade from his throat with a single finger. "If you please," he whispered as he stepped away from Linus and spun to study the gathered Ascendant before him. "Gathering your own little army, Snow? Not exactly the soldiers I'd seek out, but I admire your initiative. That voice of yours can apparently get you whatever you want"—his eyes narrowed at me—"as long as someone doesn't do something unfortunate to that pretty little neck of yours."

"Careful, or I might sing you straight to oblivion, Krage." I injected every ounce of confidence I had into my voice. "As for the company I keep, these theriodans have shown more honor and loyalty in the last few hours than I suspect you and yours could muster in a lifetime." I'm not sure Krage knew exactly how well he was pushing my buttons, but I refused to let him see me sweat. "And I'll have you know, regardless of what you may believe, that each of them is here of their own free will."

"Of course they are." Krage turned to address the leader of the theriodan pack. "Ah, Linus, you toothless old wolf. Been a while, hasn't it?"

"Not long enough."

Krage snorted a chuckle. "You know, no matter how many theriodans I meet, I never cease to feel a bit sorry for you all. The heart and eyes of a feral beast"—his eyes dropped to Linus's hands— "and no claws to back it up." His devilish grin returned. "You must all feel so...incomplete."

"We may not have claws, Krage, but blade or no blade, we can tear out your throat all the same." Linus's lips parted with a lupine grin of his own. "As you well know."

"Bygones," Krage whispered, "unless you truly wish for me and mine to start paying back debts today, wolf."

Sunil drew cautiously closer but left enough space to be able to respond if the skiomancers resumed their attack. Harold remained poised on the fire escape above our heads, blade in hand and ready to strike. Frankie assumed a fighting stance that reminded me of one of the martial arts positions Rosemary worked on with Ethan. Linus held his position, his stiletto held blade down in his dominant hand.

Meanwhile, Sumner drew close to me, but I didn't get the impression it was out of any sense of self-preservation. Deftly maneuvering her position as the conversation progressed, she kept herself interposed between me and Dmitri at all times. This woman I'd met less than twenty-four hours before was using her body as a human shield to keep me safe the only way she could. Subtle though it was, the action struck me as the bravest of the night.

"Okay," I stepped from behind Sumner and into the deserted street, "we're all here now, nobody has a knife to anyone's throat, and no one has said or done anything that can't be walked back." I channeled every ounce of energy I had into duplicating what I'd done back at the theriodan hideout, pushing my will into my voice as the words exited my lips with the subtlest of singsong melodies. *"What say we all go our separate ways and pretend that none of this ever happened?"*

Frankie and Fala both stood a little straighter at my words, Krage and Linus stared at each other as if neither had ever laid eyes on the other, Sumner met my gaze, her look of trepidation fading into one of nonchalance. Rupert, Sunil, Dmitri, and even Harold up on the fire escape all seemed to relax a bit.

I pulled in a breath to issue an even more direct proclamation when a high-pitched sonic boom I hadn't heard since I was taken from my dining room six months ago tore both the quiet night and my concentration to shreds. The sudden silence that followed only made more noticeable a new ringing in my ears, a ringing that heralded a moment I'd been dreading since Charon first led me across the Styx to my own personal hell.

A quiet whirring above my head coupled with the continued echo of the sonic attack left little doubt that a certain crimson-armored Ascendant was about to land among us. Imagine my surprise when I peered up into the darkened sky to find instead a stone-faced Asian woman in a skintight black bodysuit, her form surrounded by dozens of pieces of orbiting tech, descending under the power of a pair of what I can only describe as designer jet-boots. Damn, this outfit was even more badass than the last I'd seen her in, and black really was her color.

"Hello, Minako." I met the cold gaze of the Cardinal's technomancer and did my best to keep my voice from wavering. "Funny running into you here."

"Why, Miss Snow, I must admit," she spoke, her voice amplified by a tiny microphone at the corner of her mouth and emanating from the myriad of objects floating around her body, "I never dreamed I'd see you again, at least above ground."

"I'm just as surprised to see you here," I countered. "Last I knew, my boyfriend had you trussed up like a rodeo steer." I refocused my will, working to inject my voice with whatever it was that made me a siren. *No need for a reunion. Leave this place before my friends and I have to—*"

"I think not." She tapped the pair of high-tech noise-canceling headphones that covered her ears. "Who do you think fashioned the Cardinal's helmet? Your vocal gymnastics may be effective against the unprepared, but to me, you're as ineffectual as the human cow at your side." She descended to hover before me, her feet remaining mere inches above the ground. "Every sound, ambient and otherwise, is digitized before I hear so much as a whisper or a rustle of leaves. I still hear every word you say, if not with that unique voice of yours, so if you're trying to talk your way out of this, you're going to have to convince me the old-fashioned way."

Wow. It looked like the Cardinal wasn't blowing smoke about being immune to my ability all those months ago. Good to know.

As Minako lit on the street amid the gathered Ascendant, Frankie backed away, hiding in the shallow alcove of a nearby doorway, Harold stepped back from the edge of the fire escape, and even Linus looked on this latest arrival with respect bordering on unease. Only Sumner remained unmoved by the latest arrival to the scene, her placid features taking in every word, every move, every nuance.

She and Rosemary would get along just fine.

"My apologies for the inconvenience, Minako," Krage said, his expression still slightly dazed. "We intended to have Snow subdued by the time you arrived, but she has accumulated more allies than we anticipated, and her abilities have grown considerably since Los Angeles."

Minako's glare bored a hole through my forehead. "Free less than two days, and you've already managed to make your way to the other end of the continent. I'm impressed." She glanced briefly in Sunil's direction. "And with the elektromancer as well, no less. How did you manage that, siren?"

"I'm with Snow of my own free will, witch. We're here to—"

"I wasn't speaking to you, Jayalal." Minako's eyes cut from Sunil back to me. "I know why *we* are here seeking the Angel of Harlem, Snow, and I can guess why you and he are looking for her as well." Her gaze wandered among the gathered theriodans. "My only question is why the traveling petting zoo is in town."

Funny. I hadn't thought to ask Linus and the boys exactly why they were looking for Lady Day. It had been enough to know they'd help us, but now, that seemed a particularly important piece of information.

"Our business is our own, witch." Linus growled at Minako's words. "Now, I would suggest you and the shadow-dealers leave this place under your own power while you still can."

"What the wolf said." Sunil sent an arc of electricity from one palm to the other. "Your little machines make you a pretty tough cookie, but last I checked, they run on electricity just like the rest of the world." Sunil snapped his fingers and one of Minako's floating gadgets dropped to the ground at her feet. "You might want to go before I fry all the gadgets under your command and see how well you fare against a pack of 'lowly' theriodans."

"In any case, Snow"—Minako continued to ignore Sunil, keeping her focus on me and our conversation—"If you're with Jayalal, is it safe to assume you also freed the empath and the geomancer? Are they here as well?"

I didn't say a word and worked to keep the answer from my features as well.

"Did you know that the Cardinal was the one who allowed you and Xiao to speak all those months ago? He instructed Charon to make the introduction so that the two of you would not be lonely.

And what was the first thing you did? Attempt to engineer your escape."

"Jade is somewhere you'll never find her," my hotheaded elektromancer friend said as he tipped our hand. "I can guarantee you that."

Wise or not, I followed his lead. "Don't pretend that heartless monster gives a shit about any of us, Minako. He buried me and the others in a hole to rot."

"He let you lot live, did he not? Left you a companion, guardian, and chef. Even allowed you a friend until you overstepped." Minako let out a single cold laugh. "All the others? He simply killed them."

She was right. For six months, I'd pondered why the Cardinal had left me alive and even more why he'd apparently planned for me to stay with him in his mountain fortress before my sharp tongue had relegated me to a literal hell on earth.

He'd never visited me in his Hades, but even in his absence, there were signs that I'd been given deferential treatment.

The disappointed tone in his voice as he turned his back on me that first day and ordered Charon to take me across the Styx.

The monitor in my room that allowed me to see the sky, the sunrise, the sunset, even if only an image, from my living tomb.

The wardrobe meant for me that had gone to Jia Li after our lone argument.

A part of me wondered—a morbid part, I must admit—if I'd hurt his feelings that day, assuming a monster like him had feelings in the first place. Even more, I wondered why I cared.

"If you had even an inkling as to your true place in the Ascendant world, not to mention what is coming, you'd cling to the Cardinal as if he were the only raft in an ocean of despair, regardless of what he's done." Minako uttered the last few words more quietly than the rest, her gaze dropping to the asphalt.

"I notice he's not here with you, by the way." I attempted to turn the conversation on its head. "Everything all right between you and Big Red?"

Minako remained silent, apparently taking her turn at avoiding questions.

"Truth? I don't give a whit about what's coming. Regardless of his reasons, the Cardinal imprisoned us all and cost each of us months, even years, of our lives. Me, Sunil, Jade, Daichi, even…"

Something told me not to say the name or even mention the final prisoner that we'd freed. My gut knew there was something different about a man who required such draconian precautions, and I'd doubted the decision to set him free since the moment I made it. Unfortunately, Minako saw right through my hesitation. My lie of omission may as well have been a neon sign proclaiming the truth.

"Tell me there isn't a fifth name on that list, Snow." Minako's already cold voice went positively icy. "You, the empath, the lightning rod, Alba's earth mover. Is there another?"

"I have no idea what you're talking about."

My prior hesitation had already told Minako everything she needed to know.

"You released him." Not a question. A statement. One filled with dread. "Do you have any idea what you've done?"

"I—"

"The collar." She took a step in my direction, more than a hint of trepidation invading her tone. "Is it intact?"

"We didn't—"

"*Is it intact?*" Minako spoke each word crisply, her face so close to mine, I could smell the cool mint on her breath. "Tell me you didn't unleash that monster upon the world again." My heart raced as the technomancer seized me by the shoulders. "If that devil has been set free, the river of blood from the last few years will be nothing compared to the flood of carnage he will bring."

My breath caught in my chest. Though I stood surrounded by a quartet of murderous skiomancers, a trio of mercenary theriodans, an elektromancer with a mysterious past, and Minako herself, I suddenly felt very much the villain of the story.

"For the last time, Snow"—Minako shook me, the fear in her voice as unnerving as her claw-like grip—"is the collar intact?"

"Unhand that woman."

After a night of so many familiar voices, this one was unknown to me. Sultry and powerful, the woman who spoke the words stepped from a golden shimmer in the air and stood before us poised and unafraid. The confidence in her gaze spoke of more years than her flawless dark skin, toned body, and waist-length jet-black curls made seem possible. And her outfit would make the Real Housewives of any city on the planet green with envy.

For all our maps and plans to track her down here in the heart of the place that was her namesake, the Angel of Harlem, it would seem, had come to us.

CHAPTER 20

ANGEL OF HARLEM

Her floral top Dolce & Gabbana, her black stretch-crepe pants Safiyaa, and her black nylon gabardine sneakers bearing the bright Prada Milano logo above the chunky white sole, the woman before us had some serious style. If we all somehow made it out of this insanity alive, this Angel would be joining me for a girl's day straight down Rodeo Drive.

A pretty big if, of course.

"Quite the entrance." Krage, who had been suspiciously quiet as Minako took the lead in the conversation, immediately perked up. "Lady Day, I presume?"

She lowered her chin in the subtlest of nods, her dark eyes studying our black-clad adversary.

"At last." Rupert let out a lone chuckle. "I was beginning to wonder if we'd ever find this witch."

"Find?" Lady Day let out a throaty laugh of her own and strode over to Krage. "I've watched you and your little band of shadow-stealers bumble aimlessly around my city for weeks. The only reason we're speaking at this very moment is because I will it, make no mistake."

"But now that you're here—" Krage began.

"You will all behave, or the first to move will discover exactly how useful my talent truly is when I wish to make someone disappear." She directed a lone finger at Krage. "The crimson monster who bankrolls your Murder of Crows is responsible for the death of many of our kind and deprived the world of a dear friend last year, one more worthy of existence than any of your shadow band. Consider yourself lucky I didn't kill all four of you and avenge poor Dugan the moment you arrived in my city."

Krage and his band of dark assassins, Minako, and even the Ascendant aligned with me all held their tongue in the face of the threat.

"Now that I have your collective attention," Lady Day continued, "know that I am more than aware each of you has been searching for me, some far longer than others. For future reference, I would advise against stalking an Angel in her home, regardless of your motivation. Still, as I'm feeling rather generous this evening, I would hear each of your entreaties before I decide what to do with the lot of you."

"I'm not listening to this another second." Rupert took a step in the Angel's direction. "You will come with us now, witch, or—"

"The U.S. Capitol," Lady Day whispered dismissively, "the current head of security." She shot the skiomancer a withering smile. "This very moment."

No sooner had the Angel completed her incantation than Rupert vanished from sight in another golden shimmer. The air that swept in to fill the void left by his vanishing form crackled with electricity similar to when Sunil used his abilities.

Krage's eyes grew wide. "What have you done with Rupert, woman?"

"Weren't you listening?" She raised a dark brow as she addressed the leader of the diminished Murder of Crows. "At least it's evening. If he utilizes his shadowmancing abilities as well as I imagine he was taught as one of my Sister's Ravens, he should be able to extricate himself from such a delicate situation."

"You sent him there." Sumner's face filled with awe. "Simply by willing it."

Glad I wasn't the only one who was impressed.

"Some lessons are better learned the hard way." Lady Day returned her attention to the group as a whole. "For the rest of you, understand that the next person who moves on me gets sent to the center of the Pacific Ocean hundreds of miles from the nearest land." She directed her gaze at Krage. "How a skiomancer's talents might work on the open sea is beyond me."

Krage crossed his arms, but continued to keep quiet.

"Now," Lady Day continued, "as I was saying before I was so rudely interrupted, I would hear each of your pleas, if for no other reason than to hopefully conclude this business and put to an end this unprecedented invasion of my privacy." She let out a quiet sigh as she addressed Krage directly. "Am I to assume that you and your skiomancers are here at the behest of the Cardinal?"

"Yes." Krage kept his voice low and deferential. "My skiomancers and I are simply working a preexisting contract and performing said duties to the letter of the agreement."

"And am I correct in guessing that your master hopes to end my rather long life and add my abilities to his already prodigious list of ill-gotten Ascendant talents?"

"The Cardinal does not discuss his reasoning with those in his employ. He merely makes his wishes known."

"Just following orders, then?" I wasn't sure if my decision to speak was wise, but the words were out of my mouth before I could stop them. "That excuse always works."

"I will speak with you in a moment, Miss Snow." The Angel turned her attention on the technomancer in our midst. "I'm surprised, Minako. Has your hand not been scorched soundly enough by this particular burner you keep touching?"

Minako turned her head to one side, refusing to meet the Angel's gaze. "My reasons for being here and helping Krage and the others are my own."

"Of course they are." Lady Day returned her attention to me. "You must know, Miss Snow, that I never once believed the reports of your demise, particularly considering their source." She let out a plaintive sigh. "My sincerest apologies. Had I the first idea of where you were being held, trust that I would have secured your freedom months ago."

Compared to how she spoke with Krage and the Cardinal, Lady Day's tone as she addressed me was cordial, friendly even.

"But we've never met, Lady Day. How did you know that I'd even been taken?"

"I've been around far longer than you can imagine, dear. I have forgotten more things than most people ever learn. As for your situation specifically, though, simply know that there are many who care for you, child." She offered me a friendly smile. "Did you not guess that they would seek my aid in their desperate search for one they loved as much as you?"

Ethan. He met Lady Day in the days before I was taken. He must have come to New York seeking help, and even the Angel of Harlem couldn't send him to me.

"Unless I miss my guess," the Angel continued, "you and the elektromancer seek my help in tracking down your captor so that you might perform whatever action you deem necessary to prevent a repeat of your imprisonment."

Unable to speak, I offered her nothing but a simple nod.

Her gaze flicked to a spot across my shoulder. "And who is this woman that you bring into our midst?"

"My name, Lady Day, is Roxanne Sumner." She offered a polite bow, though her eyes kept flitting between the Angel, Krage, and Minako. "I'm merely here to help Miss Snow in her efforts to return to some semblance of normal life."

"I'm afraid she's already crossed that particular Rubicon, Ms. Sumner, but I do commend both your efforts as well as your bravery.

You do your family proud, standing among nearly a dozen Ascendant without so much as a hint of fear."

"Thank you," Sumner said, before adding a muttered, "I think."

"And that leaves you, wolf, and your pack of theriodans." Lady Day studied Linus as if he were a bug beneath a magnifying glass. "Of all those gathered, the motivation behind your pack's presence here is the only one I don't understand." She crossed her arms in a defensive posture. "As you are no doubt aware, it is rare that I deal with your kind, adversarially or otherwise." Her eyes narrowed at the leader of the theriodan pack. "For what possible reason have you sought an audience with the Angel of Harlem?"

Linus glanced Harold's way and then bowed deeply before Lady Day. "Pardon, milady, but our business with you is a private matter that I dare not discuss in mixed company."

"A contract, then," Krage said with a laugh and a flourish, "the same as me and mine, wolf, the only difference being that we don't know who is pulling your strings."

"I have no strings," Linus growled.

"No strings, perhaps," Dmitri taunted, "but clearly a leash."

Harold somersaulted down from the fire escape and landed by his pack leader's side. "Careful, shadow-man," he wheezed, pointing at the gigantic Russian, "I've never let a little thing like a lack of natural claws keep my inner hyena from ripping out a windpipe or two." His lips parted in a golden-grilled grin. "Do you truly trust your little shadows to keep you safe from us?"

"Enough." Lady Day stepped closer, her patience wearing thin. "While I'm certain your current manhood-measuring contest is fulfilling your respective tribal thirsts for validation, I have neither the time nor the desire to listen to such—"

Everyone, including Lady Day, went instantly silent as a loud metallic thunk sounded and Sunil dropped to the ground. A floating ball of steel hovered in the air where his head had been seconds before.

Minako smiled. "It occurred to me while everyone was talking that the chess piece holding everyone in check was the elektromancer." Her dismissive gaze cut in the direction of Sunil's unconscious form. "He probably should have finished zapping all my 'little machines' while he had the chance." She looked Krage's way. "Johan?"

"On it."

Lady Day immediately began to rattle off another person, place, and time, but before she could get out two syllables, a score of shadows descended upon her from every direction, encircling her neck, constricting her chest, and filling her mouth until she couldn't make a sound. The hint of golden shimmer to her left immediately dissipated into the ether.

Dmitri rushed the Angel and grabbed a hunk of her waist-length locks in one hand, twisting the hair around his fingers, and pulled a knife from his boot with the other, bringing its edge to the angle of Lady Day's jaw.

"I'm surprised, Angel." Krage laughed. "Even with your age and experience, overconfidence can still get the best of anyone, it appears."

"*Let her go,*" I screamed, channeling every iota of willpower I had into my words. "*She's done nothing to you.*"

In answer, the quartet of skiomancers stood down, their arms falling to their sides as if all four had entered some sort of trance. The shadows at their command dissipated into the surrounding darkness.

"The Louvre," Lady Day immediately began, "Monsieur—"

"You're not going anywhere," Minako said as a flying bolo-bot encircled the Angel's neck with a steel cable and cut off her half-complete incantation. "We've searched far too long to let you escape us now."

Those damned headphones of hers. Should have had Sunil fry them when we had the chance. I glanced his way. Still down. Dammit.

"That's the problem with having powers that require you to speak." Minako glanced my way. "A lesson you might want to remember."

"What are you going to do with Lady Day?" I asked as Minako hovered a foot above the ground at the Angel's side.

"The Cardinal wishes an audience with the Angel of Harlem, and my associates and I are merely executing his wishes."

"Executing is right. He's going to kill her." I met Minako's cold gaze with one of my own. "Is the death of one of the three Ascendant Angels something you want to carry on your soul?"

Breaking from his song-induced trance, Linus sniffed the air, a hint of smile crossing his features. Harold's eyes shifted left and right; whatever the wolf had smelled, he'd noticed it too. Both their expressions went stony and cool.

"That, boys, is the smell of defeat." A still groggy Krage broke from my spell as well and sauntered over to the pair of theriodans. "Remember it well."

"A question, Krage." Linus bared his lupine teeth. "You ever play cards?"

"Whatever are you going on about now?" Krage asked, exasperated.

"Just curious. I was going to commend you and your boys on your strategy."

Fala, a few feet away, cleared her throat.

"Pardon," Linus muttered, "your *people*." The man-wolf sucked air through his nostrils. "Anyway, as for holding back the technomancer and keeping an ace up your sleeve? Well played. Caught us totally off guard. I'm impressed."

Krage's expression narrowed as he tried to decide if Linus was legit complimenting him or simply setting him up for another verbal skewer.

"Funny thing?" Linus asked as the crack of a gunshot from the end of the block caught Minako in the shoulder and sent the technomancer spiraling to the pavement. "You never considered that we might have an ace or two of our own."

Another gunshot from the opposite end of the street caught Dmitri in the thigh. With a pained grunt, the skiomancer crumpled to the concrete between me and Sumner.

"The Bronx. Luther." Lady Day whispered as soon as she pulled the robotic garrote from her neck, her voice a quiet croak. "Now."

With that, the Angel stepped into a scintillating cloud of golden light and vanished from sight.

"No!" Krage shouted. "We had her."

"And now you don't." Stewart rolled from beneath a delivery truck down the street and strode in our direction. "You all right, Miss Snow?"

"You should be watching your own back, *yatsu*." Minako rocketed up from the asphalt, spun around until Stewart was firmly in her field of vision, and sent a dozen of her floating hunks of machinery flying at the man who had shot her. "Prepare to reap the whirlwind."

One after another, the various machines, regardless of their function, pummeled Stewart about the head and shoulders, the first few hits driving him to the ground and the remainder rendering him unconscious.

"Stop it, you bitch!" I hurled myself at Minako, who still hovered a few inches off the ground, and leaped onto her back, tangling my fingers in her long dark hair. "Leave him alone!"

"Or what, Snow?" she grunted, her eyes filled with pain and rage. "You going to have another one of your puppets shoot me?"

"Not exactly." With my free hand, I grabbed at one of the earpieces of her headphones and dislodged its seal. Searching for a lyric that would convey what I needed, I channeled the Queen of Pop, and sang with all my might, *"Open your heart to me."* Immediately, Minako ceased her struggle, brought us both to the ground, and removed her headgear. The fury in her gaze replaced with fear, she stood stock-still, awaiting my next order.

"Now, *beat it*." Borrowing from another member of pop royalty, I sang the repeated command. *"Just beat it."*

Without another word, Minako turned, leaped into the air, and disappeared into the halogen haze of the New York night sky.

"Andrew!" Sumner shouted, and ran to where the unconscious Stewart lay sprawled, surrounded by Minako's various abandoned machines.

"Now." I turned to speak with the remaining skiomancers. "Would the three of you care to show yourselves out, or shall I continue with the greatest hits of the 80s? I'm sure I can find some particularly devastating titles if I dig deep."

Krage looked to his two lieutenants with a calculating gaze. "Only a fool continues to fight when the prize is already lost." Without another word, he ensconced himself in shadow and took silently to the sky. Fala and an injured Dmitri followed suit, and in less time than it took to say it, we were alone. Copeland, who had fired the shot that hit Dmitri from the shadows of a nearby alley, joined Sumner as she checked on the unconscious Stewart; Linus pulled Harold and Frankie in for a quick after-action review; and I checked on a dazed Sunil who was just then sitting up.

"Did we win?" Sunil asked, his eyes struggling to focus in the low light.

"For now." I sighed. "Problem is, we won the battle and lost the war."

"How do you figure?" Linus asked, as he led the theriodan pack over to join the conversation. "Seems a pretty decisive victory to me."

"That may be true, but the only reason we're here is to find Lady Day who, last I checked, just fled for her life to the Bronx. We need her to find the Cardinal so we can end his threat once and for all and get on with our lives." My shoulders slumped. "With her gone, I don't know what we're going to do."

Sunil's features darkened like the storm cloud that rested at the core of his soul. "Not to mention, you know who isn't going to be happy at all if we don't come back with the Angel of Harlem."

"No one, including the Cardinal, could find her until she wished it. I have a sinking feeling we won't be seeing her again."

"You might be surprised." Lady Day stepped out of her trademark golden shimmer, reappearing just a few feet from where Sunil and I huddled on the ground. "I guessed that those of you remaining might still require my assistance, so I circled back and watched the rest of the melee from above." She offered me a broad smile. "I must say, Miss Snow, you comported yourself with uncommon bravery."

"Thank you, Lady Day." With a deep breath, I considered my next words carefully. "I'm glad to see that you came through all this relatively unscathed." I quirked my mouth to one side. "I apologize if our presence here in Harlem compromised you in any way."

"Bygones, child, and my apologies for my own poor display." Her voice nearly back to its previous silky smooth delivery, she let out a sad chuckle. "I'm ashamed to admit that I nearly allowed pride and overconfidence to be my downfall after all these years. Trust that I will not underestimate our enemy again, and I pray you learn from my mistake."

"You'll help us, then?"

"I will hear your plea, though I believe I already know what you have come to ask." Her astute eyes dissected me on the spot. "You're here to convince me to help you find the Cardinal so that you may return to the life you remember, but you're here at the behest of another." She drew close. "This other Ascendant, the one you freed. What does he want? Who is he?"

"I don't know," I muttered, my stomach churning, "but like you must have heard, Minako was pretty freaked out by even the suggestion he might be free."

"I did, and she was." The Angel tilted her head forward in a solemn nod. "Does this individual have a name?"

"He calls himself Metis, though I'm pretty sure that's not his actual name."

"Metis," she whispered. "That name triggers...*something* I can't quite place." She pursed her lips in distaste. "Whatever has been stirred in my soul, however, is not a fond memory, I can tell you that much." The Angel rested a gentle hand on my shoulder. "Be careful with this one, Miss Snow, for all our sakes."

Great. Even the Angel didn't know who Metis might be, though the vibe I was getting from her was very similar to the one I'd felt since I'd first met the mysterious Ascendant's dark gaze.

I knew only three things for certain.

First, I wished I'd insisted that Jade had come with us, thinly veiled threats from mysterious Ascendant be damned.

Second, after the barrage of frantic questions from Minako, I prayed that Metis hadn't found a way to get that damned collar off.

And last, the realization that even with the aid of Sumner and her people, Linus and his theriodan pack, and Sunil's powers and knowledge, I was seriously out of my league.

I'd been missing Ethan terribly for months. Not an hour had passed without me imagining his kind eyes, friendly laugh, and that smile that could melt me in an instant.

But in that moment, I wanted Rosemary.

No. *Needed* her.

She would have known exactly what to do next, and I didn't have the first clue.

CHAPTER 21

SECRET SEPARATION

Lady Day sent Sumner and Copeland with a still unconscious Stewart to the nearest emergency room with but a few words and a wave of her hand. As Sumner disappeared within the golden shimmer, my heart skipped a beat. Ascendant or not, having three trained agents with guns watching my back had done a lot for my confidence. I trusted Sunil, and I was coming around regarding Linus and his pack, but I suddenly felt very alone and very exposed.

The Angel moved our impromptu debriefing session from the street to a nearby restaurant with clientele way better dressed than any of us save Lady Day herself. No sooner had we entered the place than she shot the maître d' a quick glance, and in seconds, we were being shown to our own private room. Once behind closed doors, Linus and his theriodans agreed to give us a modicum of privacy as Sunil and I spoke with Lady Day, mostly, I suspected, so that we would honor their privacy when it was their turn to present whatever case they had to the Angel of Harlem.

But first, dinner.

As we tore into the first round of food—all of us were starving by that point—Sunil and I gave Lady Day the play-by-play of how we escaped from the Cardinal's prison; as much detail as we could about the Styx, Charon, and Metis; and the events that led to us showing up in her backyard. She seemed particularly interested in the stark contrast in how the rest of us had been treated—Daichi being drugged to keep his geomantic abilities at bay notwithstanding—and the state in which we'd found Metis: the utter isolation and complete incapacitation, the redundant security measures to keep him from escaping, and the power dampening collar with the built-in explosive, all of it designed to keep him from ever seeing the light of day again.

Or so it seemed.

"Who or what would require such draconian measures?" the Angel wondered. "I imagine the Cardinal would only take such precautions if…"

"If?" I asked. "If what?"

"I must think on this." She looked upon me with a beatific smile. "I know you came all this way to seek my assistance for both yourself as well as your fellow captives, but there are too many unknowns at the moment to even consider sending you and your friends after the Cardinal."

"Will you at least come back with us?" That had been the main thrust of the plan anyway, to bring Lady Day to Boise and then decide upon the next steps once we had a teleporter on our side. "If we bring you with us and you explain to Metis that we simply can't go after the Cardinal in our current state—"

"I'm afraid that I cannot." She offered an apologetic smile. "While I would gladly offer my services to you and Mr. Jayalal, I fear that putting myself anywhere near an individual who elicits such a response from a serial murderer like the Cardinal would be patently unwise." She peered out the window into the New York City night. "I have not lived as long as I have by putting myself in harm's way, despite my show of overconfidence and poor judgment earlier this night."

"I suppose not." My shoulders slumped. "What do we tell Metis when we go back?"

"You can't be serious." She laughed, the husky sound as delightful as everything else about the Angel. "Do not think for an instant that I would send you back to such a problematic figure mere seconds after declining to enter his presence myself. As you implied, returning with nothing to show for your absence will likely bring out a side of this Metis you have not seen nor want to. I fear not only for your safety, but that of the geomancer and empath you spoke of as well." The trepidation in her features faded into cautious hope. "Please, allow me to send you to wherever else you might wish so that you can rally your forces before again facing either of these dangerous men."

"Can you send me to Ethan?" My heart swelled with hope. "You didn't say as much, but I read between the lines of what you said earlier. He came here seeking your help to find me, didn't he?"

"Actually, it was the Delacroix girl, and that was months ago. This man of which you speak, Ethan Harkreader, who carries the Light of Neith? Delacroix said only that he was otherwise occupied and wouldn't elaborate further."

My heart broke a little at the words "otherwise occupied," but there would be time to shed those tears another day.

"Miss Snow...Persephone." She must have read either my face or my thoughts as her stern expression melted into a mother's smile. "If this Ethan Harkreader feels a tenth as strongly for you as I sense you do for him, I can only assume he was merely following another lead in an effort to get back to your side."

"Unless he's already forgotten me."

"Impossible." Her head tilted to one side the way my mother's always did when she was giving me a pep talk. "You, Persephone Snow, are unforgettable."

"Can you send me to him, though? To Ethan?"

"I cannot."

Wow. Wasn't expecting that. "Send me to the Daughter of Neith, then. Send me to Rosemary."

The Angel sighed. "Alas, the same issue prevents me from sending you to Miss Delacroix or Mr. Harkreader today as kept me from sending her to rescue you all those months ago." She took a bite of her food and washed it down with a sip of sparkling Cava. "My ability, you see, is simultaneously limitless and limited. I can send anyone anywhere in the world, and a bit beyond if I'm being honest, but I must know place, person, and time to ensure the individual arrives exactly where, when, and with whom they wish."

"And...you have no idea where Ethan and Rosemary are."

"Precisely. Without knowing either of their locations, or pardon the morbid turn, their current status, you could end up anywhere, and I would not be able to bring you back."

Ah well. Not sure why I thought one thing in this insane goose chase my life had become would come easy. "A question, then? Something's been bugging me since you sent Rupert away. Why must you specify a time? Isn't your request always 'now'?"

"Folding space is relatively easy, but I always specify a moment as well as a location lest I inadvertently incorporate a temporal shift, a lesson I learned the hard way more years ago than I care to remember."

"You can travel through time?" I asked. "That's—"

"Not nearly as impressive as it sounds." Lady Day sipped at her glass of bubbly. "At most, my jaunts have only ever shifted the person involved a few minutes back or ahead, and never predictably. To be honest, it's exhausting enough merely folding space to my will. Time, though? Now that takes its toll."

"So, no Ethan or Rosemary. How about Mr. Delacroix, or Neko, or even L.J.?"

"I've not spoken to anyone in your circle since Miss Delacroix visited me months ago. I am sorry."

"Then where do I go?" I asked. "You can't send me to any of my friends, and we both agree I can't go back to Metis. Do I just stay here with you?"

"This is the Big Apple, child. The Capital of the World, the City of Dreams, the Center of Everything. There are far worse places you could be stranded, I assure you." She studied me, her eyes filled with compassion. "But you don't strike me as the 'bury her head in the sand' type. If you want to find your boyfriend and the rest of your friends, you're going to have to look for them the hard way, but if anyone can do it, it's the woman before me."

"Can you send me home to Montecito?" I asked after running through everything the Angel had taught me about how her abilities worked. "There's no one there, but I can tell you exactly where it is."

"Now, I can certainly do that." She smiled. "Naming a living soul at the other end of a proposed jaunt only aids in my specificity and helps ensure my charge arrives precisely where, when, and with whom they wish, but a place one knows as well as they do their home is practically an entity in and of itself."

"Send me there, then. Sunil as well, if you please." My gaze stole across the room to the table of theriodans. "But not before you assure me you're safe alone with Linus and his pack."

"The embarrassment of our previous skirmish notwithstanding, I have developed a relatively reliable sense about people in general and Ascendant in specific over my many years. Minako and Krage's Murder of Crows were out for blood, but Linus and his pack? They are here to ask for a favor, and just as I have heard you out, so must I grant them an audience to discover exactly why they have come to petition the Angel of Harlem."

"I understand your reasoning for steering clear of Metis, of course, but I wish you could come with us." My chin dropped to my chest. "I feel like we came all this way and are leaving no better off than when we arrived."

"I wouldn't say that." The words were the first Sunil had spoken since we sat at the table. "We have a lot of answers we didn't have before, even if those answers raise an entirely new crop of questions." The rare bit of optimism from the elektromancer took me by surprise.

"And don't forget," the Angel added, "you have acquired a powerful ally and friend. Should you require my aid in the future, you know where to find me."

"Your Sister, Alba, said much the same thing to me back in L.A." And not only that. She'd given me her card, a gilded square stamped with only the four letters of her name and a ten-digit telephone number that now rested at the bottom of my jewelry box in my bedroom closet in Montecito.

Unlike Lady Day's open-ended invitation to return if and when I needed her, Alba's farewell overture had made it more than clear that I was welcome to reach out to her, but that such an alliance would come with serious strings. Regardless, with the Cardinal's people stalking me at one end of the country and Metis, Daichi, and Jade awaiting my return at the other, I needed as much help as I could get. Once back in Montecito, I could be in Los Angeles within a couple of hours where not one but two Angels awaited who might be able and willing to help. Though I relished the thought of seeing Alba again, I wasn't too keen on another encounter with Madame Midnight. As the saying goes, however, any port in a storm.

"I see in your eyes that you have the first inkling of a plan." Lady Day rose from our table. "Shall I send you and Mr. Jayalal on your way, then?"

"Please." I got up from my chair and Sunil stood with me. "Mom always said there's no time like the present."

"In that case, simply state the place where you'd like to be, and I will do the rest."

With a furtive glance into Sunil's dark eyes, I took the elektromancer's hand and locked eyes with the Angel.

"California, Montecito, my living room, with Sunil in tow," and with a finality I didn't expect, one final word. "Now."

"Very well." Lady Day spun her finger before her, her eyes glowing a faint gold as the air filled with static electricity. "Take care, Miss Snow. I suspect we will be seeing each other again, but until then, watch your back." The golden glow emanating from her gaze struck my eyes like the thousands of flashbulbs that had dazzled me on red carpets from coast to coast for years. "And do please send whichever of my Sisters you may encounter my *warmest* regards."

∾

Gravity went sideways as Sunil and I were pulled through a sparkling hole in space. Blinded but a second by the dazzling display, my quickly clearing vision soon revealed that the Angel had done precisely as she had promised. The setting sun poured golden sunbeams through the various west-facing windows, though my living room remained far darker than was typical. The gigantic window I'd installed to look out on the backyard pool the first month after I moved into the house remained boarded up. The Cardinal had shattered the enormous piece of tempered glass when he made his grand entrance six months back, yet another item on his ledger I planned to pay back with interest someday.

"Your house?" Sunil asked.

"Home sweet home."

I rushed to where I always left my phone to charge, but found there only an abandoned cord. Similarly, my tablet and laptop were missing in action. I sensed L.J.'s well-meaning hand in this, but it didn't change the fact that every piece of technology I had with which to contact Ethan, Rosemary, Mr. Delacroix, or anyone was gone.

I used to razz Mom about being a technological dinosaur and laughed at how she still had everyone's phone number from grade school forward stuck between her ears. In that moment, I'd have killed to be able to rattle off Ethan's phone number from memory.

Wait. Phone number.

I rushed up the stairs, praying with every step that whoever had walked off with my entire arsenal of communication devices had at least left behind the hard-won card of the Angel of the Morning.

My jewelry box, once one of my prized possessions along with the various baubles gained from my years in showbiz and the few admirers I'd let close enough to allow such gifts, now mattered only for the golden leafed square of cardboard that rested in the aged mahogany box under a set of pearls that once belonged to my grandmother.

"Where is it?" I whispered as I dug through the rings, bracelets, and necklaces, seeking the prize within. "It's got to be here." I'd almost given up hope when I spotted it there, a golden glimmer at the bottom of the box.

"Got it." I pulled the two-inch square of gold from the red velvet and held it up to the light, grateful I'd put my power bill on automatic draft before I left on the Sparkle Tour. "Now, if only the phone is still working, too."

I stepped around the bed to my nightstand where the only landline telephone in the house rested. I'd told Mom a hundred times I didn't need such an antique in my little casa, but she'd used a combination of scare tactics and a Wynter Snow guilt trip special—something about what if she was calling with an emergency and my phone battery was dead and she never got to say goodbye—and I totally caved.

Looked like my mother, the Gen-X dinosaur, was two-for-two for the day.

I dialed the number quickly, my fingers shaking, and held the receiver to my ear. The phone rang once, twice, three times, my chest growing tighter with each passing second. Whether that was because the woman I was calling hadn't picked up or because she could answer at any moment, I wasn't exactly sure.

"Why, Persephone Snow." Her voice like warm honey, El Ángel del Alba finally answered. "I thought you'd never call."

"How did you—" The question was half out of my mouth before I realized how ridiculous the question was. "Caller ID, right?"

"As far as you know." She laughed, the sound as light and effervescent as a butterfly's wings. "I'm so glad to hear your voice."

My cheeks burned with embarrassment. "I must sound so stupid."

"Now, now, my dear. You've been the captive of a psychopath for the better part of a year, and I've only just learned in the last day that you managed to free yourself and others from the Cardinal's clutches."

I considered her words for a moment. "Daichi?"

"See? Your powers of deduction are as sharp as ever."

"Is he...all right?"

"I might ask you that very question," Alba answered. "He had but a moment to speak and kept his tone hushed. He mentioned your involvement as well as a young empath, an elektromancer, and one other...?"

"Metis. He calls himself Metis."

"Metis?" Alba mused. "Can't say I've heard the name."

"Of course you haven't," I mumbled. Each repetition of the name weighed heavier on my soul, and yet, as with every other time I'd tried to find out more about the mysterious man we'd freed from the Cardinal's underground prison, my efforts amounted to nothing.

"I understand that the elektromancer is with you."

"Sunil Jayalal. He's in the next room."

"Jayalal, eh? Interesting." She paused. "My geomancer and the empath, however, remain with this Metis person?"

I swallowed back the bile in my throat. "Yes."

"I know little to nothing of this man, but between your tone and what I picked up from my short conversation with Daichi, neither he nor the empath girl are safe. I take it you have come to a similar conclusion, thus the phone call that you hoped you'd never have to make." She let me stew on that one for a few seconds before adding, "So, Persephone Snow, what would you ask of me?"

"Help me, please. I'm so far out of my league with all this, I don't know what to do." I bit my lip to keep myself from breaking down right there on the phone. "In a world with people who can call lightning from the sky, summon their inner beasts to come out and play, or send their very shadows after me, all I've got is my song."

"All?" the Angel asked. "Sweet child. You have no idea the power of your singular voice. Why do you think the entire Ascendant world was pursuing you earlier this year? Delightful though you are in person, it wasn't for your sparkling personality."

"Everyone keeps saying things like that, but no one will tell me what it means."

"What it means is that there is power in your words, your voice, your song; power that remains virtually untapped because you're too afraid to explore your potential."

"Hey." My cheeks burned at her proclamation. "I'll have you know I charmed an entire room of Ascendant and got them working together with but a single sentence, and then sent Minako and Krage's skiomancers packing with nothing but a couple of random lyrics from my mother's favorite radio station." My heart pounded in my chest. "Not bad for a—what was it Krage called me?—a 'juvenile Ascendant'?"

"I am glad to hear it." A singular laugh came across the line. "And even more glad to hear the fire back in your tone. You may be inexperienced compared to the majority of Ascendant, but you are not now nor have you ever been even remotely out of your league in relation to the others you've mentioned. Do you understand?"

"I see what you did there." The same trick my therapist pulled on me back when I was struggling with imposter syndrome during the second season of *Teen Spies*. "Point made, Alba. Thank you." I pulled in a deep breath to center myself, another trick from the same therapist, not to mention Rosemary. "Regardless, I still need your help."

"Indeed you do. I've already dispatched a car to pick up you and Mr. Jayalal at your home in Montecito. They should arrive by the top of the hour to bring you to Los Angeles so we can continue this conversation in person."

"Oh." I checked the clock. Ten minutes tops until I needed to be ready to go. "Thank you again."

"My pleasure." Several heartbeats passed before she spoke again. "I would very much like our relationship to move forward."

"Of course." I hated myself for what I was about to ask, but there was something I needed to know. "If I may inquire," I murmured quietly, "what sort of obligation comes with this assistance? I know that you were very keen to bring me to your side when we first met, but with everything happening the way it did, you didn't get exactly what you wanted."

"Newton's third law teaches that for every action there is an equal and opposite reaction. I do not help you today simply out of the generosity of my heart. I help you because you asked me for help. I help you because it is the right thing to do. I help you because it is in my best interest and the interest of one of my own to do so. And, to be honest, I help you because I want you to understand that in this world of gods and goddesses among men, you have friends."

I prepared to speak again, but before I could utter a word, she finished her thought.

"I pray, Miss Snow, that you *never* forget who your friends are in this world. Do I make myself clear?"

"Crystal."

I ended the call, packed a few items into a medium-sized suitcase, and joined Sunil in the kitchen where he was snacking on some leftover chips he'd found in the pantry.

"So," he asked, "you get what you came for?"

"Yes," I answered as I poured myself a glass of water, my hands trembling at the implications of my conversation with the second Angel of the day. "And apparently, a whole lot more."

CHAPTER 22

RUN LIKE HELL

I half expected the Driver to show up at my door at the wheel of his stretch limousine, all detailed and immaculate with its Mercedes logo glistening in the glow of the lights along my street. When he'd arrived on the scene back in Denver after my second attempted kidnapping in as many days, I was terrified out of my mind and convinced I'd never feel safe again.

Inside that finely-tuned machine of his, I'd been proven wrong. It hadn't hurt that I had a trained bodyguard, his kick-ass ninja daughter, and my own personal superhero sitting alongside me, but there was something about simply being in the Driver's presence that quelled my every fear, calmed my racing heart, and gave me hope that I would see the following day. He'd never shown any particular abilities like the other Ascendant I'd encountered—other than a baritone voice I suspected registered somewhere on the Richter scale and the smoothest driving I'd ever experienced—and yet, the reverence with which his name was spoken by Angels, skiomancers, and elementalists alike told me all I needed to know.

Nothing would have pleased me more than to spend the next two hours en route to Los Angeles feeling totally secure for the first time in three months. The green Subaru Outback at least a decade old that pulled up outside my house and honked the horn, however, was anything but a black German-built limousine.

At least there would be plenty of room for my stuff.

"You sure this is the person we're waiting for?" Sunil asked.

I checked the clock. Two past the hour.

"Unless the bad guys have tapped my phone line, I don't think—" I stopped before finishing the rest of the ridiculous thought. I'd met or seen in action not one but two people who could literally control machines with their thoughts and speak to them as if they were people. Honestly, it would have been more surprising if my phone line wasn't tapped.

Was the person waiting outside legit my ride and I was only psyching myself out? Or had the twelve minutes since I got off the phone with the Angel been enough for someone to intercept my driver and get to my house?

"Miss Snow?" The strangely familiar voice sounded from beyond my door, followed by a loud knock and a ring of the doorbell. "If you can hear me, we've got to go. Clock's ticking."

"Do you know this person?" Sunil asked.

"Maybe." I shook my head. "Can't quite place the voice." I chuckled. "Though half-recognized voices have been the standard for the last day or two."

"You going to answer the door?" Sunil asked.

"If it were anyone we should be worried about, I don't think they'd be letting a door stand in their way."

"If you're there, open up." The voice, not the Driver's earthshaking baritone but definitely male, again tickled the neurons at the back of my brain. "Our mutual friend asked me to get you to Los Angeles ASAP, and we should probably get going before anyone else shows up, if you catch my drift."

"Our 'mutual friend' wouldn't send just anyone to pick me up." I crept closer to my front door, but made sure to stand to one side, as I'd seen more than one knocked off its hinges in the preceding days. "Identify yourself."

"You don't recognize my voice?" A laugh tinged with a hint of hurt sounded from beyond the door. "It's me, Dino."

Dino? Holy shit. Ethan's backstage pal Dino.

Who, now that I thought about it, was one of the first of us to knock out a skiomancer. He basically proved himself ride-or-die back when all this started. Still, I hadn't seen him since the night I Ascended. Why the hell was he, of all people, standing on my doorstep?

I opened the door.

"Dino!" Though I barely knew the man, I threw my arms around him as if he were my long lost brother. "What are you doing here?"

Dino froze in my arms, obviously not expecting such a warm welcome. "Like I said, I'm here to drive you to Los Angeles."

"But I've only just spoken to the Angel. How did you get here so fast?"

"Alba texted me." He glanced toward his ride. "Said it was time, so I hopped in my car and came to get you."

"Time?"

"When Ethan couldn't find you in the backwoods of Idaho—and they turned that place upside down, believe you me—he, Rosemary, and Mr. Delacroix mobilized every single person who knows the real deal with you and not all the bullshit on the news."

"What bullshit?"

"You don't even want to know." Dino let out a quiet sigh. "Anyway, I've been staying a couple blocks from your house ever since, on the off-chance you or someone who knew where you were showed up." He looked past my shoulder and quickly assumed a defensive stance. "Wait. Who's that with you?"

"Sunil Jayalal," I tilted forward in a polite bow, "this is Ethan's friend, Dino."

Sunil approached the open doorway but, other than a grunted hello, didn't extend anything resembling cordiality.

"Mr. Jayalal." Dino bowed his head politely, but also kept a respectful distance, all the while avoiding eye contact.

"Wait." My brain made a connection. "The Angel herself sent you to me?"

"Well, yes."

Wow. Dino had moved up significantly in the world since I last saw him. "And I'm guessing she put you up in a house nearby to watch for me?"

"You nailed it. I've been staying here in Montecito, Neko has been staying with your mother, L.J. has been—"

"Neko's been staying with Mom?"

"Last I heard."

"My gay tiger BFF has been staying with Wynter Snow."

"For the last few months, unless something has changed."

I'd left Mom that message when I called from Idaho. Did that mean Neko knew I was free? Had he told Ethan?

"Can you call Neko?" My brain made the next logical jump. "Or Ethan?"

"Sure. I've got both numbers on speed dial."

My heart leaped in my chest. "Can we call Ethan now?" Desperation rose in my voice, and my eyes threatened to tear up. "Like, *right* now?"

"You can call from the car. Right now, we need to get on the road."

"Can't that wait just a second?" My pulse raced and I felt momentarily dizzy. "Ethan doesn't even know that I'm alive, and I really need to hear his voice."

Before Dino could answer, a whirring sound from far above filled the air.

"Crap. Not already." Dino looked skyward, squinting into the darkening sky. "How could they have made it here so soon?"

"Who?" I asked. "Who's after me now?"

Another whirring sound, this one higher pitched, joined the first. I caught a hint of movement just above the residence across the street and a flash of light on metal before whoever or whatever it was disappeared behind the house's second floor.

"We've got to go *now*." Dino took my hand and locked gazes with Sunil before pulling me toward the green Subaru. "Come on."

Far from the somewhat timid man I'd met on my previous impromptu road trip, this Dino seemed to have been taking lessons from Ethan.

"Where are we—"

"For the last time," Dino said as he dragged me across my yard, "Los Angeles." He grunted in frustration. "And now we've got Redstarts on our tail."

"Redstarts?"

"The Midnight Angel has her Ravens and Alba her elementalists, both based out of L.A." Dino opened the passenger door to his car, shoved me into the seat, and closed the door behind me. Sunil had barely made it into the back seat before Dino dove behind the wheel, turned the ignition, and jetted out of my neighborhood with the pedal to the floor. "There are similar groups all over the world."

"Northwest Africa is Redstart territory," Sunil added. "They rarely set foot out of Morocco, unless the price is right."

"Exactly." Something metallic struck the road in front of us, and Dino swerved into the left lane to avoid hitting whatever it was. "And their presence in Montecito over the last twenty-four hours would suggest just that."

I sucked in a breath as Dino hung a sharp left two blocks from my house and sent the Subaru up on two wheels for a long couple of seconds.

"Wow, someone took a crash course in driving," I whispered, then slightly louder, "not to mention Ascendant stuff." I peered over at Dino. "How have you picked up so much so fast? Seven months ago, you'd never even heard the word Ascendant."

Hell, neither had I.

"I didn't have time to explain before," Dino muttered as he took another sharp turn, this one to the right, and barreled down Route 192 East out of town. "I work for Jim Bradley now."

Jim Bradley was Chief of Security at the Santa Barbara Airport and a relatively high-ranking muckety-muck in one of the multiple secret organizations on the planet I never knew existed until all this madness began. Other than our brief interaction at my house as I worked to keep his and Mr. Delacroix's chest-beating contest from boiling over just before the Cardinal swooped in and stole me away, my knowledge of Bradley was minimal. Rosemary had assured me he was one of the good guys, at least to the best of her knowledge, and Ethan had seemed to have confidence in the man.

Figuring out who to trust and who to watch or avoid was becoming a full-time job. For God's sake, I'd allied myself with the theriodans who tried to take me in Vegas and was seeking help from the very Angel who'd sent her emissaries to abduct me in Denver. I'd confided in Jade, accepted Daichi despite our history, grudgingly became friends with stormy Sunil, and trusted Sumner, Stewart, and Copeland with my life, though I knew little more about them than what they'd told me.

But who was I kidding? Of my entire circle of the last few days, only one made my skin crawl, and knowing I'd left poor Jia Li and Daichi alone with him had plagued my thoughts from the moment we left Boise. I sent up a silent prayer that the collar Minako had been so obsessed with remained intact and that the two of them were okay. If we all made it through this, I swore to make it up to them.

One person I did trust was the man behind the wheel hopefully rocketing me to safety. Ethan's buddy, Dino, had shown uncommon bravery on more than one occasion, especially as the one normie among a crowd of super-powered heroes and villains, nearly taking a bullet for me on more than one occasion. And now, it seemed, a bit of Ethan's superhero style had rubbed off on his pal.

My tangential train of thought came to an abrupt halt along with the car as we left Montecito and took the ninety-degree curve heading south toward Toro Canyon at better than seventy miles an hour. A traffic jam on the tiny two-lane road forced Dino to slam on the brakes.

"Shit," Sunil muttered. "We're screwed."

"Not on my watch." Dino stepped on the gas and began weaving back and forth across the double yellow line between cars on both sides like an NFL quarterback on crack. Regardless, the congestion on the road slowed us enough to allow the attack from above to resume.

Flash after flash of the objects rained down as if we were caught in a metallic hailstorm. One of the projectiles pierced the roof of Dino's Subaru, revealing the silver tip of what could only be described as a feather fashioned from razor-sharp steel. What the hell was it with these people and birds, anyway?

"Redstarts out of Morocco, huh? What the hell do they want?"

"What everyone wants." Dino glanced in my direction before returning his frantic gaze to the road to navigate around a big blue dump truck, barely missing the oncoming BMW with its high beams and blaring horn. "You."

"Yeah, I get that, but who is this particular group working for? The Cardinal? Or maybe someone worse?"

"Your guess is as good as mine." Dino steered the car onto the rare bit of shoulder at our right to bypass the last bit of the long snarl of cars before yanking the wheel back onto relatively open road and punching the accelerator. "Bradley got word about you linking up with agents of the Order in Boise and your subsequent trip to New York. I was already prepped in case you showed up, and then Alba called. As for how the Redstarts knew you were not only free from the Cardinal's clutches but headed for Montecito, I have no idea."

"So, yet another band of Ascendant mercenaries is after my scalp. Great."

"The sky is so dark, I can't even see them." Sunil peered out the open window at the heavens above, electricity crackling at his fingertips. "If any of them get close enough, though, I can try to bring them down."

"I'm not sure firing lightning bolts from a moving vehicle is the best idea," Dino said. "You fry the electronics of my Subaru, we're screwed."

"I've been manipulating electricity since I was a boy," Sunil grumbled. "I'm not going to hurt your little car."

"Still, let's hold off on doing anything too drastic unless we have to." Dino kept his white-knuckled fists at ten and two as he rocketed around a wide curve to the left and hopped onto US-101. "I've got this."

The four-lane highway was relatively clear as evening approached, affording far more room to maneuver than the winding two-lane road we'd left in our rearview mirror. Dino sent his green chariot racing down the highway, shifting lanes back-and-forth and dodging the other motorists as if the Devil himself were hot on our heels. A couple minutes passed without further evidence of attack from above, and I allowed myself the fool's luxury of believing we might be in the clear.

That's when the transfer truck three vehicles ahead in the left lane whipped into the concrete median only to bounce back across to the right shoulder, its trailer coming to rest diagonally across both southbound lanes and bringing all traffic to a halt. Concrete barriers to our left and right hemmed us in, and the quickly growing mass of cars behind us blocked our only other escape route.

In other words, there I was, yet again, trapped on a stretch of highway with superhuman kidnappers coming for the bounty on my head.

Or, as I'd started calling it, Tuesday.

"What's the call?" Sunil asked, the electric popping between his fingers escalating in volume. "Do we stay in the car and wait for them to come for us or prepare to fight?"

Dino glanced my way, as if I were the one in charge. "What do you think? Do we stay put or get ready to rumble?"

"Don't look at me. You're the one delivering me to the City of Angels under the orders of the Angel of the Morning. I'm just a passenger." Another of the steel feathers impacted the hood of the Subaru with a loud clang. "Not to mention, the target."

"Target, maybe," Sunil grumbled from the back seat, "but just a passenger? You're way past that, Snow." He kept his eyes on the sky, electricity crackling at his fingertips. "The sooner you start accepting who and what you are, the better off we're all going to be." He opened his car door and stepped out onto the darkened highway. "Anyway, I only know these Redstarts by reputation. Let's see if they live up to the hype."

"You heard the man." Dino shrugged with a quiet laugh and exited the vehicle as well. "Let's do this."

What the hell? Majority rules.

I joined Sunil and Dino at the rear of the car, the two of them visually scouring the skies to either side as I peered up and down the highway for any sign of our attackers. Traffic was already backed up several hundred yards, and the roar of all the engines punctuated by the staccato honking of horns made it difficult to detect the telltale whirring sound of whatever technology the Redstarts were using to fly.

We needn't have worried, as they didn't keep us waiting for long. Landing with the grace of a trio of trained ballet dancers, the three Redstarts dropped from the still-darkening sky and surrounded us. The two women and man were decked out in stylish paramilitary garb straight from a designer's runway, jet-black and red-breasted with bright white accent stripes to resemble the songbirds I guessed were their namesake. Quiet jetpacks were strapped to each of their backs while their wrists and feet sported metallic bracers and high-tech boots with tiny jets they used to maneuver as they descended from above. As each lit around us, the whirring hum that was their harbinger cut out and only the sound of car engines, the occasional honking horn, and the gasps of various onlookers broke the relative silence.

"Persephone Snow," spoke the tall dark-skinned woman with waist-length braids standing directly in front of us, my name pronounced in a way I'd never heard before. "Come with us now, and any further unpleasantries can be avoided."

I'd heard that one before.

"No harm will befall you," spoke the shorter of the two women, her accent similar to the first woman's. Her shorn head showed off a perfectly shaped skull and unmatched features. "While we will brook no opposition, we have every intention of bringing you in not only alive, but without blemish."

I'd heard that one before as well.

"Under whose orders?" I asked. "The Cardinal's?" I cocked my head to one side. "He's already kidnapped me twice." I shot them a sarcastic smile. "Couldn't exactly keep me, though, as you can see."

"We would never work for that butcher," the first woman said. "Never."

"He extinguished the life of one of our own," the second woman added, "an affront we do not take lightly."

"As for your question, our reasons must, for the time being, remain our own." The slender man with skin like mahogany spoke with the thickest accent of all, a hint of French coloring his words and differentiating his speech from his partners'. "But please understand that we mean you no harm."

The third familiar sentiment completed the hopeful headhunter hat trick.

"I've got news for you three," I spoke, hand on hip and head cocked to the side in what was becoming my standard stance for discussing matters with Ascendant. "When you start blowing up trucks and stopping traffic on major highways just to get someone to meet with your client, the whole 'no harm will befall you' sentiment falls kind of flat."

"To be fair," the taller of the two women said, "we've not blown up anything. We merely maneuvered a relatively immovable object into your path to prevent you from fleeing."

"The driver of the truck remains unharmed, if not a bit curious as to why he suddenly finds himself stopped diagonally across a major highway." The male Redstart smiled at me, the expression nowhere near as kindly as it might have seemed under other circumstances. "That I can guarantee."

"So, you're keeping it to minor property damage and what is shaping up to be a pretty horrendous traffic jam." I shot the trio of Ascendant my most withering look. "You three should petition for sainthood."

"You have no idea," the other woman chuckled. "Compared to many Ascendant we've encountered over the years, my two associates and I embody the very definition of restraint."

"Enough talk." Sunil stepped forward, a bright bolt of electricity arcing between his hands. "Let's see how well your little jet packs work after I—"

"Enough, indeed." The female Redstart with the shorn scalp silenced Sunil with a simple raised fist, my elektromancer friend suddenly frozen in place as if he were a living statue. "Now, Miss Snow, where were we?"

CHAPTER 23

HYPNOTIZE ME

"What have you done to Sunil?" I asked as the bright arc between his fingers cut out, leaving my eyes poorly adjusted to the relative darkness. "Is this what you meant by 'no harm'?"

"Your elektromancer friend is fine, I assure you." The Redstart let her hand drop to her side, and Sunil pulled in a gasping breath.

"I couldn't move." Sunil looked my way, rare fear blossoming across his features. "Or breathe."

"Understand, however, that if he raises a hand against us again, I will hold him in stasis until he loses consciousness."

Stasis, huh? I couldn't wait to find out what the other two could do.

We each have our talents. The voice of the taller woman tickled my mind more than my ears. *My apologies, Miss Snow, but your thoughts are an open book to one such as me.*

She was reading my thoughts like words on a page. What did Ethan call that particular talent? Telepathy?

Precisely, came the selfsame voice, making my internal monologue suddenly a dialogue for the first time in my life.

Great. No sneaking up on this one.

Two for two, Miss Snow. The woman before us gave me a slight bow as she continued our mental conversation. *Not that different from your own talent, and yet oceans apart. In the future, if and when our goals are not in direct opposition, I'd be willing to work with you to help develop your rare abilities.*

Wow, that was quite the generous offer. If only it hadn't occurred in the middle of my fifth or sixth kidnapping attempt this year.

"So," I spoke aloud, locking gazes with the tall telepath, "one of you ladies reads thoughts and the other controls bodies." I shifted my eyes to the man among the Redstarts. "What exactly do *you* bring to the table?"

"Who do you think sent the truck careening into the median?" The rail-thin man offered me a polite bow. "Your pop culture calls what I do telekinesis, though I prefer to think of it as simply mind over matter taken to the ultimate degree."

"So, telekinesis, telepathy, and mind control." I kept spouting words that prior to the last few months had merely been fodder for comic books, television, and movies. "You're all psychic, then?"

"We are called psychomancers, Miss Snow, but yes." The shorter of the two women stepped forward, the glow of the sea of headlights reflecting off her naked scalp. "The powers of the mind are nearly as varied as those of the Ascendant as a whole, but we three do represent a sliver of the range of such talents among our kind." She paused, her lips parting in a smile. "Or, more accurately, Persephone Snow, we *four.*"

So, if I was picking up what she was putting down, my being a siren meant that I too was a psychomancer. I hadn't thought of my song that way, but it made sense.

As the conversation went on, something struck me as odd. A few motorists had exited their cars and were wandering the highway while, across the median, northbound rubberneckers were slowing to check out the nearly jack-knifed tractor trailer. Not one of them, however, seemed to notice the world-famous pop star standing by a man with lightning dancing between his fingers in a standoff with a trio straight out of an old Janet Jackson video.

"You wonder why no one can see us." The tall telepath smiled as she transitioned our conversation from mouth to mind. *My mind can broadcast images just as easily as it broadcasts words.* She motioned all around us. "As far as these sheep are concerned," she spoke aloud, "you three remain in your car, stuck in the same snarl of traffic as the rest. And as for my associates and me? They don't see us at all."

"This is all fascinating," Dino interrupted, the first words he'd said since we exited the car, "but did you seriously stop traffic on a major highway just to compare notes on Ascendant abilities?"

The telepath shot Dino a withering look. "You are truly fortunate, boy, that your significance is so minimal I can't bear the thought of wasting an ounce of mental energy putting you in your place."

"I'll show you insignificant." In a moment that existed firmly on the border between courage and stupidity, Dino drew a pistol from his belt and did his best to channel his inner Luc Delacroix. "You have exactly ten seconds to vacate the area and let us pass or—"

Like Sunil moments before, Dino's entire body froze, his arms and legs going into spasm as he fell to one side on the asphalt. His gun skittered across the concrete like a skipped stone and came to rest beneath a blue SUV.

Sunil raised a hand at the controller among the bunch only to drop to his knees a moment later, his palms flying to his temples as if he suddenly had the worst migraine in history.

Be warned, Miss Snow. I can speak thoughts into minds, the telepath whispered to me mentally, *or I can shout them.*

"Leave them alone." I attempted to step forward only to find myself frozen in place, though my experience seemed different than what happened to both Sunil and Dino. I still felt in control and continued to breathe, but my arms and legs were held fast as if by some invisible force. Before I could process what was happening, my body rose into the air and levitated forward until I floated helpless before the male Redstart.

"We'd hoped you'd come peacefully, but if you're intent on doing this the hard way…"

I'd had enough. I peered down at my telekinetic captor, pulled in a breath, and belted out a melodious command from another decade.

"*Please, release me,*" I sang from the bottom of my soul, "*let me go…*"

The force holding me aloft immediately abated, dropping me to the highway. I focused every iota of my attention on the thin man standing over me and, with a grim smile, sang a line from "Hurricane," one of the lesser known songs from my first album.

"*Torn apart by the winds of fate, hurled to the east and west…*"

No sooner had the words left my lips than the man turned his telekinetic abilities on his two partners, flinging the tall telepath with braids across the concrete bunker at the edge of the shoulder and the bald body-snatching mind-witch across the median and into oncoming traffic. Both engaged their flight equipment and jetted into the sky, but the momentary break in their concentration was all we needed. Dino retreated to his car and prepared our getaway as the transfer truck driver finished maneuvering his tractor-trailer back onto the road. Sunil took advantage of the brief respite and fired a bolt of lightning at the body-controlling Redstart, no doubt in an effort to make sure he never had to experience her brand of psychic ability ever again.

"Come on," Dino shouted, as the cars in front of us began to disperse, "let's go!"

"*If I run, do not follow, if I leave, just let me go…*" Another lyric, this one from the *Sparkle* album. My intent in writing "Leave Me Be" was more a chronicle of the aftermath of a heartbreak, but the words served our current predicament well. I just hoped the Redstarts heard my sung command.

I leaped into the car's front seat as Sunil dove into the back, and both doors were scarcely closed before Dino slammed his foot on the gas and we rocketed away. Barely squeezing between the concrete median and the stalled Pontiac occupying the left lane in front of us, we flew down the highway as fast as traffic would allow. With a mad combination of expert wheel handling, aggressive use of the accelerator, and selective horn bursts, Dino quickly cleared a path and got us to the front of the pack. The highway stretched empty before us, and if Dino had told me his Subaru sprouted wings, I would have at least peeked out the window to check. Sunil and I kept our eyes on the sky as Dino kept his on the road, and...nothing. Again, I foolishly allowed myself to believe we'd escaped, at least until the next exit approached and Dino took his foot off the accelerator, flipped on his blinker, and pulled into the deceleration lane.

"What are you doing, Dino?" I asked. "We need to get to L.A."

"We weren't done talking with you, Miss Snow." Dino's words, suddenly flavored with the accent of the Redstart telepath, sent an icy spike straight through my heart. "My associate has assumed control of your friend's limbs, and therefore your vehicle, while I speak to you with his lips, tongue, and vocal cords."

"No!" I shouted. "Leave him alone!"

"Don't try to exit your car, as you will find your doors and windows will not open; our third has seen to that. Nor should you attempt to break our hold over the driver, as I cannot guarantee your safety were he to suddenly awaken behind the wheel of a moving vehicle."

I kept my silence and focused on the passing scenery, not wanting to give the telepath anything more to work with than she already had, though I recognized at my core that she'd already proven more than capable of scraping my thoughts straight from the source.

Right again, came a whisper across what was usually my inner monologue. *Like I said before, your mind is an open book to me.*

Great. How do you defeat someone who knows what you're going to do or say as soon as you think it?

"That's simple." The telepath again spoke through Dino. "You don't."

We came to the end of the exit, turned right at a light, and immediately into a 76 gas station. Dino, under the control of both the unseen telepath and her body-snatcher accomplice, drove around the building and parked the car in the back. The car door locks all flipped up at once, though no one in the vehicle had touched a thing.

"Get out of the car, both of you," Dino spoke again with the telepath's tone and inflection, "and wait by the corner of the building."

My hand went subconsciously for the door handle, eliciting a raised eyebrow from Sunil.

"You sure that's the best move?" he asked.

"We don't have much of a choice," I answered. "And at least they're asking. They could be taking over our bodies like they have with poor Dino." I returned his raised brow. "And I get the impression you wouldn't like that one bit."

Without another word, we each exited the car and moved to the back corner of the gas station, away from both the highway and the local road. The lights along the rear of the parking lot provided sufficient illumination to see, and despite the terror of the moment, part of me considered myself lucky that at least the shadows at my feet remained still. A subdued Dino took position between Sunil and me, a silent guard as we all awaited the arrival of those who controlled both his words and actions.

As before, we didn't have long to wait.

One by one, the Redstarts landed around us: first the man who could move people and things with his mind, then the controller who'd driven Dino's body no differently than Dino had driven his Subaru, and finally the telepath whose voice I was already tired of hearing, regardless from whose mouth it spewed.

The body snatcher tossed a tiny package to Dino, who grabbed it out of the air. Still under the woman's control, Dino opened the package and pulled out a device similar to the silencer the Cardinal had forced me to wear when he first tried to take me back in Montecito.

"Oh, hell no," I got out before I could stop myself.

"A security measure," came the woman's voice from Dino's lips. "One that we should have instituted before."

"Not happening." I backed away from Dino and dropped into a fighting stance that Rosemary taught me. "You might be in control of Dino's body, bitch, but he's still just a man who…"

My voice trailed off as a possessed Dino produced his pistol from his back waistband. I specifically remembered the handgun flying from his grip during our highway fight and ending up beneath a big SUV, but unfortunately for us, Dino had managed to retrieve his weapon before we left.

"Understand, Miss Snow. We need you alive and well, and unless you force our hand, we have no intention of harming you in any way." Dino mouthed the telepath's words as his trembling arm leveled the weapon at Sunil. "Your elektromancer friend, however? Not so much. Unless, of course, you'd like to see him—"

The sentence was cut short by a spark of electricity that leaped from the ground at Dino's feet and struck his hand, sending the pistol flying, its tumbling arc ending atop the gas station roof.

"Not much I can do against telepaths and puppet masters," Sunil grumbled, "but no one is pointing a gun at Sunil Jayalal tonight." He glanced my way. "You sure you don't want me to light them up?" Electricity arced between his outstretched hands. "It would be my sincere pleasure."

"How adorable." The one Sunil called puppet master laughed aloud. "You two believe this represents a stalemate of sorts." She raised a hand, and my entire body stiffened for the second time that night. As bad as having my limbs manipulated by their telekinetic had been—like being manhandled by half a dozen invisible creeps— the sensation of someone taking over the motor control of my body was infinitely worse, and infinitely more terrifying.

"Now, my three little marionettes." She spun her finger in the air. "Dance for me."

As a little girl, I'd been obsessed with ballet. Mom took me to *The Nutcracker* every Christmas and once to see *Swan Lake*. Tchaikovsky and I went way back.

One time, Mom took me to see a double feature of sorts, the first and second ballets of another Russian composer named Igor Stravinsky. *The Firebird* was first, and reminded me a lot of the two Tchaikovsky ballets: the mythical settings, the magic, the monsters, the mayhem.

But the second? *Petrushka* takes place in St. Petersburg, Russia during a holiday called the Shrovetide Fair. A Charlatan arrives in town during the first act and unveils a collection of puppets that he subsequently brings to life with a magical flute: two men and a woman. The three dance at the Charlatan's whim for the remainder of the ballet, and the ending is anything but happy.

One thing stuck out very clearly in my memory: For the puppets brought to life, their every movement, regardless of the joy in their expression or the spring in their step, was torture under the thumb of their cruel master.

Entertaining to watch, but terrible to experience. Step by excruciating step, the puppet master Redstart forced the three of us to come to her side. Sunil's hands remained pinned at his sides, and though my peripheral vision could pick up the strain in his enraged gaze, the bitch had forced his face into a goofy grin. Same with Dino, who she had skipping forward as if he were a child playing hopscotch.

And me? The puppet master didn't waste an ounce of mental energy humiliating me, opting instead to have me simply put one foot in front of the other in my inexorable march toward captivity. My body was hers to command, and even if I managed to assert a bit of control, the telekinetic was positioned to put me in my place, not that I could execute any sort of plan when my every thought was open game to their telepath.

My every thought.

"I can speak thoughts into minds," the telepath had made plain, "or I can shout them." Was it too much of a stretch to imagine I could sing mine?

Hey, mind-witch, I thought as hard as I could. *Can you hear me?*

Horrifying, isn't it, her mental voice dripped with faux concern, *losing control over your own limbs and lungs and lips?*

You tell me. Lyrics leaped into my mind, and I sang them in my thoughts as if I were performing before a sold-out crowd.

Listen, as my words take root within your mind...

No!

Hear me, as your will to my every wish I bind...

No...

Free us, unleash your mental scream anew...

Echoes of her onslaught ripped across our mental link, painful for me but clearly excruciating for the other two Redstarts as both dropped to their knees in agony in the face of the unexpected telepathic assault.

Then stand aside as we bid you all a fond adieu.

"What the hell, Snow?" Sunil reassumed control of his muscles, stretching as if he'd just awakened from a forty-year nap, and surveyed the Redstarts, the two on either side of the braided telepath writhing in agony on the filthy asphalt while their torturer stood stock-still with a distant look in her dark eyes. "Did you do this?"

"Telepathy is a two-way street, apparently." I rushed for the car and motioned for Sunil and Dino to follow. "When your quarry's song can compel anyone to do anything they want, probably not the best idea to let them inside your head."

"She won't make that mistake again." Dino leaped behind the wheel and the three of us took off yet again. "Fortunately, we're out of here. Next stop, Los Angeles."

Several minutes passed with Dino's hands trembling despite his firm grip on the wheel as he navigated US 101 southeast, the Pacific Ocean appearing intermittently just beyond my window until we hit Ventura and the highway turned inland. Road signs for El Rio, Camarillo, and Lynn Ranch passed as we headed for Thousand Oaks with L.A. proper just ahead. The view alternated between businesses, homes, and undeveloped areas, with long stretches obscured by brick sound walls as we drew closer to our final destination.

"Almost there," Dino muttered, and as if in mocking answer, a sudden and strong headwind struck the car, slowing us to half our normal speed. The few other cars around us seemed unaffected and jetted past, leaving us all alone for a few seconds. "Ah," he said, "right on time."

"Right on time?" I asked as Dino pulled over on the shoulder. "What are you talking about?"

"Our escort. He's here to make sure the remainder of our trip remains as uneventful as the last half hour."

An insanely powerful gust of wind out of nowhere on the highway to Los Angeles en route to a rendezvous with El Ángel del Alba could mean only one man. As I stepped out of the car, Dietrich

Falco, dressed in his trademark white suit, Chuck Taylors, and mirrored shades, descended from the night sky, his hair pulled back in a tight ponytail, and landed silently before us.

"Persephone Snow," he said, his German accent colored with uncharacteristic warmth. "I wasn't sure I'd ever see those lovely blue eyes again."

"Hello, Dietrich." I inhaled to shout at him, angry at the unnecessary display of power and for stopping us dead on the highway, but then I noticed what he cradled in his arms as if he held a newborn baby. "Understand that we're going to have a little chat later, but first, I've got to know. Is that what I think it is?"

"Mistress Alba sent me to accompany you the rest of the way. With the late hour, I guessed you three might be famished, so I stopped for dinner." He held before him a tray of drinks and a stuffed white paper bag with red letters just visible in the highway's low light. "Hope everybody likes In-N-Out."

CHAPTER 24

TURN TO YOU

"Harkreader is going to flip." Falco held the door for me, a perfect gentleman, and escorted me inside Alba's place while Sunil and Dino waited outside. "He's never given up hope despite all evidence about your fate pointing to the worst."

"What do you mean by that?" I asked. "I'm right here, and I'm fine."

"Six months is six months, Snow. A lot can happen." He paused. "A lot has happened."

Almost verbatim what Stewart said.

"I'm sorry, but are you forgetting I was buried in a hole the entire time?"

"Buried, we figured. But alive? Pretty big shock, honestly. And no one's going to be more shocked than Harkreader."

My chest clenched. "Is everything all right? You know, with Ethan?"

"He's fine." Falco cleared his throat as he led me down an art-filled hallway reminiscent of walking through MoMA in New York. "It's just that things are different now. Complicated."

I hated the fact that the first face that filtered across my memory at that statement was Rosemary's. "What do you mean, 'complicated'?"

"Harkreader searched for you for months. North America, Europe, Asia, Africa. No matter the setback or dead end, he kept going, even when some of us frankly told him to stop." Falco held his tongue for half a second and cleared his throat before continuing. "Hell, we had to drag him off that mountain in Idaho."

"I saw you all trying to find me, you know." Something terrible waited at the end of this conversation. Something I didn't want to know, but something I needed to hear. "On the Cardinal's viewscreen the day of the fight, before he sent me away to his version of hell."

"We stayed in the wilderness of Idaho for days and didn't find a single clue as to where you might be. Minako was anything but forthcoming, regardless of the methods used to get her to talk. We knew something was up when Daichi vanished not long after arriving, and even then, nothing."

"I'm sure Alba has already told you," I offered, "but the Cardinal had Daichi imprisoned along with me." His silence was all the answer I needed.

We turned down another hallway, the urgency in Falco's steps increasing with every step.

"After Idaho, those of us in the know spread out over the globe, searching for any hint as to your whereabouts. We followed every lead, every whisper, and each led to a dead end, particularly the one that led us to your kidnapper himself."

"The Cardinal." I shivered. "Did he hurt Ethan?" I asked breathlessly. "Or Rosemary? Or any of our people?"

"Physically, no, but he did break your man in the cruelest manner possible."

"He told Ethan I was dead."

"You heard."

"Yeah. I just don't understand why Ethan believed him."

"He didn't want to." Falco continued down the hallway with me close on his heels. "It was a month or so after your capture. The Cardinal told him it happened as the two of you were vacating his latest base of operation because Harkreader, Delacroix, and the rest of your friends had yet again gotten too close. He said he was flying with you under his arm, that you struggled, that you...fell."

"Fell." I ran a quick gaze down my body, frustrated and incredulous. "Well, clearly that was a lie. I'm fine." I noted the extra muscle I'd put on my arms and upper body working out daily for half a year and wondered what both Ethan and Rosemary would think. "Better than ever, in fact." The other shoe in my mind dropped with a resounding thud. "So, that's it? Ethan thinks I'm dead."

"He never fully accepted it, but that's about to become a non-issue." Falco pulled his phone from his pocket. "I've been texting him and Rosemary nonstop since Alba notified me that you were both alive and free, but I haven't heard back from either of them."

"Are they...together?" I hated myself for letting Falco hear me stammer the two words. "I mean—"

"Not in the way you fear, I suspect." Falco removed his sunglasses and pulled an ivory handkerchief from his front jacket pocket to remove a smudge. "Upon hearing the report of your death, Harkreader became a bit, shall we say, unhinged? He's been after the Cardinal ever since, hungry for revenge. Your friend Delacroix went along to keep him out of trouble as best she could. The two of them checked in relatively frequently at first, but it's been a week since we heard from either of them.

"Wait." Another face flashed across my mind's eye. "What about Maddox? Is he traveling with them as well?"

"Oh, Snow," he whispered, shaking his head, "you have a lot to catch up on."

Before I could ask what the hell that meant, the hallway ended at a large double door of dark wood, its opulent surface finely carved with hieroglyphics like I'd seen at Chichén Itzá when I visited the horn of Mexico a year ago.

I pulled in a deep breath. "I'm guessing this is where I'll find Alba?"

"This entire compound is the province of the Angel of the Morning, and yes, Alba awaits beyond this door."

"No time like the present, then." I gave the door a gentle knock. "Hello?"

"Enter, Miss Snow," came a voice as clear as if inches of solid walnut didn't separate us. "I would speak with you."

I grasped the doorknob, the metal cool on my fingers, and opened the door. There, seated atop an ornately carved mahogany chaise lounge, the silk of the cushion beneath her as white as fresh snowfall, El Ángel del Alba studied me with her green gaze. Her concerned expression quickly shifted to one of delight.

"You look well, Persephone Snow," Alba said as Falco closed the door behind me, leaving me alone with the Angel. "I'd feared your months away might have somehow diminished you, but you appear more vibrant than ever."

"I might say the same of you." I offered the Angel a quick bow of respect as I took in her own arresting beauty. Her tawny skin held not a single blemish, and her knee-length locks twirled down her body in a spiral braid that must have taken hours. She wore what were bedclothes, and yet she appeared ready for any red carpet in the land. "My apologies for the late hour."

"No apologies are required. Did I not assure you that my aid was yours for the asking?"

"Indeed, you did." I produced her shining card from my pocket and smiled. "From the bottom of my heart, thank you."

"I don't give those out to just everyone, you know." Her friendly gaze grew pensive. "Though it certainly took you long enough to come to me."

I let out a plaintive sigh. "As you know, I was otherwise detained."

Alba shook her head slowly in disappointment. "Had you remained at my side as I asked at our first meeting, I could have prevented the Cardinal from taking you and spared you half a year of pain and loneliness."

"But—"

"*But* that decision and those months are now water under the bridge. You now seek my help." She flashed a radiant smile. "What is it you need from the Angel of the Morning?"

After all the trouble I'd gone to in order to achieve an audience with the woman who reclined before me, the biggest irony was that I hadn't the first idea exactly what it was I wanted from her.

"What is your request?" she asked when I didn't answer. "Do you want my protection? A reunion with Mr. Harkreader?" She raised an eyebrow. "The Cardinal's head on a pike?" Her head tilted to one side. "My resources, vast though they are, are not without limits."

"Maybe we start with protection. In the last couple of days, I've gone from frying pan to fire to even hotter fire, and the hits just keep coming."

"I take it, however, that you have no interest in remaining here among my company of Ascendant where I can keep an eye on you?"

"Like you said, the Cardinal is still out there. He must be dealt with once and for all, or this never ends." I let out a frustrated chuckle. "On the other hand, I've been free less than two days, and I've already run into skiomancers, theriodans, psychomancers, and even the Cardinal's own techno-witch. In fact, Linus and his pack were the only ones *not* trying to deliver me to the highest bidder."

"One of whom used to be me, I believe you're suggesting." Alba leaned forward on her snow-white chaise, a hint of annoyance coloring her otherwise flawless features. "As I've told you multiple times, I only had the best of intentions when I first sought you out."

"And I believe that." The heat rose in my cheeks, my neck, my chest. Like Tom Cruise in *A Few Good Men* questioning a decorated Jack Nicholson on the stand, I stood there, knees all but knocking, unsure if I was winning a battle while losing the war.

Talk about another major frameshift. Before all this started, it had been years since I'd considered myself lesser than pretty much anyone, what with my crown of "Reigning Princess of Pop" making me a household name across the globe, but since first hearing the word Ascendant, I'd decidedly learned my true place in the world.

"So...Ethan, Rosemary, Mr. Delacroix, and the rest. Dietrich says they're all fine, but I feel like there's something he's not telling me." I glanced back at the door where the aeromancer no doubt waited on the other side. "He said he's been trying to raise Ethan ever since you and your people first learned I was free and has yet to get a response. No call, no text, nothing. Do you know where he is?"

"Would that I could tell you." She gave an exhausted sigh. "All I can say is that when Mr. Harkreader decides upon a course of action, he is a difficult man to dissuade."

"The Cardinal told Ethan I was dead, and yet, I understand that he and the others are still looking for me."

"They were, and perhaps still are. The Cardinal's report of your demise, certainly meant to sow confusion and doubt, threw us all for a loop, unfortunately, and none more so than your lover."

Lover.

Boyfriend rolled off my tongue. Sweetheart. Bae. Even "significant other."

But to me, still just shy of twenty years old, the word "lover" sounded more like something from a book or a movie than anyone or anything who was part of my life, no matter who I might be at the end of the day.

"You have no way of contacting them?"

"Normally, yes, but at the moment, regrettably, I have no more ability than Dietrich to reach either Mr. Harkreader or Miss Delacroix."

Well, shit. Roadblock after roadblock. Back to the mission at hand, then. "Has Daichi reached out again since we last spoke?"

"Not since our one abbreviated conversation. My sincerest hope is that his silence merely connotes caution and not something far worse." Her face clouded with apprehension. "I trust he was well when last you saw him?"

"I'd only ever experienced him before as a giant sumo of rock and earth, so I have to extrapolate a bit, but as far as I could tell, he seemed fine."

"What of the others you mentioned on the phone when we spoke earlier? Though I trust your judgment in matters of character, I did instruct Dietrich to leave your friend, the elektromancer, outside."

"That's all right. He's got Dino to keep him company."

"You no doubt noticed that Mr. Harkreader's friend has grown into quite the capable agent, regardless of whom he currently reports to."

I laughed. "You should have seen him driving here like a bat out of hell. It was something to behold."

"As I understand it," Alba continued, "the three of you managed not only to escape, but you also defeated a trio of Redstarts who ambushed you on your way here."

"It was a very close thing, but yes."

"Most impressive."

Just the memory of the Redstart's various assaults on my body, mind, and soul sent a chill straight down my spine: the telekinetic's invisible touch manipulating my limbs, the telepath's foreign thoughts invading my own, and my very own muscles turned against me as I danced on the puppet master's strings.

Not to mention the unavoidable sense that the encounter was but the first.

"Between your friends who even now seek you across the globe and those who accompany you today, I must say, you certainly engender loyalty in those with whom you surround yourself."

"When it comes to working with others, I'm starting to learn that there's a lot riding on the way you talk to those who surround you, siren song or otherwise."

"Truer words were never spoken." Her eyes narrowed. "I would hear more of your fellow captives. First, this elektromancer, Sunil Jayalal, who stands outside the door of my complex. I take it he is to be trusted?"

"He's a bit grumpy, but he always comes through in a pinch." I chuckled. "Hard outer shell, sweet gooey center—you know the type."

"All too well." A hint of color invaded her cheeks. "What about the empath?"

"Her name is Jia Li, but you may know her as Jade. I don't know that much about her other than she strikes me as one of the few truly good people I've met."

"This Jade individual. I've not had the pleasure, but my various associates have encountered her before. As you assert, a respectable young woman, even if she does have questionable taste in romantic partners."

I filed that last comment away for later. Something to ask Jia Li about when we saw each other again.

I refused to think *if*.

"I take it you feel differently about the last, this Metis."

I shuddered at the name. "Honestly, he frightens me."

"And yet you left my geomancer and your empath friend alone with him?"

"He left me little choice. I'd hoped to take Jia Li with me to New York, but Metis insisted she and Daichi remain with him in Boise. His insurance policy so I would actually return."

"An impossible decision, I am sure." She crinkled her nose. "At least your gambit, however dangerous for your friend and my geomancer, has brought you to me."

"I get the distinct impression that, like you, he's been around for a while. Do you have any idea who he is? What he can do?"

"Only that the name Metis is likely an alias. Many are the Ascendant who have walked the earth far longer than they should."

"Black curly hair, olive skin, leading man chin." I paused as Metis's piercing gaze filtered across my consciousness. "Dark eyes that peer through to your very soul."

"I must ask. This man clearly fills you with dread. Why did you free him? Why include him in your grand escape?"

My cheeks burned. "You don't exactly get to pick who's on the lifeboat with you when the Titanic goes down, do you?"

And yet, I had. Sunil had warned me, Charon too, that we should leave well enough alone. That we could simply send someone back for him later after we made our escape. That we didn't know enough to free this man the Cardinal feared enough to incapacitate using such draconian measures, much less bring him into our fold. And me, Little Miss Snow-It-All, insisted on not leaving him behind. I prayed that neither Jia Li nor Daichi had already paid the price for my arrogance.

"When we found him, he was hooked to a series of machines that, as best we could tell, was keeping him alive while rendering him comatose. We released him from most of the machinery, but there remained a collar around his neck that kept him from accessing any Ascendant abilities and reportedly would explode if tampered with."

"Reported?" Alba asked. "By whom?"

"The robotic caretaker the Cardinal left to watch over us during his prolonged absence. We brought him along so that he wouldn't cause problems after we left."

"And now this artificial intelligence awaits your return, along with my geomancer, your empath friend, and this mysterious Ascendant you call Metis who we can only hope continues to wear this collar of which you speak."

I nodded.

"I'm curious." She studied me with a half-amused smirk. "Once you freed yourself, why did you go all the way to New York for an impromptu visit with my estranged sister when I had already told you that I would help you?" At my surprised gape, Alba added, "Lady Day and I may live on opposite coasts and not speak as often as we once did, but that doesn't mean we don't call and compare notes from time to time."

"My apologies, but I was following the plan I'd made with Metis and the others; like you said, trying to keep him happy."

"If you draw close to those you suspect would stab you in the back, don't be surprised at the outcome."

"Of course." Unless I missed my guess, I had a whole bunch of I-told-you-sos coming for me. "You know, Minako doesn't strike me as the easiest to alarm, but when I told her that Metis was free, all she could talk about was the collar and whether it was still intact." A shudder overtook me. "This is bad, isn't it?"

"I have no idea who this man might be that you've unwittingly released upon the world, but if Minako lost her composure"—her gaze took on a pensive cast—"then I fear the worst."

"What do we do now, then? Like my mom always used to say, that horse is out of the barn."

"As I see it, we currently share both a common goal and a similar guilt. You blame yourself for leaving your friend in harm's way, and though it was the correct decision at the time, I carry guilt for sending Daichi into the breach, as what I thought would be a relatively simple mission has led to him losing six months of his life."

"Assuming he's still alive, of course."

Her expression went cold as stone. "If this Metis has harmed Daichi in any way, know that I will send him straight to Hell."

"Back to Hell, you mean," I muttered, the joke decidedly unfunny even as I spoke it. "So, does that mean you'll help me? Sunil and I are way overdue on our return to Idaho, and I don't want to think about what will happen if we don't show up soon." Unbidden tears rolled down my cheeks. "I know I'm supposed to be this big bad siren Ascendant, but I'm just a nineteen-year-old girl who doesn't know what I'm supposed to do next."

"Of course I'll help you. Have I not made that imminently clear?"

"You'll let us borrow Dietrich, then, like you did when Ethan and Rosemary came to ask for help six months ago?"

"Not just Dietrich, Persephone Snow." Alba rose from her mahogany chaise. Michelangelo himself couldn't have carved a more graceful form as the Angel pulled herself up to her full height. "This Metis individual has not only your friend but my geomancer in his grasp. Regardless of the man's intentions, it was my decision to send Daichi on this mission that has cost him the last six months and left him in this situation, and therefore, I will be accompanying you as well." She strode to the massive double door where Falco waited. "Though I usually leave such unpleasantness to my lieutenants, I fear this matter, along with this mysterious Ascendant, will require my personal attention."

CHAPTER 25

SUPERSONIC

"Does every Ascendant get issued one of these when they graduate Ascendant University or something?" I studied the sleek silver plane that looked like something out of *Star Wars*, its polished surface gleaming in the low light of the crescent moon. "Minako and the Cardinal flew me to Idaho in a similar aircraft, and I wondered the whole way why he'd bothered with a regular private jet and all the subterfuge at the airport when he had access to such technology."

Alba raised her eyebrows and smiled. "Ascendant of every stripe benefit when all of us maintain a certain level of subtlety in our day-to-day interactions with the world."

"Got it." A helicopter flew overhead, and I wondered if the pilot could see the futuristic aircraft in the near darkness and, if so, what the hell he thought he was seeing resting atop a series of townhomes in downtown L.A. "I'm guessing subtlety is on the back burner for the evening?"

"Time is of the essence, dear." She rested a hand on a panel by the aircraft's entryway, and the door unlatched. "Dietrich, please show everyone to their seats."

Falco pulled the shiny silver door open and motioned us all inside. As we entered the relatively tiny airship, I marveled for a moment that it appeared somehow bigger on the inside. There was no cockpit, no steering mechanism, barely space for an engine, and the thing seated nine within a large oval space.

"How does this thing even fly?" I asked. "There are wings but no jets or even propellers that I can see."

"Electromagnetically, I'm guessing?" Sunil's eyes flashed silver-blue. "The power in the skin of this machine is unlike anything I've experienced before."

"A true technological marvel." Falco directed Sunil, Dino, and I to our seats, leaving the largest and most posh at the rear of the cabin area open for Alba. "What you see represents the work of no less than three of the most talented technomancers the world has ever seen working in concert, Minako among them. The Pegasus can achieve speeds up to Mach 1.6, and even without me on board to help with aerodynamics, its creators managed to keep the sonic booms to a minimum."

"Dietrich does like the quiet." Alba entered last, and the door closed behind her with a quiet click. "Always so much smoother when you're aboard, my aeromancer."

"So, this thing can get us to Boise in like an hour, then?" Dino asked as he fastened his four-point harness.

"Or less," Falco said, fastening his own and directing all of us to follow his example. "Prepare to be impressed."

"At least I know now how Ada beat Ethan and the others to the Cardinal's mountain fortress." A question that had plagued me for months popped to the front of my mind. "But how did she know where to come look for me? Ethan and the rest of my crew figured it out, but Ada was there before their helicopter showed up. How could she have known where I was?"

"Mr. Harkreader and your friends used a combination of technomancy and good detective work to discern where the Cardinal had taken you." Alba's face shifted to a knowing smile as she took her seat. "Ada, on the other hand, obtained the coordinates of your prison via more direct methods."

"In other words," Falco said, "she tracked down Krage and his Murder of Crows and put their feet to the fire."

"Literally, I'm guessing." I'd experienced what Ada was like when she was strictly business, and I'd seen her angry via the Cardinal's monitors six months back; both had made it very clear that she was not someone to cross lightly. Krage and his trio of skiomancers were tough for sure, but I imagined someone who could set you afire with no more than an angry glare would prove an excellent interrogator. "Still not sure how everyone found their way to the right mountain in the middle of nowhere but couldn't find me."

"To be honest, the Cardinal would have been better served staying below ground and trusting the security measures he had in place." Alba offered me an apologetic shrug. "It is likely that only his hubris led him to show his face and confront Ada and, consequently, your friends."

"No one was finding their way into his base of operations, were they?" I asked.

"I have multiple homes across nearly every continent of this world," the Angel said. "At any moment I wished to go into hiding, I could vanish without a trace and no one living would see or hear from me ever again."

"Harkreader, myself, and the others," Falco added, "we stayed on that mountain for days. The technomancer kid knew there was something there, but Minako had done her job well. I searched from the air while the rest scoured every square inch of that mountain, but we found nothing. Your friend L.J. even—"

"No offense," Dino interrupted, "but can we continue this conversation in the air? I'm sure Miss Snow would like to get to her friend as soon as possible."

"Oh, we're in the air," Sunil smiled as if he'd just taken a bite of his favorite food. "Can't you feel it? The hum of the electricity, the static in the air around us, the sheer power that surrounds us all?"

The craft had no windows to speak of, so if we were truly in flight, there was no way to visibly tell. I'd felt a little shift right after the door shut like an elevator going up, but nothing to let me know we'd taken off.

Technological marvel indeed.

"If I may continue, then." Falco cleared his throat, irritated at being cut off by the lone non-Ascendant among our ranks. "The same technological null that allowed your technomancer to find the Cardinal in Denver apparently kept him from discovering the Cardinal's subterranean base. The two theriodans, Harkreader, Delacroix, and her father, for all their senses, powers, and skills, could only search by foot, and the mountain in question isn't amenable to foot traffic."

"All of this still baffles me." I shook my head. "How can a mountain full of high-tech everything be invisible to a technomancer? How does that even work?"

"The same way I keep the Pegasus flying even more smoothly than it does on its own." Falco shook his head. "Having complete control over an aspect of the world not only allows you to shape it to your will, but to command even its silence."

"For instance," Sunil added, "were I feeling particularly suicidal, I could command this craft to cease functioning by willing the electricity to still itself."

"Everything, Miss Snow, is energy to be utilized, redirected, or repurposed," the Angel added, "even your song."

"But all that equipment and tech, the Cardinal's cameras and monitors, Charon." The shimmering doorway to my subterranean prison of six months flashed across my memory. "Hell, the Styx itself. How do you keep that kind of stuff under wraps?"

"Charon?" Falco asked.

"And the Styx?" Alba added, her attention sparked.

"Yeah." My cheeks flushed with heat even as all color drained from the Angel's face. "Charon was the name of the robot I was telling you about, the one in charge of keeping us all fed and watered in the Cardinal's Underworld."

Alba shot Falco a troubled look. "Dietrich..."

"No, Mistress," Falco said. "It's not possible."

The Angel's eyes flashed with blazing intensity. "Have I not taught you, my aeromancer, that anything is possible?"

Before Falco could answer, the entire craft shook as if struck, and only my harness kept me in my seat.

"What the hell was that?" Dino, who had been silent since Falco's cross glance from behind his mirrored shades, called out. "Were we just hit?"

"We're under attack." Sunil's eyes flickered with electricity. "I'll tell you that for nothing."

"What was your first clue?" Falco asked with a withering tone that took me back to our very first meeting during which he accidentally sent me flying from a building courtesy of a hurricane gust of wind.

"Visual," Alba whispered, and the craft answered in kind by rendering the smooth metal behind each of our heads as well as the ceiling and floor translucent, allowing all aboard a 360-degree view of the surrounding sky. "There." The Angel directed a finger at the starboard side of the aircraft behind my head. "Redstarts."

I craned my head around to peer out into the darkness in the direction Alba had pointed. Stars blinked above, tiny lights rushed by below, and there, just off the starboard side of our aircraft and matching our speed exactly, flew a barely visible aircraft similar to the one in which we flew, this one jet black to the Pegasus's silver.

"So, the Ascendant do all get one of these."

"If you must know," Alba whispered between clenched teeth, "I have three."

"Did our whole airship just go transparent?" I wondered briefly if we flew through the sky in a plane like Lynda Carter had in the old 1970s *Wonder Woman* show I saw once. "Like, are we legit invisible right now?"

"While the plane does have a stealth mode similar to what you describe," Falco answered, "what you now experience is merely the height of modern optical technology, made all the more clear by a little technomancer magic."

The entire interior had become a continuous video screen indistinguishable from looking through a window. That cinched it. I was getting a technomancer to work on the visuals for my next tour, assuming another tour happening was more than a pipe dream.

"I don't even want to know what a craft like this costs," I muttered.

"More than the GDP of several countries." Falco focused, and the plane in the distance suddenly dipped out of sight. "Now, excuse me while I keep these miscreants from knocking us out of the sky."

"Are they firing on us?" Dino asked.

"I don't think so." Sunil's eyes slid shut in concentration. "The ship is fine, as far as I can tell."

"It's their telekinetic." Alba scanned the virtual sky surrounding us. "The air turbulence Dietrich generated has forced them onto an alternate flight path, but they are still close." She closed her eyes as well. "I can feel them."

"Are they trying to bring us down?" I asked, my heart racing. "I thought they needed me alive."

"We can only hope that's still their plan." Falco shot me a strained grimace. "You just put them through the wringer a few hours ago, though. They might not be feeling quite as magnanimous as before."

"Magnanimous?" I reflected on the various tortures each of the psychomancers had inflicted on Sunil, Dino, and me on the highway leading to Los Angeles. "You've got to be kidding me."

"The trio of Redstarts you described as attacking you en route to Los Angeles can invade your thoughts, control your body, and rip you limb from limb without lifting so much as a finger. Anyone who emerges from an encounter with those three physically, mentally, and emotionally intact has achieved a victory indeed." Falco shot me a sidelong glance. "To be honest, they were likely showing considerable restraint, not unlike I and my fellow elementalists did during our first meeting seven months ago."

"Such high praise." The whispered words passed Dino's mouth as they had hours before, with neither the voice nor the accent his own. "My apologies for once again taking your friend's mind and tongue to use as my mouthpiece, but rather than having Emir use his talents against your aircraft a second time, I thought I might speak to you more directly."

Emir? That had to be the telekinetic.

"Are you quite certain, Latifah Lazaar, that you wish to cross an Angel this way?" Alba bristled in her seat. "Release this man immediately and be about your business." Her usually warm voice went colder than an Arctic wind. "I won't ask again."

Dino's wide-eyed gaze, a proxy for that of Latifah the telepath, shot from Falco to the Angel on her throne of steel and smooth leather. "El Ángel del Alba. We had no idea that you were attending to this matter personally. A true honor to be in your presence." Latifah peered down with Dino's eyes at his wiry form. "At least, so to speak."

"And yet you continue your assault on this young man's thoughts instead of retreating as I've ordered." Alba's eyes narrowed at Dino as if peering through him at the woman in the aircraft trailing us. "Perhaps your definition of honor and mine are somehow different?"

"I mean no disrespect, Angel of the Morning," came the off-putting combination of the Redstart's words and accent translated through Dino's voice, "but my associates and I are acting well within the Standards of Contact as I understand—"

"Do not speak to me of rules I helped codify centuries before your birth nor mistake my words as a simple request. Leave this man's mind now and let us be about our way, or trust that you will have to deal with me again very soon in a time and manner of my choosing."

"Very well," came the answer after a thoughtful pause. "In deference to one of your station as well as in appreciation of the speed at which each of our aircraft is currently moving, I and my companions will now disengage. Should any harm befall you, El Ángel del Alba, my Redstarts and I will not be the ones to blame. However, once all are again on the ground and your life is no longer at risk, we will be coming for Snow. She is not beholden to you, and therefore is open game by the very Code you helped create." Still under Latifah's control, Dino turned my way and offered a quick nod and a creepy smile. "See you all in Boise."

Dino's body slumped in his seat for half a second before he sprang back to consciousness, mad as hell.

"That witch spoke through me again, didn't she?" he spat.

"Careful with your choice of words," Falco whispered. "Alba

doesn't like that particular turn of phrase." He cleared his throat. "But yes, Latifah made you dance for her." The aeromancer looked away. "Or, I suppose, sing. Making people dance is Jamila's specialty."

Jamila. That must be the puppet master's name. God, the Ascendant world seemed tiny. Everyone knew everyone, even more so than my experiences in the tween TV and music business. Which begged the question: How was it that no one knew Metis?

"Well, I've had quite enough of that," Dino continued. "I may be the only person here who can't summon hurricane winds or lightning from the sky, but that doesn't mean I have to be everyone's punching bag."

"It's all right, Dino." I rested a hand on his shoulder and found his entire body shaking, with rage, fear, or a heaping helping of both. "It's over, and—"

"It's over until she needs to use me as her walkie talkie again."

"I'm sorry. I didn't mean to—"

"Leave me alone." He shrank into himself, turning to one side in his seat and staring at the floor. "I'll be okay. Just give me a minute."

"Of course." I returned my attention to Alba and Falco. "So, are they gone?"

The aeromancer focused for a moment. "I no longer sense a disturbance in the wind patterns consistent with another aircraft. No doubt they continue on a parallel course, as they too are apparently headed for Boise, but they are far enough away that I can't detect them."

"So, where were we?" I asked. "I mentioned Charon and the Styx, and the two of you acted like I'd just said the Devil himself was coming for dinner."

Neither Alba or Falco said a word.

"Well, what is it? Do you know who Metis is?"

"We know who he's not, if that's what the senior Ascendant on board are getting all cagey about." Sunil, who hadn't spoken since the Redstarts first struck the airship, looked around at each of us as if we were taking turns telling ghost stories. "The Lord of the Dead, the one called Hades, has been gone for millennia."

"Hades?" I suddenly wished Mom had picked literally any other name from Greek mythology for her one and only daughter. "The Lord of the Dead? He was real?"

"He was Ascendant," Falco said, "with a talent so rare, there is no record of another in the centuries upon centuries to follow."

"But he was more than simply Ascendant, Dietrich." Alba's eyes darted back and forth between me and the aeromancer. "And with that being the case, we have to consider the possibility, however remote, of not only his survival, but his involvement in all this."

"More than Ascendant?" I asked. "What does that even mean?"

Falco considered for a long moment before answering. "It involves a word we rarely use, as those individuals it applies to are so exceptional and rare that to refer to them as a group borders on offensive."

"What Dietrich is trying to say is that just as Ascendant have broken away from the rest of humanity, there are a few among the Ascendant who...Transcend even that state."

"Transcendent?" I asked. "I suppose the Angels are among that number?" I considered a moment longer. "And the Driver?"

"You're quick, Miss Snow." Alba smiled. "Such insight will serve you well."

"While all Ascendant are long-lived simply by the nature of their existence," Falco said, "those who achieve Transcendence effectively become immortal forces of nature."

I met Alba's gaze. "You cannot die?"

"At least in a manner of speaking." Alba pulled in a cleansing breath. "Left to my own devices—with a few caveats, of course—my mind and body shall continue on for centuries or even longer, unblemished by time or disease."

"But that doesn't mean she is invulnerable to those who might mean her ill." Falco's expression went deadly serious. "I must repeat my earlier concerns, Mistress."

Concerns? That was the first I'd heard Falco speak of such.

"Are you certain that you wish to expose yourself to the risk ahead?" he continued. "With Daichi on site and my abilities coupled with Snow's elektromancer, we should be able to handle whatever this Metis individual can throw out."

"*Snow's* elektromancer?" Sunil muttered. "My ass."

Alba paid him no attention. "First, Dietrich, we don't know in what state we'll find Daichi. If he has been incapacitated or worse, my absence would be tantamount to throwing you, Mr. Jayalal, Miss Snow, and her friend to the wolves, or I suppose, wolf. Second, your haunted stare reveals that you know as well as I do there is something about this situation that simply doesn't add up, and your instinct to protect me only reinforces my conviction that my direct involvement is not only called for, but inevitable." The Angel's eyes narrowed. "And third, I have relegated myself to the safety of our fortified home in the City of Angels for far too long. If this man called Metis is indeed the threat we suspect, regardless of his identity, then I will be more than happy to reacquaint him with his proper place in the Ascendant world."

CHAPTER 26

FOREVER YOUNG

"If it's not too forward to ask, how old are you, anyway?" I drew back from Alba instinctively, a part of me concerned she might strike me for asking such an impertinent question. "Are we talking centuries? Longer?"

Rather than the rebuke I expected, Alba turned to me with a smile as warm as sunshine and answered. "Truthfully, I have walked this earth far longer than even I know. In the modern day, humanity keeps meticulous count of their minutes and seconds and hours and days, but it hasn't always been this way." Her gaze took on a distant cast. "I still recall the first time I saw what you and modern society think of as the Mayan calendar. As I ran my fingers along the carved lines and caressed the cool limestone face at its center, I attempted to count the summers and winters I remembered. Even then, the number was higher than I understood."

"But that was over two millennia ago, right?" I cast my mind back to the World History class I'd crammed between filming episodes of the second season of *Teen Spies*. "How is that possible?"

"You sit among men who can call lightning from the sky and command the very air you breathe. Mere longevity is practically boring in comparison."

"Tell that to the five-hundred-billion-dollar beauty and personal care industry." I'd toyed with starting a cosmetics line a few months before my life went in the toilet. The staggering figures my manager and I discussed that day convinced me to invest in a different direction. "The fine people at L'Oréal would beg to differ."

Her radiant smile diminished a few shades. "Many seek the Fountain of Youth, my dear, but few can fathom the relentless onslaught of years."

"I don't know, Alba." I studied her flawless features, smooth skin, and lustrous hair. The Angel of the Morning, regardless of her years on the planet, didn't show even a hint of the ravages of time. "I've met countless women who would kill to remain twenty-seven forever."

"And now"—her gaze shifted into an unfocused stare, as if she stared straight through me—"you have met someone who has done just that."

"That's the price, then? Others die so that you might live?"

"In a manner of speaking." Alba withdrew into herself a bit. "Some offer their essence to me when their time is done in return for years of my protection and succor. Others have overestimated their power and place in the Ascendant world and come to try to take what is mine."

"And?"

"Not only have I shown such fools the error of their ways, but have added their power to my own even as I...removed them from further consideration."

"So, you can take an Ascendant's power, just like the Cardinal does."

"Yes." Her lips pulled down to a tight circle of distaste. "All of us can, Miss Snow, but not all of us do, and that is the difference."

A chill ran down my spine. "This Transcendence then. Is that what the Cardinal is doing? Is he attempting to Transcend into something more?"

"To truly Transcend is to forge oneself into the ultimate expression of who they already are and become all that they can be. The Cardinal, on the other hand, is nothing but a murderer of his own kind, a cold-blooded killer who must be put down." Her blank stare went icy, the whites of her eyes darkening as if a cloud had crossed the sun. "Why he is doing what he is doing is of no consequence."

Despite the million more questions flooding my mind, I held my tongue.

Alba boasted four elementalists in her stable—Falco, Daichi, Violeta, Ada—all of whom belonged to her in some way. They weren't exactly slaves nor even indentured servants, as they seemed to retain free will and were able to come and go as they pleased, but each owed her a life debt, a debt that I'd avoided by coming into my own by myself in L.A. seven months ago.

I didn't understand that night what I'd avoided nor what obligation I was taking on by accepting her help now, but one thing was certain: Alba had wanted me to join her, to be one of hers, which meant that at some point down the road, she intended for all that I was and all I would ever be to flow into her and continue her centuries-long existence.

I had no intention of saying it out loud, but after learning of Transcendence, the difference between Alba's offering of "protection and succor" and the motivation behind the Cardinal's mayhem didn't strike me as all that different from each other. Alba's was a long game whereas the Cardinal's was short and brutal, but the end result certainly seemed the same.

I wasn't sure if I'd ever feel warm again.

"We're five minutes out," Falco said, breaking my reverie. "Get ready, everyone."

I shifted my gaze left and right to study the two men I'd brought with me to Los Angeles. Dino's usually ruddy face was as white as a sheet at Alba's revelation regarding her effective immortality, and even Sunil seemed a bit taken aback. I had no idea how much or little the elektromancer had understood of Transcendence or even the simple transfer of Ascendant power at the time of our death, but he recognized, just as I did, that we sat in the presence of someone who would gladly take our life force to prolong her own without a hint of guilt.

"Once we land," Dino said, daring to speak, "I guess we're heading for the rendezvous point you and Sunil discussed with Metis prior to heading to New York?"

"We found an inexpensive motel not far from the airport that looked like it usually charged by the hour. Sunil and Jade, with a subtle vocal assist from yours truly, were able to convince the guy at the front desk to let us have a room for a couple of days while the two of us traveled." My stomach churned as Jia Li's face filled my mind's eye. "I hated leaving Daichi and Jade there with Metis, but like I said a million times, he didn't really give us another choice."

"So," Sunil said, "we go to the motel in force, confront Metis, and get our people. Got it. What do we do with him when we're done, though? With that collar on, he can't cause too much trouble, but we can't just drop him off with the police, and I'm not even saying we should. It goes without saying he gives us all the creeps, but we don't know who he is or anything about him." Sunil let out a chuckle. "Last I checked, giving off a bad vibe isn't against the law."

"We will approach this Metis as one, as you have suggested, and hope that the power differential resulting from his collar will avoid unnecessary conflict." Alba's lips drew down to a thoughtful circle. "Despite our shared apprehension, without knowing who he is and with him having committed no offense that we are aware of, the Ascendant Code demands we allow him to go about his way and he ours."

Metis didn't strike me as someone who let any code inform his decisions.

We spent the last few minutes in the air preparing for whatever was to come next. Alba and Falco conversed together quietly, their words barely registering despite my best efforts to listen in. Sunil sat in his seat focused to the point of near-meditation, static sparks popping between his fingertips as he took one controlled breath after another. Dino examined his pistol, ensuring he would be prepared to fight, if necessary, with the only weapon at his disposal.

Just as Dino was inspecting the only weapon he had, so was I inspecting mine. I cleared my throat and began a careful self-examination, as I had before every recording session since I began my singing career and every live show for two straight tours, confirming that my throat, vocal cords, and diaphragm were all in good shape and ready to rock.

~

"**M**aybe they went out for pizza?" Dino peered around the empty motel room. "I mean, even brooding Ascendant mystery men need to eat sometime."

Something in the way Dino said that last bit sent a chill up my spine.

"This top is Jade's." From under the edge of the second twin bed in the tiny room, I pulled the silky blouse Jia Li had worn as we escaped from the Cardinal's Underworld and base of operations. "It looks like she stuffed it under here for someone to find."

"These tracks are from Daichi's chair." Sunil pointed to two parallel curves left in the well-worn blue carpet. "They were definitely here."

"And now they are not." Falco sighed impatiently. "Boise may not be the biggest city on the planet, but last I checked, we're talking a quarter million people."

"Those we seek could be anywhere." Alba's dark eyes scanned the room for any clue that we'd missed. "Any thoughts, Dietrich, about where to begin our search?"

"I'm afraid not. Sunrise isn't for a couple hours, so any aerial search would be of minimal benefit, not to mention there's no guarantee they're still in the city." He turned to Sunil. "Any chance you can track Daichi's motorized wheelchair, elektromancer?"

Sunil focused for a moment. "The technology of his chair has left a certain tang in the air, but I'm not sure even that would be enough to track him and the others through a major city." He cleared his throat in apology. "Too much background noise."

"What of you, Mistress?" Falco inquired. "Do you have any sense of Daichi or any geomantic manipulation in the vicinity?"

Alba's eyes slid closed as she stretched out her arms to either side. A gentle undulation of her hips commenced, her fingers and forearms twisting before her like a pair of serpents in combat and her head rocking back and forth to music that only the Angel of the Morning could hear. Then, as suddenly as the strange dance had begun, Alba stopped, her eyes opening wide in astonishment and possibly even fear.

"Daichi is near," she whispered, her forehead breaking out in a fine sweat, "and he's not alone." Her agitated gaze swept the room, taking in Sunil, Dino, and me. "I don't know who this man is you've released upon the world, but if what I sense is remotely accurate, then I fear for us all."

Two sets of footsteps sounded from beyond the door to the parking lot, the quiet footfalls paired with the telltale crunch of gravel under wheels. Though none spoke, Alba had sensed Daichi, and even without Jade's talent or the senses of the Angel in our midst, I could feel Metis through the door, his presence casting no less a shadow than any of Krage's skiomancers.

An electronic click froze me to the spot, the sound of a keycard unlocking the door. The metal handle jiggled for half a second, and then...nothing. Not another sound disturbed the sudden silence of the room.

"What's going on?" I whispered. "Why aren't they—"

"Greetings, Miss Snow." The voice belonged to Metis, but the words, phrasing, and accent were all Latifah. "We understand that you and your friends have grown tired of me and my associates manipulating your minds and bodies."

"So," came the puppet master Jamila's amplified voice from somewhere above, "we decided to conscript those you seek instead."

Without warning, a hunk of pavement the size of my head crashed through the room's front window and flew straight at Falco. For half a second, I feared I was about to witness a gruesome death, but with a glance, Alba stopped the jagged asphalt mere inches from her aeromancer's face.

"I have had enough of my people being threatened, controlled, and exploited for one day." Alba's features went cold as ice and the jagged hunk of pavement hovering before Falco's chest shattered into a gazillion pieces, each flying to orbit Alba as if she were the sun and they her personal asteroid field. "Quite enough." With another wave of her splayed fingers, Alba destroyed the remnants of the window and tore away the wall that separated us from those we sought as if an invisible giant were parting a stage curtain. As the drywall, timber, glass, and steel pulled away, we were greeted with a nightmarish scene.

Daichi stood at the center of the parking lot, returned to the state in which I first met him. Ten feet high and formed from concrete, asphalt, and stone, the gigantic sumo glared at us with red eyes that glowed like hot coals. To his left, Jade hung in midair, her dangling form under the control of the Redstart telekinetic, while to Daichi's right, stood the one I feared most of all.

Metis, collar thankfully intact and flashing with the same series of lights I remembered, stared at us with a maniacal grin that I wasn't sure was Latifah's or his own.

"This is the man you call Metis?" Alba asked.

My answer consisted of only a nervous nod.

"I don't recognize him," she spoke, "and yet there is something about his mere presence that troubles my soul."

"You came all this way to find these three, did you not?" The telepath spoke through the man in question, her voice dripping with sarcasm. "Do you not appreciate our assistance in what could have proven quite an arduous search of this quaint little town?"

As much as I'm sure the people of Idaho would fume at having their capital city referred to as such, their irritation would barely register compared to the rage wafting off Metis. Dino's anger at having been manipulated by the Redstart telepath bordered on violent, and Ethan's backstage buddy was as easygoing a person as I'd ever met, at least when he wasn't delivering fugitive sirens to immortal Angels as mercenary psychomancers tried to run him off the highway. Metis, though? All I could say was I wouldn't want to be Latifah Lazaar once the mysterious Ascendant was no longer under her mental control.

"How did you know who we were looking for?" I asked. "Or where to find them?"

The answer occurred to me even as Metis spoke again with Latifah's words.

"I was inside your mind, Snow. Your friend's as well." Metis's eyes flicked Dino's way. "Want to know Dino's social security number? The name of the first girl he ever kissed? The password for his online banking?" Metis, under the telepath's command, tapped his forehead. "It's all up here now."

"Bitch," Dino muttered under his breath.

"Not now, Dino," I whispered, returning my attention to a Latifah-possessed Metis. "All right. If you're so powerful and all-knowing, tell me one thing."

A laugh parted Metis's ensorcelled lips. "Of course."

"Who is this man you speak through so arrogantly? You peer out at me through his eyes, hear me with his ears, and speak with his mouth." I stepped forward, and slid into the most impertinent smile I could summon. "Tell me his name."

"This is the man you call Metis. He is—"

"I think you and I both know that name is nothing but misdirection." My smile widened. "Tell me his real name." I stared deeply into Metis's dark eyes. "Make him say it, if you're so damn powerful."

As Daichi continued to look on with his hot coal glare and Jade hung in the sky like a marionette with half its strings cut, Metis's features turned up in deep concentration, as if he were solving a complex math equation.

"What? You can't summon his name?" I donned the voice of my character, Penny Sinclair, from my *Teen Spies* days and channeled the most irritating tone I could muster. "What kind of loser psychic can take control of another person's mind and yet can't make them say their own name?"

"No one controls me." No Latifah this time. Straight up Metis. "And I've allowed you as a passenger in my mind for quite long enough, Latifah Lazaar." Metis's features darkened in concentration. "Out," he spoke with a hangman's finality.

Somewhere high above, a woman screamed.

"Serves her right," Dino muttered in one ear.

"What next?" Sunil whispered in the other.

"What next, indeed, Mr. Jayalal?" Metis stepped forward, his gaze roving over the five of us standing in the demolished motel room and stopping in astonishment as he took in the countenance of the Angel of the Morning. "Is it possible? We planned for you to bring the Angel of Harlem to aid us against our shared enemy, the Cardinal, but you have instead brought El Ángel del Alba?"

"You seem to have me at a disadvantage, sir." Alba studied the man whose stare remained locked on her from beneath his thick dark curls. "You know me, and yet I do not know you." Her eyes narrowed. "And that is a rarity indeed."

"Know only that I am a great admirer of yours, albeit from afar. I look forward to our further—"

Without warning, Daichi, under the puppet master's control, swung a rocky arm at Metis. "You'll pay for hurting Latifah!" The words, shouted in anger from a mouth of stone, struck me like an avalanche. "Now."

Metis ducked beneath the wild haymaker and then dodged to one side as the unseen Redstart telekinetic sent Jade's limp body flying at him, a living bludgeon. A moment later, Jamila, Emir, and Latifah descended from the still-dark sky and landed in the parking lot behind Daichi's monstrous form. Latifah appeared slightly dazed, as if being forcibly ejected from Metis's mind had done a number on her, though the dark-skinned telepath appeared more furious than defeated. Emir brought Jade to hover before him, the very definition of human shield, as Jamila positioned herself behind Daichi's rocky form.

"Understand that we only came for Snow," Latifah spat at Metis, using her own voice, "but it would appear that the lot of you are not going to let her go without a fight." Dino stiffened at my side and turned my way, Latifah's completed thought proceeding from his lips. "If that is what is required to fulfill our mission, know that I and my fellow Redstarts are happy to oblige."

CHAPTER 27

MASTER OF PUPPETS

Something told me that letting Dino keep his weapon once we touched down in Boise was going to prove to be a bad idea, but I hadn't had the heart to say anything. Now, as he pulled his pistol from his waistband and leveled the barrel at me, I swore to myself I'd never again put sparing anyone's feelings ahead of smart tactical decisions, not that any of us were safe from someone who could carjack a mind without breaking a sweat.

"For the last time, Miss Snow," Dino continued with Latifah's words and accent, "come with us now, and perhaps we can avoid further unnecessary violence."

"I understand that everyone's presence here today revolves around the siren in our midst," Alba said, her tone shifting icy, "but hear me, psychomancers, and hear me well. When the Angel of the Morning is in attendance, you will address me when you speak." Her lips drew down to a tight circle of discontent. "And the next person who refers to me as part of a 'lot' will wish they'd never spoken the word."

"With all due respect, Lady Alba," Latifah continued via Dino, "Persephone Snow is unattached and free to speak for herself. Unless we've been misinformed, word among our kind is that she achieved Ascension on her own and lives free of obligation to you or any other. As such, our business with her is just that. We appreciate your rank and position in our society, but you do not speak for Snow."

"Respect, you say?" Alba's voice grew quiet, a whisper much like that of her Sister of Shadow. "Miss Snow came to me for assistance, and though she is neither my charge nor under any obligation, I stand here today in defiance of any who would take her against her will, regardless of who or why." She shot an affirmative glance my way. "Know that this is the last warning you will rec—"

Alba's thought cut out mid-syllable, her entire body stiffening as if she were having a seizure. I understood all too well what that meant. Unlike the subtle change in body language that accompanied Latifah's mental takeovers or the awkward marionette effect of Emir's telekinetic manipulation of limbs, this was the work of Jamila, the puppet master. I wasn't sure which I found the more shocking, that even Alba was vulnerable to such an attack or that the Redstart had the audacity to invade the mind of one of the three Angels of the Ascendant.

"You...will...pay...for...this." Alba forced out each word, her indomitable will keeping some modicum of control despite the cerebral assault. "Mark it."

"Big mistake, Jamila." Falco seethed. "The Angel of the Morning was ancient before either one of us was born. One thing about her? She forgets nothing. Do you have any idea what you've—"

Falco's voice cut out as well, his body shifting uncomfortably like his mistress's.

That left me, a suspiciously quiet Sunil, and a pissed-off Metis as the only ones potentially still available to fight for my freedom.

"I caught that glance," came Latifah's voice from Sunil's lips. "I'm no fool, Snow. I secured your elektromancer the moment I laid eyes on him."

Sunil was out of play along with all the others, cutting my side to two. Call me crazy, but I hadn't seen the whole "me and Metis against the world" thing coming at all.

Latifah no doubt planned to stay out of my head this time, considering what I'd been able to pull the last time she linked our minds, but that left either Jamila or Emir more than able to take control of me, one way or another, whenever they wanted. At least Metis, despite the collar, seemed capable of fending off a mental assault.

"What's the call, Metis?" I shouted. "You with me?"

"As if I have another choice?" He shot me an exasperated glare. "My only question is, have you learned nothing from our time together?" His flashing eyes and flaring nostrils at my confused gaze drove the point home. "Have I taught you nothing?"

I wracked my brain, my thoughts and body for the moment still my own, and replayed anything I could remember from my various anxiety-filled conversations with Metis to discern what the hell he was talking about.

That every Ascendant, no matter how strong, has a weakness?

That winning this fight was going to take more brains than brawn?

That when you face an enemy, you fight with everything you have?

No. I knew exactly what he was trying to tell me.

The one weapon I possessed on this urban battlefield was one I barely understood, and yet was so important that the entire Ascendant world was knocking down my door to bring me to their side. I couldn't call lightning or manipulate shadows or force machines to do my bidding, but I could sing. And boy, were they going to hear my—

"No, no, no." Jamila clucked her tongue as she took command of my lungs and lips and tongue and teeth. "We've already experienced your power, siren." She stepped forward and took her position at Daichi's side. "Latifah learned the hard way to stay out of your head, but because my ability requires no direct access to your thoughts, I can prevent you from singing your little song all the same."

I struggled against her, my mind screaming at my muscles to do as I commanded rather than obey the puppet master's whim, but to no avail. My hands came to my mouth, my own overlapping fingers across my closed lips effectively silencing me, not that Jamila was allowing me access to my lungs, diaphragm, or vocal cords to make so much as a squeak. With Jamila's full body control of Alba, Falco, Daichi, and me, that left Sunil and Dino under Latifah's sway, Jade dangling in the air at Emir's mercy, and a powerless Metis all alone to face our attackers.

Somehow, I still worried for the Redstarts.

"So, it is down to me." Metis turned to face the three psychomancers in their matching black, white, and red jumpsuits. "What's the matter, puppeteer? Afraid to touch my mind after watching me drive your friend screaming from my thoughts?" He turned his attention to Emir, who quickly brought Jade's hovering form between himself and Metis. "And you. You hide behind a girl whose only ability is to sense whether you're happy, sad, horny, or mad. How pathetic." He swept an accusing finger in an arc at the three Redstarts. "All of you. Pathetic."

"I could seize that collar and break your neck before you say another word," Emir answered. "Perhaps I shall."

"Perhaps you should," Metis answered. "At least then I wouldn't have to listen to your vainglorious prattle any longer." His eyes narrowed. "I remember a time when psychomancers knew their place."

"Enough!" Emir raised a hand, and an invisible force grabbed the back of Metis's collar and hauled him up from the ground, leaving him hanging before us from his high-tech noose. "Such irony, to be rescued from one land of the dead only to be escorted so quickly to another, don't you think?"

Gagging from the metal ring across his windpipe, Metis grabbed at the collar with both hands in an effort to pull the metal away from his neck and breathe, but the metal ring had been tight before. Now, with two-hundred-plus pounds of muscle and bone pulling straight down, the outcome was inevitable.

"No one is dying here today." With only those six words to

herald her arrival, a familiar female form dressed all in black dropped to the pavement between the five of us standing in the wrecked motel room and the surprised line of Redstarts. Her long, dark hair flowing as if she'd just leaped from a Pantene commercial, she spun in a tight circle and let fly a handful of shining metal objects that flashed in the LED illumination of the parking lot. A moment later, Emir doubled over in pain and both Metis and Jade dropped to the ground, released from his telekinetic grasp.

Our savior turned to look my way, and though I'd heard her voice plain as day, it was only when I locked eyes with the woman I'd declared my BFF seven months earlier that I allowed myself to believe that my ears hadn't lied to me.

"So, it *is* true." Rosemary Delacroix greeted me with a relieved half-smile and a quick nod of her head as she drew her katana from the scabbard at her back. "Hi, Seph. Pardon our tardiness. We came as quickly as we could after hearing from Bradley."

"We?" I asked, simultaneously hopeful and afraid on multiple levels of what that simple two-letter word might mean. "Do you mean...?"

The entire parking lot lit up bright as day as a muscular form I knew intimately dropped from the sky and landed amid the Redstarts like an angel cast out of Heaven. Surrounded in a nimbus of blinding white fire, he rose from the ground, the swords held in each of his hands glowing with a silver-white inner light all their own. Both Latifah and Jamila stepped back as this newcomer directed the longer blade in their direction.

"Redstarts, hear me, because I'm only going to say this once." The voice struck my ears as foreign and yet as familiar as my own. "Stand down and release the various Ascendant under your control, or face my Flame and the Blades of Neith."

My heart leaped, and yet a part of me still refused to believe. After all the months that had passed, after everything I'd done to try to get back to him, after all the sacrifices and all the pain, here he was, and I couldn't speak a syllable.

And, he had yet to so much as look my way.

"Harkreader." Jamila directed an annoyed glare at this newcomer to our battlefield. "We were wondering when you'd show up."

"Jamila Filali, you hold multiple Ascendant against their will in violation of Ascendant Standards of Contact." Ethan crossed the paired blades of his station before his chest, radiant energy arcing between them much like Sunil's lightning. "And among them, the most powerful of the Angels? That's a pretty ballsy move."

"An affront that boggles even my imagination," Metis said, rising from the pavement to address Ethan. "I can only assume that you and your lovely friend represent the Line of Neith?"

"Who are you?" Ethan turned Metis's way, though he kept his attention on the three Redstarts. "And what's that around your neck?"

Metis shot a knowing look my way. "A restraining device," he answered, "placed around my neck by my captors. Not only does this collar prevent me from using my Ascendant ability, but I've been informed that any attempt to remove it will result in an explosion that would, well, you can imagine."

Ethan studied the collar. "I'm guessing you ran afoul of a technomancer." He returned his attention to Jamila, Latifah, and the recovering Emir. "Or did you three do this to him?"

"We do not traffic with technomancers, Harkreader." Jamila cast a glance our way, reinforcing her influence over my body and the others'. "And, if you want the truth, we haven't a clue who this man is beyond his association with your lover there."

At long last, Ethan turned my way and met my gaze. In that shared moment, his eyes communicated astonishment, sadness, and elation, but above all, duty.

"Hello, Seph." The two words sent my heart racing even faster. "We were out the door the moment Bradley called, but I didn't allow myself to believe what he told us until this very moment." His voice trembled with emotion. "I'll get you out of this. I swear."

My eyes went wide as I struggled to answer, but Jamila allowed only the barest of respirations and forced my crossed fingers to remain tight across my closed lips.

"Leave her alone," Ethan commanded, taking a step in Jamila's direction. "She's done nothing of consequence to you. Let her speak."

"So that golden voice of hers can turn the tide?" Jamila laughed. "I think not."

"The Light of Neith keeps you from my mind, Jamila, and measured use of the Flame can free the rest at any moment I choose." He directed his fiery blade at the psychomancer's heart. "Now, release everyone and be about your way, unless you'd prefer I unleash them all at once and let them express their displeasure regarding their treatment at your hands?"

"Speaking of unleashing," came another familiar voice from just beyond my field of vision, "would you like me to take care of this guy's inhibitor collar, Ethan?" His shock of teal hair as bright as ever, L.J. sauntered onto the scene, his form surrounded in floating tech reminiscent of Minako atop the mountain six months ago. "Seems a relatively simple design."

No. Not now. Not when we're so close to freedom.

"Sure, L.J. Just be careful." Ethan tilted his head in Metis's direction. "According to what he said, the collar may contain some sort of bomb. We're here to defuse this situation and get Seph. We don't want anyone hurt." He cast a glance toward the still-bleeding Emir. "Any more than necessary, that is."

"Great." L.J. posted up in front of Metis. "On it."

No. Please, God. No.

L.J. narrowed his eyes at Metis. "Let's see." He sang under his breath as he focused, both the tune and lyrics unfamiliar. Something about killer instinct, sensitive cargo, time bombs, and primitive design. "Nope. No bomb here. Just a loop circuit that hijacks the part of the cerebral cortex that Ascendant use to access their abilities. I should be able to dismantle this easy-peasy."

"No need for that." Metis flexed his muscles, the fingers of both hands already between his throat and the collar, and strained against the metal ring surrounding his muscular neck. "A certain robot and I will be having words as soon as I locate him, but that will have to wait, for it would appear that my moment of freedom is at hand."

Ethan looked my way, a heady mix of confusion and apprehension filling his stare, not to mention a hint of blame, though I may have been projecting that last bit. Rosemary also met my gaze, the unspoken question in her expression the same one I'd been asking myself since I'd insisted we free the man before us: Who was Metis?

Like it or not, we were about to find out.

With a sound like a crushed soda can, Metis tore the collar at his neck asunder, the twisted metal and circuitry falling to the asphalt with a pair of resounding thuds. L.J. backpedaled to Ethan's side, and Rosemary dropped into a familiar fighting stance, her katana held before her in defense.

Though the shift was subtle, this mysterious stranger we'd freed from the Cardinal's Underworld immediately began to carry himself differently. He'd stood straight and proud since the moment he'd first spoken in Hades, but now, a certain level of arrogance and superiority beyond anything I'd noticed from him before invaded his features and stance.

"The only question now is who's going to be first?" No sooner had the words left Metis's lips than he rushed Emir, who was still recuperating from Rosemary's shuriken attack. Faster than I could follow, he wrapped his fingers around the man's throat and lifted him from the ground with no more effort than if he were holding a cup of coffee.

As the piercing crack of the Redstart telekinetic's neck breaking echoed in the space, I recalled a video Ethan showed me once of a jaguar clamping its jaws around a crocodile's neck and killing it instantly. Until that moment, the visual had been the most brutal thing I'd ever seen.

"Emir!" Jamila shouted. "No!"

"Don't worry, little puppet master." Metis glanced her way. "You're the only thing keeping the rest of the rabble in check at the moment, so you get to live a little longer." He looked down upon Emir's crumpled form as the Redstart telekinetic's body began to glow with a golden shimmer. "In any case, I have business to attend to."

"Rosemary," Ethan shouted, "get down!"

No warning for me, I noticed.

As both Ethan and Rosemary dove for the pavement, the entire parking lot filled with the golden light. Warm on my skin and blinding in its intensity, the radiance quickly coalesced into a tornado of gilded energy that flowed from Emir into Metis with a crack of static electricity and a gust of wind. Ethan had described what happened when the Cardinal took the Greyhound's essence in Denver. I'd prayed that I'd never bear witness to such a scene.

Yet another prayer unanswered.

Whatever remained of the golden glow around Emir's form faded quickly into darkness as Metis subsumed all that the man was and all he had ever been. Metis, conversely, stood even straighter, his already muscular form suddenly flush with vigor and new life. A moment later, the entire block was plunged into darkness, no doubt by the phenomenon we'd just witnessed. His body still surrounded in silver fire, Ethan charged Metis, only for his Flame to be extinguished a moment later in a flurry of movement and a clatter of steel on asphalt.

The last thing I saw before Ethan's flame went out was Metis's rabid leer as he looked my way, his expression that of a hungry predator who had tasted blood and was ready for more. Knowing he was there in the darkness filled me with a terror I hadn't felt since I was little. And it wasn't just fear for my life, but the inescapable inner voice reminding me over and over that I was the one who insisted on freeing this monster from his cage, the ever-present whisper shifting to fervent scream. My heart pounded in my ears as I struggled both to hear even the subtlest sound and to free myself from Jamila's control.

As the lights slowly came back up, the sight before us left me speechless. At the center of the asphalt battlefield, Metis stood exultant, a weaponless Ethan dangling from his grasp and an unmoving Rosemary at his feet as Daichi, Latifah, Jamila, and Jade all looked on in horror.

"I've changed my mind, witch." As Ethan struggled to free his arm from the monster's grip, Metis raised his opposite hand and pulled Jamila to his free hand with telekinetic power I had a nasty feeling he hadn't possessed two minutes earlier. "With such a smorgasbord of delights before me, I think I'll sample your ability next." His fingers clamped down on her neck as they had around Emir's moments before. "As much as I love a good fight, the thought of simply enjoying such a luxurious feast without the entrees fighting back is quite intoxicating."

Without warning, my entire body relaxed, and like a marionette with its strings cut, I fell to my knees, my body, mind, and voice suddenly again my own.

"Stop it!" I screamed. "Leave her alone!" I made damn sure not to say a word about who it was I was really concerned about. Even a hint about my feelings for Ethan would be tantamount to signing his death order. "You don't have to do this."

"But I do." His face broke into a hungry smile. "And not only do I need to take this mind-witch's life, I *long* to." And with that, he pulled Jamila around to look her straight in the eye. "It's funny, in a way. I've sensed your mistrust from the very beginning, Persephone Snow, but only now do you finally understand who among us is the true puppet master."

CHAPTER 28

TRUE COLORS

"This was all a trap?" I asked. "But for who? You had me dead to rights from the moment we pulled you out of that—"

Wait. Metis and I were the primary two who had come up with the idea to go after the Angel of Harlem and bring her back to Boise so she could help us track down the Cardinal. The rest had gone along with the plan, but mainly because I'd presented it. Looking back, however, it had been Metis who had led me to the idea in the first place.

And now? I had delivered him an Angel. Not the one we'd discussed, but an Angel all the same. As Alba pulled up at my left shoulder and prepared to fight, Metis looked her way with a ravenous stare. What had I done?

As my mind continued down the rabbit hole, my heart fluttered as realization after realization hit me. Metis had just made it clear he had no compunction murdering his own kind, he moved with strength and speed like the Greyhound had, and he spoke with the same air of superiority I'd grown accustomed to hearing from a certain crimson-armored psychopath. Had this all been a set-up? As Sunil had suggested before we awakened the madman before us, was it possible that rather than another prisoner of the Cardinal, Metis was in fact the Cardinal himself?

In this game of chess we were playing, I'd thought myself a queen. Facing the reality that I was nothing but a mere pawn sent a spike of ice straight through my chest.

"You said we needed Lady Day to help us find the Cardinal so we could finish him once and for all and move on with our lives."

"You got the first part right." He looked Alba's way. "Though you've far surpassed even my wildest imagination by bringing me El Ángel del Alba." He returned his attention to Jamila, her throat still held fast in the madman's upraised hand, and I hated myself a bit at being grateful he was ignoring the man I love held in his opposite hand. "But before dessert, perhaps a second course to help feed my voracious appetite."

I steeled myself for another gruesome crack, but instead my ears popped with a shift in pressure as a howling hurricane wind swept down from the sky and sent Metis and his two captives flying. The main gust sent Metis clear across the parking lot, his brief flight concluding with a metallic crunch as his muscular form totaled a Honda minivan.

Couldn't have happened to a nicer guy.

Jamila tumbled end over end through the air, her flailing form headed for a motor vehicle collision of its own, but half a second before impact, her airborne partner caught her by the arm and pulled her skyward and out of sight. Though their third lay dead before us, I couldn't help but think we'd seen the last of the Redstarts for the evening.

Meanwhile, the only one of the three I truly cared about was saved from splatting by a series of concentrated upward gusts similar to those that had been my introduction to what an aeromancer could do seven months ago in Denver. If someone had told me then that I'd be thankful for the man whose winds hurled me off a perfectly good building, I'd have called them a liar.

As one final burst of wind deposited Ethan safely across the lot and as far from Metis as possible, I caught Falco's sidelong gaze behind his mirrored shades and mouthed a quick thank you. He answered with a simple nod and pulled up on my other side opposite Alba. Sunil and Dino followed suit, and the five of us stepped out of the wrecked motel room and onto the cracked asphalt. A still-dazed Jade sprinted our way and hid behind Sunil while Daichi turned to face Metis as he extricated himself from the destroyed minivan. Ethan rose from the ground where Falco's winds had left him and raced to retrieve the paired blades that were his only defense. Rosemary pulled herself up from the ground and held her katana high above her head as L.J., his form surrounded in dozens of pieces of orbiting tech, appeared at her flank.

With ten of us against Metis's one, our side boasted a warrior trained since she was a toddler to fend off Ascendant threats as a matter of course, a trio of men who commanded wind, earth, and lightning, an Angel with untold power who I'd never seen cut loose before, and Ethan flush with the power of two millennia of warriors and ensconced in living flame. Still, all I could think about was how many of us were about to die at the hands of an unstoppable monster with dark locks and a devil's smile.

"Very well." Metis pulled himself up from the ground where Falco's wind had set him down considerably more roughly than it had Ethan. "With both the mind-witches in the wind, it would appear we will be doing this the hard way after all."

"You killed Emir Idrissi," Ethan said, directing the longer of his two glowing blades at Metis, "but he had just attempted to do the same to you, so by the Standards of Contact, you were within your rights to defend yourself."

Ethan sounded like a cop. I had to admit, the whole thing was pretty damn sexy, especially with the new muscles he'd put on, the accompanying confidence, and the fact that he was literally standing there engulfed in silver fire.

"Walk away," Ethan continued, "and this won't have to get ugly."

"You haven't seen ugly, Harkreader." Metis studied the constant white flame surrounding Ethan's form. "So, the Fire of Neith is yours to command, eh, boy? You have significantly more balls than anyone I've seen pull that trick before, or at least, I hope you do, for your sake." He laughed. "Fascinating, by the way. I thought that particular flame died out generations ago." He cast a disparaging eye Rosemary's way. "I'd ask how such a spark was ignited in the heart of a *man*, if I truly cared."

Ethan and Rosemary shared a look, his questioning and hers more baffled. Unless I was missing something, Metis had just spouted information about the Daughters of Neith that the only living soul remaining of that line wasn't privy to.

And she didn't like it.

With a silent nod, Ethan and Rosemary both charged Metis again, this time with the benefit of being able to see what they were doing. It didn't matter. With a wave of his hand, he sent their weapons flying, taking full advantage yet again of his newfound telekinetic ability.

"I must admit"—Metis cracked his neck as he studied the ten of us gathered against him—"it's been a long time since I've tasted of a psychokinetic. I'd forgotten how intoxicating such power can be."

"Can all of you do that?" I asked under my breath. "Take on the abilities of those you've killed?"

"First," Falco whispered, "we don't go around simply killing each other."

"At least not without cause," Sunil added.

"But to answer your question, no." Alba stepped forward and set the dozens of loose hunks of stone, steel, and drywall floating about her body anew. "Ascendant as a whole don't take on the abilities of those we defeat in combat. Their energies, their power, their essence, yes. But their talent dies with them." She glared at Metis, her angry stare met with a capricious smile. "Unless the particular Ascendant happens to be a...Lord of Death?"

"Lord of Death?" I asked. "So, Metis *is* Hades?" My mind spiraled at the bizarre coincidence of my name and the events of the preceding months. "The Greek god from all the mythology books? Is that even possible?"

"The answer to that question is complicated," Metis said, his voice filled with arrogant swagger. "I will note that the Hades of legend and myth was indeed a worthy opponent, but in the end he fell by my hand." His smile grew wider. "Just like all the others."

The bastard sounded more and more like the Cardinal with every syllable, and yet, something was off. Bradley had only been tracking the armored killer's activities for a couple of years, but the way Metis was talking, it sounded like he'd been around longer than the Angels themselves.

"So, you're not the God of the Underworld, but you took his place?" I asked, a bit dumbfounded that Ethan, Rosemary, and even Alba were letting me do the talking. "And who or what would that make you, Metis, as everyone here knows that name is nothing but a fabrication?"

"The *who* I will keep to myself for a bit longer." Metis laughed. "But as for the *what*, Alba said it herself. You've encountered individuals who control the shadows at your feet, the elements that make up the world around you, the machines that surround us in the modern day, and even the electricity that makes those very machines come to life."

"She called you a Lord of Death."

"So close, Snow. So close." Metis's eyes took on the cast of a frustrated schoolteacher. "Aeromancer. Pyromancer. Geomancer. Hydromancer." He pulled in a breath. "Technomancer. Skiomancer. Psychomancer." He raised a mocking eyebrow. "Doesn't it seem like there's one you're missing?" He chuckled. "Right there, on the tip of your tongue?"

Of course. A word I'd only ever heard in one of the fantasy movies Ethan and I watched what seemed an eternity ago.

"Necromancer."

I had no idea what that word meant in relation to Ascendant, but in myth and pop culture, at least according to Ethan, necromancers were wizards who could talk to the dead and sometimes even raise them from their eternal slumber. Metis seemed more a dealer of death than anything like that, but then again, seven months ago, my entire line of questioning would have been relegated to the part of my brain reserved for fairy tale characters and My Little Pony factoids. God only knew what the reality was.

One thing I did know: I'd only encountered one other Ascendant who could take the abilities of others. If the man before us truly was the Cardinal, then he was making it perfectly clear that, armor or not, he was not only unafraid to face a small army of Ascendant, but that he reveled in the moment.

"Sorry about the collar, Seph." L.J. looked my way. "I didn't know."

"That horse is out of the barn, L.J." I shot him a forgiving smile. "Only thing to do now is fight."

"And fight we will." Alba stood at my side, imperious. "You wield the skills of the telekinetic well, Metis. I can only imagine what other stolen talents you hide within that foul heart of yours, but ask yourself: do you really wish to face us all?"

"I desire nothing more, one at a time or all at once." He extended his arm and beckoned us to attack with a taunting wave. "Who shall be first?"

"I didn't like you from the moment we first laid eyes on your drugged-out carcass back in the hole." Sunil stepped forward, his eyes already glowing silver-blue and his clenched fists surrounded in crackling electricity. "We should have left you where we found you." He stretched an arm to the sky, and the lights all around the parking lot dimmed as the elektromancer charged his internal battery. "Let's see if I can't correct our error."

As electricity arced from the nearest light pole to his raised hand, Sunil raised his opposite arm and let fly a bolt of lightning from his outstretched fingers. With inhuman reflexes, Metis leaped into the air half a second before Sunil attacked, but the bolt still struck the necromancer center chest and blew him clear across the parking lot. Far from the flailing mass of arms and legs I expected, however, Metis's short flight appeared as graceful as a gymnast's dismount, and as he landed on his feet, my spine tingled as I realized how truly over our head we all were.

The arcing silver-blue energy surrounding Metis's muscular form continued for a few seconds longer, but in the end, he absorbed what had to be a few million volts as easily as a sponge might absorb water.

"It's been centuries since I took a bolt like that," Metis said. "I'd forgotten how exhilarating it felt."

Sunil looked on, dumbfounded. "But...how?"

"Like I've never tasted of elektromancer." Metis raised a hand and pulled Sunil's thrashing form to his grasping fingers with no more effort than pulling a hooked fish from the ocean. "Though it's been far longer on that count." His lips spread in a self-satisfied grin. "Time to refresh that particular talent."

When Metis took Emir's essence, it took the better part of a minute.

With Sunil, however, the horror was instantaneous. One moment, the elektromancer I'd considered a burgeoning friend struggled in the necromancer's grasp. The next, he withered into a limp husk, the very life drawn from his form in less than a second by the man he'd never wanted to help in the first place.

"Sunil!" I screamed as the image burned a scar across my psyche. "No!"

"He cannot hear you, Snow." Metis pulled in a breath as he looked on us all with a self-satisfied smirk. "But don't worry. You'll be joining him soon enough."

"But we helped you," Jade cried out. "Sunil, Daichi, me, Seph, all of us. How can you do this?"

"How can I not?" Metis studied her, his expression going cold. "Do you ask the lion not to hunt? The shark not to feed? The eagle to walk when it is meant to fly?"

"You're a human being, Metis, Ascendant or not." Jade stepped forward. "The difference between you and the animals is that you get to choose."

"I am Death, Jia Li Xiao, the end that comes for us all." His cold eyes narrowed at her. "Take comfort in the fact that I am saving you for last."

Ethan and Rosemary, their weapons recovered, formed up with us opposite Metis. Down to nine, we must have looked to the monster like blades of grass standing tall and proud as the mower approached.

"Enough." Alba's expression went as cold as her enemy's. "Dietrich, Daichi, incapacitate this monster."

The command had barely left her lips before tendrils of stone rose at Metis's feet and encircled his legs, waist, and torso. A moment later, my very breath was taken from me as Falco summoned a miniature cyclone from the crystal clear night sky and hit the immobilized necromancer with gale force. Ethan shot a quick look my way and shouted something, but between my ears popping with the massive pressure shift and the roar of the storm, I didn't hear a word.

A solid minute passed before Falco let up on Metis. As the cyclone faded into a gentle breeze and the dust began to settle, we all got a good look at our incapacitated foe. Cocooned to the waist in asphalt and concrete, Metis's head hung to one side, his tongue lolling from his mouth. As helpless as when we'd first seen him back in Tartarus, a part of me almost felt sorry for him.

A very small part.

Alba raised her arms to either side as if she were a bird of prey stretching its wings as a localized gust of wind pulled the Angel up from the concrete and deposited her by Metis's unconscious form. Falco and Daichi joined her, the former following Alba's lead while Daichi trundled to her side in three giant earth-shaking steps.

"It would seem this monster orchestrated some or all of this spectacle simply to draw me out, a mistake he will not live to regret." With a raised fist, Alba assumed control of the rocky shell surrounding Metis, constricting the asphalt and concrete around his limp form as easily as one might squeeze a bottle of toothpaste, and created a new collar of stone and steel to encircle his neck. "I take no joy in ending another Ascendant's existence, regardless of the situation or need, but today, for the good of many, I will make an exception." She raised both her hands before her chest, one shifting into a fist of jagged ice while the other erupted into orange flame. "Snow reportedly found you in Hell, and so, to Hell I now return—"

The stone, steel, and asphalt shroud enveloping Metis's form exploded like a man-sized grenade. Alba and Falco took the brunt of the assault, their bodies hurled backward by the shrapnel and concussive force. Dietrich landed mere inches from my feet, his trademark white suit spotted with countless circles of crimson. Alba, on the other hand, lay sprawled at the feet of a decidedly conscious Metis.

"Mistress!" Daichi cried from within the ten feet of animated asphalt and concrete and swung a gigantic fist at Metis. "No!"

Without missing a beat, the necromancer ducked beneath the rocky haymaker, grabbed the enormous arm of rock, and sent the geomancer tumbling to the ground. Straight up judo, just like Rosemary taught me.

"From within that stone golem, boy, you are indeed a force to be reckoned with." Metis directed an outstretched hand at the center of the rocky sumo's gigantic belly. "But, in the end, you're still just a boy." The necromancer narrowed his eyes at his titanic foe. "Shall we see how well you fight as I cut off the blood supply to your brain?" With a moment of concentration, Metis left the gigantic sumo of earth dissolved into a pile of destroyed pavement, no doubt with an unconscious boy resting at its core. "Hmm. Not so well, it would appear."

Metis swept Alba up from the wrecked asphalt and held her dazed form before him, their faces so close, I half-believed he meant to kiss her.

"And now, at long last," Metis whispered, all but licking his lips, "my prize."

CHAPTER 29

HUNGRY EYES

"*Stop!*" I sang, channeling Diana Ross for the second time in as many days. "*In the name of love...*"

Metis shot a perturbed look my way. "What are you doing, Snow?"

"Keeping you from doing your thing, it would seem." I gestured to Alba, who hung limp from Metis's outstretched hand, her dangling arms and legs still flush with life. "Unless you're simply playing with your food this time."

An irritated Metis returned his attention to the Angel in his grasp, refocused his energies, and still...nothing.

"You know, I hear this happens to all men eventually." I poured every ounce of contempt possible into my words. "Modern medicine, however, has made great strides in this field, and—"

"One more word and I'll rip out your throat, witch."

"Keep going, Seph." Ethan shot an encouraging look my way.

"Your voice is the first thing that's made a dent in this asshole's armor."

But what to sing? My snippet of The Supremes had cut Metis off from his necromantic talent just enough to give Alba a stay of execution, but I had no idea how long it would last.

Fortunately, I wasn't alone in the fight.

A gun roared by my right ear, and though he hadn't spoken since reclaiming control of his body from Jamila, Dino stood armed and ready for action.

His first shot caught Metis in the left thigh, the quick gush of blood suggesting Dino had hit an artery. His hold on Alba faltered, and she dropped from his grasp to the unforgiving pavement. No longer protected by his Angelic human shield, Metis stumbled backward as Dino unloaded his magazine at the bleeding necromancer. Most of the bullets went wide, but at least a couple found their target.

It was nice to know that even a Lord of Death could bleed.

With a grunt and an animalistic baring of his teeth, Metis turned and fled across the street, disappearing between the trees that lined the opposite side.

"Nice shooting, Dino." Ethan shot his friend a grim smile. "Keep that up, and Bradley's going to put you up for a promotion." He glanced my way, took a breath to say something, but in the end, shook his head in frustration and took off after Metis.

"We are all in your debt, Dino. Thank you for helping keep everyone safe." Rosemary turned her attention to my favorite technomancer. "You too, L.J. Don't blame yourself for this. None of us knew who or what this monster truly was." She glanced my way. "And you, Seph. It's so good to see you again. I wish we had time to—"

"Go." I pointed in the direction Ethan had sprinted after the fleeing Metis. "We've got the rest of our lives to catch up." I locked gazes with Rosemary, and willed the sheer gravity of the situation into my words. "Right now, I need you to make sure nothing happens to Ethan. Go get that bastard and put an end to this."

"From your mouth to God's ears," Rosemary whispered before

rushing after Ethan. "Keep your eyes and ears open," she shouted over her shoulder. "I have a feeling this isn't over."

And with that, the two people I'd fought six straight months to get back to disappeared around a dark corner, leaving me, yet again, alone.

Well, apart from Alba and her recuperating elementalists, a dazed L.J., Jade, Dino, and what was left of Sunil and Emir. I refused to even glance at the two corpses in our midst for fear I would lose whatever was left in my stomach.

I stood surrounded by half a dozen earthbound gods, and yet I'd never felt so exposed or vulnerable. We'd outnumbered Metis ten-to-one, and he'd torn through us like a sword through wet tissue. The fact that it had been Dino and his crack shooting that saved the day wouldn't leave my mind. Not the all-powerful Angel and half her team of seasoned professionals nor the combat squad of trained psychomancers, but an ordinary man with an ordinary gun. No wonder the Ascendant, for all their power and abilities, kept themselves off the world stage.

In any case, God willing, Ethan and Rosemary would finish what Dino started. Still, I didn't intend to leave anything up to chance.

"Alba," I whispered as I knelt by the Angel's side, "are you all right?"

"I will be." She raised her eyes to meet my gaze. "Ironically, after all the trouble you went through to solicit my aid, it would seem it is *I* who am now in *your* debt."

"Words that have rarely, if ever, left my mistress's lips." Falco stood and brushed himself off, his white suit stained with multiple splotches of red, courtesy of the shrapnel from Metis's attack. "Mark this moment, Snow."

The pile of rubble that had moments before been a ten-foot sumo of asphalt and concrete parted as if by magic, revealing the geomancer I'd come to think of as friend, regardless of how we met, his rail-thin legs twisted amid the debris.

"Daichi!" I stepped carefully through the broken stone and pavement and dropped to my knees by his bruised shoulder. "I'm here."

"Thanks." He shot me an exhausted smile. "Help me up?"

"Of course." I pulled him to a wobbly sit and gingerly let him go, half afraid that he'd fall over and crack his skull on one of the stones that had so recently been under his command. "Can you move?"

"As well as I could before," he grumbled with a laugh, "but I don't think anything is broken, if that's what you're asking."

"Meanwhile, another suit is ruined." Falco looked down upon his blood-stained ivory jacket through his mirrored shades. "I particularly liked this one, too. Custom, Italian, silk." He shook his head. "And quite expensive."

"Are we seriously sitting here licking our wounds and complaining about our damaged wardrobe?" Dino slapped a fresh magazine into his pistol and started walking in the direction Metis had gone. "That monster demolished us without breaking a sweat, and now Ethan and Rosemary are facing the bastard alone."

"We shall go to their aid as soon as we are ready." Alba's voice was firm, but her tone contained a hint of admiration as she looked upon Dino. "In any case, it would seem that Mr. Harkreader chooses his companions well."

I allowed Dino his seconds in the sun before getting back to business.

"How are we going to find them?" I looked Falco's way. "You've got the bird's eye view, I'm guessing?"

"As always," Falco said.

"I shall join you above, Dietrich." Alba shifted her gaze skyward. "Two sets of eyes are better than one."

"The rest of us will follow by ground," Daichi said, "and none of us will make the mistake of getting within fifty yards of that animal this time."

"I can feel his hunger and rage even from here," Jade said, "not to mention a hint of fear." Her entire body shook in revulsion. "Being in Metis's presence with the collar on was bad enough. Now that it's off, his mere proximity leaves me feeling like I'm swimming among eels."

"Sunil was right." My lower lip trembled as I fought back tears. "We never should have let Metis go free." For the first time since he fell, I allowed myself to look at the elektromancer's shriveled form just a few feet from Emir's twisted corpse. "And two have already paid the price for my mistake."

"Our mistake," Daichi said. "Any of us could have made that call, not to mention we made that decision together." He rested a hand on my thigh. "Whatever carnage Metis causes, it's on all of us."

"Agreed." Jade knelt by my side, and the two of us pulled Daichi from the rubble. "Now, let's go stop that bastard before he hurts anyone else."

"Hang on." L.J. pulled a handful of black earbuds from a pouch at his side and, after focusing on the entire bunch for a few seconds, handed one to each of us. "These should help us all keep in touch." As he approached Alba, he dropped to one knee and held the last of the earbuds before him without meeting her gaze. "Angel of the Morning, would you honor me by accepting this small token of my regard?"

"Ah, little technomancer." Alba laughed and took L.J. by the chin, bringing his gaze to hers with a wide smile. "More than once have I been proposed to with far less grace than you currently demonstrate. I find both you and your gift worthy." She extended a hand and helped him back to his feet. "Rise and join us, if you will." Any hint of mirth left the Angel's face. "Metis is about to learn why no one crosses El Ángel del Alba."

As Alba and Falco took to the sky, Daichi pulled together a mass of the rubble surrounding him and maneuvered himself into a rough chair fashioned of concrete and asphalt.

"No sumo this time?" I asked.

"Still catching my breath, I guess." Daichi's gaze dropped to the ground. "Not to mention, the armor didn't seem to help so much." He shot a look toward Sunil's and Emir's remains. "Two down already today." With a simple gesture, he gathered the remaining loose rock and debris from across the entire parking lot and formed a makeshift cairn. "This should keep them safe until we can provide a proper funeral." He raised an eyebrow my way. "Ready?"

The undertone in Daichi's voice communicated that he understood as well as I did that Metis could have broken his neck as easily as he'd cut off the blood to his brain. What we were about to do was borderline foolish, pursuing a monster who was not only capable of killing any of us with a thought but would do so without a second one.

But what choice did we have? More specifically, what choice did *I* have?

Ethan, for all his power and skill, even with Rosemary backing him up, was in mortal danger, and it *was* my fault, no matter what Daichi or Jade said. The Daughter of Neith's opening declaration that no one was dying here today had already been proven wrong not once, but twice since her arrival. With God as my witness, Sunil would be the last to fall.

We took off across the parking lot and around the same tree-lined corner where Ethan and Rosemary had vanished moments before. For the first time, I noticed the scattered rubberneckers on both levels of the motel as well as along the street who had likely observed the events of the last half hour with great interest and almost certainly with phones in hand.

As Ethan had explained it, what seemed an eternity ago, a network of technomancers kept visual and video evidence of Ascendant off both the internet and individual devices. Now that I knew of the existence of psychomancers, I suspected that memories must be subject to the constant purge as well to keep secret the presence of gods who walked among mortals, particularly in this day and age when every single thing was photographed, recorded, cataloged, and posted for the entire world to see. Otherwise, how could all this be going on under the noses of the seven billion people walking the planet?

A lot of Ascendant were going to be busy for weeks cleaning up this colossal mess.

We must have been quite the sight: a Japanese teen riding a gigantic throne of floating rock hurtling down the street accompanied by a world famous pop star, a brown kid with teal hair orbited by a dozen hunks of floating machines, a supermodel beauty in ragtag blue sweats, and a mid-twenties hipster packing serious heat, and that didn't even take into account the pair of battered superhumans circling in the sky above.

I'd watched all the superhero movies with Ethan. I never dreamed I'd find myself living through one of them.

"There, Mistress," came Falco's voice through L.J.'s communicator device as we passed another intersection. "I have visual on Metis, Harkreader, and Delacroix."

"Lead on, then, Dietrich," Alba answered. "Let's end this."

Alba and Falco took off, converging on a point just beyond my field of vision at the end of the next block. A moment later, Jade stopped in her tracks and appeared ready to wretch.

"What is it, Jade?" I asked, rushing to her side. "What do you feel?"

"Metis," she answered. "He's cornered and angry." She locked gazes with me, her eyes filled with fear. "But above all, ravenous."

"We have to get there, now!" I took off at a full sprint, grateful that I'd maintained my cardiovascular fitness during my six months of captivity. "Come on!"

I'd halved the distance to the next corner when Daichi flew past, L.J. hanging off one side of his massive throne of stone and Dino off the other.

"We'll take point, Seph," Dino shouted as they flew by.

"Watch your back," L.J. added before they rocketed out of earshot and around the house at the next intersection. "Both of you," came the remainder of his thought through the receiver resting in my ear.

"You too," I shouted, hoping L.J.'s earbud radio transmitted as well as it received. "We're right behind you."

With every step, every breath, every pounding heartbeat those last few feet, my brain ran through image after image of what I might find when I finally caught up with Ethan, Rosemary, and the others, each worse than the one before.

Nothing could have prepared me, however, for the scene that awaited as I hit the next street, the block beyond opening to our left on a tiny park lined with young trees, its parking area empty except for a dilapidated Kia from a couple decades back that looked like it hadn't budged in months. The vast grassy area beyond, barely illuminated by the few streetlights around the park's periphery, provided a darkened stage for the unfolding drama.

At the center, a wounded Metis waited in the near darkness as two figures enveloped in silver flame rushed at him from either side. As I'd seen them practice dozens of times, Ethan went high and Rosemary low as they pushed the attack, probing Metis's defenses as they worked to bring this conflict to an end.

"Perhaps if I turn up the heat a bit," Alba's voice sounded in my ear.

"It worked when Ada tried it," Falco said. "Really turned the tide."

"And who was it that taught my pyromancer everything she knows?"

Barely visible in the sky above, Falco and Alba circled, the latter's hands erupting in twin balls of fire the same color as Ethan's Flame. Just as Ada had helped to stoke the Fire of Neith in Ethan's heart all those months ago atop a mountain half a state away, so now did her mistress bring her talents to bear.

I prayed it would be enough.

Straight ahead, Daichi rested atop a park bench with L.J. and Dino on either side. Dozens of hunks of stone, concrete, and asphalt hovered in the air around him, the remnants of his rocky throne, while L.J. manipulated the various pieces of tech orbiting his body and Dino kept his weapon trained on Metis in case a rain of bullets was what the situation required.

And somehow, at the center of it all, Metis couldn't have looked less concerned.

Wounded? Yes. Cornered and angry? Definitely. But worried? Not even close.

Ethan and Rosemary converged upon Metis for another coordinated strike, the twin flames surrounding their forms glowing brighter and brighter as Alba poured her influence into them. Daichi let fly with a trio of jagged rocks that hurtled at the necromancer in the near darkness. L.J. swept left and Dino right in an effort to outflank Metis and prevent any chance of escape. Falco hovered in the air at Alba's side, the cyclonic winds holding the pair aloft pulling dust and debris up from the ground into a miniature tornado. I followed the staccato conversation over L.J.'s makeshift network, and all involved seemed to be on the same page. For half a second, I allowed myself the luxury of believing that everything was finally going our way, a belief that evaporated a moment later like raindrops on a lava flow.

The trio of stones struck Metis square in the chest, sending his body flying into the darkness and away from Ethan and Rosemary. I lost sight of Metis in the dim along with everyone else, according to the buzz in my ear. As the most dangerous man I'd ever encountered vanished into the darkness, however, one simple fact filled my heart with dread: the three most visible figures in the night, and therefore the three most at risk, were the man and woman engulfed in silver flame and the Angel hovering far above, her fists held out to either side and her lithe form coruscating with the same mystic fire.

In the time it took to understand what was happening, it was done. One of the stones flew at Ethan and the second at Rosemary, each striking its target center chest and sending the man I love and my best friend flailing to the ground. Thunder rumbled above our heads and ozone assaulted my nostrils as a bolt of lightning tore down from the sky, striking both Falco and Alba as it roared down to Metis's outstretched hand. Both the Angel and her aeromancer dropped from the sky like stones and struck the ground with a pair of sickening thuds. Meanwhile, the necromancer stood revealed by the millions of volts running down his body with only Daichi, L.J., and Dino remaining to carry on the fight.

"No!" Daichi cried out. "Mistress!" With a wave of his arm, the geomancer sent the airborne avalanche before him flying at Metis only for the dozens of rocks to fall to the ground halfway to their target. Daichi pitched forward off the park bench and landed face first in the grass. Behind where his head had been seconds before hovered the third hunk of asphalt and concrete he'd sent flying at Metis. I wasn't sure if I imagined the flash of crimson that decorated one of the stone's jagged edges.

"What a pathetic excuse for a geomancer," Metis said as he absorbed the electricity into his form, "removed from play by the very element over which he claims mastery."

With the light from Ethan and Rosemary's shared Flame extinguished and the Angel's corresponding twin balls of fire going cold, whatever poor visibility we'd had of the tiny battlefield faded to impenetrable darkness. If I knew Metis, though, and I was pretty sure I understood him well by this point, I had little doubt that he had his eye on the prize. I rushed for Alba with Jade in tow, barely making it halfway to her side before the necromancer I'd set free upon the world materialized above the fallen Angel. My brain and vocal cords and lungs all finally caught up with the horror of the moment, and I screamed in fear and rage.

"I was hungry before." A smiling Metis looked down upon Alba's twisted form. "But now I've really worked up an appetite."

"Get away from her!" L.J. ran at Metis from one side, the swarm of machines floating around him barely visible in the dim. "Leave her alone!"

A breath later, a single gunshot sounded from the opposite direction. Both Metis and I shifted our attention toward the muzzle flash to find Dino rushing straight at the gloating necromancer, a suicide play if I'd ever seen one. As Metis didn't so much as flinch, I could only guess that the bullet had missed. Before Dino could fire another, the necromancer extended a hand in my friend's direction, telekinetically seized the weapon, and pistol-whipped poor Dino about the head and shoulders until he dropped unconscious to the wet grass.

"No!" I screamed. "Dino!"

Not wasting an instant, Metis turned his attention on L.J., pulling the teen technomancer away from all his gear and to his outstretched hand. With a combination of his own strength and stolen telekinetic power, he hurled the teal-haired boy to the ground at his feet, the sickening crunch of the impact sending the hairs on my neck on end.

"Seph!" Jade shouted in my ear. "I know it's not what you want to hear, but we've got to go."

Without another word, Metis brought Dino's gun to his hand, aimed the barrel my way, and fired. The bullet passed so close, I could almost feel the heat from its steel jacket.

Still, Metis had missed.

Metis didn't strike me as the type who missed.

"Why?" I searched the necromancer's face for answers. "Why spare me?"

"Seph..." Jade croaked, her voice quiet and weak.

I glanced back and found my friend clutching her belly, blood seeping between her fingers as she crumpled to the damp grass.

"Jade." The emotion of the moment stole my voice, leaving me with only a rasping whisper. "No."

"And now," Metis said, his ravenous gaze feasting upon the sight of the fallen Angel lying at his feet, "at last I will enjoy my—"

A golden light filled the air before Metis, and before he could complete his thought, Lady Day stepped from the shimmer of radiance, grabbed her Sister, and shouted to the sky, "The Diner, Midnight, Now!"

Both Angels disappeared in a flash of incandescent sparkle, leaving me, and hopefully Metis, momentarily blinded. As my eyes adjusted again to the darkness, I found my vision filled with the necromancer's wicked grin as he pulled a pair of noise-canceling headphones from L.J.'s unconscious form and placed them over his ears.

"You've denied me my prize, Persephone Snow." He took a step in my direction. "Know that I had no particular need nor desire to feast upon a siren this night, but now this has become personal." He leveled the pistol until the barrel was aimed directly between my eyes. "Not that it will change the outcome one iota, but if you value your life, little girl, you better run."

CHAPTER 30

I RAN

I sprinted from the park as if the Devil himself were on my heels, the realization that such a statement was closer to fact than fantasy lending even more urgency to my every step. I didn't dare look back for fear that I might trip and fall and find myself at the necromancer's mercy.

What if he were right behind me, merely letting me think I had a hope of escaping his deadly touch?

Even worse, what if he stayed behind to finish the job? Ethan, Rosemary, Daichi, Falco, L.J., Dino—they were all at the mercy of a madman, and again it was all my fault. If Ethan or any of them died because of me, I would never forgive myself. I already carried the burden of Sunil's death, Emir's too. I'm not sure I could handle another soul on my conscience.

And yet, what else could I do? The only weapon I had at my disposal had been rendered useless by a piece of equipment you could buy off the shelf at any electronics store. Not that I had the first clue how I would use my siren abilities to stop Metis. My impromptu salute to 60s soul had saved Alba, but beyond that, what the hell was I supposed to do against a literal Lord of Death?

A block from the park, I cut a sharp right across a yard wet from the sprinkler and chanced my first look back the way I'd come. No Metis, no rushing footsteps, nothing. The stitch in my side that had been developing in my right belly chose that moment to come into its own. I panted like a dog, my body drenched with sweat borne from not only exertion but fear.

"He's back there killing them all," I grumbled to myself. "I'm such a fucking coward."

"Plenty of time for them later, Snow," came Metis's voice from above my head. "At the moment, however, I'm rather enjoying our little game of cat and mouse."

I peered up into the night sky and found Metis grinning down at me from atop a floating slab of concrete. I prayed this was another manifestation of Emir's telekinetic ability and not a sign that Daichi had already met Sunil's horrible fate. With a wink, the necromancer slid back into L.J.'s noise-canceling headphones, which, at least where my talent was concerned, served Metis as a bulletproof vest.

"So, this is what you do?" I shouted. "Killing out of necessity is one thing, but to enjoy it the way you do? You disgust me."

"Not that I can hear a word you're saying"—with a subtle wave of his hand, the stone holding Metis aloft descended until we were eye-to-eye—"but fear not. Another few seconds and nothing will ever bother you again."

For the hundredth time, I wondered if the man leering at me and the man in the Cardinal armor could be one and the same. They shared a unique hunger and a desperate need to rise to the top regardless of the cost, but where the Cardinal had always seemed efficient and emotionless in his quest for his next Ascendant prey, Metis was the polar opposite. Vindictive, capricious, and jubilant in the taking of life, Metis, as I'd snarked earlier, very much liked to play with his food.

Food which, at the moment, consisted of yours truly.

"Quick and painless, or a fight to the bitter end, Snow? I'll at least offer you an option about how you leave this world." Metis stretched out a hand to touch my cheek, and no matter how much I tried to force my body to recoil, I found myself frozen to the spot like a terrified rat before a swaying cobra. "Make your choice quickly, though. I have much work to do this night, and morning is almost upon us."

Death stared at me with dark brown eyes from a twisted sneer as my mind vacillated between giving in and being put down mercifully like a dog at the pound or going down swinging. I knew which Rosemary would pick and the fate Ethan would choose without question, but I was so tired. Would it be so bad to just let go and let it be over? I'd seen Ethan one last time, even if it hadn't been the reunion I'd imagined. Maybe my essence would leave Metis sated, and my running away, in a sense, would allow my friends to live to fight another day.

My cheek went cold as his fingertips drew close, and I allowed my eyes to slip closed, strangely grateful that Metis had made the decision for me.

"Snow."

Metis's voice, but not Metis's.

"Snow. Open your eyes. Now."

I didn't believe what I was hearing, as Latifah Lazaar's accent again colored the necromancer's words.

I opened my eyes to find an invisible struggle playing out across Metis's features. His arms were held out to either side as if crucified to an invisible tree, and his face shifted like mercury between frustration, agony, fear, and rage. Metis had booted Latifah from his mind earlier in the evening, an eviction that had cost her dearly based on the bone-chilling scream that still echoed across the landscape of my mind.

"What the hell?" I asked the woman lurking behind the necromancer's dark eyes. "You're saving me, now?"

"We sought to secure you mainly to gain leverage for...personal reasons." Her eyes stared out at me from Metis's enraged face. "Understand, however, that neither of us wish you any harm."

"Neither of you?"

"Jamila is keeping Metis from administering his death touch while I scramble his thoughts to the best of my ability to allow you to escape." The necromancer's face, placid one moment, twisted into a rictus of fury as he assumed a modicum of control over his own body. "Two of you this time, eh?" came Metis's unadulterated venom. "The backlash last time wasn't enough for you, Lazaar? Back for more?" His face twisted again, this time into an expression of panic. "We can't hold him for much longer, Snow. Run! Now!"

She didn't have to tell me twice. I backed away, keeping my eyes riveted on Metis's every movement as he struggled against the pair of psychomancers within his mind, and when I was beyond the range of his grasping fingers, I turned and sprinted away. But where to go? I'd seen maybe one car in the last hour, as it was still basically the middle of the night, and any house I stopped at would be tantamount to signing the owner's death warrant if Metis found me there.

Another block, and a passing helicopter gave me new direction. The airport, even in the middle of the night, would have a bazillion places to hide between the parking decks and the hundreds of parked cars. I wasn't sure of the time, but as morning approached, I'd hopefully be able to lose myself in the crowd—as long as no one got too close a look at my face, that is.

As I passed another intersection, the stitch in my right side returned with a vengeance. Like a knitting needle jammed beneath my rib cage, the stabbing pain grew worse with every step, every breath, and I made it no more than another block before I finally had to stop again. I sought shelter between the nearest house and its detached garage, squatting between their trash can and recycling bin as I did what I could to slow my breathing and get the knife in my side to let up a bit. I only allowed myself to breathe through my nose, fighting to stay as silent as possible as I strained my ears for the slightest hint of pursuit. A minute passed, then another, my fingers just below the angle of my jaw monitoring my pulse as my heart rate returned to something approaching normal.

Had I lost Metis? Was it possible that I'd escaped not only him, but death as well?

It was only a matter of time before he freed himself from the double team psychomancer attack. If he couldn't find me, would he simply return to the park and take out his frustration on the others, feasting upon their lives and essences and making himself stronger than ever? And what then? It wasn't like I could hide from the man forever. Even if I complied with the plan that Mr. Delacroix had advocated months ago and went underground until all of this blew over—not that my life as an Ascendant had any kind of expiration date—I had a feeling that Metis would still find me.

And when he did, it wouldn't be to talk.

Rosemary taught me how to breathe as much as any vocal coach I'd ever met. Before teaching me how to stand, punch, kick, or block, she'd worked to help me achieve control over the most basic function of life that each of us do every minute of every day. I utilized everything she'd taught me, attempting to control the pain in my side. My friend's stern but soothing tones filled my thoughts, bringing me to my center and flipping the final switch in my mind, as I accepted one simple fact.

This struggle of wills between Metis and me? It had to end, and not someday down the road, but as soon as possible. As the only path forward began to coalesce in my mind, I realized that not only was everyone counting on me, but I was counting on them as well. I had no idea if my insane gambit would work, the plan hatching step by impossible step between my every racing thought. My knees knocked as I rose to my feet, but I was done running.

"I'm coming for you, Metis," I muttered. "Time for both of us to face the music."

I took a different path back to the park, moving as quickly as I could with my side still panging like I'd swallowed a screwdriver. The cramping below my ribcage coupled with the inescapable thought that I'd get back just in time to witness Metis administer the coup de gras to Ethan or someone else I cared about left me on the edge of vomiting every few feet, but I soldiered on, step after step.

This time, like it or not, I was the cavalry.

After the longest three minutes of my life, my heart leaped as I rounded the corner and caught sight of the same abandoned Kia I'd seen before. I ducked across the street and hid along the park's tree line. The open grassy area remained exactly as I'd left it, littered with the unconscious forms of so many that I cared about.

At least I hoped they were all just unconscious.

After a quick scan of the area, I rushed to Ethan's side. Though his body lay askew on the grass, nothing appeared broken, and his chest continued to rise and fall every couple of seconds. Relief washed over me, shifting immediately to dread as a voice I'd already come to hate emanated from the shadows a few feet away.

"I thought you might come back to the scene of the crime, such as it is." Metis materialized from the darkness with a self-satisfied grin. I half-wondered if the monster had "tasted of" skiomancer, as he liked to put it. Bravely, he held one headphone away from his ear so that we could converse. "It took longer than anticipated to drive those two mind-witches out of my head, in case you were wondering." He let out a rueful chuckle. "Some people only learn lessons the hard way."

"Present company included, I'm guessing?"

"Your words, Snow." He released the headphone, the cushion around his ear sealing him off yet again from my voice. "Not mine."

"Exactly." I allowed myself a faint smile. "That's what I'm counting on."

And with that, the time for talking was over. Alba was long gone and likely out of commission for the foreseeable future, and even the Angel of Harlem, who I guessed had just traveled the breadth of the continent in a blink to rescue her Sister, had her limits. It was up to me to hold the line, stop Metis, and make sure everyone who had gathered to save my bacon survived to see the dawn. I had no idea whether my mad plan would work or if it was merely a fool's dream, but I was about to find out. The pieces were in place, the trap set, the target in position. All the moment required was a song.

"*Get on your feet!*" I sang at the top of my lungs. A memory of

Mom singing our favorite Gloria Estefan song as we enjoyed one of our impromptu living room dance parties when I was a kid brought a faint smile to my face. I prayed the earbuds L.J. had given everyone were still working.

"Oh, Snow, you can't be serious." He tapped the headphones covering his ears. "I can barely register that you're even singing, little girl."

"Good." I ignored Metis's withering taunt, and instead continued to sing even louder, pouring every ounce of will into lyrics emblazoned on my soul since childhood. I belted out words like strength, devotion, heart, spirit.

Action.

"You're wasting your time," he grumbled, taking a step in my direction. "I can't hear you."

"I'm well aware." I smiled. "Fortunately, they can."

As one, they rose from the ground: Ethan, Rosemary, Falco, Daichi, L.J., and Dino. All but Jade, who lay exactly where I'd left her, her lifeless form pale and still. The entire scene reminded me of *Night of the Living Dead* more than I liked, but I was relieved to discover that most of my friends not only remained among the living, but still had some fight left in them.

"*What we need now,*" I sang, channeling the Man in Black, "*is a burning ring of fire.*"

A silver inferno enveloped Ethan's body, the flame leaping body to body until all but poor Jia Li had at least a taste of Ethan's healing ability. I didn't want to think about what that might mean, but if Jade was going to have any chance of survival, I had to put such questions out of my mind. The time to strike was now.

Gloria Estefan had managed to rouse the troops, and Johnny Cash had put the wind back in their sails, but the battle itself was going to require something a bit more personal, a song that poured from not only my lips, but from my heart and soul.

I'd written the second track from my debut album, *Snowblind,* after a particularly painful breakup, and the emotion hardwired into the lyrics had gutted me with every performance since. I hadn't asked the man I was seeing at the time—or boy, if I'm being honest about the situation—to buy me expensive things or take me to lavish restaurants or fly me to faraway places. I'd only wanted him to care enough, want me enough, love me enough to fight for me.

"I want you to fight for me, stand in the breach, my one and only plea."

Metis's eyes shifted left and right as the force he'd dispatched minutes before all assumed fighting positions and prepared for another round.

"I know it's simpler when you're on your own, but we're stronger as one."

As Ethan and the others circled a surprised Metis, weapons held high, I stepped back and completed the words, the chorus of my minor hit from two years back becoming a spell of sorts, returning strength to injured limbs and fortitude to wounded bodies. The euphoria of the spotlight? Didn't hold a candle to this. Not even close.

"And if you fight for me, I will fight for you."

Rosemary attacked first, slashing at Metis with her katana. Ethan was close behind, leaping over the low arc of Rosemary's blade as he employed a scissor strike with the paired Blades of Neith that drove Metis back. The necromancer staggered backward toward a hovering Falco and a grounded Daichi, the latter's hands splayed before him on the earth and his eyes squinted shut in concentration. In answer, the grassy soil and underlying clay rock beneath Metis's feet climbed up his legs like a pair of pythons that held him fast as Falco pulled the move he used against Ethan seven months back atop a restaurant in Denver. Metis wheezed and fought to breathe as the aeromancer sucked the very air from his lungs. Another blink, and dozens of flying machines swarmed Metis's form, shocking, spraying, stabbing, and swatting the struggling necromancer as L.J. looked on from the periphery of the circle, his still-dazed eyes darting this way and that as if he were dreaming with his eyes open. Dino alone held back, keeping his sights fixed on Metis but not firing a single round.

I belted out the chorus of "Fight for Me" a second time, and the fighting force unified by my voice and words kicked it up another notch. A weaponless Metis kept his arms and fists before his face, the only defense he had against the trio of slashing blades and the dozens of tiny robotic attackers that assailed him from every direction as the earth beneath him held him fast and the air in his lungs abandoned him. Almost a minute passed before his head finally lolled to one side, the necromancer finally losing consciousness in the face of the relentless onslaught. Hesitantly, I stepped forward to take a closer look at the necromancer's flaccid form held upright only by the earthen tentacles encircling both his legs.

"Seph," came a quiet voice as a cold hand grabbed my ankle, "don't." A glance down revealed Jade's pale fingers wrapped around my leg, her dark eyes imploring me not to take another step. "He's about to—"

Another lightning bolt ripped down from the sky, striking Metis with unfettered fury. The resulting explosion of electricity and shrapnel sent the circle of warriors surrounding the necromancer flying in every direction and me flailing through the air to land in the middle of the empty street. My elbow, hip, and knee took the brunt of the impact, and I howled in pain.

Metis was upon me in an instant, those stupid headphones of L.J.'s still in place and blocking me from using the only weapon I had at my disposal.

"Enough games, Snow." My ears barely registered the words as he lunged for me, the roar of the lightning strike still echoing in my ears. "Time to die."

My final gambit a failure, I squeezed my eyes closed and prayed that death at the necromancer's touch would be painless. My every muscle stiff in apprehension of what was about to happen, I lay there trembling on the verge of hyperventilation, awaiting the inevitable.

And yet, the inevitable never came.

Forcing one eye open, I quickly learned what was responsible for my stay of execution.

Or, more accurately, who.

His crimson-armored legs straddling my body on either side, the Cardinal stood over me, his gauntleted fists wrapped around Metis's wrists as the man who stole six months of my life wrestled with the man who fought with all his might to take the rest.

"Only now, Snow, do you understand who and what I have been preparing to face these many months." His voice amplified and soulless as always, the Cardinal peered down at me, his face, as always, hidden behind his helmet's black face shield and smoked lenses. "Pray to whatever gods you may worship that either of us sees the next sunrise."

CHAPTER 31

ROCK AND A HARD PLACE

"Y ou." Metis growled the word. "A novel solution to your problem, I must say"—he gave the Cardinal's armor a quick up-and-down assessment—"if a bit flamboyant for my tastes."

"Says the man wearing a child's headset to prevent himself from hearing a nineteen-year-old girl hum a tune." The Cardinal headbutted Metis and sent L.J.'s headphones flying. "Have some dignity."

"It would appear that, since our last encounter, you've gone to a lot of trouble to fashion your entire identity after a common backyard bird." Metis sneered. "Speak not to me of dignity."

Hmm. Nice to know I could let go any concern about Metis being the Cardinal.

But it was more than that. Though Jade was the empath of the bunch, it didn't take such talent to feel the visceral hate between the two men wrestling over me. Not to mention, now that I could study them side by side, there was no comparison between the two.

For all that he had taken from me, I suddenly feared the Cardinal wouldn't live to see the morning. And strangely enough, I found that I actually cared.

Metis shifted his attention my way, the rage in his eyes leaving me breathless. "And don't even think about trying to move me with your song, Snow. A single syllable, and my only decision will be whether to crush your windpipe with my mind or flash-fry yours with a million volts between those lovely blue eyes of yours." Metis returned his cold glare to the Cardinal. "As for you, you dare to stand in my presence and claim the role of Snow's savior like some white knight after all you've done?"

"After what I've done?" The Cardinal, even with his strength augmented by the armor, strained against Metis's utter physicality. "Last I checked, you were the self-styled Lord of Death among the Ascendant. We may be cut of the same cloth, you and I, but I am nothing like you."

"Aren't you?" Metis asked, a taunting bite in his tone. "And who are you trying to convince? The beautiful siren you couldn't bear to slay who hates you regardless of your words or actions, as you took from her the only treasure worth anything in this world, her time?" The necromancer continued his struggle against his armored adversary, and he was starting to win. "Or perhaps you hope to sway the only other person on the planet who understands your unique situation as a purveyor of death?" His eyes narrowed as he let fly a solitary laugh. "Or do you perform all these mental gymnastics simply to maintain your own deluded self-image in an effort to sleep at night?"

Cut of the same cloth? Unique situation? Purveyor of death? What did it all mean?

Unless...

"She's figured it out, I think. What you are and what that means." Metis chuckled. "Even in this near darkness, I can see it in her eyes."

The Cardinal stared down at me once more, and though his

expression remained inscrutable behind the avian facade, I detected a hint of sadness in his momentary silence.

"You're a necromancer," I whispered as I pointed to Metis, "just like him."

"Just like him, you say?" Despite its modified tone and amplified volume, the hurt and rage in the Cardinal's voice came through loud and clear. "You're still alive, aren't you?"

"Not for very much longer." Metis broke the Cardinal's grip on his wrists, shoved his armored foe away, and then, in as surprising a move as I'd seen, stepped away from me and crossed his arms. "When you first encountered me, I was empty, gaunt, cadaverous, the many talents I'd taken nothing but faded memory, but as you can see, I've already begun refilling the well. Thus far, I've gorged myself on an aged psychokinetic and a virile young elektromancer, but there will be more." He threw his head back in revelry. "So many more."

"I knew this day would come." The Cardinal shifted his gaze my way for half a second. "I had not anticipated our reunion occurring quite so soon, but I have prepared for you. You would do well not to underestimate me."

"Oh, I'm quite certain that you've made good use of the handful of months that have passed since we last spoke and likely acquired a reasonable arsenal of Ascendant talents. Still, what I may lack at the moment in raw power, I more than make up for in experience." He swept an arm wide, gesturing to the unmoving forms strewn in every direction. "While your youthful energy and endurance serves you well, let me assure you that the wisdom of centuries will win every time."

"Your great wisdom didn't stop me from putting you in the ground for over two years." The Cardinal shot yet another irritated glance my way. "A deep dark hole you'd still occupy if it weren't for a certain well-meaning fool."

I was pretty sure he meant me. But how could he know?

"Greetings, Persephone Snow." The familiar grind of a particular robot's rollerball on gravel sounded from behind me. "My apologies. I know that you and the Cardinal are not on the best of terms, but I value your continued existence, so when the Redstarts arrived, I notified him of the situation and your whereabouts."

A quick look across my shoulder revealed Charon's glowing blue eye scanning my injured body like a concerned school nurse. I wasn't sure whether to scream at the little robot or leap up and hug him.

"The Cardinal? You're not calling him 'master' anymore?" Neither of the men nor the robot in our circle said a word, as I shot the robot a confused glance. "Charon?"

"Oh, Snow, you still haven't put the entire puzzle together." Metis gestured to his crimson-armored adversary, his expression filling with rage. "You think this arrogant amateur, this pretender, still wet behind the ears, could create a wonder such as the Underworld that was your home for six months? The Styx network that touches every major landmass across the entire world?" He glanced across his shoulder at my various fallen friends. "Could defeat the Angel of the Morning along with her entourage not just once, but twice in the same day?"

"So, you are Hades, and everything you said before was a lie?"

"No. That much, at least, was the truth. Conquering the previous Lord of Death and usurping his role has long been one of my proudest achievements."

"If you're not Hades, then why create an Underworld straight out of *Edith Hamilton's Mythology*? The Styx? Kerberos? Hell, Charon here?"

"What can I say?" Metis offered a humble bow. "Before you stands a lifelong student of mythology, and Greco-Roman myth in particular." He chuckled, his mouth twisted into a smug grin. "And for one such as I, the word 'lifelong' takes on an entirely new meaning."

The Cardinal laughed. "And yet, despite your many centuries walking this world, you fear to speak your own name in the presence of a 'pretender' to your throne and a songbird who barely understands her own abilities." The taunt left Metis silent for far longer than expected. "Tell her, cunning one. Before ending one or both of us, please, tell Snow with whom she speaks this day."

I wasn't sure, but it sure seemed like the Cardinal was appealing to Metis's sense of pride. Stranger still, it appeared to be working.

Metis glared at the Cardinal, the latter's avian facade all but mocking in its lack of expression. "Very well." The sudden quiet in the necromancer's voice chilled me far more than any of his rage-fueled vitriol. "Not that it matters. Soon, none shall stand against me, regardless of what knowledge they might possess." His wicked smile returned. "Not to mention the fact that neither of you will leave this place to pass on whatever you may or may not learn."

"Look," I grumbled as I pulled myself up from the ground, the pain along my side making each movement a struggle, "even I'm getting bored with all this supervillain posturing." I crossed my arms and channeled whatever remained of my inner diva from half a year ago. "Either get on with the big revelation or come at us. I don't really care which at this point." I trembled from head to toe, unclear if the anxious quivering was from facing certain death or the fact that I'd just used the word "us" to describe myself and the Cardinal.

"I have gone by countless names over my many centuries walking this planet, a few of which you know intimately, but most of which you've never heard, the latter by design. The appellation to which our armored friend here is no doubt referring, however, remains the most famed by far. I am known in this aspect of my life as an itinerant traveler, cunning warrior, articulate speaker, and quick thinker with a thirst for glory and lust for flesh, or at least that's what the books all say." Metis breathed a self-satisfied sigh. "Though tales of my travels during that time in my long life became progressively more embellished with centuries of being passed down orally, I assure you that each story is based in fact, at least at some level." He studied my dumbfounded expression, releasing a disappointed groan that I wasn't immediately deciphering his cryptic résumé. "Really, Snow? Nothing?"

"An ultra-strong, uber-smart, dashingly attractive ladies' man with no flaws whatsoever? You just described the main character of basically every book, show, and movie ever produced." I offered an apologetic shrug. "Your so-called fame, I suppose, is just another victim of the patriarchy, it would seem."

"Or the distressing state of education in this modern day," Metis countered. "Unless things have improved in my brief time away, it's like the Dark Ages all over again, but this time you and the rest of humanity pacify yourselves with cat videos as you usher in the death of our once-vibrant planet." He stared at me, unbelieving. "Your scoffing retort when I admitted I'd never heard of you, Persephone Snow, comes full circle now, for before you stands Odysseus of myth." His lips spread in a self-satisfied smile. "Though among the Ascendant, I have been called Ulysses for longer than I can truly remember." He sighed. "Ah, the Romans."

"Ulysses?" My brow furrowed. "The guy we all read about in middle school?"

"Pleased to meet you, though I'd hoped you'd guess my name." He offered me the subtlest of bows. "My exploits, the details of many of which are lost to antiquity, form the basis of Homer's *Iliad* and *Odyssey*, along with more myths and legends than I could possibly list even if we had the time." He puffed his chest with self-admiration. "Suffice to say, I am among the oldest of those who refer to themselves as Transcendent. A necromancer two years out of the gate and a siren who barely understands her own talent barely register as a threat."

"How is it then that no one knows who you are?" I asked, hoping the question would keep him talking and maybe even piss him off. "If you are who you say you are, how is it that Alba didn't recognize you, not to mention the rest? From one internationally recognized superstar to another, however do you maintain such...anonymity?"

His eyes flashed with annoyance. "When one lives as long as I have, you learn not to leave alive those who know your face, a lesson I tried to impart upon our mutual friend here upon our first meeting." He shot a look the Cardinal's way. "According to the geomancer, however, it would seem his desire for drama and recognition coupled with a soft spot for young, beautiful women has led to a string of defeats the likes of which I haven't seen in centuries." He returned his attention to me. "Simply put, for better than a millennium, I have ensured that any encounter with another Ascendant occurred on my terms and that I was the only one to walk away."

"Every encounter," the Cardinal said, "save one."

"Yes," Ulysses hissed, "save one." He dove at the Cardinal, the bare flesh of his arm missing mine by mere inches. "A mistake I shall now rectify."

The Cardinal unleashed the paired wing-blades from his gauntlets and attempted to assume a defensive stance, but Ulysses was already on top of him. Wrestling his opponent to the ground, the ancient necromancer pinned one armored arm to ground and wrestled to remove the bladed gauntlet from the other.

A gentle nudge at my calf grabbed my attention. I found Charon by my side with L.J.'s noise-canceling headphones held before him in one of the claw-like appendages housed within his torso.

"You may wish to place these over your ears, Persephone Snow." He pushed the headphones still spattered with Emir's blood into my hand. "Unless the Cardinal has altered his playbook recently, I suspect it's about to become very loud."

I immediately picked up on what Charon was suggesting and pulled the headphones over my ears not a moment too soon.

Despite the noise-canceling technology protecting my ears, the Cardinal's sonic assault still shook my teeth as if I were on stage in front of a stack of speakers. Ulysses, confident in his vicious attack one second was writhing on the ground with his hands over his ears the next. The ear-blistering attack lasted but a second, however, as Ulysses thrust a grasping hand in his opponent's direction, and with a simple wave, sucked the electricity from the Cardinal's armor into his outstretched arm. The Cardinal's movements immediately grew slow and stilted, as any help from the armor's mechanics cut out, leaving him with only his native strength and what he had robbed from his many victims. I wasn't sure how much such a suit weighed, but other than protecting the Cardinal from Ulysses's touch and most other attacks, his armor had instantly transitioned from asset to liability. I shed the headphones and maneuvered myself behind Charon as I waited for the next shoe to drop.

"Necromancer or not, I could kill you with a touch." Ulysses tore one of the Cardinal's bladed gauntlets from his arm, the bare hand beneath pale in the pre-morning light. "I could strike you down with a dozen lightning bolts and reduce you to so much ash." He ripped off the opposite gauntlet and hurled it aside. "I could cut off the blood flow to your brain with the psychokinetic's talent." He grasped the Cardinal's avian helmet and wrenched it from his head. "But, in the end, I think I will simply kill you with my bare hands and look you in the eye as all that you are, were, and ever will be fades into oblivion." He shot a glance my way. "Remember, Snow, sometimes the oldest ways are the best, not that you'll be around to utilize that advice for very much longer." His eyes grew cruel. "Behave yourself, and I will bring about your end in a much quicker and less satisfying way."

Ulysses wrapped his fingers around the Cardinal's throat, and the mysterious man who had taken me hostage six months earlier turned his head my way, his naked face beneath a close-cropped military cut revealed to me for the first time. His pale skin untouched by the sun, his eyes bulged from their sockets as he struggled to breathe. A jagged scar split his right eyebrow and proceeded up his forehead to meet his blond hairline. His revealed features triggered a memory, something deep inside I couldn't quite place, but one thing became instantly clear: no matter what he'd done, no one, ancient necromancer bent on revenge or otherwise, was killing the Cardinal until I got some questions answered.

"Hang on, Charon." I patted the little robot's head. "This might go sideways fast."

I wracked my brain for lyrics that met the criteria for "Hey, don't kill this guy until I can figure out why his face flipped a switch in my brain," and as happened when we escaped the Redstarts en route to Los Angeles, lyrics I'd never heard nor performed sprung forth complete from my mind.

"*Suspend this fight with him and me...*"

"What are you doing, Snow?" Ulysses shouted my way. "So eager to meet your own fate?"

"*Release his throat and let him be...*"

With a growl worthy of an angry theriodan, Ulysses released the Cardinal. Back on his feet in an instant, he stalked my way, a predator coming for its prey.

"*Allow us both to walk away...*"

He stopped in his tracks, an internal battle manifesting in his features as he warred with me, will against will, to take another step.

"So we can fight another day."

Frozen to the spot, Ulysses seethed. Neither his arms nor legs would obey him, but his eyes told the story of what he would do were he free to act.

An interesting thought occurred to me. My voice could control Ulysses as well as either Latifah's or Jamila's psychomancy, but where their abilities required an active connection—a fact that I'd used to my advantage just as Ulysses had—my talent simply transferred my will into song, creating an inexorable, inescapable command that even a Transcendent necromancer several millennia my senior had to obey. The Cardinal, Alba, and even Ulysses himself had tried to convince me of the power in my voice, but only in that moment, as my will alone kept a necromancer's death-touch from my flesh, did I truly believe.

Quite the insightful thought, Snow. Latifah Lazaar's voice filled my mind even as an unseen Jamila claimed my limbs as her own. *And now that you have at your mercy not just one but both Ascendant responsible for each of the tragic Redstart deaths in recent history, you shall sing for us, little bird.* Latifah crowded my mind with images of the Cardinal and Ulysses in mortal combat, my arms and legs frozen in place like a statue's and disobeying my every command. *Sing these murderers into an early grave, and rid us and the world of both of them forever.*

CHAPTER 32

THE DEVIL YOU KNOW

"The Redstarts never wanted me," I said aloud, though I answered the voice within my mind. "You only wanted to use me as bait to lure the Cardinal out into the open."

A plan that by every indication would have worked smashingly, Latifah whispered into my mind, *if you hadn't unleashed a monster upon the world in your bid for freedom.*

And now poor Emir is no more. This time it was Jamila who spoke directly to my thoughts. *Which leaves us with two friends to avenge, and the three responsible present and accounted for.*

"Three?" I continued to speak aloud, if for no other reason than to confirm I still had command of my own voice. "Wait, you mean me?"

Did you not hear what I said? Latifah asked, her mentally broadcast words so loud, I feared my nose would bleed. *You freed Ulysses from whatever hellhole the Cardinal throws all those he doesn't outright kill on sight.*

And now, Jamila continued, *not only Emir, but your friend the elektromancer has paid the ultimate price for your poor judgment.*

"You weren't there," I answered. "You don't know."

"To whom are you talking, Persephone Snow?" Charon asked. "I see and hear no one except you."

"Quiet," I answered, harsher than I intended.

I fought to turn my gaze upward to see if I could catch a glimpse of either of the Redstart women flying overhead, but to no avail. I remained frozen to the spot, able to speak but not much else.

"If you think about it, Latifah, I also freed Jade, Sunil, and Daichi. Any one of them could have been bad news, for all I knew."

Make no mistake, Snow, Latifah whispered into my thoughts. *We punish you not for your kind heart nor your heroic acts—*

But based solely on the outcome. Jamila sounded like a judge about to issue a verdict of death by electric chair. *Your actions led to the death of not one, but two Ascendant, albeit indirectly. While Latifah and I do not feel that anything you've done demands the same level of retribution we intend for the two men before you, we agree that living the rest of your days knowing that you were their executioner is fitting.*

"I'm not killing anyone." My eyes narrowed involuntarily, my anger briefly overpowering even the puppet master's control. "Not today, not ever."

You will do exactly as we command. Latifah sent a wave of pain shooting through my temples. *I wasn't prepared for your little trick earlier when you hijacked our connection and sent your song directly into my mind, but I've taken precautions this time. With Jamila's talents working in tandem with mine, you are paralyzed in mind and body, incapable of standing against us, and that wondrous voice of yours is ours to do with whatever we choose.*

I tested Latifah's claim and attempted to silently sing across our mental connection as I had on the highway leading to Los Angeles, but my effort to tap into the wellspring of lyrics and melody that existed at my core came up empty.

"What have you done to my song?" Tears welled in my eyes. "There's nothing there, as if you deleted a file in my brain."

Not so much deleted as cut off from the rest of your mind, Latifah explained. *I understand how disconcerting that must feel to one in your particular occupation.*

"But, if you've taken all that away from me, how am I supposed to sing?"

Oh, you'll sing. Latifah's triumphant tone echoed across my mind. *For the moment, Jamila holds the Cardinal in thrall while your song has left Ulysses immobilized and harmless.*

Immobilized? Maybe. But harmless? I'd never make that mistake again.

Fear not, Snow. Jamila and I will guide the words of your song and weave a spell resulting in these two dealers of death eliminating each other and ridding our world, Ascendant and otherwise, of their foul presence.

I know you feel our plans for you qualify as a form of punishment, but to many, you will be perceived as a hero: the lone siren who rid the world of necromancer filth with nothing but her song. Do take some solace in that.

"You think I'll be hailed as a hero? Simply for doing your dirty work?" I laughed. "And people call me a starry-eyed optimist."

Whether you speak of the true cause of the events that are about to occur is completely up to you, Latifah spoke into my mind.

Take the win and all the praise that comes with such an unexpected victory, Jamila added, *or admit that you were yet again a pawn of your betters and continue to flounder through your new existence among the Ascendant.*

In that moment, I seriously reconsidered my oath to not kill anyone that night.

As I fought to free my mind and body from the Redstarts and wracked my brain for anything I could do or say to prevent becoming an executioner of my own kind, the answer presented itself in the quiet hum of the Cardinal's armor coming back on line. From the periphery of my vision, I could just make out a tiny arm from Charon's metal carapace hooked into a socket along the Cardinal's breastplate.

In all my months of captivity, I'd lamented having a robotic guard that was immune to my song. Tonight, however, the fact that his little computer brain was invisible to the likes of Latifah and Jamila was just the saving grace I needed.

I mentally ran lines from my favorite movie to hide my thoughts from Latifah, hoping that a barrage of *The Devil Wears Prada* might keep her from discovering what I was planning.

What are you doing, Snow? Latifah asked.

Play games with us, and we may not be so lenient.

For the first time, the characteristic hum of one of the Redstart flight suits hit my ears from above. One or both of them must have flown close enough to try to figure out what was happening.

And if I could hear them, then they could hear me.

"*Let!*" No lyrics. Just a single syllable sung in a mid-range E.

"*Him!*" A second, this one down a full step at D.

"*Go!*" A third and final word, another full step down to end on C.

A calculated gamble, for sure. The psychomancers had cut me off from every song I'd ever written, every lyric and tune I'd sung in concert, all of pop music, every country song I'd heard, what little I knew of classical music, every hymn I learned in church growing up. Nevertheless, the opening three notes of "Mary Had a Little Lamb" are so hard-wired into all our minds, I'm not sure anyone could ever expunge such a simple childhood memory.

A moment later my gamble paid off as the Cardinal, his armor fully functional again, turned and strode my way. With me frozen in place and Ulysses simply not to be trusted, and everyone else still unconscious or worse from the necromancer's lightning strike, the Cardinal was our best bet at stopping the Redstarts and preventing a day that had already begun with a massacre from turning far worse.

At least that's what I thought until he reached out a naked hand, his bare fingers mere inches from my face and took another step. I couldn't move, my entire body still immobilized by the Redstarts' tandem invasion of my mind.

"No," my plea came out little louder than a whisper, "please."

The Cardinal stopped before me, his haunted eyes meeting mine for an instant in the rising light of impending dawn. I'd often wondered what I'd see beneath his helmet's avian facade, but where I'd expected to find cold-hearted cruelty, I found instead deep sadness and utter resignation. He stepped past me, my frozen eyes unable to follow, and I wondered with each passing second if my next breath might be my last.

"You might want these." The Cardinal reappeared in front of me, slipped L.J.'s headphones over my ears again, donned his helmet anew, and took off into the pinkening sky. His sonic cannon shook the world, the cyclical punches of sound roiling over me like a monstrous heartbeat. In an instant, my arms and legs, not to mention my thoughts, were mine to control again, the ear-splitting onslaught having shattered the concentration of the two Redstart women.

Ulysses hadn't moved an inch from where I'd left him, but the daggers in his gaze left little doubt as to what he'd do the moment he was again in control of his own limbs.

Less than a minute passed before the Cardinal again appeared before me, his features again hidden behind the black and red false face he showed the world.

Not to mention the sonic scramblers that eliminated any chance I might have of stopping him if he chose that moment to end my life.

"The Redstarts," he said, his voice again amplified and modulated by his armor's speakers, "are gone."

"Gone?" I swallowed. Hard. "Did you kill them?"

"Regrettably, no, but unless they're either braver or stupider than they have any right to be, I suspect they won't be coming back anytime soon."

"Good." I glanced Ulysses's way. "So, this has all been about him? All the kidnapping and drama and killing?"

"You think he and I are the same, but I am nothing like him." Though the Cardinal's face was hidden, I could feel his eyes grow cold at my statement. "Nothing."

"You both stalk other Ascendant, slay them, and steal their power, essence, and abilities. What makes you any different, beyond the fact he's been doing it for far longer?"

"Ulysses takes what he wants, Snow, while I take only what I need."

"And me?" I asked. "Why did you need me?"

"Didn't your song stop Ulysses today, just like the sirens of myth?"

"So, you only saved me in case you needed a pawn to throw

against your enemy?" My own eyes narrowed in anger. "You know, you could have killed me at any time and simply taken that power for yourself."

"I suppose." The Cardinal laughed. "Though I can't help but think your power already resides within the perfect vessel."

My cheeks flushed at the strange compliment. "And what of Jia Li and Daichi?" I looked away. "And Sunil? Why spare them?"

"Did I not just say that I only take what I need? I am not some monster from a storybook, but a man who discovered that, due to an accident of birth, he was an instrument of death itself. I have spent every moment since that realization living the life that was foisted upon me by fate. You are a siren, and no one questions that you have chosen to spend your life in song."

Well, if you put it that way. "So, what now?"

"Now," came a voice from behind me, "you release me to do as I please, or I end your little boyfriend before you and Harkreader have a chance to enjoy the tear-filled reunion I know you're just dying for."

A rush of movement from my peripheral vision drew both our attention. The previously immobile Ulysses now knelt by Ethan's side, his bare fingers an inch from Ethan's cheek.

"What?" The word caught in my throat. "How?"

"As you and your former captor were exploring the many ins and outs of Stockholm Syndrome, it occurred to me that your ability has its limits as well, Snow." The necromancer grabbed Ethan by his neck and stood, dangling my love from his grip with no more effort than if he were picking up a bag of groceries. "Your lyrical command prevented me from pursuing any action that threatened you or the Cardinal or kept you from leaving, but the moment I considered a less direct measure, my mind and body were again free to act."

"Put Harkreader down," the Cardinal spoke with utter gravity. "Now."

"Neither of you want that, I think." His eyes trailed down Ethan's flaccid form. "He is barely holding on as it is, but if I let him go, trust that well before that, I will have drained every drop of energy from his unconscious body." His malice-filled grin returned. "Not a peep from either of you, or Harkreader dies." He took a step in our direction. "Now, the only question that remains is which of you—"

From a shimmer of gold at Ulysses's rear stepped Lady Day accompanied by both her Sister Angels.

"Mariana Trench," the Angel of Harlem commanded. "Now."

No sooner had the three words left the Angel's lips than Ulysses disappeared in a scintillating flash of golden light, his wide eyes filled with rage the only indication that he comprehended what had just happened to him.

"You wanted me, you bastard," Lady Day proclaimed, "you got me."

No longer held aloft by the necromancer's muscular arm, Ethan slumped to the ground, the multiple shadows of the just-rising sun rushing in from every direction to catch him before he hit the ground, courtesy of Madame Midnight.

"Ethan!" Finally free to follow my heart, I rushed to Ethan's side and cradled his head in my lap. In a strange show of solidarity, the Cardinal followed, his sense of urgency almost matching mine.

"Harkreader," he asked, standing over me like a sort of guardian. "Is he...?"

I rested my fingers below the angle of Ethan's jaw, the quick thready pulse bringing equal parts relief and unease. "He's alive, but that's about it."

"My apologies for the delay, Persephone Snow." Alba strode over to my side, the rising sun behind the Angel of the Morning like a halo around her lithe form. "Both Lady Day and I needed time to recover before we could return to your side."

"Can you help Ethan?" I asked, breathless. "And the others?"

"I can." She gave the Cardinal a stern look. "But first, why exactly are you associating with this aberration?"

"The Cardinal?" My eyes danced between Alba and the man who'd stolen from me six months of my life only to arrive in the nick of time today to rescue me from certain death. "He saved me." I returned my gaze to Ethan's unconscious face. "When no one else could."

"Come away from that murderer, Snow." Madame Midnight, her

body clothed in shadow exactly as I'd last seen her in Los Angeles, came up on one side. "Now."

"You know what must be done." Lady Day joined Alba as well, and for the first time in what I understood was a significant chunk of history, the three estranged Sister Angels stood together as a united front. "When our judgment comes down, trust that you don't want to be standing with him."

"Are you going to ship him off to the bottom of the ocean as well?" I rose from the ground, carefully resting Ethan's head on the cool grass, and crossed my arms in a show of defiance even though my entire body trembled with anger, fear, and adrenalin. "I know what he's done, both to me and others, but you three don't know what he just risked for me." I met each of the Angels' gazes, searching for a hint of compassion from any of them. "Is it not possible there is more to his story? Does he not deserve a hearing? A trial?"

"You still speak as if you are one of the sheep." Alba fixed me with a disapproving stare. "Innocence until guilt is proven? A construct created by the impotent masses to give them the illusion of power over their own fate."

"Funny," I countered, "I thought such laws were put in place to protect the innocent from unfair punishment from those in power."

"And you would group this monster with the innocent?" Alba asked.

"Enough." The Cardinal looked skyward. "I don't have to listen to this."

The quiet hum of the Cardinal's armor increased in volume, but before he could move an inch, the earth itself rose around his legs like tentacles, rooting him to the spot, and every shadow across the grassy area cast by the rising sun flew at his armored head and coalesced about him in a swirling cloud of silent darkness. In an instant, the hum of his armor's circuitry went quiet as he stood immobile, blind, and helpless.

"What are you going to do to him?" I asked, my pulse spiking.

"What must be done." Lady Day narrowed her eyes at the Cardinal. "The only question is where to send him."

"Why send him anywhere?" Madame Midnight answered. "The

Cut of a Thousand Shadows should be more than enough to rid the world of this monster."

"Or we could simply leave him shackled to the earth, the air taken from his lungs, every molecule of water removed from his body, and this armor on which he prides himself melted around his desiccated corpse." Alba's lips drew down to a tight circle. "An example to others who might try to follow in his footsteps."

"No." My entire body shook as I made my decision. "No more death today."

"That is not your decision to make." Alba's features filled with ire, a side of her I hadn't truly seen before, at least not directed my way. "Now, stand aside."

"You heard what I said." I channeled every ounce of willpower I had left into my voice. *"No more death today."*

Lady Day attempted to speak, but the words refused to pass her lips.

"Release this man, my words you must obey."

The shadows surrounding my former kidnapper's head dispersed as Madame Midnight looked on me in disbelief.

"My debt to him, please know I now repay."

The strain in Alba's face slackened, her entire body relaxed, and the stony tendrils that fettered the Cardinal to the ground disintegrated.

"And as he leaves, you won't stand in his way."

Four simple lines and a melody from pop radio, and three ancient Angels of incalculable power stood before me helpless to stop whatever happened next. At no point in my life had I ever wanted that kind of power.

And yet, here we were.

"Wow. I must say, I'm impressed." The Cardinal studied me. "Though to declaw three of the most powerful Ascendant in existence as they stand before one who has hunted their kind for months?" His gaze ran between the three Angel's like a wolf before a trio of lambs. "Be careful treading the fine line between confidence and folly."

"I said 'No more death today,' Cardinal, and that included you."

"Don't forget, Snow." He tapped the side of his helmet. "With the tech in this helmet processing every sound before it hits my ears, your little voice can't get inside my head."

"Care to put that to the test?" I shot a glance at the paralyzed Angels. "Also, my 'little voice' is the only thing keeping you alive at the moment." I narrowed my eyes at the avian lenses of the Cardinal's helmet, though in my mind, I pictured the haunted gaze that lurked behind the stoic mask. "Go, before I change my mind and let the Angels have their way with you."

"But—"

"Go. Now."

The two of us stood transfixed in the moment, the silence broken only by the pounding of my heartbeat in my ears. With so much left unsaid and yet nothing more to say, we simply stared at each other in silence. Finally, after what seemed an eternity, the Cardinal stepped back, collected his gauntlets from where Ulysses had cast them, and peered up into the morning sky.

"Thank you, Miss Snow—Persephone—for my momentary reprieve." He turned his head Charon's way—I'd nearly forgotten my robotic companion was still present—and spoke one last time. "Your orders still stand, Charon. Watch over her. Keep her safe." And with that, he took to the sky, his armored form quickly vanishing into the distance.

"Orders?" I asked Charon. "But I thought Ulysses was your master."

"To borrow a common phrase from human social media that you might understand, Persephone Snow," Charon chirped, "it's complicated."

"No less complicated than the situation you have now created for yourself," Alba said as she worked to shake off the mental whammy I'd leveled on her and her Sisters. "You have freed a monster who kills his own kind without compunction."

"You mean the same fate the three of you had planned for the Cardinal?"

"We are the Angels of the Ascendant, Miss Snow." Madame

Midnight's already low voice struck my ears like a serpent's hiss. "You would do well to remember with whom you speak."

"Not to mention," Lady Day added, "I didn't hear any such protests when I sentenced the menace who nearly killed you and everyone you love to a watery grave."

"You mean Ulysses?"

"Ulysses?" Lady Day said, her surprised gape mirrored on both her Sisters' faces. "Impossible."

"Not so impossible, unless the guy who just kicked the ass of nearly every Ascendant I've ever met—no offense, Lady Alba—had reason to lie." I locked gazes with the Angel. "By the way, I noticed you named a time and place when you sent him away, but not a person."

Lady Day's eyes went colder than her dark Sister's. "I only name a person when I care that the individual I am sending away continues to breathe when they arrive on the other end."

"Back to the matter at hand." Madame Midnight stepped forward. "To my knowledge, the Ascendant known as Ulysses was history before even I was born, Miss Snow. Are you quite sure you know of which you speak?"

"You three tell me." I crossed my arms. "As you all seem quite fond of constantly reminding me, I'm the newbie here."

Alba stood in silent contemplation for several long seconds before kneeling by Ethan's side. "Awaken, Harkreader," she whispered in his ear. "Your work here is anything but done."

Alba's gentle touch at Ethan's temple brought a spark of silver flame, and within seconds, his entire body was again enveloped in the mystical fire. I looked on with bated breath as the flame swept across his body, erasing the multitude of cuts and bruises now visible in the morning light and returning the vitality to his injured body.

He sat up, his still-focusing eyes scanning his surroundings until his roving gaze met mine. "Seph." He smiled. "You're okay."

"I'm fine." I answered his warm smile with one of my own, though I was so nervous, I was about to climb out of my own skin. "Everything's fine."

"I'm glad." His brow furrowed, and the carefree grin disappeared behind a worried scowl even as the sun in the eastern sky went behind a cloud. "Wait. Where's Rosemary?"

That one simple question threatened to stop my heart.

"She's there, Mr. Harkreader." Alba pointed a short distance away to where Rosemary lay face down in the grass. "She needs your help." She swept an arm wide. "They all do."

Ethan rose from the ground and held out a hand for Alba. "Help me?"

Alba shot a pensive look my way as she took his hand. "You had but to ask."

The silver flame surrounding Ethan flowed up Alba's arm and down her own body, enveloping the two of them in a raging inferno of white light.

"Speak what you wish, Harkreader," Alba commanded with the voice of a goddess, "and it shall be so."

"Let them be healed," Ethan murmured. "All of them."

No sooner had the words left his lips than a column of silver flame descended from the heavens and struck at the center of the park. Rivers of silver fire flowed in every direction like jagged rivulets of lava, each fiery tributary finding one of my injured friends or allies and restoring them. One by one, they sat up and looked around in wonder: Dino, L.J., Falco, Daichi, Rosemary, and finally, Jade.

I rushed to her side as Ethan disengaged from Alba to check on Rosemary and the others.

"Jia Li! You're okay."

"That might be a bit of an overstatement," she said with a cough, "but I think I'll live."

"I was afraid I'd lost you." I helped her to her feet. "You were so weak."

"Still weak." Her knees wobbled and she grabbed my shoulder to keep herself from falling. "But your man's magical healing fire seems to have done the trick."

"My man, eh?" My gaze flicked in Ethan's direction. He stood in a circle with Dino, L.J. and Rosemary, his physical closeness with the woman I considered my BFF sending daggers through my gut. "I certainly hope so."

Alba finished checking on Daichi and Falco and strode over to finish our conversation as her Sister Angels watched together from a distance.

"A moment, Miss Snow?" She gave Jade a quick nod and then pulled me aside. "My Sisters and I have discussed your big revelation, and if you indeed are correct about the identity of the man you once called Metis, then there is no guarantee that even Lady Day's intervention could rid the world of such as he."

"So, he could still be out there."

"Perhaps." She studied me with a pensive half-smile. "Fortunately, I believe you have proven that you are more than capable of handling yourself, and therefore, will be doing so going forward." With a wave of her hand, the golden card burnished with the image of a rising sun and stamped with the name and digits of the Angel of the Morning reappeared in her hand. "In fact, you won't be needing this anymore." With a snap of her fingers, the golden square burst into flame before falling to the ground as metallic ash.

My heart sunk in my chest. "I'm sorry about before, but I couldn't let you kill the Cardinal right after he'd just saved me. It wouldn't have been—"

"Quiet." She hushed me with a gentle finger across my lips. "You made a decision, and though my Sisters and I may disagree wholeheartedly with what you have done, we must respect the call of a fellow Ascendant"—she cracked her slender neck—"at least until such time as any of us crosses paths with the Cardinal again, at which point he should turn tail immediately and run."

"The three of you respect my decision." The meaning of her words clicked in my brain. "But you won't be helping me again, is that it?"

She stepped away from me and turned to join her Sisters who had silently borne witness to the exchange.

"Welcome to the big time, Persephone Snow. You stand tall, indebted to no one. You're free to do exactly as you please with whomever you choose." She shot one last look back at me across her shoulder. "I simply hope for all our sakes that the choices you make going forward don't end up dooming us all."

CODA
ELECTRIC BLUE

"Ashes to ashes." I stepped to the edge of the water and poured all that remained of Sunil Jayalal from a steel funerary urn into the lapping waves of the Arabian Sea. "Dust to dust."

I'd asked Rosemary, in her role as Daughter of Neith, to be the officiant for Sunil's funeral, but she'd wisely noted that with no family or friends that we'd been able to locate, I was the person who knew Sunil best. I kept my comments brief, mostly out of necessity as I'd known the man for all of two days, and made sure to paint as accurate a picture of the elektromancer as possible: sullen yet funny, a loner yet loyal to those he deemed friends, and above all, at his core, a person worth knowing.

As I stood there, my naked feet bathing in the undulating surf of an ocean I'd never seen before, I worked to process the hours since our final battle—at least I hoped it was final—with Ulysses the necromancer and my ultimate falling out with the Angel of the Morning.

In what I guessed was their final act of kindness before I and possibly my friends were to be cut off from their support, the three Angels agreed to help us return Sunil's ashes to the land of his birth. Alba and Daichi worked in tandem to dismantle the makeshift grave the geomancer had fashioned from the shattered remains of a motel parking lot and retrieve our elektromancer's body as well as the remains of the fallen Redstart psychokinetic. In a turn that left me nauseated and angry, Madame Midnight summoned Latifah and Jamila to claim Emir's remains. In return for this gesture of respect, the pair utilized their mental abilities to keep away prying eyes and keep safe any particularly aggressive gawkers as the rest of us worked to clean up our mess. This hammered home an invaluable lesson I'd been taught countless times since skiomancers first tried to take me in Albuquerque seven months ago: with certain exceptions, there were no true friends or enemies among the Ascendant, but simply individuals with various agendas. Standing shoulder-to-shoulder with the women who had recently invaded my mind, body, and soul with only the often-bandied "bygones" as the panacea to keep us from each other's throats left me cold.

Still, it was better than fighting for our lives. I'd had quite enough of that.

Once we'd retrieved the remains of both fallen Ascendant from the mound of shattered stone and asphalt, our group and the Redstarts went our separate ways, Latifah and Jamila to bury Emir in Morocco, leaving our group to make Sunil's final arrangements.

Alba allowed us use of the Pegasus—she sent Falco and Daichi along to ensure we returned her multi-million-dollar aircraft—and then Lady Day had spoken herself and her two Sisters away to an undisclosed location to discuss "certain changes" they would be making going forward regarding interactions with the remainder of the Ascendant community. We spent a day arranging to have Sunil's shriveled corpse cremated and lining up our travel credentials, and then made our way to Pakistan.

Ethan wandered down the beach from where he stood with our group and pulled me close to his warm body as the sun rose in the east. "I understand you barely knew Sunil, but I can tell that all of this is really weighing on you."

"How could it not?" I asked, looking into those blue eyes where before I'd always found excitement and electricity. The warmth and compassion in his gaze was welcome, but something was missing, and we hadn't yet had opportunity to speak alone. "This is all my fault." The five words that had become my mantra. "Everyone but me wanted to leave Metis, or Ulysses, behind, but I couldn't leave well enough alone. That decision led to all of this."

"We all make decisions every day, Seph." Rosemary pulled up at my other shoulder. A part of me was glad to have my ride-or-die best friend back at my side, but a bigger part of me wished she were a million miles away. "We can't go backward, as Mother always said. We can only move forward and hope the lessons of the past help shape a better future."

"I wish that helped more." I shot Rosemary a sidelong smile. "I really do."

"You've got to quit beating yourself up." Jade joined us in the surf. "As I've told you a hundred times, you didn't make that decision alone. We were all there, and we all agreed that compassion was the best decision, even Sunil."

"And see where he ended up?" I buried my face in my hands.

Daichi rolled up in the high-tech wheelchair now on permanent loan from Hades. "We made the best decision we could with the information we had."

"And it blew up in your face." Falco hovered up behind him, unwilling to allow his new shoes to touch the sand or surf. "The thing about being Ascendant, Snow? Our world is not for the faint of heart."

"Understatement of the year, Dietrich."

With that, the six of us fell silent in quiet contemplation of the sunrise, the golden rays cascading across the water setting the waves afire, a roiling orange and gold that would be emblazoned upon my mind until the day I died.

And that's when it hit me.

The moment I'd dreamed of for six straight months, just as I'd told Sumner.

Ethan and me. On a beach. Soaking up some sun. Though I hadn't counted on a trip to the other side of the world, here we were. Again, the old saying about being careful what you wish for reared its ugly head.

The man I love acted as distant as a stranger, the earthbound goddess who had given me carte blanche to call upon her anytime I needed help had cast me aside, and the man who imprisoned me for six months was free to come for me again thanks to my snap decision.

And then, there was the nagging feeling that even the bottom of the ocean seven miles down wasn't enough to kill a maniac like Ulysses, a monster who now harbored a deep hatred for a certain siren who still wasn't exactly sure how to fully use her abilities.

Happy birthday, Seph. You made it to twenty. Here's hoping you see twenty-one.

AUTHOR'S NOTE

I'M ALIVE

March 2024

Surprise, surprise, I'm back at my local Caribou Coffee, having enjoyed a delicious breakfast bagel and caramel latte as I wrote the epilogue for this, the third book in my Songs of the Ascendant series. And just in time, as this book is due to my editor for her to start her work tomorrow. As I alluded to in the Author's Note from Book II, Book III was far more challenging than the two preceding volumes. I was nearly three quarters of the way to the end when I realized that the beginning simply wasn't right: it wasn't long enough or sufficiently engaging and basically needed a rewrite. And to anyone who has written long form fiction, you understand that changing the beginning creates ripple effects that flow through everything else you have written, and I was sitting at 70,000 words at that point.

This is my way of saying that Book III took far longer to create than I anticipated. Books I and II were both written, at least the original drafts, in roughly sixteen months, eight months apiece. Book III, on the other hand? I started in mid-December 2022 and am just finishing in mid-March 2024, basically fifteen months. Now, to be fair, I spent a lot of time during those fifteen months editing and improving the first two volumes, not to mention ran a successful Kickstarter for these three books along with new books from John G. Hartness and Patrick Dugan, so there were extenuating circumstances. Still, I'd hoped to have this thing done, edited, and ready to send to the printer by now, so for those of you waiting for this series, especially our fine backers from the Kickstarter, my apologies for the wait.

Writing *You Better Run*—thanks to Patrick Dugan for insisting on the better song title for the name of this book—was yet again a very different experience from writing the two previous volumes of this series: between the six month time jump necessary for my main character to truly earn her name, the temporary loss of my other two leads until the last quarter of the book, and a main character with abilities that were less obviously useful in combat, though I'd argue quite effective in the end analysis, I had to learn how to write this book. But the old saying goes, "You never learn how to write a novel. You only learn how to write the novel that you're writing." And for my tenth novel-length piece, this was again proven true.

I very much enjoyed writing Persephone Snow, and though I worried I might not find her as enjoyable to embody for an entire book as I had Rosemary Delacroix, I was proven wrong. Seph is very different from both Ethan and Rosemary, but at her core, as with the other two leads, she is a hero: a hero who is damaged, makes mistakes, and sometimes fails, but a hero nonetheless. I hope you enjoyed reading her as much as I did writing her.

As always, I need to acknowledge the fine individuals who helped bring this book to you.

To my first/alpha reader, Joelle Reizes, AKA J.D. Blackrose, thank you for your thorough read of this book and your many sage observations. You always catch the plotholes, big and small, so that my readers can have a smooth ride. Your efforts are so appreciated.

To Sarah Sover, my second/beta reader, thank you again for reading the first three books of this new series at light speed, and for all your sound advice along the way.

To Robyn Huss, my editor, thank you for sticking with me on this project and for continuing to shine a light into all the dark corners of my manuscripts so that I can get rid of the cobwebs before inviting people over.

To M.M. Schill, I asked for Persephone Snow à la Madonna's *True Blue* album, and boy did you deliver. Thank you so much for your hard work on that painting and for capturing just the right mood for this cover. Credit to Herb Ritts for the iconic original photograph.

To Natania Barron, my most excellent book cover designer, thank you yet again for bringing your skill, talent, and eye for detail to this, the seventh book cover you've designed for me. I look forward to seeing what we come up with for the remainder of this series.

And finally, as always, thank you to the woman to whom I owe everything for my Songs of the Ascendant series, Pat Benatar, and the song for which this book is named.

"You Better Run" was written by Eddie Brigati and Felix Cavaliere and was first performed by their band, The Young Rascals, and released in 1966 as their third single. Pat Benatar covered the song for her second album, *Crimes of Passion*, from which it was the lead single in 1980. It peaked at number 42 on the U.S. *Billboard* Hot 100 and appeared in the 1980 film, *Roadie*. This song has the distinction of being the second song ever broadcast on MTV on August 1, 1981 after the brand new music network premiered with "Video Killed the Radio Star" by The Buggles.

By now, you all know of my love for Pat Benatar and her music. My goal for the next twelve months is to find a way to see her and her husband Neil Giraldo live on tour. The stars have yet to align for me to see Ms. Benatar, one of my favorite performers of all time, in person, but I will be keeping my ear to the ground on any upcoming opportunities. Until then, I suppose I will have to be satisfied with the 80s station in my car and my home collection of 80s music.

And with that, the first arc of Songs of the Ascendant is complete. Fear not, however. My brain is already cooking on the next book which will again star Ethan Harkreader as he navigates the time between losing Persephone at the end of Volume II and finding her again at the final battle of Volume III. A lot can happen in six months, as Ethan is about to discover. Volume IV, barring my writer brain taking an unexpected left turn, will be titled *Fire and Ice*, and I will be getting to work just as soon as Volumes I, II, and III are all available. Until then, happy reading!

About the Author

Darin Kennedy, born and raised in Winston-Salem, NC, is a graduate of Wake Forest University and Bowman Gray School of Medicine. After completing family medicine residency in the mountains of Virginia, he served eight years as a United States Army physician and wrote his first novel in the sands of northern Iraq.

His first published novel, *The Mussorgsky Riddle,* was born from a fusion of two of his lifelong loves: classical music and world mythology. *The Stravinsky Intrigue* continues those same themes, and his **Fugue & Fable** trilogy culminates in *The Tchaikovsky Finale*. **The Pawn Stratagem**, his contemporary fantasy trilogy of *Pawn's Gambit*, *Queen's Peril*, and *King's Crisis* combines contemporary fantasy, superheroics, and the ancient game of chess. His young adult novel is *Carol*, a modern-day retelling of *A Christmas Carol* billed as Scrooge meets *Mean Girls*.

His latest series, **Songs of the Ascendant**, falls at the intersection of *Highlander*, *X-Men*, *Buffy the Vampire Slayer*, and *Chuck*, all told through a filter of 80s pop music and specifically the oeuvre of Pat Benatar. Comprised thus far of *Shadows of the Night*, *All Fired Up*, and *You Better Run*, this story is just getting started.

His short stories can be found in numerous anthologies and magazines, and the best, particularly those about a certain *Necromancer for Hire*, are collected for your reading pleasure under Darin's imprint, 64Square Publishing.

Doctor-by-day and novelist-by-night, he writes and practices medicine in Charlotte, NC. When not engaged in either of the above activities, he has been known to strum the guitar, enjoy a bite of sushi, and rumor has it he even sleeps on occasion. Find him online at darinkennedy.com.

THE BAND

Persephone Snow – Siren
Ethan Harkreader – Agent of Neith
Rosemary Delacroix – Daughter of Neith

SKIOMANCERS

Johan Krage | Rupert Martin
Fala Hawkins | Dmitri Drozdov

ELEMENTALISTS

Sunil Jayalal – Elektromancer
Daichi Kanda – Geomancer
Dietrich Falco – Aeromancer

THERIODANS

Linus – Wolf
Harold – Hyena
Franklin – Ferret

PSYCHOMANCERS

Jia Li Xiao/Jade – Empath
Latifah Lazaar – Telepath
Jamila Filali – Mind Controller
Emir Idrissi – Psychokinetic

TECHNOMANCERS

Minako
L.J.

OTHERS

The Cardinal
Metis
Lady Day / The Angel of Harlem
El Ángel del Alba / The Angel of the Morning
Madame Midnight / The Midnight Angel

You Better Run - Pat Benatar
Don't Pay the Ferryman - Chris de Burgh
Kyrie - Mr. Mister
Too Much Time on My Hands - Styx
Talk to Me - Stevie Nicks
Electric Youth - Debbie Gibson
You're a Friend of Mine - Clarence Clemons/Jackson Browne
Looking for a Stranger - Pat Benatar
The Prisoner - Howard Jones
Runnin' With the Devil - Van Halen
Breakout - Swing Out Sister
Sweet Freedom - Michael McDonald
Emotion in Motion - Ric Ocasek
Touch and Go - Emerson, Lake, and Powell
Message in a Bottle - The Police
On the Road Again - Willie Nelson
Animal - Def Leppard
Hungry Like the Wolf - Duran Duran
Fairytale of New York - The Pogues
Dancing in the Dark - Bruce Springsteen
Angel of Harlem - U2
Secret Separation - The Fixx
Run Like Hell - Pink Floyd
Hypnotize Me - Wang Chung
Turn to You - The Go-Go's
Supersonic - J.J. Fad
Forever Young - Alphaville
Master of Puppets - Metallica
True Colors - Cyndi Lauper
Hungry Eyes - Eric Carmen
I Ran - A Flock of Seagulls
Rock and a Hard Place - The Rolling Stones
The Devil You Know - Split Enz
Electric Blue - Icehouse
I'm Alive - Electric Light Orchestra

KICKSTARTER BACKERS

A special thank you to our 227 Kickstarter Backers!
You helped make this happen, and these books are for you!

~

Sheryl R. Hayes, Kiersten Keipper, Bill Feero, Chuck Teal, Beth Wojiski, Kerney Williams, Dino Hicks, Jessica Bay, Rowan Stone, Josh Minchew, V. Hartman DiSanto, Hope Griffin Diaz, April Baker, Princess Donut, Allison Charlesworth, Shanda, maileguy, Joelle Reizes, Alexandra Corrsin, Joseph Procopio, Kevin A. Davis, Robert S. Evans, Eric P. Kurniawan, Amber Derpinghaus, Andy Bartalone, R. David Grimes, Patti & Joan Holland, Scott Casey, Asha Jade Goodwin, Chuck & Colleen Parker, Jessica Nettles, Sarah J. Sover, Joe Compton, Brendan Lonehawk, Tera, James & Hannah Fulbright, Chris Fletemier, Carol B, A. L. Kaplan, Joey & Matt Starnes, Wanda Harward, Dennis M. Myers, Evelyn M, Nick Crook, Bob!, Bill Bibo Jr., Karen Palmer, Dina Barron, Charlie "Kaiju Mapping" Kaufman, Nancy E. Dunne, Rachel A. Brune, Noella Handley, Sara T. Bond, SM Hillman, C Keeley, John L. French, Anthony Martin, Lynn K, Fay Shlanda, Cristov Russell, Candice N. Carp, Samuel Montgomery-Blinn, Susan Griffith, Vee Luvian, Randy Cantrell, Gail Z. Martin, Tawni Muon, Caryn S, Jimmy Liang, Preacher Todd, Casey & Travis Schilling, The King of Rhye, Ruth Brazell, Melisa Todd, Vic Chase, Tom Sink, Nicholas Ahlhelm, Donna Berryman, Richard Novak, Liz Lamb, Angie Ross, Jonathan Casas, Christy Wilhelm, Robert Claney, Carol Gyzander, Ollie Oxxenfree, Ángel González, Caitlin Wright, Michelle Botwinick, Ashley & Cody, Amelia Sides, Nicole Rich, Ardinzul, Scott Valeri, Richard Dansky, Josh Bluestein, K.H. DeNeen, David Price, Mair Clan, Leonard Rosenthol, Vikki Perry, RHR, Jennifer & Benjamin Adelman, Everette Beach, Charlie Hawkins, Zeb Berryman, Julia Benson-Slaughter, Jesse Adams, Ash Peeples, Susan

Ragsdale, Tina Hoffmann, Robert Osborne, A.M. Giddings, Michelle LeBlanc, Amanda, Ken St Clair, J. T. Arralle, Alec Christensen, hemisphire, Marian Gosling, Zack Keedy, Dee Kennedy, Andrea Fornero, Allison Finch, Sandy Reece, Maya Barb, Shirley Kohl, Ronald H. Miller, Adrianne McDonald, James Ball III, Louise K, Elyse M Grasso, Steve Ryder, Debbie Yerkes, Brendon Towle, LB Clark, Jenn Huerta, Emily L, Eric Guy, Reverend Trevor Curtis, Jim Reader, Shauna Kantes, Stephanie Taylor, Kyla M, Micah Cash, Eric R. Asher, Cindy & Scott Kuntzelman, Avery Wild, Wes "nothing clever to say" Smith, Tamsin Silver, Steve Saffel, phoenix17, Mike Dubost, M.C. Jordan, Sarah Thompson, Cursed Dragon Ship Publishing, Venessa Giunta, Drew Bailey, Sue Phillips, LaZrus66, Scott M. Williams, William C. Tracy, Larissa Lichty, David Scoggins, Mari Mancusi, Jim Ryan, Seth Keipper, Marc Alan Edelheit, Dr. William Alexander Graham IV, Perry Harward, Liam Fisher, Jessica Glanville, Susan Roddey, Regina Kirby, Jeremy Bredeson & Leon Moses, Misty Massey, Janet Iannantuono, Regis Murphy, "Yes That Mark" Wilcox, Berta Platas, Kristen Clark, Matt, B. Y., Theresa Glover, Carol Malcolm, Dr. Keith Hunter Nelson, Adam, Leigh A. Boros & Robert A. Hilliard Jr., Aysha Rehm, Gary Phillips, Tom Savola, Audrey Hackett, Michael J. Sullivan, Annarose Mitchell, Karen M, Patrick J. Blanchard, Kayleigh Osborne, Chris Oakley, Andrea Judy, Casey, Helen Gassaway, J. Matthew Saunders, Carol Mammano, Danielle Ackley-McPhail & eSpec Books, Jared Nelson, and The Creative Fund by BackerKit

SONGS OF THE ASCENDANT

Shadows of the Night

All Fired Up

You Better Run

ALSO BY DARIN KENNEDY

<u>FUGUE & FABLE</u>

The Mussorgsky Riddle

The Stravinsky Intrigue

The Tchaikovsky Finale

<u>THE PAWN STRATAGEM</u>

Pawn's Gambit

Queen's Peril

King's Crisis

Carol: Being a Ghost Story of Christmas

The April Sullivan Chronicles: Necromancer for Hire

www.ingramcontent.com/pod-product-compliance
Lightning Source LLC
Chambersburg PA
CBHW031307210726
48287CB00005B/1446